THE CRIMSON FALCON

Safely in my room I put a light to the gas jet and sat for a few moments on the edge of my bed clutching the paper parcel in my hands. My fingers struggled with the knots in the string which bound the parcel. It was only an old pendant, I told myself, nothing to be afraid of, yet for a few moments I stared at the casket, aware of the beauty of the workmanship, before I dared lift the lid. Instead of the gleam of jewels from its satiny depths, an envelope bearing my name lay on top of the pendant and I recognized my mother's handwriting immediately. I took it out slowly and started to read.

Every word of her letter will be engraved upon my heart for the rest of my life, but I did not know then how irrevocably it was to change my own future. Never again would I be content to be the gentle daughter of an English parson, living quietly in genteel obscurity.

Sara Hylton

THE CRIMSON FALCON

ARROW BOOKS

Arrow Books Limited
17-21 Conway Street, London W1P 6JD

An imprint of the Hutchinson Publishing Group

London Melbourne Sydney Auckland
Johannesburg and agencies throughout
the world

First published by Hutchinson 1983
Arrow edition 1984

Printed and bound in Great Britain by
Anchor Brendon Ltd, Tiptree, Essex

ISBN 0 09 933390 2

Prologue

The gates were closed. My heart sank and all the old sickening fears returned. At that moment I could have cried out with anguish and frustration, believing that even now something would come to prevent me from leaving the castle. We had been travelling at speed and the horses were pulled up so sharply they screamed their protests and reared up nervously between the shafts. The coachman muttered beneath his breath, then gently he strove to calm them.

A man I had not seen before came out of the gatehouse. He was very old and bent, but then I should have known it would not be Josef who came to open the gates for us. The old man shuffled slowly towards them, but their weight seemed almost too much for his crooked arthritic hands so that once more I had time to look at the crest which ornamented those massive gates of wrought iron. I have known that crest too long, the high flung Latin words picked out in gold lettering under the half circle of dark green laurel leaves, and the beautiful proud head of the bird painted in tones of tragic crimson.

At last the gates were open and the man stood back, not looking at us, his eyes cast down upon the ground as we drove through. Before us now stretched fields of golden rye with the late afternoon sunlight gilding the heavy bunches of purple grapes ripening on the vines. In the distance, as ethereal as any desert mirage, the spires and domes of Vienna rose upwards towards the sky.

The closing of the gates behind me echoed dully, with all the trauma of finality, and now, unbidden, came the memories, and instead of the vista before me I was remembering what lay behind those closed gates.

I knew every twist and turn of that long tortuous drive which led through forests of dark conifers, so densely planted the light of day could barely penetrate into the choking undergrowth. I knew the sounds of the river, just where the path emerged from the forest and before it reached the wrought iron bridge over which the traveller must pass. Under it the river crashed and gurgled between giant boulders on its turbulent way from the distant mountains to swell the Danube winding gently across the plain below, and now, looking upwards, the road climbed steeply towards the lonely crag on which Castle Meinhart had stood for countless centuries, battered by wind and weather and the tumult of ancient wars.

It was incredible to think that it was only ten months since that morning when I had stood in forlorn amazement in the courtyard of the castle, looking up at the towers and battlements above me, trembling with nervous apprehension as my companion lifted the heavy knocker on the stout wooden door.

It seemed like a fairy-tale castle to me with its small leaded panes and lofty turrets. I had been terrified when the sound of thunder rumbled overhead and lightning flashed on dark suits of old armour and heavy polished furniture, when the wind moaned along the battlements like the anguish of a lost soul. But the castle had charmed me, too, particularly in the springtime when daffodils bloomed in great clumps beside the paths, or in winter when the sound of sleighbells echoed cheerfully across the shimmering snow.

I had thought that it would take longer than ten short months to lose one's heart completely and irrevocably. Perhaps in time I shall forget the evil that made me afraid of my own shadow, eroding my courage, creating memories that I must run from, erasing others I would have remembered always.

At last we have reached the broad highway which leads into the city and I have willed myself not to look back at the castle standing dark and lonely against the reddening sky.

The tears that are drying on my cheeks have nothing to do with Castle Meinhart or anything that has happened to me under its roof. They stem from memories of other days, and one day in particular when my eyes first fell upon the crimson falcon.

One

I had not thought to see Alan Trevellyon, my stepfather, again, so you can imagine my dismay when I received a letter from him asking me to call at his place of business between two and five on any day during the first week in October. I had no quarrel with him, indeed I had always held him in the utmost esteem.

He had been a good friend to all of us when I was growing up in that little Devonshire village where my father was the vicar. He was then a bachelor living with his elder sister in a house known as Fair Acres on the outskirts of the village. He was a solicitor by profession with a practice in Exeter, but he preferred to live in the country and three evenings every week he came to the vicarage to play chess with my father. I thought he was nice. He was a tall fair-haired man with a shy smile and always, on arrival, he pressed a new sixpence into my hand.

I don't know if he admired my mother in those days but it would not have surprised me. To me she was the most beautiful, enchanting person in the whole world. She was so graceful and her movements were those of a dancer, for that is what she had been as a member of the imperial ballet in Vienna before she had come to England to live. Her voice too, with its merest intonation of a foreign accent, was fascinating to listen to. Men always looked at my mother with that special look and I have longed to be like her but I know I never will be. She was blond and fragile, like a piece of Dresden china. Although I too am slender I am tall, with dark red hair the colour of mahogany which my mother insisted was far more unusual when coupled with eyes as blue as the ocean.

It seems very strange to be going back to Devonshire after an absence of seven years but I have never forgotten that village at the edge of the moor. It was a place of thatched cottages and pretty gardens, of winding country lanes and tall hedgerows over which the honeysuckle ran riot, where rooks swept down the sky at sunset seeking their nests built high up in the ancient trees in the churchyard.

How I have missed those soft Devonshire voices and that rambling High Street where the winds from the moor flirted endlessly with those blown inland from the sea. It would be wrong to say I have not been happy living with Miss Emily Frobisher in Kensington but I am a country girl at heart and there have been times when I have found my employer fractious and difficult to please.

She is a writer of children's books and I like to think that I have helped her in her work. She calls me her secretary, but I really think that what got me the position against several others was the fact that I had always been able to draw animals and I mentioned this fact to her at our interview. She asked me to draw a rabbit for her, so I drew one wearing a straw hat and a dapper jacket, with a bow round his neck and a cane under his arm. After that the job was mine and I have done many illustrations for her books, without any extra pay I may add, for she still refers to me as her secretary.

The letter from Alan Trevellyon came out of the blue and Miss Frobisher was a little put out by its timing.

'If you must go, Rachel, then I suppose you must, but it is inconvenient. The man has never acknowledged your existence apart from the odd Christmas card and here you are going off to meet him at the first asking.'

'It must be something very important or he wouldn't have written to me,' I argued, but she merely sniffed at this and from then on the matter was closed. I had left the house in the early hours while she was still in bed, but I had left a note to say I would return in three days' time. I knew she would not be pleased, but I wanted to visit the village to renew my acquaintance with some of my old friends. I had taken no holidays in the summer and I felt she should not begrudge me these few days.

The train was running late, but now when I looked through the window I could see that the dun-coloured soil of Somerset had given way to the rich red soil of Devonshire and on the skyline I could see faintly the rocky tors set against a pale blue sky.

I leaned my head back in my corner and closed my eyes. It seemed inevitable that I should find myself remembering the tragedies that had touched my life as well as the happy times, but in spite of the warm October sunlight coming through the window I was seeing again those wild days of that terrible January when the wind started to blow from the north east bringing with it the whirling snow, covering the ground with inches of ice. None of us had thought then that it would lie piled up on either side of the road until long after Easter.

It was on one of those days that my father went out to visit one of his parishioners who lived in an isolated farmhouse on the edge of the moor. We pleaded with him not to go, but ignoring anything we said he replied that old Mrs Marriot was ninety-five and if she had chosen that day to go out to meet her maker, then it was his duty to be by her side.

How painfully long those hours had seemed while my mother and I waited for his return, listening to the wind moaning like a banshee around the house, rattling the windows, sighing tragically through the trees in the church-yard. Our constant visits to the door showed us only the white virgin snow stretching endlessly in front of us, unblemished by footmarks or the wheels of carriages, and only the dim lights from cottage windows shining eerily through the snow. Once we had heard a crash from overhead as though one of the windows high up in the attic had broken but neither of us went to investigate and although my mother held a book in her hands, the pages never turned. It had beeen late the following morning when Mr Trevellyon himself led a search party across the moor.

Three hours later the little procession had trundled back down the village street where silent groups of villagers stood outside their cottages. The light had gone and now the men carried lanterns. They also carried a five-barred gate on

11

which reposed the unconscious form of my father. He died two days later from pneumonia without recognizing either my mother or myself.

In the days and years that followed Alan Trevellyon proved himself a tower of strength and perhaps it was inevitable that my mother eventually married him. I can hear her voice now, anxious and persuasive as she tried to convince me that once more we would be a family with a man to protect us and care for us. I have grown up with the idea that one should not put too much trust in the kindness of providence in spite of my father's calling and the faith he had tried to instil in me. I watched my mother and her new husband depart for Italy where they had decided to spend their honeymoon, happy and gay together, but tragically she contracted typhoid fever during the time they were there and I never saw her again.

My stepfather's life changed hardly at all despite his sorrow. He continued to live with his unmarried sister and for a time I lived with them also. I was never happy in their home. My stepfather was kind to me but he had been a bachelor too long and hardly knew what to do with a daughter who didn't really belong to him and who had been so suddenly thrust upon him. I wept long into the night in my unfamiliar bedroom and came down to the breakfast table bleary-eyed and desperately unhappy. Miss Trevellyon barely disguised the fact that she considered me a nuisance and something of an interloper in their home, but it was thanks to the auspices of my stepfather that I heard about the post with Miss Frobisher, who was the aunt of one of his friends.

The bustle in the corridor of the train dragged my thoughts ruthlessly away from the trauma of the past into the perplexities of the present. Always when I found myself thinking of the tragedies which had affected my life I tried to think about something else quickly, refusing to be defeated by them. Now I thought how strange it was to be visiting Exeter again after so long.

I knew it well, having spent five years in the city as a pupil at Miss Tarleton's Academy for Young Ladies, thanks to Aunt Milly in America who had left me enough money to secure me a decent education.

I could see the cathedral now standing high up above the city and its bustling streets, and such a feeling of nostalgia swept over me that I stepped down from the train with my eyes blurred with tears. My stepfather's office was in the square near the cathedral and a fair walk away. I had had nothing to eat since leaving London so I decided to find a cab that would take me to some little hostelry where I could buy a cup of tea and something substantial to eat before going on to keep my appointment. I had not told him which day I would be arriving, but from the terms of his letter I supposed any day would be convenient.

The city seemed to have changed little in the years since I had left it and I found my ears straining to catch the sounds of the voices of passers-by, soft, slow Devonshire voices that evoked memories of stability and permanence.

I paid for the cab and saw that he had set me down outside a small inn advertising home cooking and inexpensive luncheons. Obviously the cab driver had surmised correctly that I was not a young lady of wealth but one who needed to count her coppers.

The lunch was satisfying if plain fare, but after I had eaten it was still far too soon for my appointment so I decided to wander the old narrow streets which led into the cathedral square. They had fascinated me as a schoolgirl with their shops filled with antique china and bric-a-brac, and the book shops where yellowing books and great dusty volumes were being lovingly handled by old men who could never have afforded to buy them.

It was one of those clear bright days of autumn when summer still lingered hopefully, like a lover might linger with a romance that was fading. In spite of the brittle leaves which blew about the cathedral square there were others that clung tenaciously to the branches of the trees, and on the rose bushes tight damp buds struggled to open. I would have dearly liked to go inside the cathedral to absorb its peace, but I wanted to get my interview over and I was now some little walk away from the office. I looked with envy at the people sitting on the stone wall surrounding the square or in happy groups on the grass.

13

It was exactly two o'clock when I arrived at the offices of Trevellyon and Gascoigne, Solicitors, in an imposing block just off the cathedral square. My heart was fluttering like a wild thing and I waited a few moments praying for composure before I rapped on the enquiry window. A young boy answered, still chewing away at his lunch, and I was bidden to wait as Mr Trevellyon already had a visitor. I didn't see anybody leaving so I perhaps unfairly surmised the young gentleman did not want his lunch interrupted. It was all of twenty minutes past two before he conducted me towards his employer's office.

The first thing I noticed as I entered the office was that my stepfather had changed little in the years since we had last met. He stood up immediately and came from behind his desk to take my hand, then pulling up a chair he motioned for me to take it while he returned to sit once more behind his desk.

'You are looking very well, Rachel,' he said. 'It is evident London agrees with you. How long is it since we met?'

'Almost seven years.'

'Gracious me, as much as that? Are you quite happy working with Miss Frobisher? I've heard she can be something of a martinet.'

'Yes, I like the work very much.'

He was nervous, far more nervous than I, and I wondered if he had asked me to meet him at his office in order to give our interview a more business-like setting. I watched his long thin fingers playing with a pencil on the blotting paper in front of him and I longed to hurry him so that I could get out of that cold office which smelled vaguely of furniture polish.

A middle-aged woman came in to put some papers on his desk and he looked up anxiously, glad of the interruption, saying in an eager voice, 'Perhaps we could have some tea, Miss Goodwin. I expect you would like some, Rachel?'

I didn't particularly want tea, I had already had some with my lunch, but I felt it would be ungracious of me to refuse so I merely smiled and said, 'Yes, thank you, that would be nice.'

We talked pleasantries until the tea came, then he made a great show of pouring it out and handing it to me, giving me time to look round the large office surrounded by shelves filled with great legal volumes, but made brighter by the horse chestnut in the street outside which tapped its branches against the window. Before returning to his seat he put another log on the fire but after that the reasons for my visit could be delayed no longer.

'I suppose you are wondering why I have asked you to come here after all this time. I thought it would be easier for me to talk here than at home, as my sister knows nothing about my business matters.'

So I was a business matter, and because I raised my eyes at that he hurried on. 'I'll come to the point as quickly as I can. You know that several articles of furniture were left by your mother and that they are stored at my house until such a time as you might want to take them. There is a velvet chair, you remember, and an inlaid walnut secretaire, and I believe there is also a small chest of drawers and some china.'

'I remember them quite well.'

'You have never needed them?'

'No. Miss Frobisher's house is already overflowing with furniture. I would have liked them but didn't like to ask her to make room for them. Are they in the way?'

'No, they were taken upstairs to one of the attics. My sister decided she wanted the house as it was before I married, I suppose that is not difficult to understand?'

I understood perfectly. Miss Trevellyon had not wanted her brother to marry my mother. He was already well into his forties and had shown little interest in women until then, and brother and sister were very close. She had disliked the even tenor of her life altered in any way and I do not think I am being uncharitable in supposing that she had viewed my mother's death with something akin to relief, tempered, I am sure, with sorrow for her brother and his short-lived marriage. I decided not to say whether I understood her desire to be rid of my mother's furniture or not.

'It was perfectly safe in the attic, and from time to time I went up there to see that there were no signs of deterioration.'

'Are you asking me if I have room for the pieces now?' I asked. I wished I could call him Uncle Alan as my mother had wanted; to call him Mr Trevellyon seemed so stark and unfriendly.

'No, Rachel, that is not why I invited you here. Three weeks ago for no apparent reason my sister decided to clear some things out of the attic. She was alone in the house at the time and she was standing on an old trunk to reach into a corner when she fell. There was nobody to hear her cries for help and she lay there with a fractured wrist until I arrived home – but that is beside the point and she has almost recovered now. In falling, however, she had knocked over your mother's desk. One of the drawers had sprung open and this was lying on the floor.'

As he spoke he reached into a drawer of his desk and brought out an ornamental casket in mother-of-pearl decorated with silver and gold and tiny seed pearls. It was a beautiful thing and I was aware that at the sight of it the warm red blood suffused my face and throat, for I had seen it before.

'Do you know what it is, Rachel?' he asked quietly.

'Yes. I only saw it once but I remember my mother kept it locked in a drawer of that desk.'

'Do you know what it contains? The box is valuable, the contents could also be valuable.'

'It should contain a jewelled pendant. She always kept the casket locked.'

'Do you know where she kept the keys, both for her desk and for the casket?'

'There are some keys in the jewel box you gave to me with her jewellery. They could be for the desk and the casket – I don't know what else they are for.'

'If this is valuable I think it should be placed in the bank, but naturally it belongs to you. Is the pendant gold, is it something she brought with her from Vienna?'

'It is in the form of a bird, a falcon, fashioned in rubies. It is very beautiful and yes, she did bring it with her from Vienna.'

'I thought your mother had no wealthy connections in her own country. She did tell me that her father was a station-master on the border between Austria and Hungary, and that her mother was Hungarian. She was placed in the imperial school of ballet when she was little more than a child.'

16

'Yes, that is true. I don't know how she came to have the pendant or who gave it to her, but I believe it was a present.'

'It was a very valuable present,' he said dryly, and I resented the thoughts that were passing through his mind.

'My mother was a dancer, she danced before the Emperor. To people of wealth a jewel is not too much to give if they enjoyed her performance.'

'Perhaps you are right, Rachel. I know nothing of such matters.'

'Do you wish me to take the casket with me now, Mr Trevellyon?' I asked. It was easy at.that moment to address him in that fashion, although I regretted it later on when my temper had subsided a little.

'It does not belong to me or to my sister. I have looked through the other drawers in the desk but they are empty. I cannot think how that was missed.'

I knew how it had been missed. There had been another drawer in the desk, a secret drawer, and Miss Trevellyon had obviously sent the desk flying with some force to have caused it to fall open.

'Is the desk badly damaged?' I asked him.

'Only superficially. I have asked a cabinet maker to make whatever repairs are necessary. It will be put back in the attic until you decide that you want it.'

I looked at him somewhat helplessly and I was already regretting my high-handed show of temper. He really was a very nice man and I felt that he was also a sad man, a lonely man. For one brief summer he had allowed himself to love a woman and cast aside the ties that had kept him chained to an embittered unmarried sister and a domination that had gone on too long, but fate had been cruel, it had taken from him the woman he loved before they had really had a chance to make something of their life together. Now he was being fair to me as he saw it and by my brittle antipathy I was refusing to meet him halfway.

'I'm sorry you are having all this trouble. I'll ask Miss Frobisher if I can make room for them in my bedroom, but she has so many things and it is difficult.'

'There is no need for that, Rachel. There is one other point

I want to raise with you, however, and I hope you will understand what I am trying to do for you.'

I waited, watching him spread out on his desk several papers and lengthy-looking documents.

'I settled a sum of money on your mother before our marriage and on her death I transferred these assets to you. They have now matured. I did not tell you before because you had employment and a home with Miss Frobisher, but you should be aware that you have a little money of your own. I have reinvested in your name most of these monies – for which I shall want your signature – and I have also placed in the bank the sum of one thousand pounds, which I think you are now of an age to handle wisely.'

I stared at him, unbelieving. I was rich! I had thought him cold and uncaring but all these years he had had my welfare at heart, not because of me but because he had loved my mother. The tears rushed to my eyes and rolled unheeded down my cheeks. He was acutely embarrassed, his hands busy shuffling the papers. I blew my nose into my handkerchief and wiped my eyes, then he looked up and smiled the gentle charming smile I had almost forgotten. 'If you will come round here, Rachel, I'll show you where to sign your name.'

I signed without reading any of them, and he said, 'I hope if you are ever in a position when you need to sign documents and I am no longer here to assist you, you will read them carefully. I could be robbing you of a fortune.'

'The only fortune you could rob me of is the one you have given me, and that would be no robbery at all. I am very grateful for all you have done for me, there really was no need. If my mother could know of your kindness she would love you for it, I feel sure.'

He took my hand and held it in his firm grasp for several moments. 'I was dreading your coming, you know. I was afraid you would look like your mother, speak like your mother, I didn't know how I would be able to bear it. The likeness is there but it's so elusive, so fragile, I needn't have worried.'

'I wish I was more like her. My father was dark and she was so fair, goodness knows where I got this red hair from.'

'It is very beautiful red hair, and I can tell you where you get it from.'

'You can?'

'Yes, I once remarked on it to your mother and she said you were like your grandmother. She came from Budapest, she was beautiful, she loved to dance to gypsy music and her hair was as red as the beech leaves in the autumn.'

I laughed suddenly. I knew now why my mother had married him, apart from his kindness and the shoulder she had cried on for so long. He could have been fun to be with, he could have blossomed as a man should in his new-found freedom. In a sudden rush of affection I reached up and put my arms round his neck, laying my cheek for a brief moment against his own.

He was embarrassed by my show of affection but I felt he was pleased too, and he made a great thing of wrapping the casket securely in brown paper and came out onto the doorstep with me to say goodbye.

'Are you returning to London tonight?' he asked.

'I had thought of going to the village, I thought it would be nice to see some of the places I used to know. Now I'm not so sure with something so valuable in my possession.'

'The village is much the same, Rachel.'

I thanked him again and walked off down the road, turning round before the road turned into the cathedral square. He was standing where I had left him and he waved his hand in answer to mine. He had not invited me to spend the night in his house, I had noticed. It was now after three o'clock and by the time I had caught the little train which climbed the single track towards the village it would be very late. I decided instead to go inside the cathedral to think things over.

I sat in one of the pews at the back for a few moments listening to the organ and the choir practising their hymns for the following Sunday. There were only a few people visiting the cathedral and its gentle peace washed over me like a benediction. I looked at the parcel in my hands, seeing through the brown paper and ornamental casket the jewelled pendant lying against the pale blue satin lining, and I found myself remembering that other morning when I saw it for the first time.

I was just nine years old and I remember running happily into my mother's bedroom to thank her for the birthday presents I had found that morning on the end of my bed. The morning sunlight flooded the room and I stood blinking in the doorway, halted in my haste by the sight of my mother sitting at her dressing table holding up to the light a pendant on a long golden chain. It seemed to flash and sparkle with glowing colour. With my eyes filled with wonder and my hands outstretched I ran forward to stand beside her. She started back nervously and made as if to hide the pendant in the pocket of her dressing gown.

'How you startled me, Rachel, I didn't hear you come in!'

'Please, mother, let me see the pendant. Is it new, is it a present?'

Reluctantly she brought the jewel out of her pocket and it lay in the palm of her hand alive with colours of rose and crimson.

'How beautiful it is! Why have I never seen it before? Are you going to wear it?'

'Not here, darling, I am a vicar's wife and no vicar's wife would ever wear this.'

'Is it worth a lot of money?'

'Yes, a great deal of money. The stones are mostly rubies, the eyes in the bird are diamonds.'

'But what is it?'

'It is the family crest of the Meinhart family, one of the oldest and most noble families in Austria. The bird is a falcon.'

'But there are no red falcons.'

'No, but then there is a reason for its colour.'

All my mother's stories of Vienna were gay, evoking handsome men in glamorous uniforms, creamy white shoulders under the lights of crystal chandeliers, and waltzes that went on through the night until the dawn. I sensed that this was going to be a story of a different kind and I waited expectantly, perched on the side of her bed. She held the pendant up to the light and the rubies flashed as though she held a flame in her fingers. 'It isn't a happy story, Rachel,' she said sadly.

20

'I don't care, I want to hear it, please, mother.'

In the quiet of that cathedral with the late afternoon sunlight streaming through the stained glass windows I could hear the lilt of her voice and the story that would have put to shame any tale from the pen of my employer.

'Once, many years ago, just before the first crusade, the young heir to the Meinharts' vast estates lived in a big and beautiful castle set high up on top of a crag on the outskirts of Vienna. He was very happy. He had just chosen the daughter of a noble house to be his bride and they were waiting for her arrival from Salzburg.

'She came in time for the feast of All Hallows, bringing with her a retinue of young girls escorted by a company of her kinsmen.

'On the day before the wedding Ludwig decided that they should hunt for wild boar in the forest – Ludwig was the young lord's name – and he rode out from the castle with his favourite falcon on his arm. It was a beautiful bird he had trained from a fledgling, and during the morning he proudly showed off its hunting skills to his companions. Again and again he released the falcon, it caught its prey and returned to perch on his arm. Then there came a time when the bird did not respond to his call and anxiously they searched for it until the light faded, the day grew cold and the men became weary and hungry.

'The snow was already falling and so Ludwig decided to call off the search until the morning. On their return to the castle they found the falcon lying near the drawbridge with an arrow through its heart, its blood already turning the snow to crimson.

'Ludwig was saddened by the loss of his beautiful bird and offered a vast reward to whoever would give him the name of the man who had shot it. The reward was a powerful incentive and he soon learned that the man who had shot his falcon was the cousin of his betrothed, who was in love with her himself and who had shot the bird out of jealousy. The lady begged him not to seek revenge on her kinsman, so instead he returned her to her father in Salzburg and the marriage did not take place.

21

'Ludwig went away to fight in the crusades. He never came back to Castle Meinhart because he was killed by a Saracen arrow and his body was laid to rest out there in the Holy Land. From that day, however, the family Meinhart took as their crest the crimson falcon. In Vienna and in all Austria it is well known.'

'What do the words mean?' I remember asking her.

'They are Latin words, *animo et fide*, and they mean courageously and faithfully.'

'Like the falcon?'

'Just like the falcon, Rachel.'

I was drawn back into the present by a light touch on my shoulder and I looked up to see an old man looking at me anxiously. 'Are you all right, miss?' he asked.

'Oh yes, thank you, I was just thinking of something else.'

'I just wanted to make sure. You've been thinking about that something else for quite a long time.'

'Yes, but I must be going, it is getting quite dark.'

'Have you far to go?'

'I shall have to stay in Exeter tonight, it is too late to go anywhere else. Can you direct me to a small inexpensive hotel where a girl staying on her own won't be frowned upon?'

'There's the Stag's Head, miss, they only takes about four people. It's along by the station but you could walk it with your young legs in about fifteen minutes.'

I thanked him warmly for his advice and walked swiftly out of the cathedral. The streets lamps were lit and I now gave up any ideas I had had of trying to reach the village or of returning to London that night.

My room at the Stag's Head was very comfortable and next morning after a quite enormous breakfast I set out for the station. The next train to London was at noon but there stood the little country train as though it had been waiting for me, and without hesitation I booked my return ticket and ran towards it. I savoured every mile as it climbed upwards along the old familiar track. I had taken this same journey so many times going home at weekends from school, but today there

22

would be no father standing patiently waiting for me on the platform and no Angel harnessed to the smart little trap in the station yard.

Angel, the pony, had been a gift to my father from the squire after a particularly gruelling winter when he had had to walk miles to visit his parishioners in remote farms and hamlets. Her name was unfortunate because her disposition was by no means angelic. For want of a better word Angel was a hussy. She was vain and a joy to watch, but she had a mind of her own and a nasty habit of skipping onto the pavement when anything else approached her on the road. She was also not averse to stealing apples in any orchard that was within her reach. She remained flighty and bad-tempered until the day Mr Trevellyon found a buyer for her, a brewer from Ashburton, and I remember how I watched her trot jauntily down the road driven by the wife of her new owner, nor had she thought me worthy of a backward glance.

I think in my heart I had always blamed Angel for leaving my father alone on the moor during that long arctic night after she returned to her stable pulling the shattered trap behind her.

Nothing was different in the straggling High Street that started at the station and climbed upwards towards the church and the vicarage. It was lunch time and most of the shops were closed, and I knew none of the few people I met along the way. The vicarage garden was still as untidy as it had been in our time. There had always been too much to do in other spheres so that the poor garden had been sadly neglected and my father, fond of biblical terms, referred to it as the wilderness.

The swing hung crookedly from the old pear tree and the gate hung askew on its hinges. I went into the churchyard to look at my father's grave, wishing I could have brought flowers to put there, but I need not have worried. The grass around the grave was freshly cut and there was a large bunch of flowers in a new white marble urn. I also noted with gratitude that my mother's name had been added on the white headstone, presumably by my stepfather.

I knew that I would never come back to the village again

23

and if it was wrong to evoke memories that made me sad there were others that brought a great deal of joy. There was the gamekeeper's cottage which the squire had allowed us to live in after the vicarage was taken by the new clergyman and his family, but it had been I, braver than I felt, who had asked the squire to help us after I found out that my mother had been selling articles of silver and some of her jewellery to a man from Exeter so that we could live.

How bold he must have thought me, a girl of fourteen, standing in front of his big mahogany desk pouring out all my woes, inviting his help so confidently that he had been amused, throwing back his head and laughing merrily at my audacity. He had helped us, though, finding my mother a room at the hall where she could teach the niceties of the ballroom to the daughters of the gentry, as well as the intricacies of the exquisite petit point work she did.

'By Gad, girl, but I admire your spirit,' he had said as he escorted me to the door, and on the threshold he had lifted me up bodily in his arms and planted a kiss on my soft young mouth. I had hated it. His breath smelled of whisky and cigar smoke and I had wiped his kiss away with the back of my hand. Instead of being annoyed he had laughed again, saying that if I counted his kiss of such little value, a proposal of marriage at some later date was hardly likely to be received with much enthusiasm.

Oh, why were memories so hurtful? For seven long years I had put them from me, stifling them whenever they crept unbidden into my thoughts. Now the scent of the warm earth and the autumn leaves tumbling along the path brought them back most poignantly.

I had reached the stile at the end of the lower meadow and I was remembering that it had been October then, although a windier, sharper October than this one. The leaves of summer had almost gone and the fresh keen winds from the moor had already begun to taunt us with the threat of things to come.

'Meet me tomorrow morning at eleven in the bottom meadow,' the squire had said. 'I've got something to show you.' He was as delighted as any small boy with a new toy.

'I know what it is, it's a new horse, you couldn't possibly be so pleased about anything else,' I answered him.

He had laughed, tweaking my ear. 'Ay, and she's a rare beauty, Rachel, pure Arab, perhaps a little bit wild but we'll soon teach her manners.'

I had been early in the bottom meadow and hoisting myself up onto the top of a fence from where I could watch their progress down the long slow hill from the stables, I had waited. I had seen him take that journey so often and thought what a magnificent combination they made, Sir Peter and his big black stallion. They seemed like one being instead of horse and rider.

It was with me again, the foreboding I had felt that morning when I first saw them emerge from the stable yard. The mare was doing a great deal of prancing and bucking and the squire seemed to be having difficulty in turning her into the slope. I could see that she was beautiful, a warm golden chestnut with a flowing blond mane and tail. I could also see that he carried a whip which he seemed to be using lightly to encourage her to behave. She started to gallop faster than I had ever seen a horse gallop. I jumped off the gate and ran towards them shouting, 'Don't jump, please don't jump!'

Dozens of times I had seen him jump that crooked fence, freely, light-heartedly, but this horse was fighting him with every sinew in her body and he was angry. I could see his flushed face, his hands straining on the reins, and I could hear the pounding of hooves on the wet grass.

My voice was lost in the wind, but nothing could have halted that mad wild charge. I saw the horse lift into the air, but not high enough. With a sickening thud both horse and rider came to grief on the other side of the fence. Sir Peter was thrown several yards away and lay still on the top of the bank while the horse lay on her back, her hooves thrashing the air, whinnying shrilly. I rushed through the gap in the fence, tearing my dress on a rusty nail, entangling my hair in the brambles while shouts came from above where three men were hurrying down the hill from the stables.

I had run to Sir Peter first. His face was deathly pale and I saw that his head had struck a stone which lay half buried in the grass; the bright red blood poured from a cut in his head.

He was breathing, but he was unconscious. The horse too was silent now, lying on her side, her eyes glazed with pain, and I went to kneel beside her. She was so beautiful with her arched satiny neck and golden mane spread out across the grass. I took her head and laid it against my knee and she made no sound as I caressed her neck. Then the men were there, two of them with Sir Peter and a young stable boy with me. I watched his hands as they gently fingered the mare's legs. In answer to the anguished appeal in my eyes he said, 'Foreleg's broken, miss, she'll 'ave to be shot. I reckon the squire should never a ridden 'er, she weren't ready fer it yet.'

They had come with a five-barred gate and it took four of them to lift the squire onto it, then in a weary procession they plodded back up the hill. I had turned to where the horse lay on the grass and one of the boys said, 'She won't know anythin' about it, miss. Go on up wi' the others, I'll see to the mare.'

I had run up the hill with stumbling steps, my hands clenched about my ears so that I would not hear the shot that ended the mare's life. Next morning the squire too was dead and try as I would I could not imagine that man, who had been larger than life, lying still and pale in death. I could not think that never again would I hear his robust laughter ringing out in the quiet of my father's study, or see him riding his big black hunter behind the hounds through the frosty autumnal mist.

I should not have come back. Seven years was too long to expect any of my childhood friends to remember me now. I turned and retraced my steps down the length of the High Street. I could see the vicar letting himself in by the side gate which separated his garden from the churchyard. He was a stranger to me, a much younger man than the man who had replaced my father, and I couldn't help wondering if he was a Devonshire man.

That had been the first criticism one of the villagers had levelled against my father.

'It's a pity you ain't Devonshire, sor, the last one were, we understood 'im. It's allus better if the vicar be Devonshire.'

Two

'Really, Rachel, you must be completely out of your senses to comtemplate travelling to Vienna alone. It's not as though you had relatives to go to.'

Miss Frobisher was angry, and her tirade over the breakfast table was unfortunately to be the first of many. My resignation was spread out in front of her and her face was flushed, her eyes snapping, so that she reminded me more than ever of a quarrelsome robin.

'Your letter is terse to the point of rudeness, but I think I am entitled to some sort of explanation.'

'I'm sorry if my letter appears rude, Miss Frobisher, I didn't intend it to be – perhaps it is because I was feeling particularly distressed when I wrote it. I wish to leave because I have to go to Vienna and I am not sure when I shall be returning, if at all.'

The astonishment on her face was profound. 'Vienna! But why Vienna of all places? I know your mother was Viennese but I understood you to say you no longer had relatives there. Where do you intend to live, and how do you intend to live, as you have no work to go to?'

'I shall look for a modest inexpensive inn and remain there until I have accomplished what I am setting out to do. Then if I can't find work in Vienna I shall probably have to come back to England.'

'And by that time you will have lost your position here, and work for a woman with your upbringing isn't all that easy to find. What, for instance, have you been trained for?'

'I could do the sort of work I have done for you, or I could

27

look after children and teach English. I speak the German language fluently so there should be something I could do.'

'But to go to a foreign city where you don't know a soul – by this time all your mother's family are probably dead. What does your stepfather think about all this?'

'He doesn't know, there is no reason why he should. I am over twenty-one years of age and I am not his responsibility.'

'Nevertheless I shall write and tell him, perhaps he can knock some sense into your head. You have not been the same since the day you went to Devonshire to see him, moping about the house with a long face, and I've thought once or twice you've been crying in your room but I chose not to say anything. What have you got to cry about? Aren't you happy here?'

'I have been very happy here, I have loved the work, particularly the illustrative work, but something has happened which makes it imperative for me to resign.'

There was silence in the room for several minutes except for the loud ticking of the grandfather clock in the corner of the room, and the twittering of the birds on the windowsill outside. At last she looked up from my letter and said, 'I'm sorry, Rachel, but I must have a secretary and I am not prepared to hold the position open on the chance that you will come to your senses and return here. I accept your resignation but I think you are an extremely wilful and foolish girl. You came to me with excellent credentials and I had expected that the daughter of a vicar would have shown more sympathy for me and a great deal more common sense.'

I watched her stuff my letter into the copious leather handbag she always carried around. Head held high, she stalked out of the dining room without another glance in my direction.

I wished I could have taken her into my confidence, but how could I say to that proper middle-class Englishwoman that I was not what I seemed? I could hardly tell her that my father had not been that dear good man who had brought me up to observe the truth and think of others before myself, but an Austrian nobleman whose family as well as his Emperor had considered my mother unfit to be his wife, so that their ecstatic, romantic marriage had been set aside before I was born and even my name did not rightly belong to me.

The firm slam of the front door only emphasized how angry my employer felt towards me. Normally when she went to the shops I accompanied her, but this morning she obviously preferred to go alone. For a while I stared dismally out of the window at the tall stone houses along the tree-lined street, the only sound the steady clip-clop of a horse's hooves, then again my thoughts turned inwards and I was seeing mountain peaks and Alpine lakes bluer than a summer sky. This was the scenery my mother had filled my imagination with since I was old enough to understand and remember.

The house had been quiet on the night I returned from Devonshire and I had crept up to my room trying to make no sound, for Miss Frobisher was a light sleeper. Safely in my room I put a light to the gas jet and sat for a few moments on the edge of my bed clutching the paper parcel in my hands. I knew what it contained, yet I was afraid to open it. I found myself remembering my mother's words spoken to me on the morning she married Alan Trevellyon. We had stood together waiting for the carriage that was to take us to the church and she had turned towards me with a sad little doubtful smile. 'You know, Rachel,' she had said, 'I have learned from bitter experience that one should be wary of happiness, for it is a fragile thing and not something to be held captive as one would cage a bird. Always when I have thought I had found happiness it has been snatched away from me and now I am afraid it might happen again.' I had sought to reassure her with kind words and smiles, and when the carriage arrived her words were forgotten in the excitement of the day. I was to remember them forcibly in the days and nights which followed.

My fingers struggled with the knots in the string which bound the parcel. It was only an old pendant, I told myself, nothing to be afraid of, yet for a few moments I stared at the casket, aware of the beauty of the workmanship, before I dared lift the lid. Instead of the gleam of jewels from its satiny depths, an envelope bearing my name lay on top of the pendant and I recognized my mother's handwriting immediately. I took it out slowly. At that moment she seemed very close to me, and I felt if I closed my eyes I would be able to smell her perfume, hear the rustle of her skirts, see the gentle smile on her perfect face. Instead my fingers tore at the envelope until her letter lay open in my hands and I started to read.

Every word of her letter will be engraved upon my heart for the rest of my life, but I did not know then how irrevocably it was to change my own future. Never again would I be content to be the gentle daughter of an English parson, living quietly in genteel obscurity.

Behind the lines of her letter I was seeing my mother, a beautiful young country girl leaving her home in a small town on the Danube just two miles from the Hungarian border where her father, my grandfather, was employed as the stationmaster. I could imagine my grandparents dressed in their Sunday best proudly escorting their one daughter to Vienna, where she danced before a selection committee, and their joy when she was accepted as a pupil at the imperial ballet school. Then came the years of dedication and endurance for a girl who lived and breathed dancing, the striving for perfection and the endless practice which left her weary in body, but with a strengthened determination to succeed.

This was not the Vienna I had dreamed about, the Vienna of court balls and operas, of carriage rides through the Vienna woods to eat supper at some forest inn, not the Vienna of handsome men in splendid uniforms and beautiful women in exquisite gowns and glittering jewels, it was the Vienna which demanded of its musicians and artistes all that they had, their youth and beauty as well as their hearts.

The years of dedication did not go unrewarded. By dint of her talent my mother was chosen to perform solo dances, and one magical night she was chosen with four others to dance before the Emperor at the first court ball of a glittering season. That was the night she met my father, Count Carl Meinhart, an equerry to the Emperor and an officer in the imperial hussars, and, in my mother's own words, 'unbelievably handsome in his elegant uniform, particularly to a shy little country girl who was just eighteen.' That night they waltzed together and fell in love, and from then on she had no thought for her teachers who had worked with her long and patiently, or for her parents who had been so proud of her. All she cared about were the nights they waltzed in the parks and the ballrooms of Vienna, or drove through the woods in the hours before the dawn.

One night she left the ballet for the last time. He was waiting for her at the station where they caught the last train for Innsbruck and it was there, in the mountains overlooking the city, that they were married in a tiny village church with only the priest's housekeeper and his gardener to witness the ceremony.

She wrote of those blissful days in the clean mountain air, with the spring flowers underneath their feet just where the snow belt ended, the only sounds the bells around the necks of Alpine cattle. After a month Count Meinhart returned to his duties in Vienna and my mother stayed on in the village, believing in his promises to join her as soon as he had prepared the Emperor and his mother for the news of their marriage.

I thought about my mother up there in the mountains waiting for her husband to return to her, living for his letters until they ceased abruptly. I could imagine her fears, particularly when she realized she was going to have a child. Her career lay in ruins behind her for there was no going back, her money dwindling, and it was thanks to an American lady I knew as Aunt Milly that she did not fling herself into the icy waters of the lake, particularly after an envoy arrived from Vienna. He informed her that she was no longer married to Carl Meinhart. Their marriage had been set aside by command of the Emperor and Count Meinhart was now with his regiment on service in eastern Slovakia.

It was Aunt Milly who gave her the courage to go on, Aunt Milly who proved herself to be the most generous and kindest friend my mother ever had, Aunt Milly who brought her eventually to England where she met David Arden and later married him.

It had been my father, Count Meinhart, who had given the

pendant to my mother. He had told her it was always worn by the countesses of Meinhart and that one day she too would wear it proudly for all the world to see. Instead she had come to look upon it as a thing of ill omen, begging me in her letter to send the falcon back. She feared that it would bring ill luck to me just as it had brought it to her if I kept it in my possession.

Tears fell down my cheeks and splashed onto her letter and I laid it aside, opening the casket wide to look once again at the pendant lying on its bed of blue satin. I reached for it and held it in the palm of my hand where the dark red stones flashed like fire and the bright diamond eyes in the bird's head gleamed up at me with a strange penetrating wickedness. The pendant seemed to burn into my hands and I dropped it quickly into the casket, covering it instantly with my mother's letter before I locked it away. The illusion of evil had been fanciful and I was a practical person. I believed in the things associated with stability and normality, not the tantalizing terrors of the dark and secret places my mother had been afraid of. All the same, my resolve to return the crimson falcon to its rightful owners was very strong.

I knew what lay before me. I must resign from my employment with Miss Frobisher and leave the peaceful and contented existence we had enjoyed together, to embark upon a journey to a country I had only heard of, with a heart filled with pain and bitterness towards a family I did not know.

Miss Frobisher wasted no time in informing my stepfather of my determination to leave her service and he came at once to London to try to sort matters out. He stayed in London three days in the hope that he could make me change my mind, but when he realized I was adamant he did everything within his power to make the journey easy for me.

'You will travel first class, Rachel, I won't hear of you doing anything else – an English girl going abroad for the first time, and unchaperoned.'

Miss Frobisher had no difficulty in replacing me and two weeks before I was due to leave England I moved out of her home to make way for my successor, a crisp businesslike woman, a spinster, well into her forties. I had worked hard in order to leave everything satisfactory but she wasn't very grateful; I rather gathered that Miss Frobisher had already burdened her with the history of my shortcomings and she gave me the impression that if I intended to go I should go quickly so that she could occupy my place.

For the last two weeks I spent in England, therefore, I found a modest hotel in Kensington which my stepfather insisted on paying for. I would dearly have loved to have taken him into my confidence but I never knew how much of my mother's earlier life he was familiar with and rather than have him think she had deceived him, I preferred him to think that I was reckless and given to extravagance now that I had a little money of my own.

He accompanied me as far as Dover, where he saw me safely aboard the ferry for Calais. It was only then that I asked him, 'Did my mother speak of me during her illness?'

He shook his head sadly. 'No, Rachel, I was with her most of the time but she was quite delirious and I could make nothing of her ramblings.'

'Did she speak of my father or of Vienna?'

'No. She went on and on about a bird, some bird that must go back. The nurses said she could not have known what she was saying and I should discount it. She was very ill.'

The last view I had of him he was standing bareheaded on the quayside as the ferry pulled away, and I waved my hand until I could see him no more. I did not know if we would ever meet again, but hearing about my mother's delirium and her obsession with the pendant convinced me more than ever that the journey I had embarked upon was necessary.

The voyage was uneventful and I was pleased to find out that I was a confident traveller. I was assisted with my luggage in Calais and again in Paris by young men who seemed particularly anxious to be helpful, and their attentions gave me a new assurance. Now at last I was sitting in a corner seat on the train bound for Vienna.

My first-class compartment was luxurious by any standards. I shared it with a French couple and their small son, a boy of about six, as well as an extremely pampered small dog. As I moved to take my seat the boy pulled out his tongue at me. I waited until his parents looked away, then I made a face at him, instantly regretting my loss of dignity. Fortunately the boy seemed more interested in the activity in the corridor, returning only at intervals to check that his parents were still on the train.

Because of my late booking, the sleeping compartments were all reserved, but I hoped I would be able to put my feet up as the journey progressed. Any kind of sleep proved impossible because of the obnoxious child who spent half the night opening and closing the door, letting in streams of light and setting off the yapping of the dog. Consequently the first light of day found me in the tiny toilet trying to wash and make myself presentable for the remainder of the journey.

I was relieved when my travelling companions went to the dining car for breakfast and I looked forward to having the compartment to myself. We had crossed the Austrian border now and I could feel my excitement mounting as we raced through scenery I had heard of from my earliest childhood. They were so familiar, those snow-covered peaks and dark pine forests. The cold blue waters of the lakes we passed made me think of my mother staring into their depths in the months before I was born, but I was enchanted by the wooden chalets on the hillside, each with its quota of pine logs piled in orderly pyramids and ready for the months of winter, as well as by the quaint Alpine churches with their onion-shaped domes. From St Anton to Innsbruck the scenery hardly varied except for the pretty medieval villages where time seemed to have stood still. As the train pulled slowly into the station at Innsbruck I looked upwards towards the mountains surrounding the city. Somewhere up there I had been born twenty-three years ago and the urge to leave the train and go up into those mountains was so compelling it felt like physical pain.

The French family returned to the compartment and the man proffered a morning paper, which I accepted. Austrian news had little interest for me as yet and the fact that the Emperor was returning from his hunting lodge in Salzkammergut for the start of the season only attracted me momentarily. I turned the page and instantly I became alert. A paragraph informed me that the Countess Meinhart would open the first ball of the season on the Emperor's arm. I was sure my companions must hear the pounding of my heart or see the trembling of the newspaper held in my hands, and for a moment I leaned back against the cushions and closed my eyes. It was only when the French couple began to collect their luggage that I realized they were preparing to leave the train at the next stop.

I gathered my scattered wits and handed the newspaper back. The man smiled and said, 'Salzburg, Fräulein?' I shook my head and said, 'Nein, Vienna.' The boy made a further face at me. This time his father saw it and brought the palm of his hand down on the boy's bare knee with a resounding slap. A howl of protest followed, accompanied by more yapping from the dog, so it was with a feeling of considerable relief that I bade them farewell on the train's arrrival in Salzburg. Beautiful, civilized Salzburg, a city of churches and palaces, of Mozart and the music of his boyhood. But from my seat in the train all I could see was the station platform, and all my thoughts and emotions were centred on Vienna. I was impatient, now that we were so close, to move on quickly.

My attention was caught by the sudden activity on the platform as a crowd of people, both young and old, came hurrying in the wake of a young girl wrapped in expensive furs. There was much kissing and embracing, and she was laughing excitedly as they heaped boxes of chocolates and magazines into her arms. My previous travelling companions had left the door of my carriage open, and now two young men were struggling to pile her luggage onto the rack. The gaiety continued outside until the guard blew his whistle, then the girl joined me, smiling prettily and asking if I minded sharing my compartment with her. She stood at the open window waving her hand until the train rounded the bend, then she settled herself in the opposite corner. She was small and dainty, with golden hair and a delicate pink and white complexion, and she was beautiful in the way my mother had been beautiful, which made me think that perhaps it was a beauty peculiar to Austria.

35

I responded to her smile and she said in German, 'Are you too going to Vienna?'

I smiled again, nodding my head. Not waiting for me to speak she rushed on, 'I thought the train would never come, we seem to have been waiting all morning. I'm so excited, this is the first time since I left school that I have been to Vienna for the season. Is that why you are going?'

'I'm afraid not, I hadn't realized it was the season.'

'Please forgive me, I thought everyone went to Vienna at this time to enjoy themselves.'

'Not me, I'm afraid, I don't know a soul in Vienna.'

'Where are you from?'

'England.'

'England!' She made it sound as remote as though I had said that I had arrived that morning from the moon.

I didn't reply, but merely smiled a little.

'I thought everybody wanted to be in Vienna for New Year. It all starts on New Year's Eve in the Prater, with lanterns in the trees and fireworks. All Vienna will be there. Princes will dance with kitchenmaids and countesses will flirt with gamekeepers. Isn't it exciting? Then the day after there will be *Die Fledermaus* at the opera followed by the first ball at the Schönbrunn. Oh, this is the very best time to be going to Vienna . . . But you shouldn't be alone on New Year's Eve when all Vienna is waltzing. You must go to the Prater. I shall be there and I'll look for you. You will have no difficulty in finding it, everybody will be moving in that direction. What's your name?'

'Rachel. Rachel Arden.'

She repeated it – my name sounded foreign on her lips – then smiling brightly she said, 'My name is Sophia von Werenberg. We live in Salzburg but I am being met in Vienna by my cousin, Ernst von Reichman. Ernst is an officer in the imperial hussars. He's incredibly handsome and I do hope he'll be in uniform, it's so much more romantic than ordinary dress.'

Suddenly I was remembering another man in uniform who had swept my young mother off her feet, and some of the bitterness must have shown momentarily in my face because

Sophia said quickly, 'You must think I'm being very silly, but this is all so wonderful to me after that convent school in the mountains where nothing ever happened and we had to be in bed by eight o'clock in the winter months.'

I smiled sympathetically. Feeling that I should contribute something to the conversation, I asked, 'Are you staying with relatives in Vienna?'

'Yes, although we'll only be in Vienna for four days, then we're going to the country. I would really rather stay on in Vienna but Max will want to get back and I suppose Mellina will have all sorts of wonderful things planned for us. She's so terribly good at that and the country around the castle is very beautiful.'

Mellina! The name struck a strange chord in my memory. I had heard it only recently, but where?

'Your sister?' I asked.

'My cousin.'

'Such a lovely, unusual name,' I commented.

'Yes, and it suits her,' Sophia said wistfully. 'I wish I was half as beautiful as Mellina. I can't remember a time when I didn't long to be like her, but all I've got is her colouring. She's so tall and graceful and so alive.' She hunted through the newspapers on the seat beside her until she found the paragraph I had already read over and over. 'Have you seen that she is to open the first ball with the Emperor? Poor man, he is old now and so sad since his wife was assassinated and that terrible tragedy at Mayerling when his son Rudolf took his own life. Did you hear about that in England?'

'Oh yes, it was in the English papers at the time. I felt terribly sad for the girl, she was so young.'

'Poor Marie Vetsera. She was at school with Mellina. She was so sweet and pretty and Rudolf was years older and married to a woman he didn't love. Right from their first meeting Marie captivated him utterly. Isn't it sad to have to marry somebody you don't love when there are so many people in the world you could love if only you knew about them?'

She was staring out of the window, her eyes bright with unshed tears, and I too found myself thinking about Crown

Prince Rudolf and the pretty young woman who had been his mistress, taking their own lives in the hunting lodge at Mayerling rather than face life without each other. There were many questions I wanted to ask, however, and somehow or other I had to find out a great deal more about the Meinhart family. For all I knew there could be several branches of the same family, or even several different families bearing the same name.

Sophia was so enchantingly ingenuous I warmed to her in spite of her connections with the hated Meinharts, and I only hoped she was so enraptured with her cousin she would not object to answering my questions.

'You say you'll be leaving Vienna after only a few days. Do your relatives not live there permanently then?'

'Oh no, they have a beautiful house on the Ringstrasse, but their real home is a great medieval castle on the heights beyond the woods. It's like a fairy-tale castle with turrets and battlements, something the Sleeping Beauty might have lived in. Mellina hates it, she is bored by the country. Max loves it, of course, but then it is his home.'

'And Max, are you fond of him also?'

She wrinkled up her pretty nose. 'Count Alexander Maximilian Ludwig Meinhart,' she said pompously. 'Doesn't it sound grand? Honestly, I don't really know whether I like him or not.'

'Why is that?' I asked her.

I hated prying into her private life – I felt like a village busybody – but Sophia did not seem to think there was anything odd in my questions, and they were very necessary. For all I knew this man could very well be a close relative.

'Well, I suppose he is very handsome,' she replied seriously. 'He is tall and dark, but he is always so very grave and austere, not nearly as much fun as Ernst or Mellina.'

'Do they have children?'

'A little girl called Liesel. She is exquisite, just like Mellina, not like Max at all, but then I should think he would want a son for that great castle of his. My mother says she can't see Mellina having other children, she's much too fond of enjoying herself.'

'So the title might die out with the present count?' I mused.

I looked out of the window. The daylight was almost gone and we were travelling swiftly through the dusk with only the lights from occasional hamlets to penetrate the gloom.

'Where are you staying in Vienna?' my companion asked.

'Oh, at some inn,' I replied, and I handed her a card which I had in my bag. 'I expect I shall have an early night after my journey and wake up refreshed in the morning.'

She laughed merrily. 'I guarantee you won't! When you step down from the train, Vienna will take hold of you like a charm. You will feel the excitement even before it starts, then tonight there will be the waltzes and the gypsy violins, the laughter of the crowds in the park, and you will not be able to resist. I shall look for you in the Prater gardens, Rachel, and I shall remind you of your early night when we are still waltzing at dawn.'

I didn't believe any of it, but I laughed with her, falling in with her mood. Talking to this girl was easy and I found myself telling her about my childhood in Devonshire and my parents – for I still thought of David Arden as my father. I told her about the squire who had been such a wonderful friend and she interrupted me quickly by asking, 'Weren't you just a little bit in love with him, Rachel?'

For a moment her words shocked me into silence. Perhaps I had been in love with him. He had certainly been the most romantic figure in my young life, with his merry blue eyes and dark curling hair, his laughter that echoed round my father's tiny study, and the essentially male smell of whisky and cigar smoke. If I had not loved him, I had never been able to ignore him.

She was laughing at me, teasing me into admission, and somewhat crossly I replied, 'It wasn't like that. I was far too young and he was far too old. Besides, he was the squire.'

'What difference does that make?' she said, laughing merrily as though she found the whole idea of such a relationship more romantic than foolish. 'I'm younger than you are and I've been in love more times than I can remember. When I was twelve I was in love with my music master, and then they brought in a divine Frenchman who

39

taught us French and we all fell in love with him. Oh, and then there was Ernst for a while and after him there was Otto Bruch, who asked me to marry him the day after I fell in love with somebody else. Wasn't that silly of him? Do you English girls ever have any fun?'

'Quite obviously we have led very different lives! Might I ask if you are in love at the present?'

'But of course! Tonight I am in love with Vienna and you will be too when you see how enchanting it is.'

I was glad of this gay gorgeous girl who had steered my mind for a little while away from bitterness, but I wondered what she would say if I told her why I was visiting Vienna. Sophia was as airy as a butterfly, she would think it all terribly romantic and see nothing wrong in my mother's unorthodox marriage.

We were nearing the city now. I felt it. There was more activity in the corridor and the train was moving slowly, passing through the outskirts of the city, as I could see by the lights in the houses and along the streets. Sophia jumped to her feet and opened the window, but a rush of cold air and smoke filled the compartment so that she hastily closed it again.

'Another few minutes and we shall be at the station. I do hope Ernst comes to look for me on the platform, I don't want to have to wait in the cold for him,' she said hopefully.

We helped each other with our luggage. She had far more than I, but by the time the train came to a halt we had collected all our things together. I was the first to step down from the train, taking the cases as she handed them to me. I stared around me at the hurrying crowds and Sophia called down, 'Can you see him, Rachel? He's tall and fair and ever so good-looking.'

I craned my head to see down the platform and there was a young man moving from compartment to compartment, looking in each one in turn. 'Take a look,' I called to her, 'I think this could be your cousin and he is in uniform.'

With a squeal of delight she jumped down from the train and ran along the platform calling, 'Ernst, Ernst! I'm here, I'm here!'

I watched forlornly as they embraced, but in a moment she was dragging him towards me. I found myself looking up into laughing light blue eyes in a face that was certainly handsome. The uniform he wore suited his tall slim figure and his Saxon fairness. Sophia introduced us and he took my hand and raised it briefly to his lips. It was a foreign gesture, romantic and charming, but the next minute he was organizing the removal of our luggage with efficient speed.

We walked together down the platform and out of the station then he said gallantly, 'Can I give you a ride to your hotel, Miss Arden? We are in no hurry.'

'Oh no, that really won't be necessary, I believe my hotel is quite close to the station.'

'But you will require help with your luggage. I will speak to the porter.'

'You really are very kind but I can manage now, I assure you.' I turned to Sophia. 'I hope you all have a lovely time in Vienna before you go to the country. I enjoyed travelling with you, you made the journey seem much shorter.'

'Don't forget, I shall look for you in the Prater gardens tonight! You must come, mustn't she, Ernst? We have a duty to look after our visitor from England, otherwise she's going to go back there and tell them what inhospitable boors we are.'

Gallantly he added his encouragement to hers, for who could resist that gay lovely girl with the fox-lined hood of her cape pulled over her blond hair, her blue eyes sparkling with mischief?

'We would both like you to come to the Prater tonight,' he said smiling down into my eyes. 'There will be a crowd of us, many of my brother officers will be there and some girls, of course.'

'Then if I am not too tired perhaps I will be there. I will look for you.'

I was unprepared for Sophia's affectionate embrace. When they were walking away from me I felt for the first time really alone in a strange city, unsure even where my hotel was. The porter stood with my luggage, expectantly, so I produced the address of my hotel and he nodded his head, pointing to a street leading off the square.

'It is half-way down the street, Fräulein, if you would follow me.'

With every step my curiosity mounted. At last I was in Vienna and now I could feel its heartbeat in the hurrying crowds along the pavements, the lights shining through the branches of the linden trees, the smell of freshly roasted coffee and the equally delicious smell of newly baked bread.

The inn was a modest one halfway along the street and the lights from its windows streamed out into the night. I was welcomed with smiling faces and the courtesy that seemed typical of the Viennese. My room was pleasant, with shining furniture and pretty chintz drapes at the windows to match the bed covers. I suddenly felt eager to be part of this gay enchanting city and when the door closed behind the porter who had brought up my luggage I whirled round the room with a sense of anticipation. The suppressed excitement in the city streets had captured my heart too and I knew that there would be no early night for me. Instead I would follow the crowds towards the Prater and I would look for Sophia and her handsome cousin.

I surveyed my wardrobe with some misgivings. I had not been too extravagant before I left England, buying only a new coat for travelling and two warm winter dresses. The rest of my clothes consisted of skirts and blouses which in England had been almost a uniform for young women who had to earn their own living. Recklessly I had made a parcel of my oldest clothes and taken them to a hostel for fallen women. They had been accepted gladly enough but Miss Frobisher had disapproved of my action, saying, 'You may need those clothes yet, Rachel. I don't know what has come over you.' She had been far more astounded later on when she watched me packing my one evening gown. It had cost far more than I could afford and she considered it a foolish and meaningless extravagance.

'When do you expect to wear such a gown?' she had asked. 'Where in Vienna do you expect to be going in such a dress, and unescorted?'

I would certainly not be wearing it to visit the Prater gardens and my reflection in the mirror showed me a travel-weary young woman with dark smudges under her eyes and outdoor clothing that had become creased by too much sitting about in railway compartments. However, I washed in the warm water a chambermaid brought in for me, then I lay on my bed with my hair in curling rags until I felt relaxed.

I had not meant to drift off into sleep but the lack of it caught up with me and it was after eleven o'clock when I awoke, feeling chilled but rested. I could hear the people in the streets now, laughing and calling out to one another, and I went over to the window and peered out. I felt annoyed that I had slept so long, but the crowds hurrying past the hotel seemed to give little thought to the lateness of the hour as they drifted in the same direction.

I dressed quickly in one of my new dresses and brushed out my hair. This time the mirror showed me a different picture, a girl with sparkling blue eyes and shining hair. Satisfied with my appearance, I let myself out into the corridor and ran lightly down the stairs. The old man on duty in the hall smiled at me and said, 'You are going to the Prater, Fräulein? Yes, everyone goes to the Prater on New Year's Eve.'

'Shall I be safe on my own, do you think?'

He chuckled. 'A beautiful lady will not long be alone tonight. Keep with the crowds, my dear, and enjoy yourself.'

I smiled at him again before I ran out into the street. I followed his advice and stayed with the crowds, marvelling at the compelling urgency of their laughter and the sound of music as band after band joined the march. Children who should have been in bed hours before held fast to the hands of their parents, and young girls with flowers in their hair hung on to the arms of handsome young gallants in uniform. I found myself smiling back at people I had never seen before while my feet moved to the rhythm of the music and all around me lights poured out into the streets from small intimate coffee houses, nor was I oblivious to the bold admiring glances of the men who were swept along with me.

I have no memory of the buildings we passed on that first

night in Vienna, only of the avenues of linden trees gay with the lanterns. In the Prater gardens the sky was alight with fireworks and music. I stood at the edge of the crowd watching young people and old, even children, whirling around the bandstand to the tune of a waltz, and it was then some of my initial excitement left me and for the first time I began to doubt my wisdom in being there. I was alone when everybody else seemed to be part of a happy group.

Suddenly the tempo of the music changed from waltz time to something more energetic and now the dancers were whirling in a circle, forming an intricate pattern while the onlookers clapped their hands in time to the music. As I stood there entranced I suddenly found my hand seized and I too was pulled willy-nilly into the whirling throng. I looked up to see who my partner was and found myself staring into the laughing blue eyes and handsome face of Ernst von Reichman.

'I didn't recognize you at first,' he said. 'I've been watching you for some time, wondering who the beautiful snow maiden was who looked so forlorn but whose hair could melt the coldest snow.'

He was laughing, well pleased with his metaphor, then I was laughing too. The music was infectious, and if I could do nothing else I knew how to dance. I had always learned quickly, even the steps other children found difficult, and now I linked hands with other people and my feet found the beat of the music so that Ernst laughed down at me appreciatively.

I heard my name called and saw Sophia dancing with a group of young people. Immediately we were all together whirling round and round in a giant circle, and the music and the clapping hands became a torrent of sound in my ears. I had never know a night such as this one when we danced under the stars, oblivious of the cold and our breath freezing on the air. We ate hot roasted chestnuts by the edge of the frozen lake while couples skated to the music of another band, then we strolled arm in arm under trees glittering with frost watching the rockets leap into the sky to descend moments later in golden showers above the gardens. We drank delicious coffee and ate cream-filled pancakes in the café by the lake while the men sang student songs and clinked their glasses in time to the music, then back we went again to waltz to a different band until the stars paled, dawn crept slowly over the gardens, and one by one the revellers drifted away in the morning mist.

It was New Year's Day in the year 1900. Another year, another century, and I was another person. I was no longer Rachel Arden, the gently reared daughter of an English parson, I was somebody I did not yet know, somebody I had yet to discover in the months that lay ahead. But for this one night I was simply a girl in love with life and with music, a girl whose past was a myth, and whose future was burdened with mystery.

'Why so solemn all at once?' Ernst asked me, his eyes laughing into mine over the rim of his wine glass.

'I don't know, unless it is that I am finding it hard to believe that this is really me, dancing the night away with a man I had never heard of yesterday.'

'That is as it should be, a life full of surprises, happy surprises. I want to see you again, Rachel. I have duties at the palace this morning, but we could spend the afternoon together.'

'I should like that very much.'

'I wish I didn't have to go to the opera tonight, we could have gone to Grinzing. Tomorrow is the Emperor's ball at the palace and I have to be there. After that we're going to the country and I don't know what plans Mellina will have made.'

The mention of her name felt like a dash of ice-cold water thrown in my face and I wondered angrily how I could have forgotten so soon that Sophia and Ernst were relatives of Mellina and that she bore the family name I hated above all others, reminding me of my true reasons for being in Vienna.

'Don't look so disappointed, *Liebchen*, there will be other times – a great many of them, I hope,' he said, taking my resentment for disappointment.

I smiled. 'How long do you expect to be away?'

'I honestly don't know. One can never tell with Mellina, she's bound to have all sorts of entertainments lined up.'

'I wouldn't have thought there was all that much to do in the country,' I said.

'You'd be surprised at the things Mellina can find,' he said darkly, and something in his expression made me look away. The sudden shiver that swept over me had nothing to do with the cold frosty night.

The gardens were almost deserted now except for a few groups around the dance floor and still we sat on, waiting for the weary musicians to play one more waltz.

'Just one,' wailed Sophia, 'just the last one, then we will all go home. Ask them, Ernst, ask them for a slow lovely waltz, the very last one.'

We all watched as Ernst hurried over towards the bandstand where the musicians were already packing away their instruments. I saw him press a handful of money into the hands of the conductor, and once more the musicians resumed their places. This time we were waltzing to a slow haunting melody of old Vienna, unlike the spirited waltzes of Strauss.

After the melody died on the night air farewells were called and sleepy couples drifted away towards the gates, their arms still entwined.

'We'll pick up the carriages on the road,' Ernst said, but we were only halfway down the avenue when Sophia stopped suddenly, holding me by the arm. 'Oh, do listen,' she cried, 'can't you hear them?'

We listened, but at first I could hear nothing and impatiently she exclaimed, 'Violins! Gypsy violins!' She started to run in the direction of the music and we followed, hearing them plainly now.

We came at last upon a small clearing at the edge of the woodland and here we found gypsy caravans ranged around a camp fire which still burned brightly. The gypsies stood in groups around the clearing, young men and women with their arms around each other, while the old ones sat on the steps of their caravans listening to the music. Two young men were playing violins, wild, haunting, sensuous music that tantalized my senses. They wore scarlet bandeaus around their heads and golden rings in their ears and a girl danced in the middle of the circle, a dark beautiful girl with flashing dark eyes, her voluptuous body moving sinuously to the music while her bright full skirts swayed above her ankles.

I could feel my flesh tingling with excitement. This was the music I loved, the wild haunting music of the Magyars, and unable to help myself I found my feet moving to the beat of the music, my eyes closed, shutting out the leaping flames and the bold dark eyes that suddenly glared into mine as a man came forward to take me in his arms, his body moving simultaneously with mine in answer to the music.

The music stopped and the spell was broken. Immediately I opened my eyes to discover his dark inscrutable ones looking down at me with an impudent devilish smile. In some confusion I looked round to find my friends staring at me and I tried to explain that this music came to me as naturally as sleeping and breathing, that I had always loved it. Just then the gypsy girl who had danced alone came forward and snatched the man's arm away from me, and dragging him after her she glared balefully at me.

'You dance beautifully,' Sophia said. 'I hadn't thought an English girl would know how to dance to that kind of music.'

Arrogantly Ernst threw a handful of coins on the grass and two young girls grovelled for them while the man who had danced with me and the girl stood watching them in contemptuous silence.

Ernst was silent as we walked back towards the waiting carriages and I realized he was going to be in no hurry to forgive me for the folly I had committed. In an attempt to placate him I said, 'I have never been able to resist such music and tonight I have been wonderfully happy.'

His young handsome features relaxed into their customary good humour and he squeezed my arm. 'I was jealous when that gypsy fellow took you in his arms, but then you were not to know that in Vienna we only waltz. Zigeuner music is not of Vienna – it is for gypsies, not ladies.'

He had rebuffed me charmingly, but nevertheless his words stung me to a sharp retort. I was not a child to be spoken to like that by a man I had only just met, however agreeable I had found his company.

47

'But then I too am not of Vienna and I happen to think that all music is to be danced to, whether it is the waltz or the music the gypsies play.'

He looked taken aback, then he laughed.

'So beautiful,' he whispered, 'and so wilful. Ah well, it is a nice change to find a woman with a mind of her own. But you would do well not to be too familiar with gypsies, they are lazy thieving rascals and the man was too bold. If you and Sophia had not been there I would have been tempted to teach him a lesson he would not have forgotten in a hurry.'

'Oh, come now, no harm was done, and there was certainly no need for you to challenge the poor man to a duel. Besides, he looked as though he could have given a good account of himself.' I shrugged off his arm and walked quickly towards the carriage but he hurried after me, catching my arm in a firm grip so that we were staring at each other. My lips twitched with suppressed merriment and his stern face relaxed into a smile.

'I refuse to fall out with you, Rachel,' he said, 'particularly over a gypsy.'

Suddenly he picked me up bodily in his arms, put me down on the carriage seat and climbed in behind me.

'Are we not waiting for Stephan and Sophia?' I asked him in some surprise.

'The carriages are only for two people. Vienna is a romantic city where four can be a crowd.'

Vienna was just coming to life as we drove through the city streets. Men were sweeping the roads and newspaper boys whistled cheerfully as they went about their work. Ernst sat with his arms around me, and though I had had little experience of men I was happy and responded naturally to his nearness.

He made me promise that I would meet him at my hotel early that same afternoon and it was only as I watched his carriage drive away that I suddenly remembered the words in my mother's letter, 'and we waltzed together and fell in love.'

Resolutely I told myself that I was made of sterner stuff than my mother. I had not come to Vienna to fall in love; I intended to leave with my heart still intact.

Three

Youth does not call for much sleep. In spite of the fact that the pale sunlight was already streaming through the windows of my room when I went to bed, I was up and dressed by half past nine and sitting in the breakfast room where a sleepy-eyed waitress served me with coffee and delicious hot breakfast rolls. It was one of those cold bright golden mornings that come only rarely in the wintertime and I wanted to be out on the city streets to find my way to places I had hitherto only heard of or read about.

I wrapped up warmly after being told by the doorman that it was treacherously cold, and at first the outside air completely took my breath away and brought stinging tears into my eyes. After that I only found exhilaration in the biting wind as I ran lightly down the road towards the Ringstrasse, bringing smiles to the faces of passers-by and light-hearted greetings from most of them.

Already I was loving this magic city. I loved the glimpses of intimate coffee houses and the sight of delicious pastries in the shop windows. I loved the air of fashionable elegance and the romantic illusion that it was a city only concerned with the joy of amusing itself. My heart and my feet led me in the same direction, the opera house, and I found myself with a crowd of others who had come to look at the floral decorations in readiness for the Emperor's presence later on. While people came and went I stood with my face pressed against the glass looking at the luxurious carpet that covered the shallow carved staircase as it swept upward from the foyer, thinking how different it would all look that evening when the chandeliers were lit, their light falling upon exquisite gowns and priceless jewels, the air filled with the lilt of laughter and the perfume of roses. I could see it all so plainly, more so now than in my childish imagination. Bright eyes flirting over fluttering fans, and men attentive and chivalrous in their dress uniforms.

Wistfully I turned away at last and walked slowly down the steps. I thought about my mother leaving this place for the last time for the arms of her lover, forgetful of the long years of dedication and hard work in which so many people had played a part. I turned once more to look upwards at the façade of the building, my eyes blinking in the bright sunlight, and it was then I saw a man hurrying down the steps towards me, an elderly man wearing a frock coat, raising his silk hat and smiling kindly.

'I beg your pardon, Fräulein, but I have been watching you. Do you know how long you have been standing at the top of those steps staring through the windows?'

I stared at him in amazement, then stammered in some confusion, 'Why, no, but some little time, I expect. It is all very beautiful.'

'Yes, a special effort has been made, but it is tonight you should be here, watching the arrival of the Emperor and all the aristocracy.'

'I do not have to be here, sir, I know what it will be like.'

'You have been here before on such a night?'

'No, but it seems I have known about it all my life, from my mother.'

'But you are not Viennese, I know that from your accent, nor are you from Budapest. Have you come far?'

'From London.'

He raised his eyebrows in surprise. 'From London! Do you have friends in Vienna?'

'I'm afraid not, only some people I met last night, and a girl I travelled with.'

He was looking at me curiously and I began to wonder if he had some connection with the opera house. He looked more likely to be an administrator than an artiste.

He smiled, no doubt reading my thoughts.

'You must tell me, Fräulein, why our opera house fascinates you so.'

'My mother danced here a long time ago.'

He raised his eyebrows. 'I have been here since I was quite a young man but I do not recollect that we ever had an English dancer. Believe me, my dear, I would have known – I am now the Director General of the opera.'

He said it with pride and my eyes lit up with excitement. 'Oh, sir, I would be so grateful if you could tell me if you remember my mother! She was in the ballet school from when she was very young and she was just eighteen when she left it.'

He looked at me kindly, in silence, then taking my arm he said, 'Come with me, young lady. There will be old programmes, pictures, nothing is ever lost here in spite of the many alterations to the theatre and changing times. While I search you shall tell me something about your mother. What was her name?'

'Gabler, Eva Gabler.'

He stopped halfway up the steps and turned to face me, and I cried, 'You do remember her, don't you?'

'Eva, little Eva Gabler! But of course – I remember her well, a dancer of great promise, but, alas, something more important took its place. Come, I have photographs of your mother, you shall see them all.'

I sat in his sumptuous office and we talked for over an hour whilst he produced photograph after photograph, as well as old programmes where my mother's name figured. Eagerly I scanned them all until at last I looked up to find him watching me sadly.

'I have been watching you closely, Fräulein Arden. I have been trying to find Eva Gabler in your face but the likeness is too elusive, too fragile. She was a magical creature, as light as thistledown, as graceful as a gazelle. If only she had been as wise as she was beautiful, her name would have been on everybody's lips, in lights for all to see. You too are very beautiful, my dear, but it is a beauty of a different kind.'

'I believe I am like my grandmother. Did you ever know her, she was Hungarian, from Budapest?'

He stared at me for a moment, then he nodded, well

satisfied. 'Yes, of course, now I know why I couldn't take my eyes off you when I saw you on the steps outside. It was that dark red hair and those gentian blue eyes, with a grace that was once the toast of Budapest. I knew your grandmother. She too was a dancer, but she danced to zigeuner music in the expensive cafés of Budapest. It was the talk of Austria and Hungary when she married a modest stationmaster of some little border town when she had such talent and such beauty.'

'It is strange, then, that she never forgave my mother for putting love before her dancing.'

'No, it is not strange. Your grandmother was a creature of love and hate, fire and beauty. She and her husband sacrificed all they had to make your mother a great dancer.'

'You knew why my mother left the ballet?'

'There were many rumours. I knew, for instance, that she was often in the company of the young Count Meinhart, but then we heard he was with his regiment in Slovakia so it seems that perhaps we were wrong. At any rate it is obvious she found her way to England where she married a good honest English gentleman. Is your mother still alive, my dear?'

'No, she died seven years ago.'

'I am sorry. But it is evident she told you enough about Vienna to make you want to visit us, and at a time when the city is at her gayest.'

I remained silent, merely permitting myself the hint of a smile.

'I shall tell you what we will do, Fräulein Arden – you will come home with me for luncheon, my wife will remember Eva Gabler. And this evening you shall come to the theatre to see *Die Fledermaus*. It will be a night you will never forget.'

'But isn't it too late to obtain a ticket, and isn't it terribly expensive?'

'Not for the Director General, and I'd like to give you the ticket in memory of a very beautiful lady, your mother.'

There were tears in my eyes as I accepted the ticket from him.

'It is a good seat, my dear, from it you will see all the notables in Vienna as well as the Emperor, and you must wear your prettiest dress so that all Vienna can see you. Now come along or we shall be late, and that is no way to start the first day of the year.'

I looked with dismay at the clock in his office and for the first time that morning I remembered Ernst, who would by now be waiting for me at my hotel. Noticing my hesitation he said, 'You have a prior engagement, it is not convenient to eat luncheon with us?'

'No. I am so sorry, but I had completely forgotten that a friend was to meet me at my hotel, I'm afraid I have already kept him waiting.'

'A young man then, a very nice young man?' he said, his eyes twinkling with amusement.

'I think so.'

'Then you must not keep him waiting further. He is of Vienna, this young man?'

'Yes, Ernst von Reichman, I travelled here with his cousin Sophia von Werenberg, perhaps you know them.'

'Both cousins of the Countess Meinhart, if I am not mistaken?'

'Yes, that is so.'

He stared at me so seriously that I could feel the warm blood flooding my cheeks and throat. 'Be very careful, Fräulein Arden, do not go looking for trouble. Tragedies that happened in one generation have a habit of repeating themselves.'

'I'm not sure what you mean, sir.'

'I think you are, my dear. It is curious, is it not, that of all the people in Vienna the only two you know are related to the Countess Meinhart? There is no more beautiful woman in Vienna than the Countess and no woman who has been more talked about.'

'My friends are returning to the country after the ball at the palace so it is hardly likely we shall meet again.'

'Run along and meet your young man then. See, I will give you my card so that later when you are alone in Vienna you can call upon us. I want my wife to meet the daughter of Eva Gabler, she will be able to tell you more about the ballet than I can. She too was once a dancer.'

I watched him hurry along the street towards his carriage

and stood a little forlornly after he had gone.

Ernst would be cross, that is if he had bothered to wait for me, and so I took to my heels and ran, hoping all the time that I would see his tall slender figure striding down the road to meet me. I found him standing on the pavement outside my hotel, and for a moment I felt a sudden sense of elation that this tall handsome young hussar should be waiting for me.

There was a frown on his face as he called out, 'Where on earth have you been, Rachel? I seem to have been waiting for hours!'

'I'm so sorry, Ernst, I've been exploring the city,' I said, determined that I would not tell him that I too would be at the opera that night. I was hoping that he would see me there, then I would tell him how I had managed to obtain a ticket. I took hold of his hand and squeezed it gently. 'Oh, come now, don't look so cross! I'm in love with Vienna, I'm enchanted with everything I've seen so far.'

The sulky little boy look left his face and he smiled. 'There's a lot I want to show you, Rachel, and we haven't much time. Have you eaten?'

'No, but I'm not hungry. Where are we going?'

'We can eat later near the lake in the park, but first I want to show you a sight you will only ever see in Vienna.'

He hurried me along the road so that I had almost to run to keep up with his long strides. All the time he refused to tell me where we were going and what we were to see. At the end of the road he hailed a cab, and then we were riding along the Ringstrasse which curved protectively around inner Vienna like a great horseshoe.

'I know,' I said, 'we are going to the Prater to see how lovely it can be by day.'

He shook his head smiling.

'The Belvedere then, or to look at the Schönbrunn. Oh, do tell me, or I shall go mad – I hate not knowing where I'm going.'

'We are going to the Hofburg to the Spanish riding school. If you hadn't arrived when you did we should have been too late for the performance.'

I sat beside him quietly contrite as we approached the

Hofburg. I would have loved to ramble through the lofty rooms of what was still the Emperor's winter palace, although he preferred the more modern Schönbrunn palace. It was so vast and so complex, I wished I had more time for looking about, but Ernst hurried me towards the building that housed the famous riding school. We were the last to take our seats around the arena.

'Forget the ballet where men and women prance about the stage,' Ernst said. 'What you are about to see is probably the most meticulous and exquisite ballet you could imagine. See, it too is performed under chandeliers.'

Between acts Ernst told me that in all there were about sixty stallions, but probably only two or three which could perform the most difficult items. The young horses turned white between the ages of four and eight and these less experienced horses were taught by the old riders, whereas the young riders were taught by the expert horses.

One charm of the performance was the silence. We could not hear the horses' hooves on the sand as stallion after stallion was asked to perform steps a ballerina might have found exacting. There were tears in my eyes as I watched those exquisite milk-white horses with their proud arched necks and delicately poised limbs, the delicate charm of the pas de deux and the faraway dedicated look of the riders in their brown silk jackets, cream jodhpurs and Napoleon-style cockatoo hats. How glad I was that the 'valets' in faded blue who came to lead the horses away at the end of the session rewarded each of them with a tasty morsel for performing so well.

The wintry sun had gone when we emerged from the building and Ernst said, 'We must hurry, Rachel, if we are to find the café open.'

'Do you mean the café in the Prater?' I asked him.

'No, not that one, there is another in one of the smaller parks. We can get something to eat, then we can skate on the lake.'

'But I can't skate, I have never skated in my life.'

'You'll soon learn, sweetheart. I will hold on to you very tightly. It really isn't very difficult.'

Considering that neither of us had had any lunch the sweet cream-filled pastries were hardly a substitute, but Ernst didn't seem to think there was anything unusual in it. We drank our steaming cups of coffee, then tentatively I took my first steps upon the ice. A band in the wrought-iron bandstand played waltz tunes and Ernst, encouraging me with every step, took hold of both my hands and pulled me towards him. Other skaters laughed at my fears and after a little while some of my initial terror left me. Ernst came to my side and holding my hands crossways he told me to relax. 'Try not to be so stiff, and you'll see that in no time at all you'll be skating to the music.'

It was cold on the ice, our breath freezing as we laughed, but he was right, the more I relaxed the more effortlessly my feet glided on the frozen lake. When the lanterns were lit in the trees Ernst looked up in dismay.

'Gracious, is it as late as that? We shall have to hurry back now, I'd almost forgotten that wretched opera.'

To my shame, so had I, but after he had helped me off with my skates and returned them to the woman in the hut where we had hired them, we hurried once more towards a row of cabs parked near the pavement.

'I'll try to see you tomorrow, Rachel, but I don't know what plans Mellina will have made.'

'What is she like?' I asked curiously, and he looked at me in sharp surprise.

'Who, Mellina?'

'Yes, I seem to have heard nothing but Mellina, first from Sophia and then from you. Why must you always do what Mellina wants to do?'

'I don't. I don't see her all that much. Oh, I know Sophia is besotted with her, but we are her guests. Doesn't one always do what one's hostess wants to do? It's just that Mellina is pretty demanding.'

'I've heard that she is very beautiful.'

'Yes, she is. I'd really much rather stay in Vienna with you but I don't see any way out, so the day after tomorrow we shall all be returning to Meinhart.'

'You haven't told me what she's like.'

He stared at me for a few minutes as though he wasn't quite sure what he should tell me, then he gave a little shrug of his shoulders. 'You want to know what she's like? Well, she's very beautiful, you already know that. She's as fascinating as the devil, as unpredictable as the Lorelei, and she likes to have her own way.'

'Would I like her, do you think?'

'Oh, Mellina has great charm, no doubt she'd charm you like she charms everybody else.'

'And I suppose her husband is terribly in love with her? He must be if she is all the things you say she is.'

'Max! I suppose he must be, but one never knows with Max. I must go now, *Liebchen*. Think of me tonight at that boring opera, wishing every moment that I was waltzing somewhere in Grinzing with you.'

He kissed me swiftly, then I watched him hurrying away down the snow-covered street and tried not to think about his handsome smiling face and those incredibly blue laughing eyes. He was fascinating, and I was fascinated, but it was not love. What I was feeling for Ernst was the sort of infatuation my mother had felt for Carl Meinhart, but I was a girl of a different calibre, I was a girl with both feet on the ground.

In my hotel room I took out my new evening gown wishing that Miss Frobisher could be there so that I could tell her it had not been a reckless extravagance after all. Here was an occasion to wear it, without an escort.

It was a dream of a gown in cream parchment satin, cut low at the neck but quite plain at the front as most of the material was gathered at the back of the skirt into deep folds. It had only one adornment, a single crimson velvet rose, held in a loop at the side of the skirt.

I took pains with my dressing and when at last I faced my reflection in the long cheval glass my eyes sparkled with delight at the finished result. The chambermaid who came in to turn down the bed covers exclaimed with delight over the gown and asked if I would like her to do my hair since she was considered quite good at it. Now it shone like burnished bronze in the light from the gas lamps and my shoulders emerged creamy white above the narrow bodice of the gown. I needed something round my throat but the tiny gold crucifix which I normally wore seemed out of place, as did my gold locket. There was my mother's turquoise pendant and the single pearl drop Alan Trevellyon had given to her, but suddenly my thoughts were on the crimson falcon and almost fearfully I unlocked the casket, compelled by something outside myself.

It seemed to hypnotize me as I held it in my fingers, the light from the gas lamps making the crimson stones sparkle, the gleaming diamond eyes willing me to fasten the pendant around my throat where it lay shining against my skin, finding an echo in the one crimson rose which adorned the skirt.

My mother had never worn it and I had never thought to wear it, but I knew that I would, for one night only. Besides, what harm would it do? I was not known in Vienna. There would be a great many people at the opera, none of whom would be interested in me.

I was glad of my velvet cloak, a legacy from my last year in school when I had played a leading role in *The Merchant of Venice*. The cloak was a deep blue and I would have preferred it crimson, but it was warm and fashionable and as I sallied forth down the staircase I was aware of the admiring glances from those people standing in the foyer.

The little doorman greeted me warmly, saying, 'You are looking very beautiful, Fräulein. Didn't I tell you you would not remain alone long in Vienna? You are dressed for a ball, and a very grand ball.'

I laughed happily. 'Not a ball – I am going to the opera.'

'The opera! My, but you are indeed fortunate to be going there, and on such a night! The ordinary people of Vienna will only be able to stand and stare tonight. You must know someone very influential to have got a ticket for the opera tonight.'

'Yes, I have been very fortunate. Someone my mother knew years ago. Will it be possible to get a carriage, do you think?'

'It will not be easy but I will try. Wait here and I will see what I can do.'

He was gone only a few minutes and he returned to the foyer with a smiling face. 'I have been lucky, Fräulein. The carriage was on its way to pick up some people but after I had explained that it was wanted for a young lady who was going to the opera he promised to take you.'

'Oh, I do hope he isn't going to let the other people down.'

'He will be a few minutes late, that is all.'

I felt like a fairy princess as we drove through the lighted streets and even more so when I stepped down from the carriage in view of a crowd of people waiting in the square. Oh, the enchanting magic of that moment when I found myself in the foyer of the theatre mingling with beautiful women in exquisite gowns, their jewels sparkling under the lights from the chandeliers. Their escorts looked no less exciting, some in splendid uniforms, others in dark evening dress wearing silken orders and other decorations across their chests. They stood in groups, chatting easily, their laughter rippling across the foyer and up the curved shallow staircase. Some of the men bowed courteously and many of the women smiled, probably wondering who I was and whether they should know me, for only the well-known would be expected at the opera house on this night of all nights.

My seat was a prominent one in the centre of the stalls and from it I knew I would have no difficulty in seeing the Emperor when he arrived, as well as the other notables in nearby boxes. There were flowers everywhere, and in front of the Emperor's box garlands of flowers had been draped.

They were coming into the theatre now, taking their places with much laughter and chatter. I still wore my cloak although I noticed that now most of the women had removed their furs. Diamonds flashed around creamy throats and tiaras sparkled on shining hair. The man sitting next to me leaned towards me smiling, asking if he could help me remove my cloak, realizing that I was alone. I allowed him to unfasten it and ease it away from my shoulders so that now my jewels too sparkled, more dangerously perhaps, but every bit as beautifully as those about me, and if my neighbour looked at me curiously I merely smiled, thanking him for his attentions.

A ripple of excitement went through the auditorium, then

above us the boxes around the royal box began to fill with those who had waited on the stairs for the Emperor to arrive. My eyes were suddenly riveted on the box next to the royal one and I heard the whispers around me become more intense, more urgent.

I recognized her easily from Sophia's description but now I was seeing her in the flesh. Mellina was more beautiful than any woman I had ever seen, tall and slender, her pale blond hair vying with the diamonds around it and the long diamond earrings she wore, her pale orchid pink gown as delicate as the bloom in her cheeks. She smiled a queenly smile at the admiring eyes looking up at her. Sophia was there too, lovely and vivacious, laughing up into the eyes of the man beside her, a tall dark-haired man who smiled down at her indulgently, a man with a profile as coldly compelling as some ancient pharaoh on a temple wall. He wore formal black evening dress with white lace ruffles at his throat, relieved by the blue satin order across his chest and the decorations on it. I found myself staring at him, the other people in the box momentarily forgotten, but I was not sure what I was looking for in the face of this man who bore the same name as my father.

I was brought to earth by the sounds of the opening chords of the Austrian national anthem and the vast audience rose to its feet for the arrival of the Emperor Franz Josef.

I was totally unprepared for that small slender silver-haired man looking like everybody's grandfather, standing in the centre of the royal box surrounded by tall young hussars. My heart leaped as I recognized Ernst, more handsome and dashing than ever in his dress uniform.

Whilst the Emperor was acknowledging the applause with a gracious wave of his hand, I studied his face more closely. I could not believe that this man who looked so gentle and kind could have had any part in ending my mother's brief marriage, but appearances were deceptive, I told myself, a fact that was to be borne out far more forcibly in the months to come.

The lights were dimmed and the orchestra struck up the overture. It was a moment of enchantment for me when the curtain rose on that great stage where once my mother had danced to this same music, and although the spectacle and the lilt of the music completely captivated my heart, I saw the first half-hour through a blur of tears.

The applause that greeted the end of the first act was rapturous and then the lights went up to a more relaxed atmosphere. Some of the audience left their seats for the corridors outside whilst others stayed to chat amongst themselves. I looked upwards at the Meinhart box and it was then that my heart gave a sudden lurch, for the man sitting next to Sophia had his opera glasses trained upon me. Others in the box followed suit while I felt my face burning with resentment, and biting my lip I looked hastily away. From all around me it seemed the laughter and the chatter died away and one by one those in front turned to stare at me while others leaned forward or sideways, craning their necks to get a better view. They were drifting back from the corridors now, but still they stared until it seemed that from every box glasses were trained upon me. Even the Emperor was watching me.

In desperation I jumped to my feet and with barely a muttered excuse I pushed past those sitting nearest to me until I could escape along the centre aisle to the world outside.

I do not remember my escape across the foyer or my exit through the huge glass doors, only that I was out in the square and it was snowing. I threw my cloak over my shoulders, picking up the hem of my gown as my eyes searched in vain for a carriage that would take me away quickly from those hostile staring eyes.

I started to run, my thin delicate satin slippers no match for the squelching snow and slippery cobbled streets, and I was sobbing, as much with anger as with fear. Miserably I could feel the wet snow trickling down my neck, finding its way under the hood I had pulled over my hair. My slippers would be ruined, probably my gown too, but it did not seem to matter. I only wanted to find the shelter of my hotel room.

At every sound of carriage wheels or footsteps I found myself cowering in some dark doorway. This was not the light-hearted waltzing Vienna that I loved, instead it was a

61

city of dark shadows, a sinister place peopled with wraithlike creatures formed by the swirling snow, a city of narrow twisting streets where the lights could not reach. Around every corner my imagination planted some obscene being intent on my destruction.

I was lost, hopelessly lost as I stood in the middle of a tiny square peering through the snow in an attempt to read the street sign. I was so tired I could run no further, not even when I heard the sound of approaching carriage wheels, and I turned to face the oncoming carriage lumbering through the snow. I remember very little else until I was seated in the carriage and an elderly man and his daughter were patting my hands and face in an endeavour to bring some warmth into them. The man poured some brandy down my throat which made me cough and brought the tears to my eyes, but I could feel it warming my frozen body into some semblance of life.

At last I was able to tell them that I had lost my way, giving them the name of my hotel which fortunately was not out of their way. They would not allow me to pay my share of the fare and my benefactor was kind enough to escort me to the hotel desk and ask for my key. I never saw either of them again but I shall never cease to be grateful for their kindness.

It was hard to reconcile my pathetic reflection in the mirror with that of the girl who had left the hotel earlier that evening. Now my hair hung in wet strands about my tear-streaked face, and my beautiful dress was saturated with wet snow. My cloak too hung heavy and dank around my shoulders, chilling me to the marrow. Only the jewelled pendant sparkled wickedly around my throat, the diamond eyes mocking me, telling me as surely as if the bird had spoken of the enormity of my folly. What a fool I had been to wear the crimson falcon in a city where the crest and its family were as well known as the cathedral of St Stephan itself! Now I had no doubt that repercussions would come swiftly and I did not know how I was going to face them.

Four

I slept badly, and in those moments when sleep came to me it was filled with dreams of being pursued yet again down narrow unfamiliar streets, with footsteps getting nearer and the cruelly distorted faces of men and women with their opera glasses trained upon me howling for vengeance. I awoke screaming, my body bathed in perspiration. All was quiet, but I did not sleep again and I was relieved when at last the first pale fingers of dawn invaded the oppressive darkness of my room.

I went early into the breakfast room but I was not hungry. The little waitress who served me shook her head sadly when I only ordered coffee, asking me if I did not feel well. Catching sight of my face in the mirror opposite her question did not surprise me. I was very pale with dark circles under my eyes and ahead of me stretched the uncertainties of a new day.

I felt sure that Ernst would come. He would look at me with accusing eyes, hurt angry eyes, annoyed that I had kept my own knowledge of the Meinhart family a secret. Ernst must have witnessed my ignominious flight from the opera house, and he must have seen the pendant, I was sure everybody else had. I could settle to nothing, and when he had not come by ten o'clock I put on my outdoor clothes. Anything was better than sitting about in the hotel foyer.

Up and down the street outside I walked, not daring to wander too far in case he came and could not find me. Some of the passers-by gazed at me curiously but I looked sharply away towards some shop window, although I saw nothing of the goods in the window. The time passed slowly, but now it was almost time for luncheon and still he had not come. I retraced my steps, unmindful of the carriage which had slowed alongside me until a voice called, 'Fräulein Arden, may I speak with you a moment?'

I looked up anxiously to find my friend of the opera house leaning out of his carriage, inviting me to take the seat beside him.

He patted my hand gently, aware of my quivering mouth and the tears in my eyes. 'Now, my dear,' he said firmly, 'crying is not going to help. I saw you leave the theatre last night and realized something was amiss, then I saw the jewel you were wearing. My dear child, whatever possessed you to wear the Meinhart pendant on such a night and in such company?'

'I know, it was folly beyond words. Believe me, Herr Liptmann, I had never worn it before and I only wore it last night on a stupid impulse.'

'How did you come to have it in the first place? From your mother?'

'Yes. It's a long story. Now I have to return the pendant and I don't know how. I was hoping Ernst would come to the hotel this morning but he hasn't come. He must think I have been deceitful.'

'I think for the time being we will forget about your friend Baron von Reichman. It may be that he has duties which prevent him from coming. It is the ball at the palace tonight so it is more than likely that those who are going will have other matters on their minds besides the girl who fled from the opera house like Cinderella, wearing the Meinhart pendant round her pretty neck instead of glass slippers on her feet. We must think instead of how you are going to return that pendant. Do you know the Meinhart house on the Ringstrasse?'

'No, and tomorrow they are returning to the country.'

'You must not leave the pendant with servants and today they will have little time for you. I have an early appointment at the theatre tomorrow but I expect to be free by eleven. Together we will return that pendant to the Count Meinhart, but I shall leave it to you, my dear, to inform him why it was

ever in your possession and why after all these years you are
returning it.'

'But why should you take this trouble, sir? Why do you
concern yourself with my stupidity?'

'There are three very good reasons, the first to appease my
wife who was your mother's friend at the ballet school, the
second because I was never able to help your mother, and the
third because you are trying to do something she could never
have done herself, something that is right.'

I held on to his hands thanking him warmly, promising
that I would be ready and waiting on the hotel doorstep from
eleven o'clock onwards the next day.

Ernst did not come and that night I walked with the crowd
towards the Schönbrunn, standing with them in the freezing
cold watching carriage after carriage arrive bringing women
muffled in furs, their escorts clad in greatcoats over their
uniforms to keep out the cold. I felt chilled to the marrow and
the doorman at the hotel remarked, 'I thought you might be
at the Emperor's ball, Fräulein, after your visit to the opera.'

I smiled at him briefly, my teeth still chattering. 'I'm afraid
not. I stayed to watch the carriages arrive but it was very
cold.'

'And you are very pale, Fräulein. If you would like to go up
to your room I will ask one of the girls to take you up some hot
soup.'

I smiled, thanking him warmly. They were so kind,
touchingly kind, but when I thought about my brief glimpse
of Count Meinhart my spirits sank. There had been nothing
gentle in that cold aloof profile, nothing to persuade me that
the Count would receive me kindly. Indeed that sculpted
impersonal face was the last thing on my mind before I went
to sleep and the first thing I thought about next morning
when I awoke.

I was ready and waiting for Herr Liptmann in the hotel
lounge before nine thirty next morning. I knew I would have a
long wait but I didn't mind that as I sat facing the door in my
outdoor clothes, clutching a brown paper parcel in which

reposed the jewel casket holding the pendant. I had not been there long when a young serving girl came to tell me that there was a gentleman asking for me at the desk. My eyes lit up with relief for I was sure it could only be Ernst.

I hurried out of the room, my face alight with anticipation, but the only man standing at the desk was a stranger to me. As I approached him he bowed formally and with a thin-lipped smile said, 'Forgive this early call, Fräulein Arden. I am Stephan Pacherov, the Meinharts' lawyer. Count Meinhart has asked if you will be kind enough to call upon him on a matter of interest to you both.'

It was my turn to stare at him, then, seeing that he waited politely for my answer I stammered in some confusion. 'I'm sorry, Herr Pacherov, I was waiting for a friend, Herr Liptmann. It was our intention to visit the Count's residence this morning, on the same matter, I have no doubt.'

'Perhaps you could leave a note for your friend? My instructions were very precise.'

'Am I to understand that you wish me to accompany you now?'

'That is so.'

I looked at him suspiciously, wondering what kind of man this was who had appeared out of nowhere to take me to the Meinharts. He was tall and thin, probably in his late forties or early fifties, but I felt sure he was not Viennese. His complexion was like yellowing ivory and I judged him to be a man of Slavonic descent from his high cheek-bones and eyes that were slightly slanting in his lean face. His diction too was perfect, the perfection that comes with expert tuition. He smiled. 'I assure you my credentials are in order.'

I had the grace to blush, apologizing quickly for my bad manners.

He waved a gracious hand. 'It is understandable. You are very wise not to trust every stranger who professes an interest in your concerns. However, here is my card.'

I took it and scanned it anxiously. It did indeed introduce one Stephan Igor Pacherov, a lawyer with offices in Vienna, Prague and Budapest, and I handed it back to him in silence.

'You see, I am eminently respectable. My family have

served the Meinharts for many years. May I ask if you are ready to travel now?'

'Yes, of course, but first if you will excuse me I would like to write that note.'

I was not looking forward to travelling with a stranger, but it was not far to the Ringstrasse and I told Herr Liptmann in my note that I would let him know the outcome of my visit as soon as possible. I was sure about one thing. I wanted to be rid of the pendant so that my life could get back to normal. I had no wish to nurse such torturing bitterness for the rest of my life and perhaps when I had had the opportunity to meet some member of that formidable family I would be able to view matters differently.

We spoke little on the journey except about the fine morning and the air of a city getting back to normal after the holiday atmosphere of the past few days.

I could feel my heart hammering in my breast as we drove along the Ringstrasse and it was only when we turned off to drive along another thoroughfare that I looked at my companion in some surprise.

'I understood Count Meinhart's house was on the Ringstrasse?'

'So it is, but the Count left Vienna early this morning for Meinhart.'

'How far is it to Meinhart? You did not tell me you were taking me there.'

'Regrettably no, but since your business is undeniably with the Count himself it would serve no good purpose to go to the house on the Ringstrasse. You will enjoy the drive through the woods. Some of the journey will have to be taken by sleigh, as more snow has fallen in the country. Have you ever travelled by sleigh, Fräulein Arden?'

'No, never. They are not used in England. The children build sledges and take them to the parks at the first sign of snow.'

'Ah, but then your English winters are not nearly so savage as ours. The snow in Austria sweeps down from the steppes of Asia where the winters are long and the days are short. I could tell you a great deal about Siberian winters, but I guarantee you will enjoy your first sleigh ride.'

He was trying to calm my fears but at that moment I was quite sure I would not enjoy the sleigh ride, and already I was having acute misgivings about my readiness to take this journey with a stranger. We had left the city now and were travelling across the plain towards the dark forests and mountain peaks beyond. I was glad that he did not seem to expect any kind of conversation from me, but he muttered some sort of oath under his breath when the snow started to fall.

'I was hoping we could reach the inn before the snow started,' he said mournfully. 'However, it is light as yet. We will take lunch at the forest inn where the sleigh will be waiting for us.'

The inn proved to be charming and served an excellent lunch. In spite of my misgivings I realized I was hungry so I made the most of my appetite. My companion ate sparingly. As I helped myself to spiced apples and cream he left me to attend to the sleigh team, giving me time to reflect on his responses to my many questions. All I had learned was that Castle Meinhart was very old and that the estates were enormous, that the Count was undeniably rich and of ancient lineage, and that I need not be afraid. Herr Pacherov, if he but knew it, had only succeeded in making me very afraid. I was not a girl who had ever been familiar with aristocratic men of ancient lineage or visits to medieval castles on the edge of nowhere. Nostalgically I thought about the village squire in a youth that now seemed a thousand years away. He had been my nearest approach to anything remotely resembling a member of the aristocracy, but when I remembered his ruddy face creased with laughter and his merry eyes twinkling in his brown face I could find no resemblance to the lean proud profile of Count Meinhart.

In spite of my fears the sleigh ride was a joy. The two horses were fast sturdy little beasts and the sleigh was soft and comfortable as we sat back wrapped in skin rugs. More than anything the bells around the horses' necks fascinated me as they jingled and jangled musically in time with their steps. Such a joyful sound, though hardly in keeping with the blinding snow and the forest of dark conifers ahead of us.

'See, you can just see the castle from here,' my companion pointed out. 'Look upwards, beyond the forest,' and sure enough there it stood, high on a pinnacle of rock above the tall dark evergreens. In no time at all we had reached the enormous wrought-iron gates ornamented with the crest I knew so well. I sat transfixed watching a huge broad-shouldered man lumber towards the gates, making light work of their weight as he pushed them back to allow us to enter. He was a giant of a man, so powerful that I could imagine those great hands of his breaking pitilessly any creature, be it beast, man or woman, who gave him cause for hate.

He stood at the side of the road as we swept past him, and for a moment my eyes met his and I shivered. There had been no mistaking the menace in those bold dark eyes, and it chilled me far more than the snow blowing against my face.

'Who is he?' I asked my companion hoarsely.

'His name is Josef. He was born on the estate and lives at the gatehouse there. You have gone quite pale, but there is no need to be afraid of Josef. The man is something of a scoundrel but you will have no dealings with him, I can assure you.'

How dense the forest was on either side of us now! I tried to peer between the trees, planted so closely together that no vestige of light could penetrate the gloom. The long drive had recently been cleared of snow but already it was lightly covered again. We were climbing higher and in my ears was a rushing sound like water. Before I could ask any questions my companion said, 'You can hear the sound of the river now. It comes crashing down from those mountains yonder and joins the Danube on the plain below. In a few minutes you will be able to see it from the bridge we must pass over.'

The sound of the river was a crescendo in my ears now and I could feel the spray on my face as it came crashing underneath us, bringing with it great rocks and huge chunks of ice. Again my companion touched my arm and my eyes followed his pointing finger to where above us the castle stood silhouetted against the purple sky. I gasped with wonder at its fairy-tale elegance, at the slender towers and turrets and buttresses, before the drive wound round the rock towards the drawbridge and into the courtyard beyond. Like some child in one of Emily Frobisher's fairy tales I took my companion's outstretched hand to assist me from the sleigh. The jingling bells had stopped and the silence which surrounded us seemed all the more profound as we walked in the soft snow towards the massive brass-studded door and the huge bronze knocker with the face of a wolf. Above the door, this time carved in stone, was the familiar falcon crest. I could feel my heart hammering as the sound made by the knocker reverberated in the lofty corridors behind the door.

We did not have to wait long. I heard footsteps approaching long before the door was opened and I surmised that behind that door were stone floors and great lofty rooms as cold as charity. The man who opened the door was wearing dark figure-hugging breeches and a dark waistcoat under which was a high-necked peasant blouse with vast sleeves caught tight at the wrist. He was an oldish man with white hair, bowing courteously as he stepped back to allow us to enter.

In spite of my trembling knees I looked with interest around the great hall we had come into. A cheerful log fire burned in the enormous stone fireplace, the flames from it falling on suits of old armour, relics from forgotten medieval wars, and along one wall hung a tapestry depicting a sylvan scene of pastoral beauty. A shallow curved staircase led upwards towards a balcony from which pennants were hung. I followed Herr Pacherov up the thick crimson carpet that ran up the centre of the staircase and continued along the balcony above, which was lined with portraits, presumably of long-dead Meinharts. The windows in the hall were set high up, leaded with diamond panes which threw curious patterns on the stone floor of the hall. At last we came to a door at the extreme end of the balcony and after knocking we heard a voice from within bidding us enter.

It was another large room, this time panelled in oak and again a welcoming log fire blazed on the hearth. I was aware once more of suits of armour and portraits in oil, but my eyes were riveted upon the man who stood behind a dark polished table set in front of an open gun case. It was the same man I had seen at the opera, faintly amused by Sophia's chatter, but shorn of the severity of his dark evening clothes he appeared somewhat younger than I had expected.

Count Meinhart was very tall, with a lithe leanness that resembled the sinuous power of a tiger, and he was dark, with raven black hair and dark eyes. Not a tiger at all, I thought to myself sharply, a panther, a black panther, and then his eyes were on me, inscrutable in that remote haughty face, although the sound of his voice belied the severity of his expression.

It was a low, singularly musical voice speaking to me in English with the merest trace of a foreign accent, using the now unfamiliar Miss instead of the Fräulein I had become accustomed to.

'Ah, Miss Arden,' he said, 'I regret that you have had to make your journey in the snow, but January is a month of snow in these parts. I am glad that Herr Pacherov managed to persuade you to come.'

'The young lady had already decided she wished to see you, sir. I had only to induce her to make the journey with me.'

'Indeed? And when was I to have been honoured by your visit, I wonder?'

I looked at him sharply, ready to meet sarcasm with sarcasm, but he was watching me gravely, his expression curiously kind.

'I was going to call upon you in Vienna later in the morning. I was waiting for Herr Liptmann to come to my hotel.'

'Herr Liptmann?'

'Yes, Herr Liptmann from the opera house.'

'Of course. We have met but I do not know him well. You would have had a wasted journey, however, since I returned to Meinhart immediately after the Emperor's ball. You are clutching that parcel very carefully – does it contain something of particular value?'

'Yes. Something which rightly belongs to you.'

'And yet it was something one of my family thought fit to give away, I think. We will speak of that later when you have had time to rest and freshen up after your journey. We shall

71

try to make you as comfortable as possible, Miss Arden.'

'But when are we returning to Vienna? I must get back today.'

'I'm afraid that won't be possible. The snow is still falling and there is no way you can get back to Vienna tonight.'

'But all my clothes, everything I have is at the hotel. Surely they will wonder where I am, what has become of me?'

'I took the liberty of informing them that you would be away for a day or so, in view of the weather, when you went away to write that note for your friend. I did not think it was going to be possible to return to the city.' The lawyer spoke calmly, as though there was nothing untoward in taking a young woman from her hotel and depositing her in a medieval fortress miles from anywhere, where some strange man as handsome as the devil informed her she would be expected to stay. For once I was tongue-tied and my host merely smiled, relishing my disquiet.

He walked over to the fireplace and pulled a long tasselled bell-rope. Almost immediately the door was opened to admit the elderly man who had opened the front door for us.

'Find Frau Gessler, Otto. Inform her that we have a guest and ask her to prepare the Rose room. In the meantime perhaps you would like some tea, Miss Arden? I believe it is an English custom at this time of day. Come, sit here before the fire, you will not be accustomed to the size of these rooms or the cold.'

He pulled a chair forward for me to sit on, and because I couldn't think of anything else to say or do I accepted it. The two men started to speak to each other in rapid German which I was only able to follow in places and was not very much interested in anyway. I was bothered about my clothes. I had only the things I was wearing, not even a hair brush or a tooth brush, and all sorts of grim possibilities were stirring up my imagination.

Tea arrived, served with lemon or milk, and with it were rich pastries which I was determined not to eat. I accepted the tea gratefully but I didn't want either of my captors to think I was sufficiently at ease to gorge myself on cream cakes.

About half an hour later the door opened again and this

time a plump woman with a round peasant's face came in to announce that my room was ready. The Count turned to me with his most charming smile and said, 'Go with Frau Gessler, Miss Arden. She will find anything that you are short of and perhaps later I may have the pleasure of dining with you.'

I followed Frau Gessler along several narrow halls and corridors, all of them richly carpeted, until at the end of a long corridor she stopped to open a door for me.

In spite of my fears I gasped with delight at the room I entered. I had dreamed of this room in my childhood fantasies. My feet sank into a thick rose-coloured carpet and there were heavy rose-coloured velvet drapes at the window and rose and turquoise bed coverings on the four-poster bed. In the grate a fire burned brightly and I saw that the dressing table was equipped with brushes and combs even before Frau Gessler opened another door to my own private bathroom. I had never known such luxury and some of my fears evaporated in the warm comfort of that room, allowing my face to relax into a smile as I thanked the servant for her efforts on my behalf. She bowed her head and bobbed a little curtsey, but her stolid Teutonic face hardly relaxed it expression of surly indifference. Frau Gessler at least, I decided, was not too pleased at my arrival.

She spoke in a guttural accent I had difficulty in following, and when I asked her to repeat her words she strode over to the vast wardrobes which stretched along one wall. Opening the doors she showed me that inside was hung anything I might need in the way of clothes, and after she had left me I could not resist examining them for myself. Hanging from one corner of the wardrobe to the other were gowns. Tea gowns, dinner gowns and morning gowns, cloaks edged with priceless furs, riding habits. In the drawers I found delicate underwear, fairy-tale nightgowns and rich velvet robes as well as an assortment of shoes and slippers. Quite obviously the Meinharts didn't stint themselves when it came to caring for their guests.

Next I inspected the view from the diamond-paned windows which jutted out above the window seats upholstered in rich turquoise brocade. I caught my breath at the vast panorama of snow-clad mountains and pine forests and the swiftly flowing river. The sun was setting in a bright red ball, its glow turning the snow to some semblance of pink icing like that on a birthday cake, and I shivered, suddenly afraid, when I caught sight of the grim battlements above me and the turrets reaching pointed into the evening sky.

A serving girl came in with a pitcher of hot water, and Otto came to inform me that the Count would be dining promptly at half past seven and I would find everything I needed in the wardrobe. Count Meinhart would expect me to dress for dinner.

Well, he could go on expecting, I thought irritably.

I felt better after I had washed and brushed my hair, but I had no intentions of availing myself of any of the clothes in the wardrobe. The dress I had travelled in was blue – the colour of my eyes, so the saleswoman who had sold it to me had said – and if it wasn't entirely suitable for eating dinner in the company of a man of ancient lineage and great wealth, at least it was my own, which left me with some sort of dignity.

At a few minutes before seven thirty Otto appeared to escort me to the dining room and if he was surprised at my attire, nothing showed in that stolid retainer's face. As I followed behind him I tried to remember the corridors but they looked so much alike that I was soon lost.

The room we entered was far smaller than I expected but the table shone with crystal and silver, and tall slender candles in elegant candelabra vied with the firelight. The Count was smiling down at me, explaining that as there were only two of us he would not subject me to the formality of the large dining hall. He wore a claret-coloured velvet dinner jacket and if he was surprised that I had not availed myself of the dinner gowns at my disposal he made no comment.

Through the courses of an excellent meal he chatted easily and naturally, but I do not know to this day what we spoke about. I was aware of his black enigmatic eyes above the candle flames and the rare smile which softened his lean brown face.

Over coffee he asked my permission to smoke and I

watched him lighting a long black cigar with sensuous pleasure.

'Forgive me, Miss Arden,' he said, breaking the silence, 'but I omitted to extend Herr Pacherov's apologies that he could not join us for dinner.'

'Has he returned to Vienna?' I asked startled.

'No. As I told you, that is impossible at the moment. He wished to dine in his room so that he could work on a matter of some importance.'

'How long must I stay here?'

'You mean you are determined not to enjoy your stay? Some young women who live not too far away would be vastly intrigued to be spending a winter's night in Castle Meinhart, particularly when the host is the Count himself.'

'I don't happen to be some young women, sir, but it seems to be the Meinharts' prerogative to take what they want, when they want it, and to discard it just as easily.'

He threw back his head and laughed, then he leaned forward with narrowed eyes staring into mine. 'I dare say I should know what you mean by those words, Miss Arden, but I assure you I do not. Perhaps it will put you at your ease if I make it quite plain that there is nothing I want from you which I should take pleasure in discarding. Now, do you think we could open that parcel which has caused my family some discomfort and you quite obvious distress?'

The parcel had reposed at my feet throughout dinner and now I picked it up and handed it to him intact, a gesture which brought a swift smile to his lips and a gleam of amusement into his eyes. I watched his strong slender fingers coping with the string and unwrapping the paper to reveal the casket. For some considerable time he sat staring at it, as though he was reluctant to open it, then slowly he raised the lid and took out the pendant.

He sat with it in his hands and I could see the jewels flashing as they caught the light from the candle flames. Then he held it up so that the chain was twined through his fingers and the pendant itself was caught in the leaping flames of the fire.

When at last he looked at me his face was again a grave

remote mask and some of my earlier fears returned. He laid the pendant on the table and rose to his feet. I watched him walk across the room to a heavily carved dark walnut desk into which he inserted a key he had taken out of his pocket. I couldn't see what he removed from the desk but next moment he was placing a casket on the table, a casket more ornamental than the one I had brought, but nowhere near as delicate. He opened it and, to my astonishment, took out a pendant exactly like the one I had brought to Meinhart. He laid them side by side on the table and I rose to my feet and stood looking down at them.

'You are surprised, Miss Arden?' he asked quietly.

'I am astonished,' I replied. 'How many of these pendants are there?'

'Only the two. Now I leave you to guess which is the real one.'

'But aren't they both real? They look exactly alike.'

'One of them is a fake, a beautiful, clever and most ingenious fake.'

'I don't understand. Why should there have to be a fake?'

'Many years ago a thing of great beauty vanished from this house and was never seen again. It was very old and quite priceless. Originally it was worn by the men of this family, but more recently the women wore it. When the pendant was missed the Countess Meinhart of that day ordered it to be copied by the best jeweller in Austria from photographs and paintings. He did an admirable job, don't you think?'

'But which is the real one and which is the fake?'

'The real one is that worn by you at the opera, the fake is the one I have just removed from the desk. It would interest me to know why you suddenly had a conscience about the pendant when you never did before.'

'The pendant was not mine to have a conscience about; it belonged to my mother.'

'Your mother!'

'Yes. It was given to her by a Count Meinhart who presumably had every right to give away something which belonged to him.'

'A foolish besotted man gives many things to a woman who

76

for a brief hour makes him believe he is in love with her. Usually it is something he regrets in the sober light of day. I can't imagine why that particular count was willing to give away his heritage, or why, when he had fallen out of love, it was never retrieved.'

I turned on him then in righteous anger, an anger which made him start back as though I had struck him, which I had half a mind to do.

'If that Count Meinhart was a foolish besotted man, it is certain that my mother was more foolish to believe in his promises when he was neither honourable nor kind. She was his lawful wife. They were married at a little church in the mountains and later their marriage was annulled by the command of the Emperor and the Meinharts. If she took the pendant it was all she took. For all he knew she could have died destitute – he gave her no money and there was no way she could go back to the ballet that had been her life. How dare you think my mother capable of stealing such a thing, when in fact it was given to her by her own husband? She never even wore the pendant and it is because she wished to return it that it is lying there now.'

We stared at each other like two angry adversaries and I was glad that I was tall. I had never been so sure of my young steely strength, even though I doubted it would avail against the man standing before me. Suddenly he smiled.

'I congratulate you, Miss Arden. I had always heard that auburn hair inspired a temper to match it, but I never realized how stormy such eyes could be or that they could flash like blue steel. I very much fear that I have said things which caused you to be angry, but as yet we are on opposite sides of the fence, you and I. Perhaps if you would accompany me along the corridors and through the halls of this castle, we could find the Count Meinhart who caused your mother and you so much distress.'

He didn't wait for my answer, instead he picked up a candelabra holding six tall candles, indicating that I should carry another. He strode towards the door and stood waiting for me in the open doorway.

I do not think I shall ever forget my first tour of Castle

Meinhart in the dead of night, with only the flickering lights from our candles to light the way. In no time at all my head was spinning with the names of long dead counts and countesses, as well as with the names of their children. Grand dukes and duchesses, barons and baronesses, it seemed the Meinharts had contributed to and replenished half the noble houses of Europe, but all the time my eyes were searching for just one face, the face of my father.

I listened to his voice extolling their virtues or deploring their vices. I listened to tales of feudal lords who had not been ashamed to take their privileges at the expense of servile countrymen and their shy young brides, and to stories of chivalry and high purpose. There were other tales too, concerned with betrayal and faithlessness. Then we came to a gallery on whose walls were hung portraits of a more contemporary style. I held my candelabra higher, as did my companion, for now we were standing before a vast picture depicting a slim military-looking man in uniform standing behind a couch on which a beautiful woman sat. She wore a tiara on her dark cloudy hair and carried a spray of mimosa against the gauzy material of her gown. She had her arms around the shoulders of two children, a little girl of about five and a small boy a little younger, while standing next to his father was a tall handsome boy in his early teens. I bent down to look at the plaque under the portrait which told me that this was Count Alexander Meinhart and his wife Elisa with their children Max, Ludmilla and Franz, and the year was the one after I was born.

There was something I did not understand here but although I longed to ask questions I remained silent, moving on with him to the next portrait. It was the same woman but this time alone, wearing a white evening gown with a dark blue silken order across her breast. I looked with awe at her pale proud face but it was the pendant around her throat which captured most of my attention. Surely the Countess Meinhart must have been miserably aware that it was a fake pendant she wore so proudly? Did she spare a single thought, I wondered, for that other woman who had thought to be the next Countess Meinhart?

'You have brought me here so that I might see this picture?' I accused him.

'Not entirely, Miss Arden. I brought you here so that you might find the man who took it upon himself to dispose of our family heirlooms. This is a portrait of my mother, and the previous one shows her with my father Alexander and my sister and younger brother.'

'And you too, Count Meinhart.'

'Yes, but as you can see it is a long time ago.'

'I take it your father is dead, but what about your mother and the two children?'

'My mother lives in Paris. She always hated our winters and as she is French she was happy to return there. My sister is married to the Austrian ambassador at the court of St Petersburg. My brother Franz died soon after that portrait was painted, after a fall from a pony.'

'Oh, I am sorry, he looks such a nice little boy,' I murmured.

'Yes, Miss Arden, I remember that he was, a very nice little boy.'

We moved on to the next portrait and now we were looking at a young man on horseback, a handsome debonair young man only too conscious of his virile appeal, a young man whose bright blue eyes looked into mine with apparent recognition.

I felt my knees trembling and my companion's voice seemed to be coming from a great distance. I staggered and would have fallen if he had not put his arm out to steady me, and then as suddenly as it began the room stopped spinning and I was calm again. The Count was looking at me keenly and under his regard I could feel the blood flooding my face so that I looked away quickly.

'This portrait disturbs you, Miss Arden. Why?' he asked severely.

'Please tell me first who he is,' I implored him.

'It is a portrait of Count Carl Meinhart, my father's cousin.'

'His cousin!'

'Why, yes. Count Carl was killed in Slovakia, in a shooting

accident, I believe, although I never heard precisely what happened. He had no younger brother to succeed to the title so it came to my father, a much older man with a growing family. My father didn't want the title. He was happy wherever the army sent him, but my mother was glad, for she hated living in strange towns – as soon as she became accustomed to one place, the army sent him elsewhere. Besides, she loved Vienna, it was her favourite city.'

'Yet you say she chooses now to live in Paris?'

'That is so. She is not fond of my wife and one Countess Meinhart at the castle is enough. You believe this is the man who gave the pendant to your mother?'

How adroitly he had changed the subject, but I could only nod my head miserably.

'Then you are saying that Carl Meinhart loved your mother but that their marriage was set aside. I know nothing of this, of course. He was a brave and dashing officer, a favourite with the Emperor, but not such a favourite, it would seem, as to be able to confront Franz Josef with the woman of his choice. Still, I am glad that your mother recovered her faith in men sufficiently well to allow her to marry your father.'

'Count Carl Meinhart was my father.'

I made the statement baldly and without subterfuge. There seemed no point in trying to hide it. We were kindred, the Count and I, whether he liked it or not.

He looked down at me with narrowed eyes but I met his look fearlessly. After all I wanted nothing from him. I had returned the pendant and I was prepared to leave the castle as soon as the weather permitted, the next morning if I had my way. He would never be able to say that a strange girl had popped up out of nowhere expecting to claim her rightful inheritance.

Some of my thoughts must have communicated themselves to him because quite suddenly his expression softened and he said, 'It seems, cousin Rachel, that we have a great deal to talk about. Return with me to the warmth of the fire and you shall tell me about yourself, your childhood, the years after you were born and how your mother came to marry an

Englishman. Perhaps it is not too late for the Meinharts to honour their obligations.'

'There is nothing I want from you, Count Meinhart. My mother married a good kind man and brought me up to believe that he was my father. It was a grievous shock when I learned that he was not, a shock that caused me to feel a great deal of hatred and bitterness against your family, but what good has it done? The past is over and it is useless to nurse either bitterness or anger about something that had nothing to do with me. When I leave here in the morning I shall try to forget the Meinharts. I shall do as my mother wished and continue to think of the man who raised me with love and kindness as my father. He was the only man who ever deserved that title.'

I did not return to Vienna next morning. When I awoke it was still snowing, great dry flakes that in no time at all obliterated everything within sight, and I stared through the window of my room helpless and frustrated. The same serving girl I had seen the night before brought a tray to my room containing tea and toast as well as a note from the Count. He regretted for my sake that I would not yet be able to return to the city, and advised me to wear something warm from the wardrobe as the temperature was well below freezing.

Wearing my own clothes had provided me with an independence I was reluctant to part with, but my winter dress was not proof against the elements. Swallowing my pride I selected a black woollen skirt and bright emerald green blouse and cashmere shawl, and instead of my impractical shoes I was happy to find that the fine leather boots fitted me perfectly. I wondered whom the clothes belonged to. The Countess was tall, that much I had noticed at the opera house, but somehow I did not think these were her clothes.

I decided I would try to find my way about the castle, keeping to the main corridors and hoping not to open doors which might label me as an intruder. I soon forgot that the snow had made me a prisoner as I wandered through corridors where portraits and ancient weapons were displayed, through rooms not often used but obviously intended for great occasions, until I came at last to a ballroom that made me gasp with its beauty.

The orchestra was intended to play from some sort of minstrels' gallery set high up above the floor. From the roof hung three rows of crystal chandeliers and round the edge of the floor couches and gilt chairs upholstered in red brocade gave the ballroom a festive air. I stood in the middle of the floor looking up at the chandeliers like a child in an enchanted forest, then humming a little waltz to myself I started to dance smoothly and effortlessly on the polished floor. Halfway through my dance I was brought to an abrupt halt by the sound of applause and I spun round to find the Count standing in the doorway, his eyes filled with laughter.

'I hope you don't mind,' I stammered, 'but I have been trying to find my own way around.'

'Not at all. You dance as though you loved it. One day you shall dance in this ballroom to an orchestra and wear your most beautiful gown. I am glad to see that you took my advice and selected something warm.'

'Do you always provide your guests with wearing apparel or do they belong to some member of the family?'

'They belong to my sister. Ludmilla loves Vienna and came here often, whenever she wanted a change from whatever country her husband was sent to, but now she comes very seldom.'

'She no longer cares for Vienna?'

'One never stops caring for Vienna, my dear. People, yes; Vienna, never.'

'I see.'

'Do you? If you do, you saw far more quickly than I ever did.'

'I don't understand.'

I thought he would have continued the conversation, but with a brief smile he put his hand under my elbow and said, 'Come and look at the portrait of your father in the light of day. Tell me if he is as you imagined him to be.'

By the light of day he was more handsome, more debonair, and I could well understand how my young mother, protected and sheltered in the rigid environment of the imperial ballet, found herself in love with him.

Somehow he reminded me of Ernst, perhaps it was his fairness and his laughing blue eyes, but there was no resemblance whatsoever to the man who walked beside me, pointing out things I might find interesting on the way. He took me to the library where massive leather-bound volumes occupied every wall from floor to ceiling, and to the drawing room, decorated in white and gold.

'How beautiful it is!' I exclaimed, standing in the middle of the room and staring around me. 'It is hard to imagine these lovely rooms when the castle looks so gloomy and forbidding from the outside.'

'That is only because you saw it for the first time on a winter's day with the snow falling and the sky dark and dreary. In the springtime it is different. I hope you will see it for yourself.'

'That won't be possible, I'm afraid. When I leave here I do not think I shall ever come back.'

'We shall see.'

'Is there much more of the castle?'

'I won't burden you with it today. The guests' bedrooms are along the corridors where your room is situated, the family bedrooms are in the other wing. My wife's suite is at the side of the castle, my rooms are on the front overlooking the lake, and my daughter's rooms are also on the front.'

'Ah yes, of course, I had forgotten you had a daughter. Is she here or is she in Vienna?'

'She is in Innsbruck with her mother's family at the moment. I expect she will be returning as soon as the weather permits.'

'Her name is Liesel?'

'Yes, how did you know?'

'Sophia told me. I travelled with her from Innsbruck.'

'Oh yes, of course. I had forgotten for a moment that you have met both Ernst and Sophia, and yet it was Ernst who told me your name and where you were staying in Vienna.'

'Tell me, please, was Ernst very angry that I hadn't told

him about the pendant and my connections with the Meinharts?'

'Do you mind whether he was angry or not?'

'I didn't want to hurt his feelings. Ernst and Sophia were very kind to me in Vienna, particularly on that first evening when I didn't know a soul in the city.'

'Why shouldn't Ernst be kind to you? A beautiful girl alone and without friends, just the sort of situation I am sure Ernst found entirely to his liking! Sophia, of course, is a sweet child.'

'You don't sound very fond of Ernst, actually I found him charming.'

'I am sure you did. He comes from a very charming family, a family whose charm can cover a multitude of sins. Believe me, Rachel, I should know. However, you may well get another opportunity to charm Ernst if they arrive at Meinhart before you decide to leave it.'

'If it is fit for them to travel, then surely it will be fit for me.'

'Of course, but it may not be convenient for me to travel with you and Herr Pacherov goes from here to Prague. Unless you would prefer to travel with one of my servants?'

He was the Count again, arrogant and distant. I followed meekly behind him along one corridor after another until we reached another great hall which proved to be the entrance to a private chapel.

The floor was marble in all sorts of designs and colours. He told me it had been brought from Italy in the fifteenth century and had originally been in another chapel under the present one. The altar was beautiful, ornate with gold and silver and jewels, the family pews upholstered in rich crimson velvet, the stained glass windows behind the altar showing a scene of Saint Paul on his way to Damascus. If the Meinharts embellished their castle to suit their creature comforts, they also did not stint themselves when honouring their God.

'The old chapel must have been hewn from the rock, then?' I asked.

'That is so, but one of my ancestors became too old and infirm to climb the steps leading to it and so he had this new chapel reconstructed on the same level as the rooms of the castle.'

'And what of the old chapel?'

'Standing idle and no longer consecrated. It has not been used as a chapel for centuries. I haven't been in there since I was little more than a boy and we thought we were very brave to go down there to explore.'

'Are there other rooms down there then?'

'The old family burial crypt is down there and there are dungeons. It is many years since I ventured into the dungeons – they are dark damp miserable places where once men no doubt were beaten and tortured, in centuries more violent than our own. I take it you would not wish to see the dungeons?'

'Why, no! I have a vivid imagination, and if I went there I would only imagine all those desperate tortured people with broken bodies, and great brawny men wearing masks.' I shivered, for I was thinking of Josef the gatekeeper. I could well imagine those huge gnarled hands and that evil leering face enjoying the struggles of his victims.

'Is the crypt no longer used for private burials now?' I asked, wanting to change the conversation but wishing it could have been on a brighter note.

'No, there is another burial ground on the other side of the lake. That has been in use since 1780, so you see it is quite modern by Meinhart standards.'

He was smiling again, that cynical, half amused smile which did not always reach his eyes. As he held the door open for me to pass in front of him he asked, 'Can you ride a horse, Rachel?'

'I can, but not too well, I'm afraid. The squire of our village in Devonshire allowed me to ride a very docile mare called Betsy, and occasionally a more frisky one, but the second one only when he was with me.'

'You would enjoy riding in and around the estate, I think. If I thought you would be with us for any length of time I would personally find a mount for you.'

Herr Pacherov was waiting for us in the gun room and I occupied my time by staring out of the window while they conversed in low voices.

The sky outside was lighter now and the snow had stopped.

There was even a pale sun struggling to break through the clouds and the scenery outside the window seemed to take on a timeless beauty, like that on an old Christmas card. I was interrupted in my reverie by Herr Pacherov, who came to shake hands with me and bid me goodbye.

'My apologies, Fräulein Arden,' he said courteously. 'I feel your enforced stay has been largely my fault, but at least it has enabled you to see something of Meinhart. Not many people are afforded that opportunity. The weather is improving, so soon you will be able to return to Vienna.'

I wished him a pleasant journey. After luncheon the Count left me, saying he had calls to make on the estate, advising me to go where I wished and amuse myself in any way I could.

I had an enchanting afternoon. I looked again at the portraits, I walked through the rooms looking at priceless porcelain and ivories and I marvelled that only a few years ago I had been plain Rachel Arden going to London for the first time in search of employment, and that once, as a young girl, I had stood in front of the squire's desk asking him to help my mother because she was selling her few valuables so that we might eat.

That evening I did a reckless thing. Instead of my own blue woollen dress I chose a dinner gown – not too ostentatious – black velvet with a tiny bodice and full billowing skirt. There was no ornamentation on the gown beyond the dark sable on the collar and edging the wide medieval sleeves. The little chambermaid smiled with delight but Frau Gessler, who met me in the corridor, did not allow her stolid face to relax a quarter of an inch. So much for that, I thought, there is a woman who does not like me.

Oh, those corridors leading from one hall to the next, all looking exactly alike, or so I believed in those first few days! I lost my way again and this time I found myself in yet another hall, a magnificent hall from which a wide marble staircase descended lit by Grecian goddesses holding aloft lighted torches. I had stumbled into what was evidently the main hall and now I was looking at two more portraits, those of the present Count and Countess.

I was surprised to find the Count in a splendid decorated

uniform, but the portrait had been painted when he was much younger. The Countess was in white silk with the crimson pendant, the fake falcon pendant, resplendent round her slender throat. There was something about this portrait that made me feel uneasy, yet it was simply that of a Viennese beauty wearing a ball gown and carrying a closed fan in her long delicate hands. I tried to analyse the portrait. Pale blond hair graced by a diamond tiara and long diamond earrings, a short straight nose and delicate coral lips. As I moved the eyes of the portrait seemed to follow me, but I knew this was only the art of the painter, nothing more. They were blue eyes, as innocently china blue as a child's, but still I felt a revulsion for that portrait which was totally unreasonable. I shook myself angrily. This woman had done me no harm, she was young and lovely and no doubt entirely gracious, yet I was glad to turn away from those eyes which seemed to mesmerize me. I was startled at what appeared to be another portrait, but this time I was looking into a huge mirror at my own reflection. For a moment I stood transfixed, intrigued by the stranger that stared back at me, the tall slender girl in her rich black gown edged with fur whose dark blue eyes looked afraid in her pale beautiful face.

I turned away abruptly and started to walk down the stairs. I was only halfway down when the door on the right opened and the Count came out accompanied by two massive Great Danes. He paused, looking up at me, and the expression I surprised in his face brought the blood up into my face, causing me to lower my eyes in some confusion. He came forward to meet me, cautioning the dogs to lie down in the hall. As I reached him he bowed over my hand, kissing it lightly.

'Did anyone ever tell you that you have a strangely compelling beauty, Rachel, one that a mere man might find very disturbing?' he asked lightly, and although I was aware of my blushing face it was a question I did not answer.

Dinner that evening was a light-hearted affair over which he set himself out to be charming and entertaining. He talked about a multitude of things and I was surprised to find how knowledgeable he was about many places in England which he seemed to know far more about than I. When I showed surprise he laughed. 'I had an English nanny when I was small, and later she came to us again to care for Ludmilla and young Franz. I remember that she was a martinet with a sharp tongue, although she was always just. We were all very fond of her. She took me to her home in England several times for holidays in the summer. Her family lived in Cornwall, they were fishermen. I loved those times in their cottage close to the sea.'

'Then you must know Devonshire also,' I said eagerly. 'It is the next county to Cornwall.'

'Yes, it is a gentler county. I remember its red soil and those ridiculous hedgerows one had to climb to see over the top.' I watched the expression flit across his face in the light from the candles, reflective, perhaps a little sad, before he continued. 'I like to think that that good woman taught me values which have served me well. The English have values, I think, they are not given to light-hearted meanderings which mean nothing, but they have an awful knack of making some other nations seem pale and flighty. Perhaps that is why we all tend to get rather cross with them from time to time.'

For some reason I felt inordinately pleased, yet what had I to feel pleased about? There was nothing English about me except a name I hadn't any right to. Guessing my thoughts he smiled. 'I have no doubt, Rachel, that you absorbed all their good qualities and none of their bad ones. What do you intend to do when you leave Vienna?'

'I don't know. Look for work, I suppose.'

'Work?' He said it as though he had never heard of the word.

'Yes, work. I gave up a very pleasant job to come here to return that wretched pendant and my employer replaced me before I left London.'

'But what kind of work, what can you do?'

'I was a secretary to a woman who wrote children's stories about animals and fairies and hobgoblins.'

He laughed, and somewhat crossly I retorted, 'She was very sorry to lose me, and I don't suppose my successor is able to draw.'

'Draw? I thought you said you were a secretary.'

'So I was, but I used to draw pictures which she was able to make use of in her books – rabbits in frock coats and silk hats, hens in bonnets. You must have seen them in children's stories.'

He was looking at me quite seriously now. 'I would like to see some of your drawings one day. I know a man in Vienna who might be able to put some work your way, that is if you decide to stay here.'

'I don't think that is very likely. You are quite right, I have absorbed all those qualities which make me feel far more English than Viennese. I shall go home to London and look for work.'

'But have you a home to go to, friends you can stay with?'

'I haven't had a real home since my mother died. I shall probably stay in a girls' hostel or something until I can find work. I have a little money, I might even stay in some small inexpensive hotel.'

'I feel in some way responsible for your welfare, Rachel. You are here on account of the pendant, you would still be in your employment in London but for that "wretched thing", as you call it, and I don't see why your mother's sufferings at our hands should be visited on her lovely young daughter. I have been giving the matter a lot of thought but I had to know first what your future plans were.'

I looked at him puzzled, unable to follow his train of thought, and he went on to say, 'I have been thinking for quite some time of employing an English governess for Liesel. She has not been good with governesses. The last one, a German woman from Bavaria, stayed longer than any of the others, but the child is hopelessly spoiled and needs taking in hand badly. I have spoken to Mellina about sending her away to school in Switzerland but I am not really sure if that is the answer. Would you consider the job, Rachel?'

'But I have not been trained to be a governess, I have never taught children. As a matter of fact I have had very little to do with children.'

'Except to draw rabbits in frock coats for their books!'

'Oh, that! I never knew if the children who read those books liked my drawings. Why should you think of me as suitable material for a child's governess?'

'Because you have had a reasonably good education and a happy home life, because you have a sense of humour and a bright young courage, and because of those special English qualities my daughter might benefit from.'

I was looking at him in some amazement. He was asking me to stay at Meinhart to teach his daughter, a possibility I had not even remotely considered, and although my first instinct was to say it was out of the question, a familiar recklessness was urging me to jump at the offer.

'Think about it. There is no hurry, but it has decided possibilities, don't you think?'

'Countess Meinhart might not agree with you. In fact, she may object strongly to the idea.'

'She may, that is a possibility, but not one that is insurmountable. There are certain aspects of my wife's life with which I do not interfere so long as they do not injure my honour, my name or my home. Mellina knows well how far she can go. I do not think she will oppose me in this.'

His words chilled me, they were so cold and uncompromising. I would not like to make an enemy of this man, but what were the aspects of Mellina's life he found so distasteful?

My train of thought was interrupted by his next words.

'Why not accept the challenge?' he urged. 'Try it – six months, a year – you have nothing to lose. It would be work, and I will see that you are amply rewarded. You will not be a servant in this castle, you will be treated like one of the family – which in fact you are. You will have a part in everything that goes on within these walls, the balls, the dinners, the boar hunts, all those things your mother told you about in your childhood but never herself experienced. Come now, what do you say?'

Against all my better judgement, against all those stolid English values which an army of Englishmen and English-women had tried to instil into me throughout my childhood, I agreed to think about it, and I knew such values would have little weight against the fascination this man was beginning to have for me.

Five

I lay sleepless for most of the night. It was so still, it seemed that the blanket of snow which covered the earth had hushed all the normal sounds. There was no wind, but I had been brought up in the country and had always been familiar with the sounds of the night, the barking of foxes, owls hooting and the distant sounds of night trains. Here there was nothing, and once I went to the window and pulled back the drapes, letting in the bright silver moonlight. Twinkling stars shone in a clear frosty sky but after a while I was glad to pull the curtains and return to my bed. The stillness was eerie, it was as if we existed in a fairy-tale castle divorced from reality, but the problem on my mind refused to go away and it was dawn before I finally slept.

In the morning it was back with me and still I wasn't sure. The prospect of returning to England with no employment waiting for me and only a small amount of capital was a daunting one. Most of my money was invested and inaccessible and after all, what was a year, six months even? Nothing at all when most of my life lay in front of me.

I already knew and liked Sophia, and there was Ernst, too; I felt strangely comforted when I remembered his gay blue eyes and tender admiration. Liesel was a child, I felt sure I could handle Liesel, but I hadn't met Mellina. Would Mellina accept me?

I had always been able to be honest with myself. My father had said it was a quality which might serve me well in my adult life, but now I was not too sure. I did not think my common sense would be proof against Count Meinhart's persuasions and I knew if I did stay at the castle it was because he fascinated me hopelessly and completely, and that I would do well to run from such emotions. Ernst was a man to flirt with, to tease and laugh with, whereas Count Meinhart was a man I could not even try to understand. I thought him cynical and remote, I felt embarrassed when his black inscrutable eyes smiled into mine with an amusement I did not understand, and there were those other times when I felt that he could never be my friend but could well be my implacable enemy.

An army of peasants were clearing the drawbridge and the road towards the river, and I had no doubt that there were others already making an attempt to clear the long drive towards the gates. A pale wintry sun shone in a delicate blue sky and I looked at it doubtfully. It was a day which would certainly allow me to take that journey back to Vienna, and to help me to make up my mind I wore the dress I had arrived in. I breakfasted alone after Otto informed me that the Count was out on the estate, and after breakfast I went into the library and played endless games of patience until I heard the door open and looked up to find the Count watching me.

'I see you are dressed for travelling, I take it you have decided not to accept my offer,' he said quietly.

'I don't know. Your offer is very tempting, I have nothing to return home for, no home or family and no job, but I still doubt that I am the right person to act as governess to your daughter. I am not trained to be a teacher – as a matter of fact I am not trained to be anything. In England the daughters of vicars usually stay at home until somebody asks them to marry him.'

'And did anybody ask you to marry him?'

'The matter didn't arise. I was only a schoolgirl when my father died, and because of our circumstances I had to grow up very quickly.'

'But there must have been some young man in your life, or perhaps several?'

'No, I assure you, there is no young man in England I am anxious to return to.'

'In that case why not accept my offer, perhaps for six

months? If at the end of that time you are unhappy here or have become homesick, I shall not seek to detain you.'

My answer was deferred, because at that moment the merry sound of approaching sleigh bells came to our ears and I watched him stride over to the window where he could see the courtyard below. There was a frown of annoyance of his face which gave to the severity of his features an added formidability. He was not pleased at the interruption and now I could hear the sound of laughter and women's voices.

'It appears our solitude is at an end, Rachel. My wife and her friends have returned to Meinhart.' He said it with such a lack of warmth that I could not help wondering why a beauty such as Mellina could not elicit a greater show of welcome from her husband.

He did not go out to meet them, but instead went to stand near the fire grate looking silently into the flames, and I got to my feet, the playing cards forgotten, aware of my trembling knees. In a moment there were light footsteps outside the room and unceremoniously the door was flung open and Mellina was there, sweeping into the room with outstretched hands, wrapped in a grey velvet cloak edged with blue fox, the hood still covering her pale hair. I watched as the Count stepped forward dutifully, bending his head to kiss her briefly on both cheeks.

'What a journey!' she trilled. 'The roads in Vienna are quite terrible but the sleigh ride was a joy. I've brought Sophia and Ernst, of course – oh, and Baroness Bruchner. I do hope Frau Gessler has remembered to get their rooms ready . . .'

For the first time her bright china blue eyes caught sight of me and in that split second they seemed to change from gay inconsequence to narrowed contemplation.

'Well, well,' she said, 'and who have we here? Dear Max, have I come too soon, should I have given you more warning?'

Not in the least disconcerted the Count said, 'Permit me to introduce Miss Rachel Arden, who has come all the way from London to return that bauble you have regrettably never been able to wear. Now, my dear, you will be able to dispense with that poor copy you insisted upon wearing for your portrait.'

'All the way from London, Miss Arden,' she mused. 'And how did this bauble, as my husband calls it, come to be in your possession in the first place? No doubt some old love affair and perhaps a delayed attack of conscience?'

I stood without speaking, my eyes meeting her amused cynical ones without flinching, and she laughed a little. 'No matter,' she said lightly. 'Now that you have accomplished your mission you will be wanting to return to England as quickly as possible. It will have to be by sleigh, Max, at least until she reaches the outskirts of Vienna.'

'I don't think we need to concern ourselves about Rachel returning to England just yet, Mellina. I have been trying to persuade her to remain with us for a while as a governess for Liesel. If you remember, we did speak about the matter a few weeks ago.'

'Yes, but that's all we did, nothing was decided upon. Is that your vocation, Miss Arden, are you a governess?'

'I should try very hard to be a good governess under the circumstances, Countess Meinhart,' I replied, suddenly aware that my mind had been made up for me by this assured woman who was regarding me with unconcealed dislike. For a moment I met the Count's eyes before I quickly looked away, having surprised a look of quiet satisfaction in their steely depths.

'Under what circumstances?' she wanted to know.

'I gave up my employment to come to Vienna, and I shall have to find other work when I return to London. If I can work here it will solve my immediate problems.'

'You appear to have put yourself at great inconvenience to return the pendant. One day you shall tell me all about it, but not now. I take it you have been given Frau Ebber's room, she left us in the summer. It is quite a pleasant room and I have no doubt you will be comfortable there.'

I looked at the Count quickly, and just as quickly he said, 'At the moment Rachel is in Ludmilla's room. She did not come equipped to stay but the weather made it impossible for her to return to Vienna. I told her she could wear Ludmilla's clothes until she could make arrangements for her own to be brought here or until she returned to Vienna. There is no reason why she should not continue to occupy that room.'

'I take it that Rachel' – she emphasized my name sarcastically – 'is no ordinary governess. Max, perhaps you would explain why.'

'She is related to the Meinharts, in spite of the Englishness of her name.'

'Related! To the Meinharts?'

'I'm afraid so. A dubious blessing, I'm sure you will agree, but we owe her the same hospitality we would extend to any of our kinsmen. I suggest she remains in Ludmilla's room; in time she may prefer to choose one nearer to Liesel. Perhaps we should let her decide for herself.'

He smiled, a cool unconcerned smile which quite plainly said as far as he was concerned the matter was at an end, and Mellina spun round and walked back towards the door. Opening it she called out, 'In here, all of you. Max is here with a long-lost relative, it would appear.'

Next moment Sophia was there, squealing with delighted recognition, rushing over to embrace me, followed closely by Ernst who stood beside Mellina staring at me in dumb-founded surprise. The thin aristocratic woman who came with them was being greeted by the Count, stiffly, without the suspicion of a smile as he bowed his head briefly over her hand.

I went through the rest of that afternoon in some sort of daze, responding automatically to Sophia's embrace as well as her chatter, refusing to meet Mellina's amused cynical eyes and Ernst's more doubtful ones. Later I excused myself on the grounds of having letters to write. It was not an untruth, I had not written to my stepfather since sending him a brief postcard to say I had arrived safely, and I decided I should write to Miss Frobisher, if only out of politeness.

'You will find stationery in the library,' the Count said. 'If you will leave your finished letters on my desk in there, Otto will see that they are mailed.'

I thanked him quietly, more than glad to make my escape. The letters were more difficult to write than I had thought they would be. Both my stepfather and Miss Frobisher would be left wondering how I had suddenly acquired the position of governess to an Austrian nobleman's daughter, so I decided to say simply that I was well and happy, and that I had obtained employment. Writing the letters did not take me very long and I was on the point of leaving the library when Ernst came into the room, quite obviously with the intention of finding me there.

'I say, Rachel, Mellina tells me you are staying on here as some sort of governess for Liesel. How on earth have you managed that?'

'I haven't managed it at all,' I snapped, resenting his question the moment it was put. 'Count Meinhart asked me to consider the position and I have accepted for a trial period. I don't even know if I am capable of being a governess.'

'And what's all this about you being a long-lost relative? You never told me anything about it.'

My expression softened. I supposed he had every right to be angry and to ask questions about my connection with his relatives. 'I didn't mean to be secretive, Ernst, and I'm sorry I wore that stupid pendant at the opera. But for that I could simply have returned it with a polite note and I needn't have met the Count or any of you again.'

'I don't suppose you've given a thought to what you're letting yourself in for.'

'You mean living here when Mellina quite obviously doesn't like the idea?'

'I mean about Liesel.'

'What's wrong with Liesel?'

'She's already had a procession of governesses, mostly German. She's like no other child I know – spoiled and strange. Mellina spoils her, and Max . . . well, I don't know about Max, perhaps he's never quite got over his disappointment that she was a daughter instead of a son.'

'Do you mean that he has little love for her?'

'I don't know what I mean. You'll be able to judge for yourself when she comes home in the morning. I say, Rachel, you won't have to spend all your time with that child, will you?'

'I shall expect to earn my salary, but I suppose like any other employee I can expect some time to myself. Why?'

'Because there's a lot we have to talk about and there's a lot we could do together. I'm here for at least two weeks, and we could ride together over the snow. You'll come, won't you?'

How I warmed to Ernst at that moment. He seemed so normal and uncomplicated and he so obviously admired me and wanted my company. I badly needed a friend in that household and dinner that night merely accentuated the fact.

Over coffee Mellina said, 'I have told Frau Gessler that Rachel will be taking over the duties of governess but that she will be staying in Ludmilla's room for the time being.'

The Count merely acknowledged her remarks with a brief smile.

'Frau Gessler was not pleased, Max,' she went on as though I was not there.

'It is no concern of Frau Gessler's.'

'I think it is. She has cared for Liesel since she was born.'

'Hardly an achievement when one thinks of the finished product.'

'You do not think her private feelings should be considered, then?'

'Frau Gessler is a servant in this house. I do not think we should ask her advice on the way we bring up our daughter.'

Oh God, I thought, I wish the conversation would end. He was high-handed and firm, she was provocative, and when my eyes met hers across the breadth of the table I found them filled with cold hostility.

'Now that the snow has stopped falling I should like to show Rachel something of the estate, Max – perhaps in the morning before Liesel arrives,' Ernst said, little knowing how grateful I was to him for changing the trend of the conversation.

'Do you intend to tramp in the snow then?' the Count answered him acidly.

'I thought we could ride.'

'Rachel tells me she is inexperienced on horseback.'

'There is that little mare, she seems docile enough.'

'Very well, by all means Rachel can try to manage the mare.'

'I hope that you are not going to forget that we have guests,'

Mellina said. 'It would be gallant, Ernst, if you remembered my guests first and Liesel's governess later – much later.'

I knew that my face was flaming, I only hoped I was far enough from the candlelight to hide it. Before Ernst could answer her, however, the Count said, 'I suggest you wear Ludmilla's riding habit, Rachel, I expect you will find it in your wardrobe.'

'How fortunate that Ludmilla's clothes fit you so well,' Mellina said, with a sweet smile that quite belied the acidity of her words.

'Come with us if you like, Sophia,' Ernst said, but I could tell from Sophia's delicately flushed face that she too was unhappy about the battle of words that had taken place over the dinner table. She shook her head. 'Oh, no, Ernst, not tomorrow, I have other things I want to do. It really isn't necessary to entertain me.'

I could feel resentment boiling up inside me. I hated them referring to me in an oblique manner as though I wasn't sitting at the table with them. I was prepared to be a governess, to do my duty and earn my money, but I was not prepared to be treated like some poor relation, even if I was one. I made an early excuse to leave the table, feigning a headache, but promising that I would be happy to accompany Ernst to the stables the following morning.

When I reached my room I surprised Frau Gessler leaving it. She passed me quickly with her head averted. She carried nothing in her hands and I wondered idly why she had found it necessary to visit my room at all. There was nothing disturbed, and feeling suddenly contrite I thought that perhaps I had misjudged the woman. The fire burned brightly and the curtains were drawn against the night, so perhaps she had entered my room merely to attend to these things.

For some quite obscure reason I bolted my bedroom door that night. I had not done so when the Count and I were alone in the castle apart from the servants, indeed I had never remotely suspected that cold austere man of having sinister designs upon my virginity, but now in bolting my door I recognized an admission that there were things to fear in that enigmatic environment.

My sleep too was not dreamless and calm as it had been before Mellina came back. It was interspersed with whispering voices and footsteps, with doors opening and closing somewhere in the regions below, as well as with the wind moaning along the battlements. In the sober light of day, however, I accepted my disturbed slumber for what it was, too much imagination and nightmares I couldn't even remember.

It was morning and the sun was shining. Hesitantly I donned Ludmilla's pearl grey riding habit and the plumed tricorn riding hat that went with it. I pushed my feet into her soft grey riding boots and the mirror assured me that I looked every inch an aristocratic lady of fashion about to mount her palfrey. I was feeling far from brave. I had not been on a horse for eight years at least and no man living could ever have called me an experienced horsewoman. I liked horses, and had never been afraid of them, but what Ernst called a docile little mare could well be a flighty filly as headstrong and unmanageable as Angel had been.

I had almost finished breakfast when Ernst and Sophia arrived. The Baroness, it appeared, did not eat breakfast, and Mellina never left her room until mid-morning. Max had evidently breakfasted early and was already somewhere on the estate.

'Come with us,' I said to Sophia, without any encou. - ment from Ernst to do anything of the kind, but she shook her head, smiling a little. 'I don't feel like riding this morning, you two go. I'll go out presently to see if I can find Max.'

I fell in love with the mare as soon as I saw her. She reminded me of Betsy with her gentle brown eyes and the way she affectionately nuzzled my shoulder. They quickly saddled her and led her to a mounting block. At first I was diffident and all too sadly aware of my lack of practice, but she was a calm, quiet little beast and soon I forgot that I hadn't ridden a horse for years in the sheer joy of cantering along the snow-covered paths. Ernst was a brave sight riding beside me on his big chestnut.

'Happy?' he asked, smiling down at me.

'Oh yes, deliriously happy! I'd forgotten how exhilarating

it was to ride with the wind against my face.'

'You sit a horse well, Rachel. I'll make a horsewoman of you in no time!'

'I doubt it – I shall never have enough time to become experienced.'

Instinctively I reached up to touch the little gold crucifix that I always wore. It always gave me reassurance, almost like a good luck charm, but now I was disconcerted to find that I was not wearing it. I remembered it lying on my bedside table while I tried on Ludmilla's riding habit and felt momentarily cross with myself that I had forgotten it. Oh well, I knew exactly where to find it when I got back to my room.

We rode for most of the morning, only returning to the stables in time to wash and change for lunch. At the stables we found Max and Sophia dismounting from their horses and I thought how pretty Sophia looked in her green velvet riding habit with the cock plumes falling against her flushed cheeks. Max towered beside her, elegant and at one with his big black stallion, and as his dark eyes looked into mine I was aware of a certain cynicism, although his remark was courteous enough.

'You appear to have enjoyed your ride. When you are more proficient perhaps a more lively horse could be found for you.'

'Oh no, Count Meinhart, I am very happy with this one. I could become very fond of her. What is her name?'

'Greta.'

'I think that suits her very well.'

I walked back to the castle with Sophia, who whispered to me on parting, 'I'm so glad you're staying, Rachel, I do hope you won't find Liesel too difficult.'

'First Ernst and now you, Sophia – you both make Liesel sound like a pretty terrifying proposition. Why does everybody think Liesel will prove too much for me?'

'Oh, I'm sure we don't. She's really a most enchanting child but she has been terribly spoiled.'

'By her father?'

'I don't think so. By Mellina, of course, and the servants. Frau Gessler idolizes her, and so do her grandparents in Salzburg.'

'Well, I can only do my best,' I said, with more conviction than I felt.

'I'm sure you'll do marvellously, Rachel, and you will adore her – she's just like Mellina.'

Just like Mellina! Sophia couldn't have said anything to make me feel more inadequate.

Back in my room I went immediately to the bedside table to look for the crucifix, and was dismayed to find it wasn't there. I searched the bathroom but it was not there either, and painstakingly I set about examining every inch of the floor. I turned back the bedcovers and searched through the drawers, but the little gold cross and chain seemed to have disappeared into thin air.

For a while I sat on the edge of my bed close to tears. That little cross had always seemed like my one true link with the happiness of the past. Every time I touched it I was reminded of long summer evenings and soft country twilight, of church bells on Sunday and the low timbre of my father's voice filling the little stone church at the edge of the moor. Now it was lost and I felt as though my youth and my memories were lost with it.

I searched every passage and room where I had been that morning, and in spite of the time returned to the stables in case it had fallen there. Even as I searched I had little hope of finding it. I could still see that little cross lying on my bedside table waiting for me to pick it up.

I was the last to arrive at the dining table and took my place in some confusion, then realized with horror that I was still wearing my riding apparel.

'You look very attractive in your riding habit,' Mellina said, 'but the smell of horseflesh is hardly likely to encourage our appetite.'

'I'm so sorry to be late. I didn't change because I went back to the stables to see if I had dropped my crucifix. I was so sure I had left it on my bedside table this morning, but it isn't there now. I thought perhaps I was mistaken.'

There was silence around the table, all eyes upon me, then Mellina said, 'Is the crucifix valuable? We must ask the servants to look for it in that case.'

'It has great sentimental value. I'm sorry it's lost.'

'I'll help you look for it after lunch,' Sophia said. 'Perhaps we'll find it together.'

'There won't be time, darling, Liesel arrives after lunch. Of course you can look around on your own if you like,' Mellina said quickly.

I looked once at the Count's face and it was dark with some annoyance I couldn't understand. Was he annoyed that I had kept them waiting for lunch, or with Mellina's flippant acceptance of my loss? Whatever it was, I began to feel very apprehensive about the afternoon before me. He was angry about something, I was to be confronted by his daughter who was so like Mellina, and the two together succeeded in robbing me of any appetite I might have had.

As soon as I could I excused myself again and hurried upstairs to change into something more suitable for a governess's introduction to a new pupil. I wore my own dress, which seemed to restore some of my lost courage, and spent another half hour searching for the crucifix, crawling round the floor on my hands and knees. I was kneeling in this posture when the little chambermaid came in to tell me the Count wished to see me in his study and I took the opportunity of asking her if she had found my pendant. She blushed furiously and seemed afraid, but not guilty. Puzzled by her manner I probed further. 'You do remember my wearing it though, last evening for dinner perhaps?'

She nodded mutely, then with a little awkward curtsey she beat a hasty retreat. I was on the point of leaving my room when Otto appeared to say his master wished to see me immediately, and it was the 'immediately' which sent me marching downstairs with squared shoulders and a determination not to be browbeaten by this autocratic family.

The Count was sitting behind his huge oak desk and opposite him sat the most exquisite young girl I had ever seen. She was tall for her age, as tall as Sophia, but she had a beauty as pink and brittle as porcelain. She resembled her mother with her silver fair hair and bright blue eyes, but where Mellina seemed vitally alive, the child sat strangely quiet, apathetic almost, and who could tell what thoughts were there behind the enchanting façade of her face?

'This is Miss Arden, Liesel. She has come from London and is related to us, strangely enough. For that reason we call her Rachel, and she might prefer it if you were to call her Rachel also.' His voice was kind, as kind as I had ever heard it, but the girl merely acknowledged my presence by a nod of her head, as queenly and unconcerned an acknowledgement as any her mother might have afforded me.

'Well, what do you say, Liesel, is it to be cousin Rachel?'

'I should prefer to call her Miss Arden, if she is to be my governess.'

Some of my courage evaporated and I saw a quick frown of annoyance cross the Count's face.

'As you wish, Liesel, but Rachel is here at my invitation – she is not a Frau Ebber or a Fräulein Brückner to be treated to either tantrums or discourtesies. Do you understand?'

'Of course, papa. I didn't like Frau Ebber or Fräulein Brückner, they were such silly women. But I thought I was to go away to school in Switzerland?'

'When you are older perhaps, or if Rachel grows weary of you. I have business on the estate now so I propose to leave you two together to see how you get along.'

He turned towards me with a grave smile on his face. 'Well, Rachel, see what you can make of this child here and let me know immediately she gives you trouble.'

With this admonition he left us, and Liesel and I sat staring at each other like two cats weighing up what each might conveniently expect from the other. I decided to make no immediate effort and eventually had the satisfaction of seeing her eyes waver, then she said surprisingly, 'Didn't you like England that you came to Austria?'

'Yes, I liked England very much, it was my home.'

'Why come here then, and to be a governess of all things?'

'Why not? It's work and I might enjoy it, that is if you and I can be good friends. Is that going to be possible, Liesel?'

'A governess is not a friend, she is a teacher.'

'That too. But if we are friends it might make learning a happier thing for you, and teaching more pleasant for me.'

'Fräulein Brückner said I learned very quickly. I speak

103

French and German as well as English, how many languages do you speak?'

'Only two, I'm afraid, so you have the advantage of me there. I speak English and German with a smattering of schoolgirl French.'

'I hate history and geography, is there anything else you can teach me?'

'Can you draw or paint?'

'I did some watercolours once but they were not very good.'

'Well, we will explore together. I shall have to try to make history more exciting, and there are probably a great many things you could teach me.'

Her eyes opened wide. 'What sort of things?'

'You could tell me about this castle. No doubt it figures prominently in the history of Austria if those portraits in splendid uniforms are to be believed. I know how the family came to adopt the crimson falcon as its emblem, but to live in such a beautiful castle and not to know its history would be ridiculous.'

'What is the point of my father paying money so that you can teach me if I am expected to teach you?'

I laughed, even though I didn't altogether feel like laughing. 'Your father escorted me round the castle the first night I came here and told me stories about some of the men and women whose portraits are on the walls. I was merely hoping that you could do likewise.'

'Did my father show you the dungeons?'

'No, he said they were dank dismal places, as I expect they are.'

'Or the crypt?'

'No.'

'I could show you those if you like.'

'Couldn't you show me something a little more cheerful?'

She looked at me with amused narrowed eyes, then in an offhand voice she said, 'Perhaps we could find something.' She rose from her chair in one swift graceful movement and made for the door, looking round as she reached it and evidently expecting me to follow.

Once more as on my first night at Meinhart I was taken round the castle, but this time we found portraits of long-dead Meinharts who had fired the child's imagination by their wickedness and their propensity for evil deeds and swift punishments. She took obvious delight in retelling stories of violence and torture and abruptly I interrupted her by asking, 'Who told you these terrible stories?'

'Oh, there are books in the library,' she answered airily. 'I used to read them until Frau Ebber told my father and he took them away. I'm far too old for fairy-tales, and I was bored by those silly romances Fräulein Brückner used to read. They were all about kitchen maids who married counts and lived happily ever after in castles such as this one. Did you ever hear of anything more ridiculous?'

She had moved on to stand in front of a portrait of a lovely graceful woman in medieval dress and thoughtfully I followed her.

'This is my favourite,' she said eagerly. 'This is Ginevra, Countess Meinhart. She was beautiful and so wicked. It says in the history books that she worshipped the devil and that the Emperor and all the court were her lovers. When her husband came back from the wars he poisoned her and then killed himself. She's the one I'd like to be like when I grow up.'

'Oh Liesel, of course you wouldn't like to be like her. That was another age, this is now. We are not concerned with medieval wickedness. When you grow up, surely you want to be a loving and happy wife to some nice young man of noble birth, not a harridan like this.'

'She's very beautiful.'

'I agree, but beauty isn't enough. A man wants more than beauty from a wife if she is to make him happy.'

'Is this your first lesson for my daughter?' Mellina's sweet lilting voice interrupted us and I spun round with my face flaming, while Liesel ran forward into her outstretched arms.

Her blue eyes were mocking in her laughing face, and I stood there without speaking. Indeed there was nothing to say.

'I want to come with you now,' Liesel said. 'I'm tired of showing Miss Arden round the castle.'

'You must be, darling, but you and I shall spend some time together later on. In the meantime I suggest you continue with your tour. Did you know that Rachel is related to the Meinharts? No doubt that is why she is so interested in our common ancestors.'

She hugged Liesel, then with a small swift smile in my direction she said, 'I'm sorry to have interrupted such a valuable lesson, Rachel, please continue.'

Disconsolately Liesel moved ahead and I followed. 'Haven't you other stories besides those of cruel times which have fortunately gone for ever?' I asked her. 'We live in more enlightened days now, Liesel.'

'Do you really think so?' she said sweetly, and something in her amused cynical eyes made me feel suddenly cold, as though an icy hand had touched my bare flesh.

We came at last to the hall which led into the chapel and she asked, 'Did my father take you into the chapel?' Before I could answer her she was going through the door.

'How often is it used?' I asked her.

'On saints' days and whenever the Abbe comes from the monastery in the mountains. My father invites him to spend a few days here two or three times during the year, but last year he didn't come at all. Perhaps he is afraid to come.'

'Why should the Abbe be afraid?'

'Perhaps he is sensitive to atmosphere. Perhaps it is the dungeons he doesn't like, they are under here. Come, I will show you.'

'No, Liesel,' I said firmly, 'not today. I don't want our first day together to be spoilt by visions of old evils.'

Even as I spoke she had opened the thick brass studded door which led towards a flight of steep stone steps, only dimly lit from the chapel above.

'Liesel, stop, you might fall and hurt yourself. It is so dark in there,' I called after her.

'Come down, Miss Arden, there are candles in the old chapel. Don't say you're afraid to come.'

I was afraid. I had always been nervous in the dark and of things I could not see. I feared that the spectres of ancient evils still haunted those places of torture and already I was hating the cold dark smell which was creeping up the stairs. Liesel had gone, however, and she was in my charge. I had to follow whether I liked it or not. Reluctantly I began to walk down the steep stairway, feeling my way by the wall until my hands discovered a cold iron stair rail. She met me at the bottom of the steps and she carried long candles, one of which she handed to me, then she struck a match to light them both.

'We'll go into the chapel first,' she said, 'then we will go into the dungeons.'

I followed, holding my candle up high so that the light from it fell upon the walls and the altar. I was surprised to find it still furnished with pews although it was bare compared to the chapel above. The small mosaics on the floor looked interesting but it was impossible to see their colours by candlelight. Wrought-iron chandeliers hung from the ceiling but I did not expect they would contain candles. Before me the altar was bare except for two enormous and probably very valuable candelabras and I couldn't help wondering why they had been left there instead of being taken to adorn the chapel above us. I looked curiously at the candle in my hand. It was tall and black and stupidly I racked my brains trying to remember what I had once heard or read about black candles.

'I don't suppose my father told you about this chapel,' she said from somewhere behind me.

'He said it was no longer in use but he didn't bring me here.'

Somehow it didn't have the appearance of a disused chapel in spite of the bareness of its altar. My feet were standing on a deep pile carpet and there were those beautiful silver candelabras. I looked round for Liesel only to see the light from her candle disappearing down the corridor outside.

I made a hasty retreat, calling after her, 'Liesel, come back! I don't want to see the dungeons, we can see them some other time.'

She took no notice, and in some sort of panic I followed after her, half running, half stumbling, with the candlelight flickering on bare rock which told me plainly that we were somewhere within the pinnacle of rock on which the castle stood. She was waiting for me some distance ahead, and as I drew nearer I could see in the candlelight eyes shining with undisguised devilry. She was laughing at me, amused by my quavering voice and chattering teeth.

'Why are you so afraid?' she demanded. 'There's nothing to be afraid of, all those people who were killed and tortured centuries ago have been removed and there are only dead Meinharts in the crypt. See here, you can still see those rings high up on the wall. Do you suppose that once some man was lashed to them? And look at those instruments there, what do you suppose they were used for?'

I didn't look, and I was angry now. This headstrong child both terrified and nauseated me with her love for cruel hurtful things, and I took hold of her wrist, my fingers digging deep into the soft young flesh.

'We are going back now, Liesel, whether you like it or not. You are trying to frighten me and there are other things in this world more important than this cold, dark, nasty place.'

I started to drag her after me and she resisted so that I had to put both my hands around her wrist, surprised at the strength of her slender childlike body. I wasn't sure of the way, it was dark ahead and the rock above us and around us looked the same wherever the light fell. She was coming with me willingly now and in a small voice guaranteed to lull my suspicions she said, 'You don't need to hold me, I'm tired of being down here. I should go first, I know the way better than you.'

I stepped back so that she could pass in front of me. We could not be far from the old chapel and sure enough there was the door ahead of us, a stout wooden door through which she passed, waiting for me to follow. I stood beside her, peering into the darkness, then, before I was aware of her intentions, she blew out both the candles and plunged us into sudden darkness. For a moment I heard her laughter, then she pushed me further inside and I heard the heavy closing of the door.

I found the door, running my hands over it, finding the brass studs that adorned it, but try as I might I could not open it. The darkness moved in upon me, oppressive, heavy with unseen menacing things, and with a sob of despair I sank to the floor, hugging my knees fiercely as though by that act alone I could recover some of my lost courage. I hammered on the door until my hands were bruised and aching and I shouted for help until my voice became a dry whisper in my throat. It was mid-afternoon, I would not be missed until the family sat down for dinner, and even then that terrible child was capable of telling them I had a headache and had retired for the night. I knew those candid blue eyes could be pitiless, she had probably already forgotten my existence in pursuit of some dubious pleasure of her own.

I crawled a little way along the floor and found a shallow step, then I crawled further until my hands found something carved in stone and my fingers started to explore. There was a design of some sort, and lettering. My hands moved upwards until they came to a sharp edge and searched over the rim until they found a face, a face carved out of stone. I groped along its length finding armour and a cloak, then a sword, all carved in stone. I recoiled in horror; I was in the crypt and what my fingers had found was the stone effigy of a knight in armour, supposedly a likeness of the man within the tomb.

I crawled back up the steps and found the door against which I leaned my head, frantic with terror and the smell of decay all around me. Somewhere in the darkness I heard a scuffle and high-pitched squeaks. Oh God, no, not rats, I thought, with visions of their horrible furry bodies scampering over me in the dark.

I willed myself to think of other things which had lain dormant in my thoughts for a long time, things far removed from that terrible place. I thought about the haze of purple heather on the moor in the early autumn and the scent of wood smoke in mist-laden mornings. I thought about London in the early evening and the theatre crowds happily bent on enjoyment, but then unbidden came a vision of the dead falcon with an arrow through its breast and its blood turning the snow to crimson.

I shall never know how long I lay on that cold stone floor, shivering with cold, my ears straining for every sound, my eyes trying in vain to see into the darkness. I only know I was sobbing with terror when the door opened, letting in the lamplight from the corridor before I felt myself lifted up by strong arms and heard a voice whisper, 'Here, take this lantern, I shall have to carry her up the stairs.'

Oh, the exquisite torture of feeling my cramped limbs relax and the ridiculous joy of ordinary lamplight as I was set down gently upon the floor. I threw my arms around my rescuer crying, 'Oh Ernst, darling Ernst, how glad I am to see you!' A man's voice, low and charged with amusement, answered me. 'I regret I must disappoint you, Rachel, your knight in shining armour is not Ernst.'

I looked up into his face in wide-eyed astonishment. It was the Count who stood looking down at me, his face now a polite mask, and then Ernst and Sophia were there enquiring if I was safe and what had happened to me.

'Liesel said she had lost you in the dungeons, Rachel, she said the candles had blown out and she was unable to find you.'

So Liesel was an accomplished liar as well as a mischievous child. I raised my eyes and found the Count watching me. At that moment I could have told him the truth but Ernst and Sophia were there, solicitous in their endeavours to comfort me. I was taken to my room by Sophia who made arrangements for a meal to be served to me. Quite honestly I would have preferred to have eaten with the rest of the family but when she stayed to fuss I wanted her to go. I wanted to be alone with the door locked if I was not to be allowed to go downstairs.

I lay quietly watching the firelight and the lamplight playing on the ceiling of my room. Outside the castle the wind had risen and it moaned dismally along the battlements like some tormented lost soul from the dungeons below.

Something beyond my ordeal in the crypt and Liesel's perfidy was bothering me, but I wasn't sure what. This way and that my thoughts pursued the happenings of the last few days but still their troublesome meanderings evaded the thing that worried me. Lulled by the comfort of my warm bed and the sighing night wind I closed my eyes and dreamily drifted off into a state of half-sleep, to be suddenly thrust into wakefulness. I sat up, staring in front of me with all thoughts of sleep forgotten. I knew now what had troubled me since that moment I stood with Liesel in the old chapel holding our candles high so that we could see into the darkness.

It had been the overpowering scent of incense in a chapel that I had been told was never used – that, and the heavy silver candlesticks as well as the tall black candles. I felt a vague crawling sensation on my flesh, an unmistakable chill as though I was on the fringe of a rare and terrifying discovery. Again I began to explore the hidden chambers of my mind and again I was on the verge of sleep when it came to me like an illuminated picture and I was back in the past, sitting in the cosy comfort of the vicarage on a cold winter evening trying to do my homework while my mother sat over her embroidery and my father and the squire argued as they loved to argue about all manner of things under the sun. That night my father was troubled because some vestments had been stolen from the vestry, together with candlesticks from the altar itself and several silver chalices. The squire in his usual bantering tone was saying, 'I don't know what you're worrying about, David, the thieves won't get far with that sort of stuff. They've obviously been stolen from a church. And what in God's name they want vestments for I can't imagine.'

My father's face had been so thoughtful in the firelight that the squire had said, 'Come on, David, the church won't fall apart because a few ornaments have gone missing. You have others, I take it?'

'Yes, that's not what is worrying me.'

'I'll give you a donation if they don't turn up. If it's their value that's worrying you, that should set your mind at rest.'

'It's not their value. I'm wondering why they've been stolen. What sort of thief would steal from a church where the objects he steals are easily recognized, and why would he steal vestments and altar cloths, and why would he steal a crucifix which no ordinary person would want to buy?'

My homework was forgotten, and I remember that my mother had raised her head from her embroidery and sat watching the two men with rapt attention. The squire too was

111

thoughtful. He sat in his favourite chair with his legs stretched out towards the fire, a glass of whisky warming in his hands, while my father sat looking quietly into the flames of the fire, more troubled than I had ever seen him.

'What are you thinking, David, that they've been stolen for a lark?' the squire asked.

'Perhaps. But a very dangerous and foolish lark, if it is that.'

'How dangerous?'

'There was a case in the next county several years ago of a group of spoiled young people with too much money and too little sense stealing things from a church to hold what they called the Black Mass. Graves were robbed, and all sorts of heinous crimes were perpetrated in the name of the devil before the culprits were found.'

'I remember, wasn't one of them Sir Godfrey Lawson's son and his wife? I don't know much about it, what happens exactly?'

'Oh, a crowd of people get together who are bored with normal everyday living and the worship of God. They revert to the middle ages and invoke the devil. They turn the crucifix upside down and put black candles on the altar. More often than not they make some sort of sacrifice, like a young animal or a cockerel, but in medieval times it would more than likely be a young virgin or a newborn child.'

The squire was staring at my father speechlessly and when he became aware of the silence in the room and of my mother and myself looking at him fixedly he said lightly, 'I'm not sure that we should have embarked upon this subject. I have no doubt that the stolen articles will turn up and that we shall find they were stolen by one of the village lads who had had a bit too much to drink and for nothing more sinister than a bout of high spirits.'

My mother had quietly set aside her embroidery, saying she was going into the kitchen to make supper and inviting me to follow her. When we returned to the fireside my father and the squire were discussing more mundane matters.

Soon after that I went to my new school in Exeter and in the face of an entirely new way of life I quickly forgot the talk on

112

that night, nor had I ever known if the stolen vestments and silver came to light. Now, in my bedroom within Castle Meinhart, with the moaning wind rattling the windows, I became very afraid.

Six

My dark suspicions seemed to have no foundation in the light of a new day. The night before I had been all for telling the Count that I wished to leave Meinhart immediately, that I had no interest in trying to teach his mischievous daughter, but in the sober light of day I could see my defeat at the hands of a child as something to overcome, not something to run away from. Besides, the alternative – to return to London and the weary round of job hunting in a lonely city – was hardly more encouraging, although I fully expected life at Meinhart to move from crisis to crisis in the months ahead.

I had risen early in the hope that I might encounter my employer before he left the castle, but he was on the point of leaving the breakfast room at the moment I arrived there. He raised his eyebrows maddeningly, and faced with a cool half smile I blurted out, 'I propose that I should start Liesel's lessons as soon as possible. Is there some room set aside for that purpose?'

'I think that is very sensible of you, Rachel. For one moment I thought you were here to tell me you had changed your mind.'

'I thought about that too, but I don't see why I should allow a girl of Liesel's age to get the better of me.'

He smiled and indicated that I should accompany him. 'There is a room set aside for her tuition next door to her bedroom, I will take you there now. The room is quite adequately equipped but if there is anything at all you are short of, let me know and I will try to obtain it for you. I propose that you keep a similar timetable to the one used by

114

Frau Ebber. She was with Liesel from half past nine in the morning until luncheon and from two o'clock until four. That way she had some time to herself and of course I shall not expect you to work at the weekends. There may be whole days when Liesel is out with her mother, in which case you may do exactly as you please. May I ask how you intend to handle the situation you found yourself in yesterday?'

'I intend to ignore it.'

'I think that is very wise. There are two women who come to the castle every Tuesday and Thursday. One of them teaches Liesel to play the piano, the other one teaches her dancing. You may like to keep an eye on her progress, or you may prefer to have that little time to yourself.'

'I think for the time being I would like to stay and watch.'

'Very well. Have you any other questions about the arrangements?'

'I don't think so – they seem most adequate to me, sir.'

He looked at me thoughtfully for several moments, then smiling a little he said, 'I would prefer you to call me Max, Rachel. Do you address your other relatives as sir?'

'I do not have other relatives.'

'In that case, perhaps you might try to be a little more friendly with this one.'

I was very aware of him at that moment. He stood very close to me, so close that I could smell the soap he used and the faint odour of cigar smoke. He looked down on my blushing face with undisguised amusement. I was comfortable with Ernst, it was so easy to laugh and tease a little, even to flirt with him, but I was not comfortable with this man and I was relieved when he said lightly, 'Come, let us take a look at the schoolroom and you can tell me if it meets with your approval.'

It was a warm comfortable room overlooking the lake, lined with glass-fronted bookcases. There was a huge sphere representing the world on the floor near the fireplace and I was happy to see that a fire had already been lit. Fires were never any problem at Meinhart but I never saw who lit them. Underneath the rooms used by the family and their guests I supposed there must be an army of servants in quarters I was never likely to see, who carried out their duties most diligently as well as unobtrusively.

In the centre of the room was a table and three chairs, and there was a chintz-covered window seat which jutted out alarmingly above the sheer face of rock beneath. Appreciatively I turned to say, 'Oh, but this is charming! I am sure I shall find everything I need here.'

'Liesel has been told she must be here promptly at nine thirty so perhaps you might like to eat breakfast now. I do not know how much of her story about the happenings of yesterday afternoon has been believed by the rest of the household, but I can assure you, Rachel, I didn't believe a word of it.'

Taken somewhat aback I looked at him enquiringly, but he only said, 'I have to go to Baden this morning and shall be gone all day. If you have any queries about Liesel or the facilities here perhaps you will speak to me after dinner.'

He smiled briefly, then stepped aside to allow me to leave the schoolroom before him.

I was somewhat apprehensive about the day in front of me but I need not have been. It passed pleasantly enough, and Liesel seemed happy to allow me to forget the previous afternoon, although she did arrive in the schoolroom with a sulky look on her face. As the morning progressed, however, and I did not refer to the incident, she brightened considerably.

She had a quick intelligent mind but not an academic one. She read well, both in German and in English, but she quickly became bored and I decided to ask her to write an essay on a subject of her own choice while I prepared the lesson for the afternoon. She wrote quickly, I was pleased to see, as though the subject she had chosen interested her, and I looked forward to reading something which gave her so little trouble and which I hoped would enable me to understand her a little better.

The morning passed so quickly that I was surprised to hear the luncheon gong reverberating through the rooms and corridors, but Liesel sprang to her feet with undisguised relief saying, 'Good, I didn't think there was anything else to write.

Will you be lunching with us, Miss Arden?'

'I expect so, I haven't heard of any other arrangements.'

'Frau Ebber never lunched with us, she ate with the rest of the servants in the kitchens.'

I bit my lip, smothering the instant retort on my lips, and said, 'Go and wash your inky fingers, I shall see you in the dining room.'

I saw the sulky look return to her face but I felt a small moment of elation when she had no choice but to do as I asked.

It was a short-lived victory, I soon discovered on reading her essay. This was a piece of witty, caustic writing with several spelling mistakes, in which I figured prominently. I sat with it in my hands at the schoolroom table bristling with annoyance. The essay was entitled 'My New Governess', and the unnamed governess was a distant relative who had come out of nowhere, with no clothes and no money, a woman who was afraid of the dark shadows around her but a woman possessed of a strange beauty with dark auburn hair and deep blue eyes. I might have found that flattering if the essay had not gone on to suggest that I was desperately in love with Liesel's father and was embroiled in a passionate love affair with her handsome military cousin. It was a story some trashy romantic novelist might have written and I had little doubt that Liesel had read a number of them herself to be able to write such rubbish. In anger I tore it into small pieces and consigned them to the flames.

She returned to the schoolroom promptly at two o'clock and although I knew that she was watching me with sly speculative eyes I was determined to ignore the essay just as I had ignored my sojourn in the family crypt.

'I've decided to find out what you know about history,' I told her.

'You know I don't like history, I told you yesterday.'

'Your father didn't say I was to leave it out of my curriculum simply because you don't happen to like it. That goes for any other subject you are not keen on, too.'

She slammed her writing case on the table and dragged up a chair which she jarred against the table legs with some force.

I ignored her attitude and tried to find out how much she knew about the Napoleonic wars, but soon discovered that what Liesel was really interested in was the royal divorce whereby Napoleon put aside the Empress Josephine in order to marry the Austrian Princess Marie Louise. His defeat at the hands of Nelson was merely an excuse to discuss that brave soldier's love affair with the beautiful Emma Hamilton. In short, whenever some historical figure was mentioned, it was his or her private life she was interested in, not the deeds that had made them famous.

'Who told you about such events?' I asked her. 'They never figured in my education! Was it Frau Ebber?'

'Of course not, Frau Ebber probably never knew of them. She was very plain, I don't suppose any man ever looked at her.'

'You shouldn't say such things about people, Liesel, she was probably a very cultured woman. Beauty isn't everything.'

'I'd much rather be beautiful than cultured.'

'Why?'

'Well, I shall never be expected to earn my own living but I do want to marry a rich and powerful man.'

'You'll be far more likely to succeed in that quarter if you can discuss the events of the day intelligently. Beauty without intellect is merely a façade, and a man can find that easily, he doesn't have to marry it.'

'My mother is very beautiful and she has married one of the most powerful men in Austria. She told me herself that she hated school and that the only things she was interested in were those which would make sure of a brilliant marriage when she was old enough. I don't suppose that will happen to you.'

'Why do you say that?'

'You are very beautiful, but here you are teaching me things I don't want to learn and I don't suppose you'll meet anybody interesting here.'

'I am not here to meet anybody interesting, I am here to work. There is plenty of time for the other.'

'But you are getting older all the time, aren't you? Do you never think of the wasted months and years spent teaching me

118

when you could be enjoying yourself in Vienna?'

She had risen from her chair and I stared after her to where she had gone to gaze out of the window. Her remarks were impudent, not the sort of remarks one expected to hear from a young girl, and I was inordinately vexed by them. I didn't feel like letting her have the last word, but on the other hand I didn't want to get into any sort of argument with her about either my past or my future.

As I joined her at the window I saw that she was watching something or someone outside with rapt attention, and was surprised to see that she was staring at her mother. Mellina was mounted on a bright chestnut horse, wearing a black riding habit which complimented her delicate fairness, but it was her companion who astonished me most.

She was laughing down at Josef the gatekeeper with every evidence of amusement, and he was holding the rein of her horse. They were an incongruous couple, the beautiful aristocratic countess and the huge man with his handsome dark face and enormous gnarled hands.

'Josef admires my mother,' Liesel said, 'and I think my mother admires Josef. They always laugh together when they meet and although he is a peasant he is very handsome.'

'Josef is an old servant, Liesel, that is why your mother speaks to him. It is good for servant and mistress to converse amicably.'

She looked up at me with wide guileless blue eyes, but I was aware instantly of the mockery they contained. 'My mother is not on familiar terms with any of the house servants or any of the gamekeepers, only Josef, but then none of them have Josef's power, that is what attracts my mother.'

To my shame I said nothing. I had no armour, no weapons against this girl who in spite of her years was more deviously sophisticated than I was ever likely to be. I did, however, make a firm resolution that I would speak to her father immediately after dinner, and speak to him I did, in the library, considerably chagrined when Mellina came in to hear the conversation.

Not to be put off I told him about the essay I had asked her to write, leaving out the part where I was supposed to be in love with him, then I told him about her weird and singular notions of history. He looked at me gravely, but Mellina laughed, saying in her lilting amused voice, 'I really don't see what all the fuss is about! My daughter finds you beautiful enough to write an essay around you, and what young girl isn't intrigued by the love affairs of famous people? I know I was.'

I looked at her in some exasperation. Of course, Mellina would have been. I was beginning to realize the enormity of the task I had set myself. Beautiful rich young women did not have to be interested in learning for learning's sake. They would never need to put it to the test, they would never need to earn a living, except by marrying some rich young man from a noble family who would expect to find a cheerful companion, an obliging hostess and a passionate bedmate.

I looked at the Count for some indication that he was going to assist me, but he was standing quietly beside the fireplace looking down into the flames, not at Mellina lounging gracefully against her cushions, and I suddenly wondered if either of them knew what I had been talking about.

At last the Count looked up, still ignoring his wife. 'Of course you will change this pattern, Rachel. I don't know who has filled her head with all this nonsense, but it is time women became something more than pretty ornaments about the place. Times are changing, even in Vienna.'

'Oh Max,' Mellina chided, 'how are things changing? Vienna is just as she always was. The Emperor is getting old and he has no son to follow him, but in ten or twenty years' time we shall still be looking forward to the ball at the Belvedere just as we are now. If Rachel wants to turn Liesel into a bluestocking I suppose she must, but it's not going to do the child any good. Men hate clever women, they only make them feel inferior. They want a woman to be beautiful and amusing. What man wants to return home to a bookworm?'

'I think a man might hope to find some stimulating conversation in his own home,' I couldn't resist saying. 'I think at least women should be educated to the same standard as men. The time is fast approaching when women may not be content to sit at home and wait for their lord and master to return – some of them might conceivably want to go out into the world and earn their own living. Besides, what man wants to listen to gossip all night or talk of the latest fashions when he has had a wearisome day? No wonder men go out and find other company.'

'Well, of course they do, darling, in the houses of pleasure or in their stuffy old clubs. I hadn't realized you were such a feminist, or is it that you really don't like men very much? I must be sure to put Ernst in the picture before he becomes any further embroiled.'

I met her mocking eyes bravely and stood my ground. 'Why should women be inferior to men? It has nothing to do with whether I like men or not – it is simply ludicrous to believe that women are incapable of learning anything beyond the ability to be somebody's pet or plaything. Surely we are above that?'

I saw a gleam of anger in her eyes at that moment and I bit my tongue. I had gone too far, and I heard the Count laughing before he said, 'I should forget this argument, Mellina, I believe it's one you are not going to win!'

'It is one I have no wish to win,' she said bitingly. 'I want my daughter to grow up with a knowledge of music and art, to be able to dance and talk amusingly with both men and women, not to bore them with talk of stocks and shares and wars everybody has forgotten years ago.'

She rose from her couch and swept gracefully from the room. Although the Count watched her with narrowed amused eyes, he smiled at me when she had gone in a friendlier fashion than I had expected.

'You are Liesel's governess, Rachel, and as such you are responsible for her education. Do what you think is necessary. Rich, bored and beautiful women have a nasty habit of getting into mischief. If it is not already too late, perhaps you may have a hand in saving Liesel from such a fate.'

After that interview I was insistent that Liesel worked hard, although she did so with bad grace. I believe she was more afraid of her father's reprovals than mine, but at least I did not have to suffer any of her tantrums. The two women arrived from Vienna, and I decided that instead of going off on some pursuit of my own I would stay to watch her dancing lesson as well as her performance on the piano.

'There is no need for you to stay, Miss Arden,' she said haughtily. 'Why don't you go riding with Cousin Ernst? He would like that.'

'I have made no arrangements to do so,' I answered her calmly, 'and I would prefer to see you dance.'

'Why should you – unless you want to learn too?'

'I can do all the dancing I want to do. Come, we're wasting time and these two ladies have come to teach, not to listen to an argument.'

I was surprised to find that it was ballroom dancing and not ballet that Liesel was being taught, but watching her waltz was sheer joy. Her slender body seemed to float effortlessly as a cloud, gracefully, beautifully, her exquisite face alight as she whirled to the music. Her efforts on the piano, however, were less spectacular. They were adequate enough to amuse herself and probably her guests at a small dinner party, but I had expected to hear glorious melodies played by those small slender fingers.

The two women left and I couldn't help wondering how much money was spent week after week in bringing them by carriage or sleigh from Vienna for the sole purpose of teaching Liesel how to waltz and perform pretty, light pieces of music on the piano.

'You waltz beautifully,' I told her, 'but does your teacher need to come every week? The waltz doesn't change!'

She looked at me scornfully. 'It's not just the waltz she teaches me, we do the polonaise and the quadrille.'

'But how can you without any other people?'

'Oh, we imagine them. Just so long as I can do my part it doesn't matter about the others.'

'I don't hear you practising the piano very much. Don't you enjoy it?'

'Oh, it's all right, but at the moment it is more important that I learn to dance properly in time for the ball at the Belvedere palace.'

'Aren't you a little young to be thinking about going to such a grown-up affair?'

'You don't know anything, do you, Miss Arden? The daughters of the most important men in Vienna open the ball while everybody watches. Last year was my first year so naturally I shall be there this year.'

'I always thought the dancers from the imperial ballet opened the ball.'

'They do, but the waltzing proper is opened by us.'

'I see. You must forgive my ignorance, Liesel, but I would ask you to remember that I am a foreigner in Vienna and have a lot to learn.'

After that she came a little more willingly to her studies.

My ignorance of the social life of Vienna was not at an end. It was to be demonstrated once more over luncheon when Mellina said, 'Liesel will not be taking lessons tomorrow – she is returning to Vienna with me this afternoon and we are staying overnight. Perhaps you will drive us, Ernst?'

Ernst looked up with the same sulky expression I so often saw on Liesel's face. 'Why me, Mellina? You have a host of unemployed coachmen,' he muttered with bad grace.

'They're a nuisance in Vienna, and Sophia is coming with us. You could take us to a concert this evening, it would be gallant of you.'

'I didn't intend going back to Vienna until I had to. After all, there aren't many days left of my leave.'

I sat with bowed head, concentrating on peeling my fruit. Mellina said sharply, 'You'd better come, Ernst. Sophia already has her gown for the ball and she will need a companion in Vienna while Liesel and I are at the dress-maker's.'

'Oh, very well then, but I thought you hated the carnival season in Vienna. I can't think why we didn't stay on there, nothing very exciting has happened here so far.'

I didn't miss the baleful look Mellina turned upon him before she snapped, 'Ernst, you really are a bore, just because you can't go cavorting off with Rachel here! Let Max amuse her, if he comes back in time. They seemed to be amusing themselves very nicely before we arrived here.'

I said nothing but merely sat there with my face burning. Aware of my embarrassment Sophia said, 'I don't have to go to Vienna, Mellina. I have my gown for the ball, I could quite easily stay here.'

'Like Ernst said, there has been no excitement at Meinhart and that is what you came for, isn't it? No, Ernst will drive us into the city and Rachel must amuse herself.'

I was glad when luncheon was over. The long afternoon stretched ahead of me and I wondered how I should occupy myself until it was time to retire for the night. I spent the first hour wandering about the rooms of the castle looking again at the portraits on the walls. Then, when I reached the hall leading into the chapel, I felt a sudden draught and my skirts blew around my legs. I looked round sharply and saw Frau Gessler closing the door leading to the dungeons below. She was just extinguishing her lamp, and she seemed to jump several inches when I addressed her.

She was looking at me through narrowed eyes, her broad peasant's face redder than usual. I had not seen the woman for days and I took the opportunity to ask her about the missing crucifix.

She shook her head. 'I would have given it to the mistress if I had found it,' she answered me shortly.

'You don't remember seeing it lying on the table near my bed?' I persisted.

'No, Fräulein, I do not go into your room.'

'Oh, but you do, Frau Gessler, I remember seeing you leaving it.'

'Are you accusing me of taking your crucifix, Fräulein?'

'Not at all. I only wondered if you had found it when you went about your duties.'

'No, like I said, I would have handed it to the mistress. Perhaps you lost it outside.'

'Perhaps. Have you also duties in the old chapel, Frau Gessler? It must be very cold and uncomfortable working down there.'

'I went to see if the traps had been set. There are rats in the cellars and sometimes the men forget to set the traps.'

'Not a very pleasant occupation for a woman, but then perhaps you are not afraid of rats? They terrify me.'

'Is that so, Fräulein?'

She gave a stilted grimace which I presume passed as a smile and walked away. She hadn't liked my questions and I had a strong feeling that I was chancing my luck in posing them. However, there was no doubt that there were rats in the crypt and perhaps she had been speaking the truth when she said she had gone down there to attend to the traps.

About an hour later I was sitting in the library with my head in a book when Mellina came in all dressed and ready for travelling.

'Oh, forget that book for a while, Rachel,' she said, and I was surprised at the charm and friendliness of her manner. 'Why don't you ride in the park? It's a beautiful day and the fresh air would bring some colour into your cheeks.'

I admitted that I didn't feel very confident riding on my own.

'Nonsense. I've taken the liberty of telling Gottfried to saddle one of the horses for you, he knows which one you will be able to manage. It's all very good practice and much better than sitting here all afternoon with these stuffy old books.'

She gave me another dazzling smile which I returned, thinking happily that at last Mellina had decided I was destined to be an adjunct to the family for some time and that she might just as well accept me with good grace.

I thanked her for her kindness, saying that I would take advantage of it, then with another swift smile she was gone.

One of the horses, she had said, and fervently I wished that it was Greta as I donned Ludmilla's riding habit. I was not relishing riding alone and I thought the groom gave me a long searching look as I entered the stable yard. It was not Greta who waited for me beside the mounting blocks but another horse, a much bigger horse, although he stood patiently enough beside the steps.

'I thought I would be riding Greta?' I said to the groom.

'Countess Meinhart said I was to saddle this one, Fräulein. Keep to the paths, do not be tempted to ride into the forest, and you should come to no harm.'

'Is he quite docile?'

125

'I have heard no reports that he is not. His name is Hassan. The master bought him two years ago, he is a purebred Arab.'

I mounted him and off we set along the path which led down towards the lake below. I couldn't help thinking about that other Arab whose beautiful head had lain against my knees before they put a bullet into it. She too had been a thoroughbred, and angry with myself I turned my thoughts to other things. The horse seemed quiet enough and Mellina was right, the fresh air was better for me than the warmth of the library. The sharp wind brought the colour into my cheeks and as we skirted the lake I experienced a newfound joy in the majestic beauty of my surroundings and the snow-covered mountains in the distance. We came at last to the river pounding savagely between the rocks under the bridge and I felt the horse shy nervously away from the sound. Ahead now stretched the long curve of the drive with the forest on either side of us, and at the end of the drive were the great iron gates which I could not yet see.

Filled with a sudden spurt of courage I induced the horse to canter, and I was loving it – I even began to feel like a horsewoman – when from the forest to the left of us there came the sudden crack of a rifle. As the horse reared nervously I hung desperately on to the reins; then he bolted along the path ahead and I had to hold on for dear life, more afraid than I had ever been before. I was remembering that morning when I had run down the hillside shouting 'Don't jump! Oh, please, don't jump!' and then the sickening thud as both horse and rider hit the ground. In spite of my own predicament I was unable to rid myself of that moment from the past. I was hanging on to the horse's mane now, having lost the reins, aware of the flying hooves beneath me kicking up clouds of ice and melting snow. Straight ahead of me loomed the gates, closed and enormous, and I wondered how soon it would be before I was flung against them. I had no thought of others on that icy road, I did not hear the sound of other hoofbeats, but suddenly I felt myself lifted bodily from the horse I was riding and thrown unceremoniously across the back of another horse while a man's voice said, 'Hold on, try not to move.'

I hung on, feeling the horse rear on his haunches as he was

pulled up sharply, hearing the high-pitched whinny of resentment. Then we were still, and I was sobbing with relief. I felt the man's hold on me relax and next moment I was standing on the road beside the big black stallion and Max was holding me against him so that I could feel the beating of his heart. I looked ahead of me, expecting to see the horse I had been riding injured against the gates, but instead I saw the gatekeeper Josef walking back to where we were standing, leading him by the reins.

'Mount him,' the Count said to me in a stern voice, and when I cowered back he said more gently, 'You must ride him, Rachel. If you don't, you may never ride a horse again.'

I didn't care, I wouldn't have cared if I had never seen another horse, but both men were watching me, the Count gravely, willing me to mount, the gatekeeper with a sly smile on his face. Although I was still trembling visibly I took the reins he offered me and mounted the stallion. I looked once at the gatekeeper, and now his eyes met mine boldly as they had done on the day of my arrival. He was a giant of a man, making the tall Max seem almost delicate beside him. His face had the tanned ruddy hue of one who spends most of his life outdoors and I looked again at his huge hands which seemed capable of crushing a skull in their palms.

'Where were you when you saw the horse bolt?' Max asked him coldly.

'I was in the forest, master, I have set traps there.'

'Was it you who fired the gun?'

'Yes, sir. I saw movement in the trees, some predator, I thought.'

'You should have made sure, it could well have been a deer wandered from the herd. Did you fancy venison for supper, Josef?'

The man was looking at the ground now, mumbling something beneath his breath, and the Count asked, 'Well, did you discover your predator?'

'I did not have time to look, master, I heard the horse and saw the lady here trying to keep on his back. I did not know what would happen when he reached the gates.'

'Very commendable of you! But you knew the horse, so you

knew what to expect when you fired that rifle. You also knew how to control him.'

'How should I know the young lady would be riding that horse, sir?'

'How indeed?' the Count said.

I was calmer now, but surprised by the turn the conversation had taken. Seeing my look the Count said, 'Come, Rachel, we will return to the stables. Who arranged for you to ride Hassan?'

'Mellina,' I said miserably. 'Oh, but I am sure she never expected that he would bolt, we were doing marvellously until he heard the rifle shot.'

He nodded absently, nor did we speak again until we reached the stable yard, then he said, 'Go on up to the castle, I need to speak with the groom. Join me in the library – I think we could both do with a glass of cognac after such a fright.'

I refused to contemplate that Mellina could be capable of that much wickedness. How could she have known that Josef would fire his wretched rifle just as I approached him along the road? How could she have even known that I would ride that way?

That night I dined alone with the Count, wearing my own blue dress, and he raised his eyebrows slightly as he handed me a glass of wine.

'Why are you so reluctant to wear Ludmilla's clothes?' he asked, smiling a little.

'Because they make me feel like a dancing girl making herself beautiful for her lord and master. After all, they are not my clothes,' I answered him boldly.

He laughed. 'Well, I can assure you I don't think of you even remotely in the role of a dancing girl, but I do expect a woman to look her prettiest when we are dining alone, and by candlelight. And that reminds me, do you have a suitable gown for the carnival ball at the Belvedere?'

'The carnival ball!'

'Why, yes. Everybody in Vienna goes to the Belvedere. Some of us dance, some of us merely sit on the balconies and watch, but everybody who is anybody in Vienna expects to be there.'

'But I am a nobody in Vienna.'

'A matter of regret, and one which I am sure your father would have tried to put right if he had known of it.'

'But I am merely a governess in this castle and I shall not expect to be invited.'

'Nevertheless you will be invited, Rachel. But you haven't said yet if you have a gown worthy of the occasion.'

'I haven't. I had such a gown but it was ruined in the snow the night I ran away from the opera house and all those staring eyes.'

'You can wear my sister's clothes.'

'Oh no, Count Meinhart – Max – on such an occasion I would prefer to wear my own, and since I have nothing suitable I shall not go.'

'In that case I shall enhance your salary. As soon as you reach Vienna there is nothing to stop you going out to buy something suitable.'

'Perhaps we should ask Mellina.'

'Not satisfied with her finding a horse for you to ride, you are willing to put yourself in her hands over a ball gown! Is it not possible that Mellina would find one the colour of your hair, over-embroidered with sequins, so that you might look like a fugitive from one of the town's houses of ill repute?'

'I am sure you misjudge her,' I protested without conviction.

He looked at me with some degree of cynical amusement before he said, 'Do I, my dear, do I?'

No further mention of the Belvedere was made, but in spite of my earlier feelings I enjoyed dining with him. I enjoyed listening to his views on world events and I learned a little more of the history of Meinhart. Later we played chess, and although he was more skilful than I he was surprised that I acquitted myself as well as I did.

'I often played with my father,' I said. 'Of course he always won, and I'm afraid I am a little out of practice.'

Before we left the room he went over to a small desk and took out a little parcel, handing it to me with the words, 'I don't suppose this will ever replace the original, but I would like you to wear it, Rachel. When you are not wearing it, see that it is carefully locked away. I would not like you to lose another.'

In some wonder I took the parcel from him and unwrapped it. Inside was a velvet jeweller's box and on opening it I found a delicate gold chain and a beautifully chased crucifix.

'This is beautiful!' I exclaimed. 'But why should you feel you must replace something I lost so carelessly?'

'I am not so sure that you did lose it, for it obviously meant a great deal to you. I hardly think you would have treated it carelessly. Of course there is always the chance that the clasp became worn with age.'

'You are very kind to have bought this for me. I can't tell you how much I shall treasure it.'

'I didn't buy it, it belonged to my mother.'

'It is very beautiful, but shouldn't it belong to Mellina?'

He laughed, but it was not a laugh of amusement. 'Mellina would have little interest in wearing a simple crucifix. Her taste runs to more flamboyant jewellery like the crimson falcon, but diamonds and emeralds are her favourites, the bigger the better.'

He was not being cynical, he was merely stating a fact. He expected Mellina to choose the exotic jewellery she knew he could afford, but at that moment I would not have exchanged the crown jewels for that beautiful crucifix once worn by his mother, and I was touched by the warmth of a gesture I had thought this cold man incapable of.

He walked with me to the end of the corridor where my room was situated and on leaving me he took my hand and lifted it to his lips. I could feel my face blushing as my hand lay trembling in his, then, taking me by surprise, he bent his head and lightly brushed my lips with his.

Seven

Nothing, it seemed, mattered now except the ball at the Belvedere. It was the sole topic of discussion over the breakfast, luncheon and dinner table until Max informed us he was fed up with it and had half a mind not to go.

Liesel was more animated than I had ever seen her and even Mellina became talkative when I asked questions about the event. It was to be held at the beginning of February, she informed me, and the family were to leave Meinhart two days before. That night I made a point of asking Max if I could go back to Vienna with them to retrieve my belongings from the hotel and perhaps call upon Herr Liptmann and his wife. He looked at me in some surprise saying, 'But of course, Rachel. As I told you, I am expecting you to accompany us to the ball.'

I bit my lip vexedly. I had nothing to wear for the ball if it was to be the grand affair they said it would be, and Mellina rightly guessed why I seemed unsure.

'I don't suppose you have a ball gown, Rachel. A girl who comes to Vienna for a short time and stays for much longer is not likely to have a ball gown in her wardrobe.'

'That is no problem,' Max said quietly. 'I have already told Rachel I will advance her salary in order that she can go out and buy one.'

'That shows how little you know, darling,' Mellina trilled. 'The shops in Vienna will have run out of ball gowns days before, only the ones nobody would be seen dead in will be left.'

'In that case she will take one of Ludmilla's,' he answered

131

her patiently, 'or she could borrow one of yours, something you would not be ashamed to wear yourself.'

I looked at him sharply but Mellina ignored his remarks, turning instead to the Baroness who sat listening to her quietly. I wondered again if she ever smiled.

I looked in Ludmilla's wardrobe that night out of curiosity, but it did not contain a single gown I could have worn for the Belvedere. There were dinner dresses in plenty but the absence of a ball gown seemed to settle the matter for me. It was evident I would not be there.

On the day when Ernst had to return to his duties in Vienna I overheard him speaking to Mellina in the corridor outside the library. I was in there to make sure of my facts before embarking on the afternoon's history lesson, and they were on their way back from the dining room, obviously unaware that their conversation could be heard.

'You'll come to the house for dinner on the night of the ball, Ernst? I shall expect you around seven.'

'I suppose so,' he answered her with poor grace.

'Don't be such a baby, Ernst! I'm sorry the holiday hasn't turned out the way we expected, but it hasn't for me either. Max didn't seem disposed to organize a boar hunt and Sophia's got a sulk on. The weather was a nuisance, I couldn't arrange anything here when we had to stay longer in Vienna and now Sophia's being difficult. Besides, Rachel is here.'

'I'd like her to come to the ball with us.'

'Oh, darling, don't be so difficult – there'll be more girls at the ball than you'll know what to do with, every bit as beautiful as Rachel and with the right sort of background.'

'Even so I'd like her to come.'

'Well, we'll see.'

I stood in the library feeling resentful as their voices faded, wishing at that moment that I was back in London looking for work. On my way back to the schoolroom Ernst caught up with me and in an eager boyish voice he said, 'Rachel, you are coming to Vienna at the end of January, aren't you?'

'I have to be there to collect my things from the hotel.'

'You have to be at the ball, to see Liesel in the opening ceremony and to dance all night with me.'

'Isn't Liesel rather young to be attending such a grown-up event?'

'Not at all. She dances beautifully and the daughter of Count Meinhart will be very much in demand by a host of young gallants.'

'All blue-blooded, I have no doubt,' I couldn't resist saying.

He threw back his head and laughed. 'That was most unkind of you, Rachel, but very true. Will you sit next to me at the dinner table before the ball?'

'Oh, Ernst, I shall not be going to the ball! I'm so sick of the ball – even if I could go I don't think I should want to.'

He was looking at me so searchingly I wanted to move away, but we were standing in a narrow corridor and he had me captive against the wall with an arm on either side of me, so it was impossible to get away without an undignified struggle.

'Really, Ernst, do let me by! Suppose somebody comes and sees us like this,' I said sharply.

'Who's to see? Max is out and Sophia will think it all beautifully romantic, Mellina might be amused and who else is there?'

'There's Liesel.'

'It would take more than this to shock that child, I can assure you! You haven't said you are sorry to see me go.'

'Well, of course I'm sorry, you seem to be the only friend I have here.'

'Oh well, I suppose that will have to do for the moment.' Before I could stop him he had swept me into his arms and was kissing me passionately. I didn't hear the door open, but Liesel's silver-toned voice interrupted our embrace. 'Aren't we to have a history lesson then? I seem to have been waiting a long time.'

Unabashed he merely ruffled her hair, and after a gay smile in my direction I heard him running down the stairs. Somehow his departure left me feeling very vulnerable and that night I missed him sitting at the dinner table, his impudent blue eyes laughing into mine whenever he thought we were unobserved. I supposed Sophia was missing him too.

133

She was very quiet and for once everybody seemed engrossed with other matters apart from the ball. I was glad when the meal was over and I could retire to my room to prepare lessons for the next day. Max, Mellina informed us rather crossly, had gone to Linz on business and would not be back until the end of January.

'Does that mean that he will not be coming to Vienna with us?' Liesel asked.

'He is joining us later. Really, it is too bad of Max to arrive after all the arrangements have been made, then he will just stand around looking bored and aloof from it all. He never professes to like any of my friends.'

The Baroness raised her thin arched eyebrows at that statement and Mellina leaned forward to pat her hand. 'Oh, not you, darling,' she said. 'After all you are unobtrusive enough, even for Max.'

The house on the Ringstrasse overlooked a small park and I was left to saunter in behind the luggage. I loved it immediately I entered it, and stood in the centre of the hall looking round with me with delight. It was there that Ernst found me, entranced like a child in an enchanted palace, looking at the crystal chandeliers that hung from the ceiling and the beautifully carved staircase which swept up from the hall.

'Oh, Ernst,' I said in awe, 'I love it! It is as beautiful as Meinhart but a much gentler place. One can imagine all sorts of dark happenings at Meinhart but only happy things should happen here.'

He laughed and said, 'What an imagination! Have you looked around?'

'No, we've only just got here.'

I was standing at the bottom of the stairs looking up at the portrait of a woman which hung at the curve of the first landing. She was young, with dark auburn hair and intensely blue eyes. She was wearing a pale blue gown, and in her hair and falling from the waist of her gown were white gardenias. I stood fascinated by the portrait, until Ernst said, 'You know,

Rachel, you are rather like her, it's probably that hair of yours and those blue eyes. A very interesting combination, I've always thought, as well as unusual.'

'Who is she?' I whispered.

'Oh, probably some Countess Meinhart, the house is full of them.'

'But this isn't an old portrait and she isn't Max's mother.'

'There's another portrait of her in the drawing room; there might be a plaque under it. Come and look.'

I followed him into the drawing room, a beautiful room in colours of pale rose and turquoise. My eyes were immediately drawn to the portrait over the mantelpiece. It was the same woman, but this time she sat on a long velvet sofa and curled into the crook of her arm was a small fair-haired boy. Ernst bent his head and read out to me from the plaque underneath the portrait, 'Countess Theresa and her son Carl.'

For a brief moment I found my legs trembling under me and felt so faint I had to catch hold of the back of the chair.

'I say, what's this, are you ill?' Ernst asked solicitously, putting his arms around me.

'No, just a little faint, that's all. It's probably the journey – I didn't eat much breakfast.'

I was not ill, nor was it the journey; it was the shock of suddenly being confronted with a portrait of my grandmother and my father as a child.

As we turned to leave the room we found Mellina standing in the doorway. I had no idea how long she had been standing there but there was a taunting amusement on her face as she looked up at the portrait. 'How strange,' she said. 'I hadn't noticed it before but you are very like the Countess Theresa. You could almost be her daughter except that you are too young. I wonder if this is the scandal Max refuses to talk about, a little indiscretion on the part of the beautiful Theresa, or that little boy who looks so innocent and grew up not to be.'

'It's a pity we can't retrieve the dress from that portrait in the hall,' Ernst said. 'It would be a sensation at the ball.'

'And quite out of fashion, but then only a man could make such a fatuous remark,' Mellina snapped. 'I wish you'd go and talk to Sophia, Rachel. I don't know what's the matter with her and I've no time to spend worrying over her sulks and silences.'

'Is she in her room?' I asked.

'No, she's in the room across the hall. I can't understand her being so unreasonable at a time like this.'

Sophia was in tears when I found her, a crumpled letter in her hands, and when I put my arm around her the tears flowed faster.

'Whatever has happened?' I asked. 'You were so happy this morning and thrilled to be returning to Vienna, now look at you!'

'The letter's from Stephan. I told him I would be back in Vienna for the ball, but now Mellina's arranged for some man I've never even met to escort me.'

'Didn't you tell her you had already arranged to be with Stephan?'

'She said it would be discourteous to her guest and that I had to write to Stephan and explain. How can I explain that I am going with somebody else when I want to go with him?'

'Well then, Mellina will surely understand when you tell her you have promised to go with Stephan.'

'No, Rachel, Mellina would not understand,' came Mellina's voice from the door behind us. 'I shall have a houseful of guests for dinner before the ball and Stephan von Winckler will not be one of them. Really, Sophia, I invite you to Vienna for the happiest season of the year and so that you can meet eligible men of quality with lands and money and all you can do is moan about this impecunious young man. I suppose Ernst introduced you to him.'

'He's handsome and nice, and I don't care whether he has money or not,' wailed Sophia.

'Then you are a bigger fool than I thought you were. I promised your mother I would do my best for you and that's what I've done. Don't I have enough to worry about at the moment without you weeping and wailing all over the place? This young man will go the ball without you, but there's nothing to say you can't dance with him if he asks you. And please, Sophia, do try to look a little bit less like an abandoned puppy, or no man is going to look at you.'

She swept from the room in an attitude of righteous indignation and miserably Sophia gathered up her travelling case and other belongings. Still in tears she climbed the stairs to her room. I followed, although I didn't know where I was to sleep and by this time Mellina was out of sight.

'You are to have the room next to mine,' Liesel called out from the door of her bedroom. 'I'll show you.'

It was a smaller room than Liesel's, but pretty, as I imagined every room in that fashionable house would be. Liesel flung open my wardrobe door and said, 'There is nothing in the wardrobe. I hope you have brought some of Ludmilla's clothes, otherwise you are going to have nothing to wear.'

'I am going to the hotel to collect my own clothes this afternoon, but I haven't very many of them, I'm afraid.'

'Then you can't go to the ball, can you?'

'I very much doubt it.'

'My gown is coming later today, I'll show you if you like.'

'Yes, Liesel, I would like very much to see it.'

She went back to her own room and I unpacked the one black velvet dinner gown which rightly belonged to Ludmilla, made myself more presentable after the journey and let myself out of the house. It was still snowing a little, but the streets were wet after rain and the snow hardly settled before it melted. There was a sparkle about the city streets, more glittering than the falling snow, and I decided that I would call at the Liptmanns' house before I collected my things from the hotel. Unsure of the direction I took a cab from outside the park and in a short time I was standing outside their front door – half-way along a fashionable street of tall stone houses.

The door was opened by a spruce maid in a starched white apron who informed me that both Herr Liptmann and his wife were at home, and I was ushered into a comfortable parlour. It was in no way as sumptuous as any of the rooms in the Meinharts' house, but the room had a happy, lived-in air with photographs of children here and there as well as a fat black cat which dozed comfortably on the hearth rug.

Both Herr Liptmann and his wife welcomed me warmly

and soon I was sitting down to delicious coffee and warm scones and butter. Frau Liptmann was a pretty plump woman with a happy smile and a gay bubbling wit. I warmed to her instantly and soon we were talking about the days of her youth when she and my mother danced in the imperial ballet. Out came the inevitable photographs and I spent an enchanting afternoon looking at them and talking about the past.

I did not miss the look of consternation which passed between husband and wife when I told them that I had accepted the post of governess to Count Meinhart's daughter. I hurried to explain that I looked upon it as something of a challenge, and that in any case there was nothing waiting for me in England.

Herr Liptmann shook his head doubtfully. 'I have no doubt that Count Meinhart is a gentleman of integrity, but the Countess has a doubtful reputation.'

'I'm not very sure what you mean.'

'Well, it is rumoured that the Meinharts go their separate ways. The Countess has some very unsuitable friends, not, you understand, when her husband is in Vienna, but when she is in the city alone. I don't suppose you will be asked to meet any of them.'

'There is a Baroness Bruchner who has been staying at Meinhart, but I can hardly say I know her.'

'Baroness Bruchner,' he mused. 'I know the Baroness too, an old woman with too much money. She is Polish by birth. I believe her first husband was a prince in that country but he died before she came to Vienna. She too has quite a reputation for devious pleasures.'

I could not believe that the Baroness was capable of revitalizing herself to enjoy pleasures of any kind, she seemed so apathetic, but seeing the doubts on my face Herr Liptmann said, 'There is always talk about a beautiful woman who loves life, but the Countess chooses her friends unwisely: dilettantes, faded royalty, exiled aristocrats, rich people with more money than purpose in life, pleasure seekers bent on seeking it in ways that are unusual and often bizarre.'

My face must have look so troubled that Frau Liptmann cut in. 'You are frightening the child. I am sure the Countess has been most gracious and will continue to be so. Now then, Rachel, you must tell us if you are here for the ball at the Belvedere and what you are going to wear.'

'I am very much afraid I shall not be there. The Count has offered to advance my salary so that I can buy a ball gown in Vienna, but at this late stage there will be very little left worth buying.'

'That is unfortunate, but you are right, there will be nothing of any worth left in the shops. Isn't there a gown you can borrow?'

'I have been wearing the Count's sister's clothes which fit me, but unfortunately she has left no ball gowns at Meinhart. No, I shall simply have to resign myself to staying away. I really don't mind.'

'Oh, but you should mind! It is the event of the year, far more popular than the Emperor's ball which is for a favoured few. The Belvedere is the most beautiful palace in Vienna and on the night of the ball it is a fairy-tale palace. Thousands of scented carnations fill the place, one can hardly breathe for the perfume. My dear child, somebody as young and beautiful as you should mind very much. You *must* go. Your mother would have wished it – how she danced at the Belvedere! We can't let a little thing like a gown defeat you.'

I smiled at her enthusiasm, but it did not bring the gown any nearer.

She looked at her husband with merry twinkling eyes, her head on one side like a little robin, and suddenly he smiled also as though they shared a secret.

'Come with me, Rachel,' she said, 'I think I can help you with a gown.'

Wonderingly I followed her up the stairs and into a bedroom at the front of the house.

'This is our daughter's bedroom when she comes to visit us,' Frau Liptmann informed me. 'She and her husband were to have come in time for the ball but unfortunately the children have measles, so this year they will have to miss the event.'

She opened the wardrobe door and took out a gown enveloped in sheets of tissue paper and laid it across the bed.

When she had removed the tissue I gasped with delight. It was a fairy-tale gown in pale blue heavy satin with a tiny draped bodice and voluminous skirt. It was decorated with tiny seed pearls and glittering blue beads and with it were long gloves of exactly the same colour. It was a gown adoring parents had bought for a beloved daughter and I looked at Frau Liptmann in some consternation.

'But Frau Liptmann,' I protested, 'I couldn't wear your daughter's gown – it's new and I should be afraid in case I damaged it in some way.'

'My dear, you must wear it! We only have one daughter and we don't see her nearly as much as we would like to. She won't be wearing the gown, and it seems such a waste to see it lying there in the wardrobe when there is a young lady who is longing to go to the ball and has no gown to wear. Besides, I was so fond of your mother, it's nice to think we can do something for you.'

Impulsively I bent down and put my arms around her, and when I released her I saw that there were tears in her eyes.

'Come now,' she said briskly. 'Let us see how well it fits in case it has to be altered.'

It needed no alteration. The bodice moulded my figure before it fell away in graceful folds to the floor. The colour complimented the colour of my eyes and my dark red hair, and Frau Liptmann went into transports of ecstasy, dragging me downstairs to show her husband the finished result.

'You need some jewellery. Have you anything suitable?' she asked.

'I have a pearl drop, I think that is all this dress needs, and I can get flowers for my hair.'

'And have you a cloak?'

'Yes, the cloak I wore at the opera. I got it wet that night but it had been wet before, so I am sure it will be all right.'

'You can wear Gerda's cape. It is blue and will look quite lovely over that dress.'

She produced the cape, a paler blue than mine and edged with luxurious blue fox fur, including the hood. I thanked them warmly, my voice trembling with emotion at their kindness, and promised to return both the dress and the cloak the morning after the ball. They waved my gratitude aside, insisting only that I enjoy myself and promising to look out for me at the ball.

For the first time in weeks I felt entirely happy as I made my way to the hotel to collect my belongings in a carriage which Herr Liptmann insisted on paying for. Not even the sight of Sophia's doleful face across the dinnner table and Mellina's studied indifference could dampen my enthusiasm.

There had been an air of excitement since dawn. I could feel it within the house as well as on the streets outside. Before it was properly light I could hear the laughter of passers-by, the wheels of carriages and the whistling of errand boys, while inside the house there were the hushed voices of the servants as they went about their duties.

I dressed quickly after attending to my toilet, creeping on tiptoe past other bedroom doors, but there was little chance that my footsteps could be heard on the deep pile of the carpet. The hall was already filled with flowers which the servants were removing to make way for the caterers. I let myself out of the front door and hurried along the street. I was going to the florist's. I had ordered my flowers the day before and the girl in the shop had advised me to collect them early since they were inundated with orders and would have very little time to attend to late arrivals. Indeed I was surprised to see that a queue of ladies' maids had already formed outside the shop. I joined them and waited with my collar turned up against the cold, shivering a little in the flurrying powdery snow but vastly intrigued by the sprays and bouquets that were being handed over to the waiting girls.

Carnations, the young assistant had said, were out of the question. All the carnations in Vienna would be on display at the Belvedere palace, so I had chosen camellias. I didn't want to draw too much attention to the likeness between myself and Countess Theresa by wearing gardenias as well as a blue gown. The flowers were handed to me in a beautifully decorated box, and not even their price had the power to dampen my anticipation of the evening ahead.

The day passed in an unreal haze of dressmakers and hairdressers, beauticians and manicurists. Sophia was pale and apathetic, Liesel feverishly excited, and Mellina conspicuous by her absence. In the late afternoon Max arrived. It seemed incredible that it was dusk and the lamps were lit outside along the Ringstrasse, shining through the bare branches of the linden trees, while inside a quiet descended on the house which told me that all within it were getting ready for the ball.

I went into Liesel's room to see if she wanted any assistance but she said she did not, her mother's maid would attend to her, so I spent some time over my hair, donning my gown last of all. Nervously I tried the flowers on my hair, arranging the spray this way and that before I was satisfied, hardly daring to look at my reflection in the long cheval glass in the corner of my room. I knew there would be women at the ball adorned with priceless jewels, but the mirror showed me a tall slender girl with an unusual kind of beauty. I stared at myself with wide eyes, finding it hard to believe that the girl in the mirror was really me.

Both the hall and the drawing room were crowded with guests when I finally descended the stairs, and as I stood on the bottom step looking for a familiar face Ernst came promptly to my side, his blue eyes filled with admiration and a happy smile on his face. 'Rachel, how wonderful you look! I feel as though I'm really seeing you for the first time.'

I returned his smile, allowing him to lead me across the hall and place in my hands my first glass of champagne. I enjoyed him flirting with me while my eyes scanned the groups of people. I blushed under the admiring glances of the men and the curious gaze of the women, and then I saw Max, elegant in his evening dress with the blue satin order sweeping diagonally across his chest. Over the heads of the other guests our eyes met and he smiled briefly before he resumed his conversation with an elderly man.

Suddenly some of the sparkle went out of the evening, although I could not have said what I had expected of him. I responded only half-heartedly to Ernst's chatter and I felt vexed with myself. Surely I hadn't expected him to leave his guests and come running to my side to tell me how beautiful he found me? Illogically, that is exactly what I had expected and sternly I told myself not to be a fool.

I was a long way away from him at the dinner table, but once I caught Mellina's eyes upon me, appraising and unfriendly, though as usual she was captivating all those near her with her beauty and sparkling wit.

Sophia's escort proved to be a small portly man in his forties, and when I remembered the handsome and dashing young hussar she had been with at the Prater I could sympathize with her unhappiness. He would not find her cheerful company, I felt sure, and Mellina's eyes flashed dangerously whenever they viewed her young cousin. I remarked to Ernst that Sophia looked far from happy but he merely said, 'No doubt Mellina has plans for Sophia to marry well, and Stephan won't be at the ball – he decided not to go.'

I remember sitting on the edge of the carriage seat so as not to miss a single thing on that ride to the Belvedere. The streets were thronged with happy cheerful people, the lights from coffee houses and restaurants shone out into the night, and outside the Belvedere the lights blazed over crowds of people waiting tirelessly in the falling snow. Suddenly I felt part of that happy bright-eyed throng as we alighted from the carriage, and there were smiles and waving hands from the crowd, as well as exclamations of delight at the sight of me in my borrowed gown and cloak with its fur warm and luxurious around my throat, and Ernst, tall and distinguished in his splendid uniform by my side.

We went to the balcony to watch the opening ceremony performed by the dancers from the imperial ballet. Then came the official opening, a polonaise performed by young men in full evening dress and white gloves, and lovely, very young girls in white dresses with white flowers in their hair and long white gloves on their hands. Liesel was one of them, more enchanting and fairylike than I had ever seen her, partnered by a young man a little older than herself, impeccably dressed, and every inch the perfect escort. How well they all knew the intricate steps of the polonaise! At last came the first waltz of the evening and I was spinning round in Ernst's arms to the entrancing music of the Emperor Waltz.

It was a magical night, the music and the dancers, the champagne and the jewels, the carnations and the laughter. To the music of the Acceleration Waltz I found myself dancing with Max, his arm lightly about my waist, my hand in his, while his eyes looked into mine with all the admiration I so desperately wanted from him. I never wanted the waltz to end, I wanted it to go on and on to the end of time, but all too soon it came to the final brilliant flourish of a Strauss waltz and I was walking with Max to the edge of the ballroom.

He smiled down at me. 'You are looking particularly lovely tonight, Rachel. Even if I had not already decided to believe your story I would have been convinced after seeing you standing underneath the portrait of Countess Theresa.'

I blushed in some confusion and said, 'Liesel and her partner performed splendidly in the opening polonaise. Who is the young man she was dancing with?'

'The son of the French ambassador, I believe, although I have never met the young man. I can always rely on Mellina to see that her daughter only speaks and dances with the right partners.'

'Mellina is doing that for Sophia too, but it isn't making her very happy,' I said sharply.

'Indeed, and where is Sophia? I haven't seen her since we arrived.'

'Hiding somewhere, I shouldn't wonder, from the man Mellina insisted on putting her next to at dinner. There he is over there, that small plump man with the scarlet ribbon across his chest.'

Max smiled his sardonic thin-lipped smile. 'I know him, a Russian, but his name for the moment escapes me. He is quite a powerful man in diplomatic circles, a widower, and a grand duke, I believe. Probably just the type of man Mellina wants for Sophia.'

'Sophia, on the other hand, doesn't want him.'

'Perhaps not, but it isn't always possible to have what one wants in this life. The Meinharts, for instance, invariably marry their Salzburg cousins or their Parisian half-cousins.

144

Sometimes the marriages work remarkably well, others are disastrous and should never have taken place. There is no Meinhart of Sophia's generation for her to marry, but she will no doubt marry to please her family – or Mellina, which is the same thing.'

'But that is unfair and outdated! She should be free to choose for herself,' I stormed indignantly.

He smiled down at me, a slow tired smile, but there was no bitterness in it. 'Yes, my dear, you would say that, but if you will forgive me for saying so, you are young, very young and very lovely, and you have a lot to learn.'

With a formal grave bow he left me staring after him. Next he was waltzing by with Mellina in his arms and I could not help hearing the words spoken by an elderly lady standing beside me. 'Count Meinhart and his wife make a very handsome couple. What a pity they have no son.'

'Yes, indeed,' said her companion. 'One wonders if all the gossip about the Countess is true . . .'

Somehow, after that moment, the ball ceased to entertain me. All those sparkling, exquisitely gowned women and handsome men were like actors and actresses in costume, taking part in some Ruritanian operetta, and the Belvedere palace was a stage setting as romantic as it was unreal. It was life in three-quarter time, as heady as champagne and just as frothy, the talk and the laughter too forced and brittle, a façade covering innumerable little hurts and disappointments like Sophia's. But even as I stood at the edge of the ballroom watching the dancers with sad cynical eyes, a young man was bowing before me and there was I whirling with him round the ballroom to the strains of yet another waltz.

Eight

The days of the carnival were over and back at Meinhart the days and weeks passed quietly. It was incredible to think that I had already been almost four months at the castle. I had not seen Ernst since the night we left Vienna, and Sophia had returned to Salzburg. She wrote to me occasionally, long jumbled letters about her latest young man, and she always asked if I had seen Ernst and if by any chance he had mentioned Stephan. Ernst too wrote, romantic letters which made me smile a little. I was not in love with Ernst, but I was flattered that this dashing handsome young man professed a love I did not think he really felt. He wrote of hoping we should meet at Easter and on other occasions in the future, but there was nothing substantial in our friendship. Mellina once caustically informed me that Ernst would need to marry well since he had no money of his own, and that although he might think himself in love with me he knew where his duty lay.

I saw Max at dinner most evenings, polite or distant according to who was present. There were whole weeks when Mellina became bored and returned to Vienna or went to stay with friends of hers. I never knew who they were.

I spent most of my time with Liesel and she never ceased to amaze me. I found her capable of absorbing knowledge like a sponge absorbs water. She had a quicksilver brain, but unless I made her lessons both exciting and interesting she quickly became bored. Liesel was beautiful and intelligent, but try as I would I could not become fond of her. I did not really even like her. This worried me. It seemed wrong to feel antagonism

146

towards such a young girl, but I couldn't help it. She questioned my authority and made me feel inadequate; I hated the half smile that hovered around her lips when I tried to explain the questions she posed, and at other times she tried to trick me by her questions. There were other things too which troubled me.

She alluded to her mother's friends and seemed to know more about them and their scandalous activities than was natural in a child. Again and again she tried to get me to go down to the dungeons with her, and later I would hear her chuckling over my refusals with Frau Gessler.

Twice I saw Frau Gessler leaving the door which led down into the old chapel, her big peasant face flat and expressionless, but I had the sense to stand back into the shadows so that she did not see me. More and more I wondered what she had been doing there.

Sometimes in the evening when Mellina was away I dined with the Count alone. Our conversation was always confined to ordinary everyday things and soon after we had eaten he would leave me to my own devices. I kept him informed of Liesel's progress and he seemed satisfied. I hoped I was able to disguise my own feelings about her from him, but one evening he looked at me pointedly across the dining table and asked, 'What is Liesel's attitude towards you, Rachel? You only tell me about the work you are doing together – you do not tell me if you are friends, which is equally important, don't you think?'

I blushed under his severe regard but I determined to answer him truthfully. 'I don't think Liesel looks upon me as a friend. I am merely her governess, like the women who were here before me.'

'Then you are managing her better than they did. She made their lives a misery. Is my daughter capable of friendship, or does the fault lie with you? Perhaps you do not like her. We do not always like the people we come into daily contact with.'

'I have never had any difficulty in making friends, indeed I always had plenty of them, but she is different, I don't know why.'

'I would like to know what makes her different. Is she cold, uninterested, more intrigued by the bizarre, the devious, things you find distasteful?'

By this time I knew my face was flaming with colour but I forced myself to meet his searching eyes. 'That is part of the trouble, and I don't think Frau Gessler helps. I believe she has filled Liesel's head with stories of evil and witchcraft from the days of her own youth and does so still. They are together more than is necessary or even healthy.'

I was appalled at my boldness, and when he didn't immediately answer me I was sure I had said too much. He was looking gloomily into the fire and at that moment I sensed a great loneliness in him, a need for an outstretched hand of warm understanding, but I clenched my hands together under the table and remained silent.

After a while he looked up as though he had reached a decision and said, 'I will speak to Frau Gessler in the morning. She has duties here which do not include my daughter and which should keep her fully occupied. She came here with Mellina when first we were married, she had been with the family for a great many years, but I have never quite known why Mellina is so fond of her. She comes originally from a small village in Bavaria, a district rife with stories of hobgoblins and dark deeds. She was probably reared on them and saw nothing odd or dangerous in retelling such stories to Liesel. The woman is unintelligent but that does not mean that she is incapable of some form of low craftiness and she could make a dangerous enemy. We must not underestimate her influence on Liesel, and I will speak to her in such a way that she will not think you have had any hand in it.'

'I think I could be very afraid of Frau Gessler.'

'Her influence will not disappear overnight, we cannot expect that. There are times, Rachel, when I regret having asked you to stay on here.'

'You think I am not right for Liesel?'

'On the contrary, I think you are very good for Liesel. No, it is something else, something you wouldn't understand.'

'I can try.'

He smiled, that sudden sweet smile that robbed his face of

148

its accustomed severity. 'We are getting altogether too serious. This castle has that effect on one at times and perhaps I am becoming fanciful. You will see great changes in the countryside during the next few months now that the snow has gone. Spring is an enchanting time, the park is filled with flowers and the lake will be alive with wild fowl. I have invited the Abbe to come down from his mountain retreat, he arrives on Friday. I think you will enjoy meeting him.'

I was surprised how quickly he could change the conversation from deep gloom to something lighter, but I couldn't help wondering what would be the outcome of his instructions to Frau Gessler to stay away from Liesel. I did not have long to wait.

Liesel came to me, her small face spiteful and contorted with fury, accusing me of interfering, saying she would go to her mother, that her mother would send me packing immediately and that she had no intention of ever learning anything from me again. After her outburst she rushed back to her room, banging and locking the door behind her. All day she refused to open it, even for meals that were left hopefully outside her room, but that night her father knocked on her door and sternly demanded to talk to her. She let him in slowly and reluctantly. I never knew what he said to her that night, but next morning she was back at her desk. She was sulky and uncooperative, but as the day progressed she mellowed and by the time we put our books away we were at least on speaking terms.

The Abbe proved to be a small plump man with merry twinkling eyes and an impish sense of humour. He had a lively, much travelled mind and I enjoyed my first meal in his company. Listening to the Count and the Abbe chatting together in a relaxed companionable atmosphere restored some normality to an otherwise troubled week.

Liesel was quiet and respectful to the Abbe and he teased her in a gentle bantering way that brought dimpled smiles to her lips although not into her eyes. Coming back from our walk across the park, with Liesel scampering ahead of us, the Abbe said, 'She is something of a trial to you, that beautiful child?'

I smiled, 'Sometimes,' I admitted. 'She resents authority, perhaps she has been spoiled.'

'And sometimes it is within herself, with or without the spoiling.'

'She is very young, she will mature.'

'Ah, yes, she will mature. A leopard is a beautiful and delightful thing when he is a cub; he too matures, but does he change his spots? No, my child, he does not, he only becomes more deadly.' His eyes had grown suddenly grave in his round good-humoured face.

'Abbe, Liesel is little more than a child. She has no vice in her, only high spirits. All children have a streak of cruelty in them. Now that Frau Gessler is no longer so much in evidence I am sure I shall be able to control the leopard in Liesel.'

'It is a calm and quiet faith you have, my child, and I hope it does not let you down. I see you wear a crucifix – it is a very beautiful one.'

'Yes, I lost the one I had when I arrived here and the Count was kind enough to give me this one. It belonged to his mother.'

'You say you lost one?'

'Yes. I thought I had left it in my bedroom but I must have been mistaken. I probably lost it somewhere on the estate.'

'And do you always wear that one?'

'Most of the time.'

'All of the time, Fräulein Arden, you must wear it all of the time – it may help to protect you from evil.'

His voice had been stern, so stern that I looked at him anxiously; then suddenly he smiled, patting my hand gently. 'Don't look so worried, my dear, I am just an old man who likes to see some show of faith in the tools of his trade.' He touched the heavy gold cross he wore on his chest. 'See,' he said smiling, 'I would sooner lose my vineyards than lose this cross. It is a philosophy you too would do well to remember.'

Somehow our conversation worried me for the rest of the day, and particularly when Liesel said over lunch, 'I don't know why my father invites the Abbe to come here. I don't like him very much.'

*

Next day Mellina returned from Vienna. We heard her voice through the open window of the schoolroom and instantly Liesel put down her pen and without asking to be excused rushed from the room. I went to the window in time to see her flinging herself into her mother's outstretched arms. Mellina was laughing happily, piling parcel after parcel into Liesel's arms. They were joined by Frau Gessler who walked into the castle with them, all three deep in conversation.

I felt troubled. I had been happy throughout the Abbe's visit; now I was sure it would all be changed. What would be the conversation round the dinner table this coming evening, I wondered? With Mellina back I could not think it would be the agreeable companionable sort I had come to look forward to.

Liesel returned to the schoolroom with Frau Gessler. The woman gave me a long hard look, then without another glance in my direction she put down the parcels she was carrying and went out through the door. Liesel was busy tearing the wrapping papers from the gifts she had received and I watched, fascinated by the expensive presents which were revealed: dresses and exquisite underwear, a large floppy doll for her bed, boxes containing bracelets and other jewellery. Impatiently she thrust them all aside and looking at me with hot angry eyes she said, 'It isn't here! It isn't here and she promised!'

'What were you expecting?' I asked her, but she took no notice of me. Instead she jumped to her feet and rushed from the room and all I could hear after that was a succession of banging doors as she passed through them. I stood looking down at the opened boxes on the floor and at articles which must have cost a great deal of money. Automatically I started to rewrap them, putting them in a neat pile in the centre of the table. It was almost four o'clock and I knew there would be no more work done that day so I made my way towards the drawing room, where I suspected Liesel had gone to confront her mother over the missing gift.

Mellina was lying on the sofa sipping tea while Liesel was stamping about the room in a fine rage, accusing her mother

151

of forgetfulness. Mellina was watching her with a half smile on her face, enjoying her rage, quite unperturbed by her daughter's outburst. She turned and favoured me with an amused glance.

I looked appalled at Liesel's tear-stained face until, bored by the outburst, Mellina said, 'Enough, Liesel! Can't you see I'm tired after my journey? I don't want to hear one more word.'

'But you promised, you promised,' wailed Liesel.

'All right, I promised, but it wasn't ready. You'll just have to wait until they can send it. I wasn't staying another day in Vienna merely to pick up your fancy-dress costume.'

So that was it. Almost immediately the tears ceased and all dimpled smiles again she rushed into her mother's arms asking, 'When will it come, will it come tomorrow?'

'Tomorrow or the day after. Now go away and let me have my tea in peace.'

I looked curiously at her as she poured herself another cup of tea. She was thinner and there was a strained look on her face which made me wonder about the week she had just spent in Vienna. She seemed edgy. The crack of a rifle from the park outside made her jump nervously, and the hand which held the cup to her lips shook a little.

After Liesel had gone back to the schoolroom to look again at her presents, Mellina said, 'What a tiresome child she is. One would have expected her to be satisfied with all those things but all she is interested in is that wretched fancy-dress costume, and the ball isn't until the end of April.' She laughed a little and added, 'I expect I was much the same at her age.'

'Did you enjoy your stay in Vienna?'

'Yes, but it was far too hectic, rushing here and there so as not to leave any of my friends out. If you want tea I should ring for some fresh.'

'I don't really want any, we were late eating lunch. What is Liesel's costume to be?'

'Oh, I mustn't tell you, it's a secret. If she wants you to know she will tell you herself.'

'Is the ball held in Vienna?'

'Why no, it's here at Meinhart. There wasn't one last year,

152

we were in the South of France, but this year I have decided there should be one. The house is full of people but it can be a bore. Sophia will be here, and Ernst, I hope, so no doubt you will wish to join us.'

'I shall have to think of something to wear if I am invited – fancy dress balls have never been part of my social life.'

'They do not have them in England?'

'Oh yes, I'm sure they do, particularly at New Year, but I never went to one.'

'I have something you can wear – I saw it in Vienna and bought it specially for you. Come to my room and I'll show you.'

I looked up, touched by her unexpected kindness, but she wasn't looking at me, she was pushing the tea tray aside. As I walked behind her towards her bedroom I was aware again of an air of weariness about her, an unusual fragility which I put down to the journey she had just taken.

Frau Gessler and a young maid were putting away her clothes but Mellina dismissed them unceremoniously. Frau Gessler scurried past me with her head lowered and Mellina laughed. 'You have antagonized Frau Gessler, Rachel. She thinks you are responsible for the Count's instructions that in future she stays away from Liesel.'

'She isn't good for Liesel. She fills her head with all sorts of horrible stories about evil and witchcraft.'

'Well, there are such things, or have you been blinded to the influence of evil all these years? It is just as potent as pure goodness but not nearly so boring.'

I stared at her but remained quiet. I didn't want to enter into an argument with Mellina on a subject of this kind.

I had never been inside her bedroom before. It was a beautiful room although I was startled by the colour scheme. The heavy drapes at the windows and the bedspread which covered the huge bed were in a deep glowing crimson and gold. The walls were white but the carpet too was gold. Somehow Mellina's porcelain beauty struck an incongruous note in a room which seemed entirely theatrical. I watched her hunting through her wardrobe and couldn't resist asking, 'Have you brought the costume from Vienna?'

'I ordered it some time ago – it should be here but it isn't.'

She went over to a white and gold wardrobe on the opposite wall and suddenly exclaimed, 'Ah, here it is!'

She brought out a tissue-wrapped parcel which seemed heavy from the way she tossed it onto the bed, then she took off the wrappers. Lying there was a thick silk skirt which seemed to have been fashioned from all the colours of the rainbow. It was beautiful, gaudy, and like nothing I would ever have worn. With it were petticoat after petticoat, all frilled so that the skirt would stand out above my ankles and swirl whenever I moved. There was a fine lawn blouse with a drawstring neckline and black shoes with high heels and silver buckles. Mellina even produced long gypsy earrings which she let fall inside one of the shoes.

'A gypsy costume!' I exclaimed. 'It's something I wouldn't have thought of. Do I look like a gypsy?'

'No, but Ernst informed me that you could dance like one – and look at this, I managed to get hold of it from a friend of mine who lives in Budapest.'

She thrust into my hand a photograph of a woman in just such a costume, a woman who was beautiful and spirited with dark laughing eyes and thick curling hair.

'She is lovely, who is she?'

'I had the photograph copied by an artist who painted this picture.'

Suddenly I was looking at the same woman but this time in colour, bright swirling skirt, white blouse worn off her slender shoulders, long swinging earrings and dark red hair, and hoarsely I asked again, 'Who is she?'

'Your grandmother. You did not tell us that she was once the toast of the café society of Budapest, only about your mother, who was a dancer of a different kind.'

I looked at her quietly for a few moments. Her eyes were mischievously amused. 'I thought you had found me a fancy-dress costume out of kindness and I was grateful, but now I can see that it was purely out of malice. Do you expect me to thank you for it?'

She shrugged her shoulders indifferently. 'It is immaterial. Kindness or malice, what difference does it make? Wear the costume and enjoy the ball. I always invite the Romanies to play for us, my guests would be delighted if you would dance for them.'

'May I keep the picture?'

'Of course, I have no use for it. Why don't you show Max? He is probably unaware of the relationship.'

'I shall not be ashamed to show it to him, but perhaps not tonight. The Abbe is a guest here.'

'The Abbe! What is he doing here? Max didn't tell me he was coming.'

'I understood he was a constant visitor to Meinhart.'

'But not for some time. Why now, I wonder?'

She had recovered her composure and stood with her back to me looking out of the window. There was a strange look on her face, just such a look as I had seen on Liesel's face when she was frustrated about something, before she turned towards me with a bright smile and said, 'Take the things off the bed, Rachel, and put them in your room. You will look beautiful in them, very beautiful and I hope not nearly so innocent.'

I wanted the evening to be over so that I could escape to my own room to forget the veiled sarcasm that had been tossed around the dining table, the barbed shafts of disenchantment between husband and wife.

Mellina was wearing a ruby red velvet dinner gown in what I suspected was an act of bravado, for I had never seen her wearing anything other than pastel colours which complemented her nordic beauty. She looked ill at ease whenever she found the Abbe watching her.

'I had hoped you would be here to celebrate Mass on Good Friday,' the Count said. 'It is regrettable that you must return so soon.'

'Yes, my friend, but I have a duty to my little flock up there in the mountains,' the Abbe replied. 'I have no doubt the priest from the village would be delighted to assist here.'

'It is of no consequence. I have to be away for a few days and perhaps Mellina too has plans to be away.'

'You are not a Catholic, Rachel,' the Abbe said, 'but Max tells me your father was a clergyman.'

'I am an Anglican, but in spite of his calling my father was not bigoted about religion.'

'Ah yes, there are many strange and obscure beliefs in the world, and each one of us supposes ours is the right one.'

'Then there are others who feel no need for religion,' the Count said smiling. 'Mellina, for instance. How long is it since you prayed for your lost innocence, my dear?'

'I have all the religion I need. We all lose our innocence, but I have kept my beauty,' Mellina retorted.

'I sometimes wonder how much it has cost you to keep your beauty.'

'I don't understand you, Max.'

'I was thinking of the beauty parlours in Vienna who welcome you with open arms.'

His tone was bantering, but Mellina and I both knew that he was not thinking about the beauty parlours in Vienna. His words were an accusation that in some way or another she was paying a price for the retention of her beauty.

'Gracious, but it is cold in here,' she complained, shivering. 'Why does it always feel so much warmer in Vienna?'

'Yes,' mused the Abbe, 'it is cold, as cold as Lucifer. I have never been able to understand why one associates the devil with warmth when it is the cold he so happily engenders.'

They were talking in riddles, but Mellina understood. She sprang to her feet and went swiftly towards the fireplace, holding her hands out to the flames. In her glowing red dress, with the flames from the fire lighting up her face and leaping towards her hands, she appeared like a pagan high priestess calling upon her master to wreak dreadful vengeance on some pitiful soul.

I stood in the courtyard early next morning to bid the Abbe farewell. The Count had already done so before he was called away, and Mellina was still in her bed.

The Abbe took my hand in his and said, 'Why don't you spend a few days in Vienna at Easter? You will be on holiday

156

from your duties and Vienna is very beautiful in the springtime. You can walk in the parks and visit the museums, you can go to the opera and hear Mass in the cathedral. What does it matter that you are not of our faith – are we not all the children of God? Have you no friends you could visit?'

I looked up eagerly. 'I think I could stay with the Liptmanns, they are nice people and have already been more than kind to me. I will write to them and ask if it is convenient.'

'Do that, my dear – you will not be happy here, nor will you have anything in common with Madame the Countess's friends. Most of them are foreign aristocrats, faded royalty, and you will stick out like a sore thumb in such a gathering.'

'Sophia or Ernst may be here, I would have liked to see them again.'

'Sophia is a dear child, the young man I have not met. Go to Vienna, child. Come back when Mellina's friends have gone, then all the summer will be before you.'

'Yes,' I said doubtfully.

'Something else is troubling you?'

'There is to be a masked ball on the last night in April. Mellina has given me a costume to wear but I am not sure I want to be there.'

'The eve of the first day in May, that is very singular,' the Abbe mused.

'Mellina tells me it is an old custom, that there has always been a masked ball at the castle on the eve of May Day, except for last year when they were away.'

'You call it May Day, and for a moment I had forgotten that you were English. Well, as you can see I am not a man who has ever been familiar with masked balls – I should cut a pretty figure, to be sure! Wear your crucifix, my dear, and pray to the good Lord for guidance, that is my advice to you.'

I watched his carriage drive away, waving my hand as it crossed the drawbridge and turned towards the river, then slowly I returned to the house. His words had disturbed me but I did not know why. When he saw that they disturbed me he had turned aside in an effort to be jocular. Still I was puzzled. What was wrong in celebrating May Day with a ball?

That night I wrote to the Liptmanns asking if it was convenient for me to spend Easter with them. They replied regretfully that they always visited their daughter at Easter, but they pressed me to stay with them for as long as I wished at a later date.

So I had no choice but to remain at Meinhart over Easter.

Nine

Easter and April, the first Easter I had ever spent outside England, and I was feeling homesick. I thought about all those other Good Friday mornings when the church bells rang out from the grey stone tower above the old churchyard gay with daffodils, with the hawthorn bushes bursting into pale green leaf and primroses blossoming underneath the hedgerows. From my window high up in the castle I could see that daffodils were blooming here beside the lake and it had been the sight of their nodding golden heads that had first stirred this homesickness in my heart. The first brood of baby swans were following their parents in close formation across the lake, but how I missed the soft rolling countryside and the church spires across the fields.

Most of Mellina's guests had arrived and the castle seemed full of people. Max had gone away and was not expected back until late, and I dreaded sitting at the dining table with the people I had seen arriving. They had laughed a lot and too loudly, the women elegantly dressed for travelling, the men with limp fat jewelled hands and bored voices, and others who seemed more feminine than masculine, with long white hands they held aloft for me to take and shrill giggles at every witty remark passed round the group. Through it all Mellina floated, elegant and lovely in pale blue velvet, while I in my dark blue skirt and white blouse had been introduced fleetingly as Liesel's governess and a distant relative. 'I don't know how, darlings,' she had trilled. 'Max knows but he isn't saying, so try not to ask too many questions if he happens to be there.'

After that I responded churlishly to their knowing smiles and open curiosity, and took the first opportunity I got of making myself scarce. I could hear laughter in the room next to mine, and it seemed that all the castle hummed and buzzed like a hiveful of bees. It was several hours to dinner so I sat in my room and tried to get interested in a book I had taken from the library. It was not to my taste, I was really in no mood for something as heavy as this, and I wondered whether I should put on my outdoor clothing and walk in the park. I was slipping into my coat when there was a knock on the door, so putting my coat down on the bed I went to open it. Sophia was there, flinging her arms around me and saying, 'I'm so glad you're still here, Rachel! I wouldn't have come if I'd thought you'd gone back to England.'

'But why should you think that? I told you I had promised to stay for a few months at least.'

'Well, Liesel's such a brat, isn't she? I should have thought you would have realized that and gone home.'

'You didn't tell me she was a brat when I asked you. You said she was enchanting. She is, but it's a witchlike enchantment and not a fairy-tale one.'

'Ernst is coming, Mellina told me. I can't wait to see him, he will be able to tell me all I want to know about Stephan.'

I looked at her doubtfully. 'I thought you had found another young man in Salzburg?'

'Oh yes, darling, but not for keeps, just a nice young man who took me to concerts and tea dances. Stephan was different, I really believe I'm in love with him.'

'Then I would advise you to keep it to yourself in this house. You know what Mellina was like the last time you talked about him.'

The laughter suddenly left her face and a sad doleful look took its place. 'She's already told me she's invited Sergei and that she expects me to be pleasant towards him. Oh, Rachel, I don't even like him but I have the awful feeling that my mother and Mellina between them think he's a good match for me. He's very rich and has vast estates in Russia, but he's been married before and he's far too old for me. I thought Mellina invited me here because she was fond of me, not to find me a husband. What shall I do?'

'My dear, I don't know. I don't know anything about matchmaking cousins or arranged marriages, thank goodness. Be pleasant to the man but don't allow him to think you look upon him as anything but a friend. Speak to Ernst, he may be able to help you.'

'Ernst will have quite enough to do looking after himself. He hasn't any money, you know, and I think he's always known that he will have to marry a wealthy woman who is looking for a title. I wouldn't be surprised if Mellina hasn't already found someone amongst her friends. Oh, Rachel, I really believe that I hate her.'

I was startled by the vehemence in her lovely face and I couldn't resist saying, 'I haven't forgotten our train journey when your entire conversation was about Mellina and how much you loved her.'

'That was before, this is after. There are other things about Mellina that I don't like quite apart from what she is trying to do to me. Look what she's done to Max, for instance.'

'What has she done to Max?'

'Well, before they married he laughed a lot and was fun to be with. I wanted to marry somebody just like him, but he seldom smiles now and when he does it is that aloof cynical smile that keeps everybody at a distance. I don't even think he's in love with Mellina any more – as a matter of fact I've been wondering if he ever was.'

'But you don't know that, Sophia, they're still together.'

'They would be. Max isn't one to wear his heart on his sleeve and no breath of scandal will be allowed to touch his name or his castle. Whatever Mellina does to him will not be made public property. I think he must know about the gossip surrounding her but as long as he remains with her nobody knows whether it's true or not.'

I didn't want to know about Max and Mellina, it was too important to me and I didn't want it to be. I was determined that I would be my own woman, that no man would ever make me suffer as a man had made my mother suffer. When Sophia saw that I had walked away and was feigning indifference she said, 'Can't we go somewhere together? I don't want to spend all the afternoon talking to those people in the drawing room, can't we go outside and walk?'

'That is just what I was about to do when you came knocking at my door,' I answered her, and so the problem of the next few hours was happily resolved.

I was the last to arrive in the dining room that evening. I immediately saw that Sophia had been placed next to the Russian and that Ernst had arrived and was sitting next to Mellina. I apologized for my late arrival and took the only vacant seat, between a blowsy woman with obviously dyed blond hair and a pale delicate young man who lapsed into poetry whenever the conversation flagged.

The woman insisted on calling me deary and I was surprised to learn that she was English but married to an Eastern gentleman who kept his European wife well supplied with money whenever he returned to his country and his other wives. She had no hesitation in relating to me the most intimate details of their life together, and seemed well pleased with the arrangement. She had been a dancer in a Paris nightclub when they met, but her ungrammatical English would have immediately let her down in English society and I wondered what Mellina, with her proud patrician beauty, was doing in such company. She seemed happy enough, however, queening it at the head of the table. There was no sign of her husband.

Several times Ernst looked down the table and meeting my eyes he smiled, but it was impossible for us to speak together because immediately after dinner Mellina had some sort of amusement planned for the evening and she and her guests drifted into the drawing room. I said I had letters to write and she appeared to accept my excuse with relief.

I put a match to the ready-laid fire in my room because the night had grown chilly, then I settled down in the chair in front of it to read. The heat of the room and the dull book made me feel very drowsy and I must have gone to sleep almost immediately. When I awoke the house seemed very still and silent. The fire had burned low and although I tried to stir it into some semblance of a blaze it was too far gone, so I decided to undress and get into bed. I heard a clock strike ten but I felt sure it was long after that time. Outside the night was pitch black with not the faintest glimmer of starlight, and the hooting of an owl from somewhere deep in the forest disturbed the silence.

I was not sleepy now and I lay on my back looking through the window. It had been a mistake to sleep in the chair because now I was so wide awake that the problems of the day seemed intensified. For what seemed like hours I tossed and turned, then finally I decided that I would try to read a little more of my book. I thrust my feet into my slippers and hunted round for my robe, then I walked across to the window to draw the curtains. I did not expect anybody but the gamekeepers to see the lamplight in my window, but I preferred them to see the castle in darkness.

I reached up to pull the tasselled cord when I became aware of lights from somewhere deep within the forest. At first they were stationary, then they seemed to move from a circle to a line and I stared, rubbing my eyes in case they were deceiving me. I was shivering a little, pulling the robe closer around me. There was little wind and the torches – I had decided that was what they were – shone brightly in the pitch darkness. As I watched I became aware of a low murmuring sound, the like of which I had never heard before. I rubbed the glass where my breath had misted it, and the circle was there again, but moving now as if those who held the torches swayed in some sort of rite. At first the sounds defeated me, then in a blinding flash I realized that the figures were chanting, a slow monotonous chant which was hypnotic and spellbinding.

Again the circle broke and then they were moving in one long straggling line through the forest clearing and towards the bridge. They moved slowly, as though they were in a trance, but as yet I could only see their torches and figures. They divided into a column of two as they crossed the bridge and they were coming towards the drawbridge now, their torches held high. Vaguely I could see that they wore dark cloaks, looking like a procession of monks as they came nearer to the castle.

It was an eerie sight to see them crossing the drawbridge with the glare from their torches shining into the waters of the moat, and I pulled the curtains closer together. The chanting was louder now, but as suddenly as it had started it stopped, and now in a silent procession they were walking underneath the castle walls and I could see them more plainly. They all wore dark dominoes with the hoods pulled well over their faces. It was impossible to distinguish any of them, but here and there was the gleam of a woman's gown where the domino fell away, and I watched fascinated as they moved slowly through the great centre door.

I moved back and sat on the edge of my bed shivering in the cold that suddenly seemed to invade my room, and I remembered at that moment the words the Abbe had said, that it was the Lord Lucifer who dispensed the cold. I couldn't think straight. Was it some strange medieval rite they performed out there on the night of Good Friday, or was it some other more sinister ritual that I had witnessed? There was no priest at Meinhart to officiate at such a ceremony. I could hear it again now, a faint monotonous chanting, and it came from somewhere below me, somewhere within the great pinnacle of granite on which the castle stood.

Overcome with curiosity, I tightened the robe around me and crept out into the corridor. I carried a single candle which I could easily extinguish if I heard a door opening or saw a light, and I moved quietly, hugging the wall, opening and closing doors carefully so that not a sound was made. When I reached Sophia's room I turned the knob slowly, not daring to knock, but the door opened silently on the thick carpet and I crept inside raising my candle on high. The bed covers were turned down but the bed had not been slept in. I looked round quickly for the gown she had worn that evening at dinner. There was no sign of it, nor of her shoes or jewellery, and I stood trembling and suddenly afraid. They must not come back and find me here, so much my muddled brain warned me of, and I fled from Sophia's room, stumbling and bruising myself against doors and corners, for I had put out my candle and was relying upon instinct and my sense of direction in a darkness which seemed to close in upon me, filled with menacing things.

My bed was cold and I lay shivering between the sheets, still wearing my robe, until the first faint pearly grey streaks appeared in the sky. I had only seen the dawn come up twice before, once on the morning after my father went out across the moor, and the other from my seat on the train from Paris to Vienna. Now I was seeing it for the third time and never more gladly. Although I had lain awake I had heard little sound, a few whisperings in the corridors and suppressed laughter from the room next to mine. Once, just once, I had heard somebody turn the knob of my bedroom door, only to find it locked. That had been the moment I sat up in my bed feeling the hair rise on my scalp, my knuckles clenched against my mouth to suppress a scream in case the night prowler should prove insistent. When they went away the relief was indescribable. I could hear the hammering of my heart shutting out every other sound.

I had to behave as though nothing had happened, go down and eat breakfast with them, talk normally, respond to overtures of friendship, and I was terrified that my hollow eyes and pale face would betray me. I need not have worried, however. The breakfast room was empty and I had to wait until after nine o'clock before a sleepy-eyed servant came, surprised to see me there. I ordered coffee, saying I did not want anything else, and I had finished drinking it and was out of the castle before anybody joined me. It felt good to be out in the cold fresh air with natural growing things and the birds singing in the branches of the trees.

I took the path the procession had taken the night before, my eyes on the ground, although I did not know what I was searching for. The ground was hard, there had been no rain for several days, and still unsatisfied I took the path towards the river and the forest beyond. I would not dare to go into the forest in case I was being watched from the castle, but I would go as near to it as I dared. I was halfway across the bridge when I saw something on the ground, glittering in the morning sunlight. I stopped and picked it up, and stood looking at it lying in the palm of my hand. It was a diamond earring, a beautiful thing shaped like a tear with a ring of small diamonds hanging from it. Hastily I dropped it into the pocket of my coat. I knew that it was valuable, and I determined to look round the guests that evening. If one of them had its fellow, or if any woman was not wearing earrings at all, I could produce it nonchalantly, saying I had found it that morning on my walk. At least I would know the identity of one of those torch-bearing anonymous figures.

By the time luncheon came around I was walking briskly back to the castle, not wishing to miss a moment of the meal ahead. I had worked up quite an appetite, but mainly I wanted to look again at those people who had walked underneath my window in the dead of night. I had almost reached the drawbridge when I saw Ernst striding forward to meet me.

'What energy!' he said laughing. 'I looked for you at breakfast but when you didn't appear I thought you had decided to have a lazy morning. Where have you been?'

'Walking in the park. I was having coffee soon after nine, so it seems it was the rest of the household who decided to have a lazy morning.'

'It must be the country air, it always has that effect on me. We're not used to it.'

'Have you seen Sophia this morning?'

'No, but I believe she intended to go riding with Sergei. I don't know whether they went or not.'

'With Sergei!'

'Why not? I know Sophia's head is more often in the clouds than out of it but she can't be entirely blind to the fact that he's a very rich man and is extremely interested in her.'

With his fresh young face Ernst did not have the appearance of a man who had been up half the night and I longed to tell him what I had seen, but prudence got the better of me and I remained silent.

'Have you settled down here looking after Liesel?' he asked me.

'As much as anybody could settle down looking after Liesel! She can be a problem, but I expect you know all about that.'

'She'll be a beauty one day, though. Mellina won't exactly

166

like having competition from her daughter.'

'But they're a generation apart!'

He grinned at me impudently. 'That is something that has never worried Mellina – ask Max.'

'Max isn't here.'

'He came home last night, but I haven't seen him yet.'

I stood still, staring at him. If Max was home then he must know something of the events of last night, perhaps he was even a participant. I felt suddenly angry, almost sick. What kind of people were they, whom could I trust in this great castle? Never in my life had I felt so alone.

Many of the servants were visiting their families so luncheon was a buffet meal eaten in the entrance hall where I had first been admitted into the castle. The food was laid out on long tables and the guests helped themselves to venison and duckling, roast lamb and freshly caught trout. A huge log fire blazed on the hearth and I stood near the window looking around me, at suits of armour and at fading standards hanging from the balcony above.

'We are going into the woods this afternoon, Rachel.' Ernst had followed me and was entreating me to join some excursion. I declined the invitation, pleading a headache and saying I would rest instead. I realized my mistake as soon as I had spoken.

'Didn't you sleep well, Rachel? I had not thought you were subject to headaches.'

There was a lull in the conversation nearest to us and Mellina was watching me closely with narrowed eyes.

'I think the problem is that I slept too well, I don't remember a thing after I put my light out around ten thirty.'

Apparently mollified, Mellina turned her attention elsewhere.

I looked for Max but he was not in the dining hall and luncheon came and went without him putting in an appearance. Ernst was attentive but I wished he would go so that I would have the opportunity to talk to Sophia, who had spent most of the time sitting by the window looking across the park. She seemed listless, almost apathetic and quite unlike her usual bubbly self. When I remarked upon it to Ernst he merely smiled and said, 'Oh, she's probably sulking, she's decided she doesn't care for Mellina now, but she's always like that after one of her love affairs comes to an end. Disenchantment with Mellina has probably had the same effect.'

'Perhaps I should go over and talk to her.'

'I don't think that's a good idea, *Liebchen*. Let her bounce back of her own accord, she always does.'

I watched them set out in their carriages in groups of two and four, and although I didn't exactly see Mellina I felt sure she had gone with them, and probably Max as well. The castle seemed unnaturally quiet and I decided to take a look in the schoolroom, more for something to occupy myself with than for any other reason. Liesel was staying in Salzburg with her grandparents and the room seemed too orderly and unused for me to remain in it long.

Passing from the schoolroom to the main hall I chanced to look out of the window and saw Josef dragging a long heavy box up the steps from somewhere down below. I wondered if there was a way into the dungeons from the path without going through the main hall. I stood watching him man-oeuvre his burden onto a long low cart and set off in the direction of the forest. Before he reached the drawbridge he looked back once at the castle, spotted me and gave a little bow. It was an insolent gesture rather than a respectful one, and angry that I had allowed him to see me I turned away and went towards the hall.

The chapel lay before me in darkness and I went inside, leaving the door open. I knelt for a few moments in one of the pews before I walked up to the altar. Spring flowers had been artistically arranged in gold vases on the altar and around the font, as well as in two copper urns standing on the altar steps. Tall white candles stood in silver candelabras and there were others placed at intervals along a ledge on the wall. I moved out into the hall, wrinkling my nose at the scent which seemed to hang in the air. A little nauseated I realized that it was incense – incense in a chapel that had not been used since the visit of the Abbe several weeks earlier.

Impulsively I tried the door leading to the crypt but it was locked and I was about to turn away when I saw a bunch of keys hanging on a hook outside the door. My heart started to race and I found myself listening for any sound outside the castle but it was as quiet as the grave. I wished I hadn't thought of that particular metaphor so close to the old crypt below, but all the same I hurried back to the chapel for a candle, lit it and returned to the door in the wall. I was not brave, indeed I was anything but that, but there were strange things going on in the castle and I had to know what they were for my own peace of mind. If there was evil for evil's sake then I must leave Meinhart, even though I left with my heart dead and my future a barren wilderness.

After trial and error I found the right key, surprised when the lock turned easily as though it had been recently oiled. The door was heavy even for my young strength but at last I had it open and now the candlelight fell on rough-hewn rock walls which I remembered from my last visit. The smell of incense was stronger now, making me cough so that the tears filled my eyes, but I forced myself to go on.

At last I stood at the doorway looking into the chapel, surprised to find it as before. The candlelight flickered on the bare walls, the pews stood in orderly rows, but on the red carpet were smudges of earth and one or two dried and shrivelled leaves. They could not have blown into the chapel from outside and again my heart raced with excitement. I reached the altar and looked up. There was no crucifix, but above the altar was a sort of cupboard, closed and locked by a chain and a heavy padlock. Only the two heavy silver candlesticks adorned the altar and I picked up one of them, examining it closely. However careful they had been, they had not been careful enough. Two drops of black melted wax had been left on the base of the candlestick, and there were one or two others on the white marble top of the altar.

Some time quite recently candles had burned on that altar, and well satisfied with my find I retraced my steps to the realms above. I did not look towards the crypt or the dungeons behind me, but as I mounted the stairs I heard the door open above me and the next moment I was blinded by the light from five candles held aloft and Max's voice saying in some annoyance, 'Rachel, what the devil are you doing down there?'

Unceremoniously I was pulled upwards into the hall and he was looking down at me with anger in every line of his stern forbidding face.

'I wanted to see the old chapel,' I stammered.

'Why, for heaven's sake? You've seen it before.'

'I know. I wanted to see if I would have the courage to go down there again.'

'Why put your courage to the test – or was it simply that you were curious and took advantage of the absence of my wife to satisfy your curiosity?'

I didn't answer him, but my eyes met his unflinchingly. I was afraid of him at that moment but I too was angered by his arrogant assumption that I had something to hide. It was he who had something to hide, and wild horses were not going to make me tell him my real reason for being in the old chapel.

There was a look of veiled amusement in his eyes now as he asked, 'Did you find the door open?'

'No. I took the keys from the hook behind the door.'

'You must have had other reasons for going down there. I would like you to tell me what they were.'

'I had no other reason. I have been looking at some of the old books about the castle and wondered why the old chapel had been left with its altar intact. It is very beautiful and very valuable and I believe it came from Jerusalem. I would have thought it might have been placed inside the new chapel when it was built.'

'You are misinformed, Rachel. The new altar came from Jerusalem. I have no idea where the old one came from – a relic from the Dark Ages, I shouldn't wonder. I suggest you now return to the part of the castle which belongs to this century instead of wandering about old rooms that are never used.'

He stood aside and I passed before him, my head held high, my cheeks burning indignantly. I wanted to spin round and cry out that the chapel *was* used, that he knew very well it was used, but for what evil purposes I had yet to discover.

'May I suggest that you return to your room and try to look

a little less like the chimney-sweep's boy before we eat dinner?' he said. 'If you are quick there is still time to drive through the estate, and I could show you some of the beautiful countryside around these parts.'

He was smiling, but it was not until I returned to my room and looked into the mirror that I understood his remarks about the chimney-sweep's boy. There were smudges of grime on my face and my hands as well as on the front of my dress where I had held the candlesticks. I was looking decidedly more presentable when I sat next to him in the open chaise half an hour later.

Although it was still only early April the afternoon was warm and sunny as we drove through the extensive grounds of the estate. We did not go towards the main entrance but in the opposite direction, through vineyards and beside the babbling river, and eventually through other gates which also carried the crest of the crimson falcon.

The countryside was beautiful, green flat fields rising upwards to the distant snow-capped mountains, and churches with golden onion-shaped domes standing out against a clear blue sky. The villages we drove through were pretty, the houses decorated with painted murals. Along the roads we passed carts drawn by great lumbering oxen, and the men and women walking beside them acknowledged our presence with respectfully bowed heads and light curtsies.

We came at last to a small village and here Max suggested that we should leave the chaise and walk on up the straggling street towards the church. Outside the door of the church a smiling priest came forward to meet us.

Max introduced me as Miss Arden, a distant kinswoman who was staying at the castle, and did not mention that I was there as governess to his daughter. The priest took us inside where I exclaimed at the beauty of the altar, which was indeed magnificent for such a tiny church. He replied that it had been brought from Jerusalem at the same time as that in the Meinhart chapel and that it had been given to the church by Count Leander Meinhart. Max was watching me searchingly, and suddenly I realized that it was my grandfather who had donated this beautiful altar. That was why he had brought me here, after our conversation on the steps leading down into the old chapel, proving me wrong.

'The Abbe has been visiting you, I gather,' the priest said. 'He called here on his way to Meinhart.'

'Yes, that is so. It is a pity he had to return home before Easter.'

'I will celebrate Mass with you at Meinhart any time you wish, you have only to call upon me, Count Meinhart.'

'Thank you, father, I shall remember your offer. We must not linger now. I am anxious to show Rachel as much of the countryside as possible before dusk.'

The priest stood outside his church while we walked down the road, and we had almost reached the chaise when two little girls came running towards us, their hands clasping posies of wild flowers which they handed to me with dimpled smiles and low curtsies. They were blond children with long flaxen pigtails tied with bows of blue ribbon to match their cotton dresses, and I exclaimed delightedly over the charming picture they made.

'I had no idea how beautiful it was in these parts,' I told Max. 'I know the Tyrol is beautiful but I had thought the district around Vienna would be flat and ordinary, not nearly so picturesque.'

'Yes, it is beautiful, but it was not always like this. In medieval times these people were little more than serfs scratching a bare living from the soil. A few goats, a few scrawny chickens. For a family it was a disaster when their one cow died and for the most part they were in revolt, without pleasures of any kind, the miserable victims of a great injustice which gave to a handful of nobles all the colour of the world and to the rest nothing but hardship.'

'When did it start to change for these people?'

'Only gradually over the years. Before they had a church they used to hold their sabbaths in some forest glade or old burial ground, and one can well imagine them working themselves into ecstasies of blasphemy and superstition, cursing to eternity those rich nobles who kept them in servitude.'

'You mean they worshipped the devil?'

He looked at me gravely. 'No, Rachel, they worshipped

God the only way they knew how. The church was built for them as late as the seventeenth century and you heard the priest say the altar was given to them by your grandfather.'

'You recognize that he was my grandfather?'

'Of course. Did you think that I did not?'

I was silent for so long that he turned gently towards me. 'What are you thinking about now, I wonder?'

'I would very much like to show you something before dinner.'

'Of course. You sound very mysterious.'

I merely smiled, but I intended to show him the portrait of my grandmother that Mellina had had copied.

When I handed it to him in the dining room in the early evening he took it in his hands and moved over to the light so that he could see it better.

'She is a very beautiful woman. I don't recollect ever having seen it before. How did you come by it?'

'Mellina gave it to me. She had it copied from an old photograph.'

'How did Mellina come by it, and why give it to you?'

'I don't know, but the costume in the portrait is exactly like the one she had provided for me to wear at the masked ball.'

'Who is the woman?'

'My grandmother. I told you she was Hungarian, what I didn't tell you was that she too was a dancer before she married my eminently respectable grandfather. She danced in the restaurants and cafés of Budapest. That may have been why she wanted my mother to be a dancer, although of a very different kind. The imperial ballet was the most respectable thing she could think of for a daughter who had inherited her talent.'

He handed the portrait back to me with a swift smile. 'Why are you suddenly so defensive? I accept that your grandmother was a dancer, your mother too – what difference does it make? It is as much a part of the past as those poor serfs I told you about.'

'It also confirms that perhaps the Meinharts were right when they would not allow my father's marriage to my mother to stand.'

His eyes were inscrutable as they stared into mine and at that moment I wanted to run from him, I felt so shaken by the feelings he aroused in me. I could not move, I could not even take my eyes away from his which were gazing into mine with burning intensity. Then his arms were around me and he was murmuring against my hair, 'Oh Rachel, Rachel!'

I had never known passion; now I was aware of it, raw and searching as our lips clung together and I was giving him back kiss for kiss, until as suddenly as he had embraced me he let me go so that I would have fallen had my hands not found the back of a chair.

For a long moment we stared at each other, then as though nothing had happened between us he walked over to the fireplace and pulled the bell rope.

'Dinner is late, perhaps you will join me in a glass of brandy?'

That night I paced about my room telling myself that I could not stay at Meinhart, for there was too much danger – danger to my heart in addition to any danger there might be to my well-being in other respects. I heard the laughter of Mellina and her friends returning to the castle long after midnight, but still sleep eluded me. In the morning I would tell Max that I must leave, that I had made a mistake, that I wanted to go home to England as I had never wanted anything in my life before. Liesel would not miss me, indeed she would be glad that I had gone, and there was no future for me here in love with a man who was married to a woman he would never leave, a beautiful aristocratic woman from his own world, the mother of his child.

What possible hope for the future was there in such a situation? I arrived at the breakfast table heavy-eyed, filled with a stern resolve to do exactly as I had planned. My well-laid schemes, however, met with disappointment when I was informed that Count Meinhart had already left for Munich and would not be back until the end of April.

Ten

How vain and foolish are promises when one is young and desperately in love for the first time! I knew now that I would no more be able to leave Meinhart than the bird which adorned the gates would be able to take wing and fly. I resolved instead that I would show my love in different ways. I would try to like Liesel, I would be a good teacher and try to be her friend, but there too I was fated to meet only disappointment. I did not like Liesel and she did not want my friendship.

Easter had come and gone but the days were filled with warm sunshine and I saw little of Mellina. She was so engrossed with plans for the forthcoming masked ball that she seemed to have time for little else. I asked her one morning if I could be of any help and for once she welcomed it, involving me in writing out invitations on gold-embossed cards, each one bearing the Meinhart family crest, to people of standing both in Vienna and as far afield as Munich, Berlin and Paris. Huge marquees were erected in the grounds and orchestras were invited to play for the dancing. Catering establishments vied with each other to receive her patronage and a fortune was spent on flowers, both for the interior of the castle and for the huge stone urns which stood along the paths.

'I suppose I should invite the Emperor,' Mellina mused, 'but it's always such a problem entertaining reigning royalty, and besides he's far too old. I shall have to invite him, however, and hope that he won't come.'

Ernst was invited, I was happy to see, as well as Sophia, and I imagined how excited she would be, particularly with

Sergei miles away in Russia.

'What kind of masks are we expected to wear?' I asked Mellina.

'Oh, the usual kind. There is a man in Vienna who makes them, I have his address somewhere. You'd better order a few extra ones in case some of the guests forget to bring them. Ordinary black masks will do, unless some of the guests favour those on a stick. I prefer the other kind, they're less bother.'

I was glad of the extra work, it stopped me thinking too much. In any case Liesel was far too excited to settle down to lessons and when I asked her what her costume was to be she merely tossed her pretty head, telling me to wait and see.

The last day of April was warm and bright. Many of the guests had arrived the day before and were already staying in the castle, but I was up very early, before most of them had made an appearance. Liesel and I wandered in the park looking at the preparations and it was there Ernst found us the morning after his arrival. The Emperor had declined the invitation, much to Mellina's relief, but there were other guests just as difficult, like the Grand Duchess who drank nothing but herbal tea, and the German actress who discovered an old lover amongst the guests with his new wife to whom she was abominably rude. Ernst and I laughed about it all as we walked back to the castle.

The ball started at dusk and as I donned my costume I could see that already the lanterns had been lit in the trees. The beautiful skirt with its half-dozen petticoats swirled above my ankles as I had known it would but instead of the shoes that went with it I decided to wear soft leather boots like the ones in the photograph. I let the gathered neckline of the blouse slip daringly off one shoulder, adding the earrings last of all.

My eyes looked back at me startled as I confronted my full reflection in the mirror for the first time. This was not the prim and proper governess in her starched white blouse and severe black skirt. It was not even the girl who had waltzed round the ballroom in her borrowed blue gown. Now I was a Magyar, a gypsy, a woman of fire and passion with a mane of dark red hair rippling round my shoulders and with a figure of voluptuous grace. It was a vision which at once sobered and startled me, but my resemblance to the grandmother who had captivated Budapest was there for all to see.

There was an orchestra playing in the ballroom where the older and staider guests preferred to stay. For those who wished to dance outdoors, there was also a band which usually played in one of the bandstands in the parks of Vienna and Ernst and I decided this was the place for us. Ernst had chosen a Viking costume with a great horned headdress on his blond head, and I had to admit it suited his Scandinavian fairness.

I looked for Liesel and Sophia amongst the guests but there were so many people it was impossible to find them. Unmasking time was scheduled for twelve o'clock in the clearing outdoors and Ernst told me it would be a time of great hilarity and shocks of surprise for many of the guests. I looked for Max in the crowd, wondering what costume he had chosen, but there were other men with his tall lean grace and it was difficult to find him without looking straight into his dark eyes. I danced with pierrots and Roman emperors, Red Indians and rajahs, Egyptian pharaohs and Napoleons, until the last waltz before the unmasking. In the arms of an Arabian sheik in a white burnous over riding breeches I finally saw Max's dark eyes laughing into mine, and felt his arm strong and firm around my waist. I knew before he removed the black mask from his eyes that it was he, and I knew that he had recognized me long before by the dress he had seen in my grandmother's portrait. Now when I looked around I could see that Mellina was wearing the dress of a Roman matron, a white, beautifully draped gown. Max murmured in my ear, 'She has done well to adopt the gown of her namesake, the Empress Messalina. I wonder if my wife is aware of the full story of her wickedness?'

I was, for ancient history had always fascinated me. Messalina, the wife of the Emperor Claudius, had been an adulteress and a poisoner, as evil a woman as any in history, but Mellina looked confidently beautiful as she moved around her guests. My eyes found Liesel now, exquisite and fragile, dressed as a Dresden shepherdess. Still there was no sign of Sophia and I asked Max if he had seen her.

'No, but she is here. There are too many people. Why Mellina had to have this spectacle I can't imagine – she only grumbles about the upheaval.'

Into the circle of guests came a band of Romanies and instantly I recognized them as the same gypsies who had played in the Prater on New Year's Eve. The two young men who had played their violins so skilfully were there, as were the bold beautiful girl and the man who had danced with me. They started to play the music I had always loved, haunting, wild, melodious music, and I wanted to dance as I had never danced before. Instead I clenched my hands together and stood with my feet planted firmly on the ground.

After the applause Mellina stepped into the centre of the circle and with her sweetest smile said, 'I have a surprise for you all. We have a young cousin staying with us who, although she is English, dances beautifully. She is already dressed for the occasion so I am going to ask her to dance for you as she once danced for these gypsies here in the Prater on New Year's morning.'

She moved towards me, her hands outstretched, her smile of welcome belying the mockery in her eyes. I felt the gentle push Max gave me and heard him whisper, 'You must dance, Rachel – you must not let Mellina defeat you.'

I met her smiling face bravely. If she was hoping that I would make a spectacle of myself I would prove her wrong, and the gypsies knew it too. They started to play and after the first few notes, I began to dance. I knew the tune they were playing, it was a czardas, and for a while I danced alone, unaware of the circle of faces and the leaping flames from the bonfire, then beside me was my partner of New Year's morning and all around us was a tremendous silence.

It lasted for a few moments after we had finished our dance. Then came the applause as we took our bows, and the congratulations of a host of people who came forward to greet us. Mellina stood next to Max, her face frozen into a set smile while he applauded enthusiastically. They too came to congratulate me on my performance, then with a tight little smile Mellina said, 'Thank you, Rachel, that was charming. My guests were surprised when I told them that an English girl was going to dance for them, and I shall now feel obliged to explain from whom you got your talent.'

'You must do as you think fit, Mellina. My grandmother was not the toast of Budapest for nothing.'

The older guests were now drifting away from the festivities and only the younger ones were left to dance around the dying fire. Ernst returned to my side and I couldn't resist asking, 'Why did you tell Mellina that I had danced with the gypsy on New Year's morning?'

'No reason really, only that she was going on about getting some real Romanies to play for us and I said she could do worse than ask you to dance.'

Slightly mollified I said, 'I still haven't found Sophia. Will you come with me while I look for her?'

'Oh, she's here somewhere. She's probably with Sergei. We don't want to interfere with that, do we?'

'A few months ago she would have been highly delighted for us to interfere. Has she suddenly changed her mind?'

'She's had it changed for her, I shouldn't wonder.'

'All the same I intend to find her,' I said, marching off in the direction of the castle.

I found her at last sitting on the stairs of the empty ballroom looking alone and dejected. I stared curiously at the costume she was wearing, unaware at first what she was supposed to represent.

She was wearing what seemed to be a boy's Sunday suit of black velvet, with knee breeches, black silk stockings and black buckled shoes. Over this she wore a short white surcoat. It had no sleeves and was cut low at the shoulders, and it was edged with a border of rich heavy lace round the bottom. This puzzled me until it dawned on me that Sophia was not wearing a page's costume but the garb of an acolyte, the boy who swings the censer at the celebration of the Mass.

I felt as though a bowl of cold water had been thrown into my face, but I went forward to sit beside her on the steps. 'Sophia,' I said, putting my arm through hers, 'why haven't I seen you before? Where have you been hiding?'

She looked at me through lacklustre eyes and shrugged her shoulders. She seemed so totally unlike the girl I had met on the train journey to Vienna that I stared at her dismayed. A little more sharply I asked, 'Sophia, what is the matter? Are you ill? Haven't you enjoyed the ball?'

'Yes – and of course I'm not ill. Why are you making all this fuss? I am simply waiting for Sergei.'

'But you don't like Sergei,' I insisted.

She looked at me crossly, and in a flat unemotional voice she said, 'I do like Sergei, I like him more every time we meet, and I would rather you forgot what I said to you previously.'

'You mean you have forgotten Stephan and that you and I were friends – in other words you have decided to do what Mellina wants?'

'Yes, Rachel, that is exactly what I mean,' she said, rising from the steps. She walked away and left me staring after her.

It was almost dawn when I heard the chanting again, this time from within the castle. I went to the window but there was no torchlight procession of black hooded figures. I knew that something was going on below and I had a pretty good idea what it was. I slipped into my robe and hurried along the corridors to Sophia's room. I did not need a candle, for the first light of dawn was already feeling its way through the windows and I knew I had to hurry. Those people in the act of selling their souls to the devil would have little desire to linger once the light of day filled the rooms. My feet made no sound as I ran towards Sophia's room. As before the door was unlocked and as before the covers had been turned down but the bed remained unslept in. I knew that she was busy performing her part in a rite as vile as any abomination practised by the decadents of ancient times. But who, I wondered, were my friends in this castle – if there were any? Who could I turn to and ask for guidance to save Sophia while there was still time?

I could not tell Max. I loved him, but he was Mellina's husband and probably as much involved as she. I had no friends amongst her guests except Ernst. Remembering his blue-eyed, open face I made up my mind to trust him. He would know what to do, and when I thought of his tall Viking figure dancing happily the night before I could not believe Mellina had yet corrupted him.

All that day I felt restless. Most of the guests had already left by the time I saw Ernst walking along the path from the bridge in the company of another man and I hurried down the path to meet him. He smiled at me, immediately making an excuse to leave his companion, and on reaching my side he said, 'I looked for you earlier this morning but I couldn't find you.'

'I was with Liesel, but she was too excited to do any work today and her mother wanted to show her off in the drawing room.'

'Would you like to go riding or have you other plans?'

'I want to talk to you, Ernst. I feel if I don't confide in somebody I shall go mad, and you're probably the only person I can trust.'

He looked pleased. 'Well, that's a step in the right direction. Shall we walk towards the gates or the other way?'

'The other way. I don't want Josef watching us; I don't like him and I don't trust him.'

'Poor Josef! And to think he's such a lady-killer amongst the village maidens!'

He listened to me in silence while I poured out all my suspicions, leaving nothing out, not even the afternoon I had gone down to the old chapel and found the black wax on the candlesticks and the altar. When I had finished my story I waited for him to say something, searching his face for signs that he too was uneasy, that he agreed with every word I had said.

'You don't really mean all this about worshipping the devil and strange rites in the middle of the night, do you, Rachel? I've been coming here for years and I've never seen or heard anything I couldn't understand.'

'You mean you don't believe me?'

'I mean I think your imagination is running away with you. It's this old castle, I've always said that it plays tricks with one's imagination. It's so old and hostile, just the right sort of place for ghosts and vampires.'

'I'm not talking about vampires or ghosts! I'm talking

about evil, real wickedness, not the sort found in horror stories. Something is happening to Sophia – she isn't the lovely happy girl she was six months ago. Mellina is different too.'

'How do you mean, different?'

'She's nervous and highly strung. She jumps out of her skin at the least unusual sound, and then there was the Abbe.'

'The Abbe?'

'Well, it was the conversation round the dinner table one evening – veiled, hinting at things I couldn't fully understand, and the way he told me always to wear my crucifix.'

'I thought it was lost.'

'So it is, but Max gave me another that belonged to his mother.'

'The devil he did!' I looked at him sharply, but he smiled. 'I would rather I'd given it to you than Max, I don't like to think of anybody else giving you jewellery! Are you wearing it now?'

'Yes, but I'm not here to talk about me. What are we going to do about Sophia?'

'She's going home tomorrow so we shan't be expected to do anything, and honestly, Rachel, I can't think there's anything in this nonsense about the Black Mass and such. Sophia is going home and I know for a fact that the Russian has been recalled. Perhaps she's feeling a bit lovesick – Sophia falls in and out of love as often as she changes her dresses. You'll see, she'll be altogether different the next time she comes to Meinhart.'

'When will that be?'

'Oh, Mellina always has a big party for All Hallows' night on 31 October. That and the eve of the first of May are the highlights of her year, far more exciting than carnival time.'

'So Sophia will be back here for Halloween. I can understand Halloween, but hardly May Day.'

'You are thinking of the English calendar, *Liebchen*. In Germany and Austria we celebrate Walpurgis Night on the last night in April. This is the night when witches are supposed to hold revel and dance with the devil. What you heard last night was one of our ancient customs, just like you celebrate Halloween – a night of high spirits, nothing more.

Do forget these silly notions about something sinister happening here, you've too much imagination for your own good. Max would think it hilarious if he knew the things you were thinking.'

'You mean you are going to tell him?'

'Not a word, not to Max or Mellina or anybody else for that matter, if you promise to forget all your dark suspicions about my friends and my family.'

I said nothing more to Ernst but I determined that during the next few weeks I would familiarize myself with the events of Walpurgis Night if I had to search through every book in every shelf of the library. I should not have involved Ernst in my suspicions, I realized that now, and I would tell him nothing more, indeed I would trust nobody at Meinhart but myself.

Before I went to bed that night I unlocked the small drawer at the back of my dressing table and took out the earring I had found on the path leading to the forest. I didn't want it, and I had looked in vain for its owner. Whoever had worn that earring preferred to lose it rather than report it missing. I wondered if I should take it to Mellina and ask her to advertise amongst her friends, but then I thought better of it. There were other festivities ahead of us which might give me an opportunity to bring up the matter of the missing earring.

Contrary to what Ernst had told me on the morning we talked in the castle gardens, Sophia did not return to Salzburg. Instead she stayed on at the castle after all the other guests returned to their homes. She spent most of the time with Mellina, they rode together and walked in the park, and I often heard their laughter in one or other of the rooms as I passed the door. We never returned to the easy happy companionship we had enjoyed. She avoided me whenever she could and when we passed in the corridors or on the stairs she gave me a small swift smile and hurried on.

Liesel surprised me one day by asking, 'How long is Sophia staying here? I thought she was returning to Salzburg.'

'I thought so too, Liesel.'

'I never see my mother now that Sophia's here,' she complained. 'Why are they such good friends suddenly?'

'I don't think there's anything sudden about it. Sophia admires your mother tremendously. Haven't they always been friends?'

'I used to think Sophia was pretty, but I don't think so any more.'

'Oh, but she is – she's very pretty.'

'Well, I don't agree with you. My mother is beautiful and she won't ever change, but Sophia has.'

'Your mother too will grow old one day, we all change as we grow older, but that's a long time away for both your mother and Sophia.'

'My mother gets more beautiful all the time, do you suppose she's stealing some of Sophia's prettiness?'

'What an outrageous thing to say! Of course she isn't, who on earth put such a notion into your head?'

Unabashed she laughed and said, 'Frau Gessler used to tell me about an old woman in the village where she was born. The villagers used to pay her to put a spell or a curse on someone they didn't like and in no time at all the curse started to work and their hair and their teeth would fall out.'

'I'm not surprised your father told Frau Gessler to stay away from you if she filled your head with that sort of rubbish.'

'I just hope Sophia doesn't stay here until Halloween, that's all.'

'What do you know about Halloween?'

'There are not as many people invited and we play charades in the drawing room after dinner before the ball starts. I expect my mother's invited a lot of those silly people who were here for Easter.'

'Don't you like your mother's friends?'

'Not the ones with dyed hair and flashy jewellery, and I hate those men with squeaky high-pitched voices and effeminate mannerisms. My father doesn't think much of them either, I can tell.'

'Your father will be here for the ball, though?'

'He wasn't last year, he went away to stay with the Abbe in

the mountains. He doesn't mind the ball, just so long as it keeps my mother amused.'

I hated having to pump Liesel for my information, but I found her willing to talk, particularly if she thought she was shocking me.

She was wrong about Sophia, however. At the beginning of June she and Mellina were invited to spend a month on the yacht of a German princeling in Adriatic waters and they departed amongst a profusion of suitcases and trunks, nor did Sophia come to say goodbye to me. Mellina left Liesel angry and sulky so that there was no doing any good with her, and I was glad when Max returned to the castle, packed her off to her grandmother in Salzburg and told me that I could take a month's holiday.

I wrote to the Liptmanns and got an immediate reply to say I was very welcome to spend my vacation with them. Max had to go to Vienna on business so he drove me into the city, a drive made more enjoyable by the golden sunlight slanting through the trees as we passed through the woods, and even more by Max sitting beside me, his hands slender and firm on the reins.

We went straight to the Liptmanns' house. I introduced the Count to Frau Liptmann, who immediately invited him to eat luncheon with us. He charmed them both by his cultured air as he talked knowledgeably about the theatre, music and great paintings, and on leaving he kissed first Frau Liptmann's hand and then mine, wishing me every enjoyment during my stay. He said he would send the carriage for me when I informed him what day I intended to return to the castle.

As I watched him drive down the street all I could think of was that he was going to be in Vienna for several days, only a few streets away, yet it might just as well be a thousand miles.

In spite of the hopelessness of my yearnings, however, I was happy in Vienna. Frau Liptmann took me to the most expensive and exclusive shops where we wandered through the scented rooms and I could imagine Mellina choosing her gowns from amongst those displayed by bored, supercilious models. At other times we visited museums, walked in the parks and listened to bands playing endless waltz tunes.

One day I was standing on the edge of the pavement watching a troop of hussars riding towards the palace, when I spotted Ernst at their head. When he saw me his eyes lit up, and that night he turned up at the Liptmanns' house. Frau Liptmann was charmed by Ernst, but as we said goodnight outside our bedroom doors later that night she said, 'That young man is attractive, my dear, but it is the other man who is more dangerous.'

'Dangerous?' I echoed, surprised.

'To your heart, I mean.'

'Oh, Frau Liptmann, Count Meinhart is my employer, a married man with a young daughter I am being paid to teach. I can assure you, if he had any interest in me he would not have left me here in Vienna to be entertained by Ernst.'

'He is also a man of honour, and there are many barriers.'

'I agree. There are Mellina and Liesel, as well as our stations in life.'

'That is not so important as it once was.'

'But it's important to me, Frau Liptmann. I'm not my mother to be swept off my feet by a handsome face and a title to go with it.'

She looked at me kindly, her head on one side, then she leaned forward and gently kissed my cheek. 'Your mother never cared about the title, my dear. I was her friend and I knew her very well. She only cared about the man, and you will too when the time is right.'

Dear Frau Liptmann, she was such a romantic at heart. Her own life had been so happy that she wanted the same sort of happiness for every person she was fond of. I cherished no such illusions, I was only too aware of the barriers of class in spite of her assumption that times were changing.

I allowed Ernst to take me out whenever he was free to do so. Strangely enough, Ernst's title did not worry me. He flirted charmingly but I knew that when the time came he would marry for money, for he had confirmed Mellina's words by telling me that he came from an impoverished though noble family and would probably be expected to marry a woman who looked like a horse with a doting father and a bottomless bank account.

We laughed together about his plight, and although he professed undying love for me I never took him seriously. Still, I enjoyed being with him. We danced and rode through the woods, we sailed on the Danube and walked in the parks and I was no more in love with him at the end of my holiday than I had been at the beginning. One thing I did feel reassured about was that never once did he allude to our conversation in the grounds of Meinhart and I thought he had probably forgotten about it. On our last evening together, however, he surprised me by asking, 'I hope you didn't hear any more chanting in the old chapel after I left Meinhart? Or see any ghosts roaming the battlements?'

'No, of course not, and I'd rather you forgot all that nonsense. It was stupid of me.'

'You were very serious at the time.'

'Yes, and I don't want reminding of it. How was I to know that you celebrated Walpurgis Night? My father used to tell me I had too much imagination and that it would get me into trouble one day. Besides, Meinhart lends itself to all sorts of weird imaginings.'

'Didn't I tell you that it did?'

He seemed well satisfied with our conversation and I hoped he would never refer to it again. He was going on a tour of duty with his regiment in Hungary and said he would not see me until the end of October.

Eleven

The rest of the summer passed happily enough at Meinhart.
Long clear days in the warm sunlight made the castle stand
out golden against a blue sky and even the river became less
turbulent on its way to the Danube. I always rode Greta now
on my rides through the park but I still dreaded meeting
Josef. Somehow he treated me with a degree of insolence
entirely out of keeping with his position.

There were many times when I saw him talking and
laughing with Mellina. She was normally aloof and distant
with the house servants and even with the grooms, but she
and Josef seemed to have developed a rapport which was
completely at variance with their different life styles.

One afternoon Mellina came into the schoolroom whilst I
was trying to introduce Liesel to the mystery of algebra.
Whenever she interrupted us the lesson was immediately
forgotten. Liesel looked up from her book and said slyly, 'I
saw you in the park this morning, mother. I was riding
Marcus but you didn't see me.'

'No, darling, I didn't see you. Why didn't you join me?'

'Because you were with Josef. I don't like the way he looks
at you. I don't like the way he looks at anybody.'

'Josef is a good servant, there is no need to be afraid of him.
Why don't you like him?'

'I've told you, he looks at you as though he knows what you
look like without your clothes on.'

'Darling, what a thing to say, and in front of Rachel too!
You should teach your pupil to mind her manners, Rachel –
and you, missy, are too old for your years.'

With a shrug of her shoulders and a swift irritable smile Mellina left us and I said, 'That was not a very nice thing to say to your mother. I think you should go after her and apologize.'

'Why should I? It's true. He looks at you the same way. Did you know that once my father hit him with a riding crop because he caught him molesting one of the gamekeeper's daughters?'

'No, but I expect he deserved it.'

She grinned. 'Oh yes, but he doesn't like my father. One day he will kill him if my father doesn't kill him first.'

She was quite serious, and I shivered a little. Emotions at Meinhart seemed too primitive, it was a world divorced from the gentle normality of life as I had known it. I seemed to be back in the Middle Ages, in a world of dark deeds and unleashed passions, of inquisitions and raw instincts.

There was one other incident which troubled me and that occurred at the beginning of September. Liesel had been confined to her room with a temperature and Mellina gave instructions that Frau Gessler should take her hot drinks and soup until she was well enough to resume her lessons. There were other servants who could have performed these services just as well but Max was in Paris visiting his mother and there was no way I could countermand any of Mellina's orders.

Frustrated and helpless I had to watch Frau Gessler entering Liesel's room where she remained for hours talking to the girl, filling her mind with who knows what stories. Mellina and I dined alone. Conversation had been minimal at luncheon and in the afternoon she had left the castle to go riding. Over dinner she seemed distracted and I retired to my room as soon as I had eaten on the pretext of writing letters. We were no company for each other and I had sensed a highly strung restlessness in the way she had picked at her food, pushing the plate away impatiently halfway through.

I wrote to my stepfather and then found that I had to go down to the library for an envelope. The drawing room and the library were in darkness and as I passed along the corridor which looked out towards the drawbridge I saw Mellina walking along the path wearing a dark blue cloak over her dinner gown and carrying a lantern in her hands. It was still only dusk but obviously the lantern was to light her way on the return journey. I stood watching her as she crossed the drawbridge and turned towards the river. She was hurrying and I could not help wondering if she was going to Josef's house. It was a long walk to the gates in her light slippers, but where else could they meet, except in some forest clearing?

There was a slight sound behind me and I turned, startled, to find Frau Gessler watching me with narrowed eyes and ill-concealed dislike on her flat peasant's face.

'How is Liesel?' I asked her quickly.

'It will take time, Fräulein, she is not fit for schoolwork.'

'It is only a bad cold, Frau Gessler. I am sure she will be able to take up her studies after the weekend.'

'The Countess will decide. I take my orders from her.'

I had no intention of bandying words with Frau Gessler then or at any other time, so I gave her a long cool look and went on my way. That night, however, I was awakened from my sleep by Liesel's screams of terror. Throwing on my robe I lit a candle and ran out into the corridor towards her room. As I drew nearer the screams became louder and I wondered who else in the castle could hear them. By the time I reached the corridor nearest to her room the screams had ceased. I could hear her sobbing and the deep guttural tones of someone else in her room, striving to calm her. I flung the door open and saw Liesel crouched in the corner of her bed, while Frau Gessler was trying to reach over to touch her.

As calmly as I dared I walked over to the bed and asked, 'What is the matter, Liesel, what frightened you?'

'Nothing frightened her – it was a nightmare, nothing more,' Frau Gessler answered me.

'She is not subject to nightmares, I have never known her have one before.'

'I have, many times.'

'When you were with her, Frau Gessler, terrifying her with your evil tales, but never once since you were told to keep away from her! Now that you are back the nightmares have started again. I shall speak to the Countess, Frau Gessler, and have you relieved of your duties, either that or I will wait until the Count returns from Paris.'

Her face puckered into lines of anguish and to my horror she started to weep, grovelling on her knees, clutching at my robe with her long clawlike hands.

'No, Fräulein, no!' she sobbed. 'Miss Liesel is my baby, my *Liebchen*, always I have cared for her, always she wants to hear the stories I can tell her. You are cold, and cruel to try and take my baby away from me!'

'Pull yourself together, Frau Gessler. Maybe you meant well but the results are unfortunate. Please return to your room now and leave Liesel with me.'

She looked at me piteously but seeing that I was adamant she scurried away, leaving me with the sobbing girl.

'Would you like me to bring you some hot milk, Liesel, to help you to sleep?' I asked her.

She shook her head. 'No, Frau Gessler brought me something.'

'There is nothing to be afraid of. See, I will draw the curtains back, it is almost dawn, and I will leave the lamp burning on your bedside table. There are no shadows in the room now, nothing to frighten you. Try to sleep now, and no nightmares this time.'

She allowed me to pull the bedclothes up under her chin and I waited until she seemed to have settled down. As I walked back towards my room I wondered why Mellina hadn't heard the screams when her own bedroom was just around the corner. I paused, undecided. I did not want Frau Gessler to get to Mellina before I did, so I retraced my steps and knocked gently on Mellina's door.

It took several minutes before she came to open it and I began to think she wasn't there. When she appeared she was still wearing the dark blue cloak she had worn the evening before, though I couldn't see what she wore under it. Her blond hair was hanging loose and dishevelled, and her eyes were startled as they looked into mine. She did not invite me in.

'You didn't hear Liesel screaming?' I asked her.

'No. What is wrong?'

'She is calmer now and I stayed with her for a little while. It

191

was a nightmare, brought on, no doubt, by one of Frau Gessler's bedtime stories. Perhaps you will speak to her before the Count returns.'

Her teeth were chattering and she seemed distraught.

'Is anything wrong, Mellina?'

'No, nothing, what could be wrong? You woke me out of a deep sleep, that is all. You say Liesel is all right now?'

'Yes, I have left a light burning in her room.'

'Very well. I'll speak to Frau Gessler in the morning.'

She closed the door firmly to show me that the conversation was at an end and I returned slowly to my room. I was sure she had not been sleeping, indeed I was sure that she had only just returned to the castle, and I wondered if she had been somewhere in the forest with Josef. It was a balmy night but I shivered, remembering those huge strong hands of his and Mellina's white slender body, picturing the kind of passion those two might have aroused in each other.

After that night nothing was the same. Between Mellina and me there was a sort of uneasy peace born out of her guilt and my knowledge. She was afraid that I would tell Max of my suspicions. She did not know me well enough to plead for my silence, nor understand me well enough to know that I would never betray her, not because I liked her, but because I liked him too well. Anyway, from that night on Frau Gessler stayed away from Liesel's room. Another woman now attended to her needs, a courteous unimaginative country-woman who went about her duties efficiently and quietly, making no effort to linger with Liesel after they were done.

Restless as always, Mellina informed me that she was going to Vienna to make arrangements for the ball on the night of 31 October. When I offered to help she said all the invitations had already gone out and everything that needed to be done at the castle had already been attended to.

'I don't suppose you will object to dining alone,' she said. 'If you wish, meals can be served in your room.'

'Whichever is most convenient,' I replied.

'I'm sorry Max is extending his stay in France. His mother is very demanding, more so as she grows older, and Max has always been a dutiful son.'

'His mother doesn't visit the castle. Does that mean that she is no longer interested in the festivities held here?'

'She is happy in Paris, where many of her old friends have taken up residence. Paris is a civilized city and knows how to take care of the world's exiles.'

'But she is not an exile.'

'She is a voluntary one. We have never been close, nor is she fond of Liesel. One would have thought she might have cared for the child even though she disliked me. Countess Elisa surrounds herself with old aristocrats from her youth and an army of cats, living in splendour in one of Paris's most fashionable streets. She will keep Max with her as long as possible.'

'I see.'

'What do you see, Rachel? Max and I understand each other perfectly, that is why our marriage has lasted when other marriages in Vienna have ended dismally. Have you decided what you will wear for the Halloween ball?'

'No, I haven't given it much thought.'

'It will not be as big an affair as the one on Walpurgis Night but it is still one of the most sought-after events in Vienna. You may look in my wardrobe if you like and choose a dress from there. I shall get something new in Vienna.'

'You are very kind, Mellina, but there may be a chance for me to visit Vienna before the ball. There are one or two things needed for the schoolroom and I would like to buy them myself.'

'Just as you wish, but I did say it was going to be a very select affair, any gown you pick must do it justice.'

'I shall remember.'

Clashes of this nature left me feeling frustrated and angry, but I had trained myself not to let my feelings show in my face and this time was no exception. She stared at me long and hard, then biting her lip she turned and walked from the room.

For the next few nights I dined in my room and then one bright morning I heard the sound of Max's voice in the courtyard. I rushed to my window in time to see him entering the castle. I wanted to run along the corridors and down the stairs to greet him, but it was not my place. I wanted to tell him how much I had missed him, that the day was more golden because he had returned, that the castle felt more like home because he was in it, but the right wasn't mine. Instead I wrestled with Liesel on the discovery of America, feeling at the end of the day that she didn't much care whether it had been discovered or not.

I had thought that with Mellina in Vienna and Max once more at the castle we might have resumed the easy friendship we had enjoyed previously, but it was not to be. He avoided me whenever he could. Herr Pacherov returned to the castle and they spent long hours in the study poring over maps and documents so that I was left more or less alone, and when they did condescend to dine with me I was aware of Max's dark eyes resting upon me with sombre indifference. Although he was courteous, I felt that the gentle irony coupled with warm regard I had come to expect from him had gone for ever.

I did not know if he regretted the night when he had shown his feelings for me too strongly, or if he had dismissed the incident as merely the proximity of man and woman in a setting of intimate understanding. Now I was put firmly in my place; I was his daughter's governess, nothing more, and I felt hurt and bewildered by it all.

Liesel, too, always ready to pounce upon any new development, remarked, 'I used to think my father was attracted to you but not any more.'

'Don't be silly, of course your father is not attracted to me, he is married to your mother.'

'That doesn't make any difference. I know dozens of my mother's friends who come here time after time with different people, even though they are married to somebody else.'

'That may be so, but you should be glad your parents are not like that.'

'I don't really care. He's going away with Herr Pacherov at the end of the month – I heard them talking in the study. That means he won't be here for Halloween.'

'He's probably far too busy anyway to be bothered with another ball.'

'Perhaps they're going to stay in the mountains with the Abbé.'

'Perhaps.'

'Don't you care that he won't be at the ball?'

'It isn't for me to care or not to care. Your father has every right to please himself in what he does, I am merely here as your governess. I would be happy if you could remember it too.'

She was smiling at me quite unabashed, then she said a curious thing.

'I wonder if Sophia left her costume here, the one she had for the masked ball?'

'I have no idea, but why should she unless she intends to wear it another year?'

'Oh, nobody wears the same costume twice, otherwise we would all know who everybody is. I expect she has left it here, she may need it.'

'You mean for another masked ball in Vienna perhaps?'

'Perhaps. She could have given it to the Abbé for one of his acolytes.'

I had forgotten Sophia's unusual costume, but Liesel's remarks set me wondering if indeed Sophia had left her costume at the castle, and that afternoon while Liesel had her piano lesson I decided to find out.

Sophia's room was at the other end of the castle from mine and I expected that by the middle of the afternoon the corridors would be empty and most of the household tasks would have been finished. From high up in the castle I could see men and women working in the vineyards gathering the ripened grapes, and there was an air of peace and stability about the countryside in keeping with the solid permanence of the medieval castle. I met no one on my journey from my room to Sophia's room and I turned the knob of her door gently, fearing it might be locked. It opened to my touch easily, however, and I stepped inside.

It was a beautiful airy room, similar in proportions to my own, with a bathroom leading off it, but it had an unlived-in look that was almost clinical with its white walls and carpet. Only the peacock blue drapes at the windows and the bedspread gave it colour. I left the door unlocked and was ready with more than half a dozen excuses should any of the servants come in, and quickly I started my search. I began with the chest of drawers but they were all empty. Sophia had taken everything out of the wardrobe and the empty hangers on the rail gave it a huge cavernous look. I searched the bathroom and every other place I could think of but there was no sign of the costume.

It was only when I was letting myself out of the door that I remembered the wide shelf placed high up in the wardrobe, normally reserved for travelling cases. I pulled forward the dressing table stool to stand on, I reached into the dark recess of the shelf and drew out a parcel shrouded in tissue paper. With my heart racing like a mad thing I pulled the paper aside to reveal the black velvet breeches, then the surplice, and I was busy searching for the shoes when something fell on the floor. I glanced down and then froze in horror; for staring straight up at me was the face of a damned soul. I choked back a cry of dismay as I felt my heart lurch sickeningly, so shocked I could hardly stop myself falling from the stool.

I got down clumsily, scraping the back of my ankle on the stool, but quite unaware of the pain. For a moment I could only stare at the thing on the floor with horror, not realizing what it was, then slowly I reached forward and picked it up. It was a mask made out of papier-mâché. Whichever way I held it it leered at me with livid white features in a cloud of bright red hair, beautiful and sad – the saddest, most wicked, most exquisite face I had ever seen. The lashes were long, black and silky to the touch. I walked over to the mirror and slipped the mask over my head. Although I knew I was seeing an illusion I was appalled by the vision confronting me; a creature indescribably evil, abominably wicked, but whose timeless beauty made me fearful that I had sold my soul to the devil and that the face of the mask would be imprinted on my own face for all time.

I took it off with trembling fingers, looking closely at my reflection, hardly daring to believe that my face could be unchanged. I felt cold, so cold that my teeth were chattering in spite of the warm autumnal afternoon, and I looked at the thing in my hands with revulsion. In spite of the bright red hair and deathly white face, in spite of the mocking curves of the purple mouth, it had a terrible fascination. I rose to my feet and hid it in the folds of the costume, pushing them all once more to the back of the wardrobe shelf.

I sat on the edge of the bed for several minutes before I felt I could face the world outside that room. My eyes never left the wardrobe door in case the thing should have a life of its own and open the door. Pulling myself together I let myself out into the corridor, relieved that I was unobserved. Back in my own room I scrubbed my hands and face as if they might have been contaminated, then I went back to the schoolroom to see if Liesel had finished her piano lesson.

A little while later I asked as nonchalantly as I dared, 'Why were you so curious about Sophia's fancy-dress costume, Liesel?'

'I just wondered, that's all.'

'I didn't see her until the ball was over, and by that time she had removed her mask.'

Liesel said nothing, so recklessly I went on, 'Whatever sort of mask did she wear with that costume? She looked like a boy sitting there.'

'She was supposed to be a boy. It was just an ordinary mask, a black one like most of the other people wore.'

'I see.' She was looking at me now and I made myself smile and say airily, 'I thought you looked far prettier in that costume of yours and it was far more suitable for a girl.'

'I shan't wear anything so silly next year, I shall be older. I shall go as Cleopatra, not some little ninny in frills and flounces.'

'Oh, come on, you're not a bit like Cleopatra with your Saxon fairness. I expect she was dark and sultry and very sophisticated. Besides, you're too young.'

'I thought you were supposed to teach me history! Cleopatra was only fifteen years old when she was delivered to Julius Caesar wrapped in a carpet, and not very much older when Mark Antony fell in love with her. Beautiful bad women are so much more exciting that beautiful good ones.'

'But was Cleopatra a bad woman? She was a beautiful

woman living in a man's world, fighting men with the only weapons she had available to save Egypt from the domination of Rome.'

'Why did they call her the serpent of the Nile then?'

'I don't suppose the Romans were very kindly disposed towards her when she captivated first Julius Caesar and then Mark Antony. She even defeated them in death. Octavius was unable to keep the promise he made to the Senate that the queen of Egypt would walk behind his chariot in chains.'

'Then I shall just have to think of somebody else who *was* wicked, won't I?'

What was it about this precocious child that made me feel inadequate? In many ways she was years older than I and although I longed to make a cutting remark that would remove the mocking smile from her face, I only told her with some asperity to return to her books.

I made up my mind that I would speak to Max that night after dinner whether Herr Pacherov was present or not, and that I would wait for him no matter how late it was if he failed to join me for dinner.

I need not have worried. They were both in the dining room before me and as I sat down at the table Herr Pacherov handed me a glass of wine. Max did not look up from the letter he had just opened and sat frowning at it in a thoughtful way until the servants came in to serve the meal.

After that we exchanged the usual pleasantries but I could tell that Max's thoughts were elsewhere. Herr Pacherov entertained me with some story about the village where he had been born, and the long hard winters when the wolves came down from the mountains to scavenge along the village streets, but I found it difficult to attend.

After the meal the two men excused themselves on the pretext of having work to do but I said quickly, 'I need to speak with you for a few moments, Max, it is very important.'

He raised his eyebrows slightly, then turning to the lawyer he said, 'I will join you in a few moments, after I have heard what this young lady has to say.'

He returned to his chair at the table and sat waiting expectantly for me to begin. For once I wished he would make it easier by adopting a friendlier and less remote manner.

'I need to obtain one or two new books for Liesel and I'd like to select them myself.'

He raised his eyebrows still further. 'Books! What sort of books? My dear girl, the library is full of them.'

'I am aware of that, but they are not altogether suitable for our needs. I was thinking in terms of one or two history books about the Americans. Liesel is familiar with the more colourful aspects of European and ancient history, but American history is relatively new and has not yet become too scandalous.'

He smiled wryly. 'I see you are still having trouble with your pupil's lurid imagination. If you will give me a selection of what you need I will have them sent here as quickly as possible.'

'I would really much rather go into the bookshops in Vienna. I shall only be away one evening – I wouldn't ask if I didn't think it necessary.'

He looked down at the table thoughtfully as though my request to go to Vienna was indeed a momentous one, and for one awful moment I believed he was going to refuse. Idly he picked up the envelope he had been handling earlier and took out its contents. I could see that it was a large white card which looked like an invitation. Suddenly he seemed to make up his mind and rising from the table he said casually, 'I have to go into Vienna before next Tuesday, so if you can arrange to travel with me on Monday you will have all the next day to get whatever you need. Liesel's ballet and piano teachers are here all Tuesday so she will be fully occupied. How does that arrangement suit you?'

'Very well indeed, I can stay at my hotel near the station.'

'That will not be necessary. In case it has escaped your memory we do have a house on the Ringstrasse, you needn't go to any hotel. My wife is in Vienna, I believe, and she may be glad of company.'

Not my company, I thought as he left me with a brief smile.

How I looked forward to that drive into Vienna with him! It was true I was going there in search of new history books for the schoolroom, but as soon as he left me I hurried to the library to search in the desk for the address of the mask maker in Vienna. I did not know if the same man had made the particular mask I had found in Sophia's room, but I would visit the man in Vienna and try to find out. It had been the work of an artist as well as a marvellous craftsman. That night I busied myself by writing down a description of the mask; I even made a sketch of it from memory and painted it in watercolours. I could not capture the pervading sadness and evil of it, my painting was simply a face without character, but surely he would know from my poor effort if he had been the maker or the designer of such a mask.

Monday morning dawned golden bright and long before breakfast I was up packing a small case with my needs for the next few days. I helped myself to one of Ludmilla's dinner gowns even though I cherished no illusions that there would be an occasion to wear it.

Josef's face was surly as he came forward to open the gates and the Count favoured him with only a curt nod as he urged the horses forward. In the distance the spires and domes of Vienna rose ethereally beautiful against the blue sky and I tucked the rug more closely about me in the fresh autumnal breeze.

Max turned his head and smiled, a smile that lifted my heart and made my pulses race. 'There is a saying in Austria, Rachel, that if one is alone in the autumn, one is alone all the winter long. Perhaps you have heard of it.'

'No, but many of those old sayings have a grain of truth in them.'

'You have a favourite one, perhaps?'

'None. Most of them are concerned with the wasting of time, and I seem to have wasted so much time on vain and stupid things.'

'We all do that, I'm afraid, and no poet ever put it half so well as the Persian one when he wrote, "The Moving Finger writes; and having writ, Moves on: nor all thy Piety nor Wit Shall lure it back to cancel half a Line, Nor all thy Tears wash out a word of it."'

I looked towards him but he was watching the road ahead, his face at that moment immeasurably sad. I longed to put my hand in his but I only clenched it tighter under the fur rug that covered our knees. I knew the translation of the Rubaiyat. The poem had been a great favourite with my father; he had called it a poem of surpassing beauty written by a cynic with little faith.

Perhaps he had been a cynic but he had also been a realist. Here was I, young and desperately in love for the first time in my life, and the future did not matter, only the present with Max beside me. I found myself thinking about another famous line from Omar Khayyam, 'The Bird of Time has but a little way to fly – and Lo! the Bird is on the Wing.'

I never spoke those words. One cannot lightly ignore the conventions of a lifetime. Instead I sat prim and decorous next to him watching the road pass swiftly under the pounding hooves and the wheels of the carriage. Soon, too soon, we would be in Vienna and Max would be with Mellina.

He let himself into the house on the Ringstrasse with his latchkey and immediately a manservant came forward to relieve us of our outdoor clothing. He did not seem surprised to see us, but when Max asked if the Countess was at home he shook his head saying she had left the house two days before without leaving an address and the servants did not know when she would return.

Max said nothing, but the frown deepened on his face and I felt this was due to Mellina's cavalier behaviour.

'If you wish to go to the shops I should do so immediately after lunch,' he advised me, 'in case you have plans to meet the Liptmanns while you are here. Or have you something more romantic on your mind?'

'Romantic!'

'I was thinking of Ernst, perhaps you are expecting to meet him here.'

'I have no plans to meet Ernst or visit the Liptmanns, but please do not concern yourself about me – I am quite capable of amusing myself.'

He smiled at that, then said quickly, 'Perhaps you will dine with me later. By that time Mellina may have returned.'

Mellina, Mellina! She was the one going off into the blue and leaving no messages behind – why should he need to feel so considerate towards Mellina when she was so inconsiderate to everybody else?

I went first of all to the bookshops where I managed to find three new history books on the Americas as well as an up-to-date life of Cleopatra, then just along the street I hired a cab and gave the driver the address of the mask maker. It proved to be a small shop in the old quarter of the city, on a narrow cobbled street, and I looked around me with interest after I had paid off the cab driver. In the window of the shop were all the usual paraphernalia of his trade, carnival hats and lanterns, masks and decorations of every kind, but nowhere was there anything remotely resembling the mask I had found in Sophia's room.

Plucking up my courage I entered the shop, hearing the bell ring above the door and echo in the corridor beyond. It was an untidy shop with shelves piled high with bric-a-brac in no particular order, and I had to wait quite some time before I heard the shuffling of footsteps approaching from behind the door at the back of the counter. When the door opened an old man came forward wearing steel-rimmed spectacles at the end of his nose. He was bald except for two lengths of wispy grey hair at either side of his head and he was wearing a greasy waistcoat over a peasant's shirt which was none too clean.

He peered at me shortsightedly over his glasses and I smiled at him, more confidently than I felt. 'I have been given your address by a friend,' I lied. 'You make all kinds of masks, isn't that so?'

'Masks and other things, it says so in the window, Fräulein.'

'Do you make masks for special occasions?'

'Didn't I just say so? Carnivals, fancy-dress balls, all sorts of special occasions.'

I produced my painting and laid it on the counter. 'Can you remember making this one?'

He returned his glasses to their proper place and held my drawing up to the light, then he laid it down on the counter

202

and without looking at me he muttered, 'I can't remember, I can't remember it at all, I would need to see the mask.'

'But you must remember, you can't have been asked to make many like that one. I know my painting cannot capture the beauty of your workmanship or the sadness, but you must know if it was your work or not?'

'No, like I said I don't remember it and I am busy now.'

Dimly I heard the bell above the door but my disappointment was so intense that I urged him again. 'It is very important to me, please try to remember! Did anybody at any time ask you to make a mask like this?' I tried flattery: 'I was told that you are the only mask maker in Vienna who could have made anything so sad and so beautiful.'

'And so evil and terribly alive,' a voice said from behind me and I looked round startled to see the Abbe standing there. He reached forward and handed my painting again to the old man behind the counter. Startled, he took it and studied it.

'Think again, my friend,' the Abbe said. He smiled gently at me and together we waited for the old man to speak.

He handed the painting back to me and said in a tired voice, 'Perhaps I did make such a mask, but I did not design it, oh no, that was done by another. It was brought to me as a painting and I was told to copy it, for a fancy-dress ball, you understand. I am an old man and I am not rich, I was offered a good price for my work.'

'Who offered it, a woman?' the Abbe asked.

'I don't remember.'

'You mean you are afraid to remember?'

'I forget faces, and I forget names even more, they do not mean anything any more; I only want my customers to pay me for what I do and go away.'

'We shall get nothing more here, my child,' the Abbe said, 'but at least we know that this old rascal made the mask. No doubt the police can soon find out whom he made it for – we can go there now if you like.'

'No, father, no, not the police,' the old man whined. 'It was a long time ago that I made that mask, for a lady and a gentleman who came to see me, a beautiful lady and a gentleman, very much in love they were, she knows exactly what she wants and he pays me everything I ask without a murmur. I am a poor man, there is not much money in this kind of trade, the lady told me it was for a fancy-dress ball and who am I to ask questions of my betters?'

'Who indeed?' said the Abbe. 'But you thought it was a strange mask, did you not? What sort of a man or woman would want to look like that?'

'Yes, father, many times I ask myself that question, but I got no good answers.'

'There are no good answers, my friend, for the mask is concerned with evil, and only with evil. And now, Fräulein Arden, you and I will go and drink an excellent cup of coffee at the little café in the park where we can breathe God's good clean air. Do you believe in God, my friend?' he asked suddenly, turning towards the old man.

'Oh yes, father, yes indeed.'

'Then I charge you as you believe in eternal salvation to say nothing of this young lady's visit to your shop – nothing – or it could well be that the police will be made aware of that evil thing which I can assure you was never intended for a fancy-dress ball.'

I was trembling as we left the shop, walking quickly towards a tiny cobbled square and the delicious aroma of roasting coffee. We sat outside the café in a pretty park where we could watch two small boys sailing their boats on a pond, and during the next half hour I poured into the Abbe's ears all I had been afraid of over the last few months.

He listened without interrupting me and when I had finished he said, 'You are in great danger, my child, and I implore you to tread warily. I too have known that all is not as it should be at Castle Meinhart but my hands have been tied. I do not know how much or how little the Count himself is involved and I fear for the child Sophia. I watched you alight from your cab this afternoon and I followed you at a discreet distance. When I saw you go into that shop I came after you, for something told me that by asking questions you could put your own life in terrible danger. It was brave but it was foolish, my child.'

'Will he tell them about my visit, do you think?'

'I do not know how much more he fears those children of Satan than he fears the Vienna police or the God they have forsaken. We can only hope he fears God more than he fears the devil.'

For a moment neither of us spoke until at last he looked up and said, 'Are you staying with your friends the Liptmanns?'

'No, I am at the Meinhart house. Max brought me to Vienna but Mellina is away and we do not know where.'

'It is not possible for me to call upon the Count before I return home to the mountains. I have been in Vienna almost a week now for an ecclesiastical conference, and it is time I went home.'

We left the park together, but some little distance along the road he found a cab for me. It was late afternoon when I finally returned to the house on the Ringstrasse. I was about to go upstairs when Max called to me from the room in which my grandmother's portrait decorated the wall above the fireplace. He was standing on the hearthrug with the same envelope in his hands that I had seen in the dining room at the castle.

'I have a problem, Rachel,' he said. 'This is an invitation from the Emperor to a concert tomorrow evening at the Schönbrunn. It is addressed to my wife and myself but in her absence I do not know whether to accept.'

I waited without speaking, and when I didn't say anything he went on, 'Would you like to accompany me in Mellina's absence?'

'To the palace!' I exclaimed.

'Certainly to the palace – I don't suppose the Emperor is inviting us to a musical evening at the Prater.' He was irritable, but it was not I who had made him so. It stemmed from his wife's absence, I felt sure.

'Perhaps Mellina will return in time for the concert.'

'If she does, then the three of us will go. I take it you have brought a suitable gown with you.'

'I brought one of Ludmilla's dinner gowns.'

'Dress at the palace is very formal. I suggest you look in my wife's wardrobe and select something of hers. Don't look so doubtful, Rachel, Mellina already has more clothes than she will ever wear, so I am sure she will not resent your wearing something of hers.'

All the next day I waited in some trepidation for the sound of Mellina's musical voice in the house, but when late afternoon had arrived and she still had not returned I knew I would have to start dressing. I did not like having to choose a gown from Mellina's wardrobe but when I saw the array of clothes hanging from one wall to the next I could hardly think she would begrudge me the loan of one of them. They were mostly new, all expensive and very beautiful, and I finally selected a deceptively simple gown in heavy ivory parchment satin with satin slippers to match. Max looked at me with critical acclaim and remarked, 'You look very beautiful, but you need some jewellery. It will be a glittering occasion as always and not one where your youth and beauty alone will be enough.'

I watched him go over to the safe in the wall concealed behind the picture of my grandmother and take out a dark blue leather jewel case. I gasped with delight at the diamond necklace which lay against the dark blue velvet and the bracelet and long earrings which matched it. I fastened the bracelet round my wrist and the earrings in my ears. Max clasped the necklace around my neck and I could feel myself blushing furiously as he touched my skin. Then he produced a diamond tiara from the safe and asked me to wear it.

'You will see that all the other women are wearing them, there is no need to be afraid,' he said, placing it over my hair.

'I feel I should not be wearing Mellina's jewellery even though I am wearing her gown,' I said unhappily. 'Now I really do feel like a dancing girl adorning herself for her lord and master.'

'No dancing girl ever did her lord and master more justice, or looked more beautiful,' he said smiling, 'and if the jewels worry you, think of them as belonging to my mother rather than Mellina.'

I went through the first part of that evening in a dream. I do not remember the drive through the city streets or our first entry into the Schönbrunn palace, I was only aware that everywhere there was a dazzling light from a forest of crystal chandeliers and that the marble and gold staircase we climbed was peopled by other guests, beautiful women in exquisite gowns, their jewels vying with the light from the chandeliers, and men who bowed gallantly over my hand. The feel of Max's hand under my elbow was the only real sensation I was aware of as we were greeted with smiles and bows and polite words of greeting. I felt that my own smile was fixed and forced, but soon we were standing in two long lines waiting for the Emperor to appear at the top of the staircase.

We did not have to wait long. The doors were opened and he came forward, standing to attention while the Austrian national anthem was played, then he came down the stairs towards us. He was followed by high ranking officers but my eyes were only for the slight, silver-haired man who walked slowly, nodding first to one person and then the next, occasionally pausing to speak to one of his guests while the men stood with bowed heads and the women curtsied. At last he stood before us and I too curtsied. I heard his voice speaking to Max as I rose to my feet.

'Welcome, Count Meinhart, we see you too seldom in Vienna these days. I am sorry that the Countess is indisposed, please give her our good wishes for an early recovery.'

He was looking at me kindly and slightly puzzled, and I was aware of his faded blue eyes and tired sad face, then he smiled, murmuring softly, 'Charming, most charming. I grow old, and although my memory is not what it was, you remind me of the Countess Theresa. A new and beautiful face at the palace is very pleasing.'

'Thank you, your majesty,' I stammered, and then with another smile he moved on.

Later we followed him into the music room where we sat on small gilt chairs while the orchestra took their places on a raised dais at the end of the room. I knew that many of the eyes of those present were on us, some curious, some admiring, others merely speculative, but through it all Max sat unperturbed, always charming, invariably attentive, and at last I relaxed and allowed the music the Emperor had chosen to fill my senses with its melody. We listened to the music of Tchaikovsky and Borodin and the *Liebestod* from *Tristan und Isolde* which Max told me had been the Empress Elizabeth's favourite, and afterwards we ate delicious assortments of food in one of the side rooms leading off the music room. Once I caught the Emperor looking at me from across the room, his eyes sad, brooding, as though he was trying to remember. Bitterly I said, 'He is still remembering my grandmother. I wonder if he remembers that young equerry whose marriage he so callously put aside.'

Max looked down at me with a faint smile and with gentle irony said, 'I very much doubt it, Rachel. The ending of a marriage when it is not one's own is a small thing for a man to recall when he remembers the suicide of his only son and the assassination of his Empress.'

I felt suitably chastened, and when the Emperor looked my way again I smiled at him across the room.

'Do I really look like my paternal grandmother?' I asked Max on the way home. 'I was always told that I resembled my Hungarian grandmother.'

'Perhaps you do, but it was the Countess Theresa the Emperor was remembering.'

'I suppose she was often a visitor at the palace?'

'Of course, and there was also a rumour that at one time the Emperor was very enamoured of the beautiful Theresa.'

'Gracious me!' I snapped. 'There's no end to the scandal that goes on in these exalted circles! How can they possibly stand in judgement on anybody?'

He chuckled in the darkness of the carriage but refrained from commenting further.

We had entered the hall of the house and Max was reaching out to relieve me of my cloak when from the stairs above us Mellina's voice taunted, 'Well, well, and what a delightful picture you make in your borrowed finery, with your borrowed escort!'

I looked up startled and Max's face registered dark annoyance.

'So you have returned to us, Mellina,' he said dryly. 'That was gracious of you.'

She came slowly down the stairs and I wondered how long she had been in the house. She was wearing a red velvet robe over her night attire and her pale blond hair hung loosely on her shoulders as though it had just been released. She looked pale and tired and she swayed slightly as though with fatigue. She walked into the drawing room and went straight over to a small table on which glasses and brandy were kept, and poured some of the warm golden liquid into a glass which she held to her lips.

'I hope you are going to tell me where you have been in all that finery, splendid enough to dine with the Emperor, no less.'

'That is exactly where we have been, Mellina, how perceptive of you! Of course I had to make a suitable excuse for your absence so I informed the Emperor that you were indisposed, and he sends you his good wishes for your early recovery.'

'And how did you introduce Rachel here, as a kinswoman, or as a governess?'

'As a kinswoman, naturally, and you will be pleased to hear that he was completely captivated by her.'

She turned and was in the process of pouring out another glass of brandy when Max stretched out his hand and took the decanter away from her.

'I think you have drunk quite sufficient of that for one night, don't you agree? I should go to bed, Mellina, we are returning to Meinhart in the morning and that is only a few hours away.'

She placed the heavy goblet on the table so sharply that I was afraid it would break. Without looking at either of us she swayed uncertainly towards the stairs.

'If I am awake I will return with you, if not it will have to be another day,' she called out to us, and miserably I looked at Max's face which registered neither anger nor sorrow. It was as coldly remote as the faces of his ancestors on the walls of Meinhart.

Twelve

I was not looking forward to the journey back to Meinhart. Mellina would be with us and if her attitude on the evening before was any criterion she would be fractious and I could expect to bear the brunt of her ill humour. I rose early and started to pack the few things I had brought with me, then reluctantly I went down to face them over breakfast.

I was surprised to find Max breakfasting alone, and already dressed for travelling. He greeted me with a smile and as I helped myself to coffee and rolls he said, 'I regret having to ask you to stay on in Vienna for a few days, Rachel. Mellina's maid informed me that my wife has been ill during the night and will not be fit to travel. It is imperative that I return to the castle this morning but if she is ill I don't think it should be left to the servants to care for her.'

My heart sank dismally, but I said, 'Oh, I'm sorry. Has she caught a chill or is it likely to be something more serious?'

'I have sent for the doctor and I will wait until we have his verdict. Do you mind staying on for a while?'

'No, not if you think it is necessary. But what about Liesel?'

'Liesel will be quite all right with Frau Schultz. You need not be afraid that Frau Gessler will have access to her, she knows better than to disobey my wishes.'

'I thought Mellina seemed very tired last night – she was quite unsteady with fatigue.'

He smiled cynically. 'She was quite unsteady from too much brandy, my dear, but your observations were meant to be charitable, I have no doubt.'

I looked at him in surprise. 'But I have never known Mellina to drink brandy!'

'She drinks when she is troubled, when her plans have gone awry, or for other devious reasons. Last night she was angry because we had gone to the palace without her, even though it was entirely her own fault, but she was also troubled about some other matter, perhaps something which has happened during her visit here.'

'You do not know what it is?'

'I have no idea and I stopped asking questions about her personal life a long time ago when I realized she did not take kindly to questioning or criticism. It could have been a new gown that she doesn't find as becoming as she had thought it would be, perhaps a broken dinner engagement, perhaps even a fading love affair. Whatever it was has contributed to her indisposition this morning, either that or for some reason unknown to me she does not wish to return to the country today.'

'I see,' I murmured, not seeing at all and more than a little confused by his mention of a fading love affair.

His smile deepened but there was no mirth in it.

'I doubt if you do, my dear. Mellina's rages are entirely unpredictable, nor are they concerned with matters you could have any idea of. She will not be pleased that I have asked you to stay. Can you bear her annoyance when she knows I have returned but you have been asked to remain here?'

'I believe so. I have never flattered myself that Mellina liked me, my life at Meinhart would be happier if she did, but I have always maintained that I must make the best of it. I suppose I shall suffer her displeasure and adjust to it.'

'Thank you, Rachel. There is the front door bell, it could well be the arrival of our good doctor.'

He rose from the table and went to stand near the fireplace waiting for the doctor to be announced.

He was a middle-aged man, obviously well known to the Count who greeted him in a friendly fashion and after introducing us suggested that he go upstairs to see to his patient. I was surprised when Max did not offer to go with him, but the doctor himself showed no surprise.

About five minutes later he returned and in answer to Max's unspoken question he said, 'She is suffering from

211

exhaustion and has a slight fever but I have left some medicine which will quickly bring it down. She appears somewhat emotionally upset, do you know if anything is troubling her?'

'Nothing to my knowledge. She has been in the city for several days before my arrival, but where and how she spent those days I do not know.'

The two men looked at each other long and hard, then the doctor said, 'She should be fit to travel in two or three days, but I have issued a warning to the Countess which I feel you should hear.'

'I shall be glad to hear it, although whether she will take your warning is another matter. A great many people have been issuing warnings to Mellina for a long time and I have never known her obey any of them. What have you said to her?'

'I told her that too many late nights, too many parties and too much alcohol were not likely to contribute to her wellbeing.'

'And what was her reply?'

'Merely that I fussed too much. I have left her a sedative to calm her, though I have the feeling it will be fighting a losing battle against a host of other matters which feed her emotions.'

Max permitted himself a small smile. Shaking hands with the doctor he said, 'Thank you, my friend, for coming so promptly. Is it necessary for you to call again?'

'I hardly think so if she obeys my instructions. If I am passing tomorrow I might just call in to see how she is.'

'Rachel will be here. She is my daughter's governess and also a distant relative. You can give her any information about my wife which you think I ought to know.'

The doctor departed and I looked at Max a little doubtfully.

'Don't worry,' he said. 'Mellina has a strong constitution. If she is suffering from some emotional disturbance it is one she has brought on herself.'

Later that morning I watched him leave the house with some misgivings, then I walked slowly upstairs and tapped lightly on Mellina's door.

She lay propped up against her pillows but she was not asleep. Her pale blond hair seemed to have lost some of its lustre and her eyes were sunken and surrounded by dark smudges of tiredness, making them seem too large for her pale face. She fixed me with cold angry eyes as I went to stand at the side of her bed.

'Why didn't you go back to Meinhart with Max?' she accused testily.

'Max had to go back urgently, but he didn't think we should both go and leave you alone.'

'Very commendable of him, I'm sure, but I am hardly alone in the house. I have a perfectly adequate maid and the house is full of servants.'

'He asked me to stay nevertheless, and I am hardly in a position to refuse.'

'Why ever not? You are in charge of Liesel, not me, and I am constantly being informed that you are not a servant and should not be treated as such. I suppose Max left you here to spy on me and to report to him later about my friends who come to the house.'

'I am sure he did not. I have no intention of reporting to Count Meinhart about anything which takes place here, none of it is my business. I am merely here to see that you obey the doctor's instructions and stay in bed until you are well enough to leave it.'

'I am well enough now. I shall get up immediately after lunch.'

'That is quite ridiculous. You should drink the sedative the doctor left you and try to get some sleep. You will feel much better in the evening, I'm sure.'

'Why don't you mind your own business, Rachel, and send my maid to me?'

'But the doctor's sedative . . . '

'I don't intend to take it. I am expecting a friend and I want to know the minute she arrives.'

'But you are ill, Mellina! Can't I see her and explain? She could come back tomorrow or the next day, whenever you are feeling well enough.'

She glared at me balefully. 'I have given instructions to my maid that this woman is to be brought upstairs the minute she arrives. Why don't you go out, Rachel? You don't get many opportunities to visit Vienna, and anything is better than hanging around the house when you are not needed.'

I looked at her helplessly, but I could see that she did not want me in her room, or even in the house when her visitor arrived.

It was raining, that fine clinging rain that makes one feel more miserable and wet than a steady downpour, and in spite of her encouragement to leave the house I was not going to tramp the city streets in the rain. I went to sit in the drawing room with a book. Mellina's maid hovered expectantly in the hall until I was tired of seeing her there, so I went to ask if there was anything she needed.

'Madame the Countess is expecting a friend, Fräulein,' she said. 'She has asked me to remain in the hall until she arrives so that I can show her upstairs immediately.'

'What time is she supposed to be coming?'

'At two o'clock, Fräulein.'

'It is now only a little after one, and there are menservants to attend to the door. In the meantime what are we going to do about the sedative the doctor has left for the Countess to take?'

The girl looked afraid. She was only quite young, a pretty girl with big brown eyes which looked at me with helpless appeal.

'I have been up half the night with her, I don't think she slept a wink, but I can't get her to take the medicine and if I mention it again she will be terribly angry.'

'You are afraid of her, aren't you?'

'She could dismiss me, Fräulein, and employment is not easily come by in Vienna.'

'How long have you been with the Countess?'

'Only five months. I was lucky to be chosen, there were about twenty applicants for the post.'

'Why did she choose you?'

'She said I looked as though I could mind my own business and needed the job badly. Indeed I did, Fräulein, my mother is an invalid in Baden and I have to send money home every week for my sister who takes care of her. I explained all this to the Countess and she was very kind. I think she gave the job to me because she was sorry for me, and I must do my utmost to keep it.'

'Yes, of course you must, and you are in no danger of losing it. What is your name?'

'Lily'.

'Well, Lily, I suggest you take your mistress a hot drink and put in some of that medicine left by the doctor. The Countess has a fever and should be made to rest – it is no use sending for the doctor and then disobeying his instructions.'

'But if she knows what I have done she will dismiss me.'

'I will take the full blame, Lily. Please do as I say, and if the Countess's friend arrives I will explain that she is ill and ask her to come back tomorrow. If she is a good friend she will understand and sympathize.'

The girl looked doubtful, then making up her mind she bobbed a little curtsey and went back up the stairs while I returned to the drawing room to wait.

The afternoon passed slowly and the friend did not arrive. Shortly after four o'clock I went upstairs to Mellina's room. She was sleeping soundly and for a few moments I stood at the side of her bed staring down at her. Sleep had erased the lines of strain from her face and left it as peaceful and serene as a child's. It could have been Liesel sleeping there, childlike and carefree. The door opened and the maid looked in, so I followed her outside into the corridor.

'Did you give her the draught?' I asked her.

'Yes, Fräulein, she went to sleep almost immediately. Did the friend she was expecting arrive?'

'No. Please don't worry. I am sure she will feel much better when she awakes, perhaps well enough to see her friend if she arrives later.'

'Oh, I do hope so. I am afraid of her when she is angry.'

'And is she often angry, Lily?'

'Not always with me, Fräulein, but she is often angry about other matters.'

'What other matters?'

'I don't know. Sometimes when she comes back after she

has been away for a few days, and once with Baron von Reichman when he called to see her, and him such a nice friendly young gentleman. They quarrelled all afternoon and there was no doing any good with her after he left. All night she paced the floor, I was glad when she went away again the next morning.'

'Well, don't worry about it now, Lily. I'm here so if you have any problems when the Countess wakes up, please come for me.'

I smiled at her more reassuringly than I felt, then thoughtfully I went downstairs.

I couldn't understand why Mellina should quarrel with Ernst. They always seemed to be the best of friends and Ernst was not difficult to get along with. I couldn't help wondering if she had quarrelled with him for the same reason she had quarrelled with Sophia, because he too had refused to conform.

The rain persisted for the rest of the afternoon so I resigned myself to spending a day in front of the drawing-room fire. I looked up at the portrait above the fireplace, at the charming little boy and the beautiful woman who held him in her arms with such pride, then, a little curious, I went across to the mirror and gazed for a moment at my own reflection. We were very much alike, the Countess Theresa and I. We had the same dark red hair and blue eyes, and a mouth which I thought was a little too large for true beauty although there were those who said it was my best feature. It was not a chocolate box beauty, my face had too much determination in it, but it was strange that both my grandmothers had possessed the same colouring.

I ate my solitary dinner alone, disliking the idea of the long night ahead of me, but at just before seven o'clock the front door bell rang and I heard one of the menservants going down the hall to answer it. Next moment Hans was standing before me with a doubtful look on his fresh young face.

'There is a person at the door, Fräulein Arden, asking to see the Countess,' he said.

'Who is she, Hans?'

'She is a Madame Pickarde, a Frenchwoman I believe.'

'Have you shown her into the reception room?'

'No, Fräulein,' and the doubt on his face increased so that I asked sharply, 'Why ever not, Hans, if she is the guest the Countess has been expecting?'

He blushed and in answer to my look of puzzlement he said, 'The woman is a strange sort of visitor for this house. Perhaps you will know what to do with her, Fräulein.'

More puzzled still I went ahead of him out of the room and towards the front door where a dark shape hovered on the threshold. I hoped my surprise didn't show, but the woman who stood there was indeed a strange visitor for the house on the Ringstrasse.

She was tall and so thin the skin seemed stretched tight across high cheekbones, and her eyes were sunk in a face which was splashed with black as though even before her death her body had begun to corrupt. She wore a stiff rustling dress of black taffeta which had once been rich and probably expensive. It was now stained over her flat chest where food had been allowed to spill down it, and the beads which had once adorned it were hanging on thin threads as though they were about to fall away. She smiled at me, if one could call it a smile, for it looked like the grimace of a death's-head, showing long yellowing teeth with several gaps.

I stepped back at the door inviting her in and as she passed in front of me I felt nauseated by the stench which came from her, an unwashed smell of stale perfume and nicotine. I asked her to follow me into the reception room and as she shuffled after me I noticed that she wore threadbare carpet slippers on her feet.

She stood before me in the light and I could see now that in spite of her air of poverty her long bony fingers were encased in valuable rings and there was a thick gold chain around her neck ending in some sort of talisman. I looked at her enquiringly and she smiled again, saying ingratiatingly, 'Madame the Countess is expecting me, two o'clock she said, but I could not come then, I had business to attend to.'

'I am sorry, madame, but the Countess was taken ill in the night and the doctor had to be called in. She is sleeping at the moment and will not be able to see you.'

The sunken eyes narrowed still further and she came closer to peer into my face. I backed away swiftly, a gesture which caused her to chuckle softly to herself.

'She is not here then, she has returned to the country?'

'I have told you, she is upstairs in her bed fast asleep. Her maid had to give her a sleeping draught. I doubt if she will awake in time to see you this evening.'

'Yet I think if you were to rouse her she would see me, Fräulein,' the woman said, and I sensed a threat in her words, a threat which momentarily made my blood run cold.

'Is it possible for you to come back tomorrow, madame? I am sure she will be much better then and able to see you. She will not be fit to travel for several days.'

'I don't know if I can come back yet again, I am a business woman and I live some distance away. Carriages cost money for a poor woman such as me, the great ones do not seem to realize that.'

'I am sure the Countess will willingly pay your carriage fare since you have had to make the journey twice.'

'That's as it may be, Fräulein, but it may not be convenient. Tell the Countess that when she awakens. I could visit her in the country, yes indeed, that may be the best solution for all of us.'

Again there was the veiled threat in her argument, and sharply I said, 'If it is expensive to call upon her here, I am sure you will find it considerably more expensive to visit her in the country.'

The sunken eyes gleamed in the yellowing face and she wheezed, 'The young lady is sharp, very sharp, but I have friends who could take me to the country, an afternoon's drive, you see, a little outing for an old woman, it could be very pleasurable.'

'And profitable, madame?' I retorted. The words had sprung too swiftly to my lips and I regretted them as soon as they were spoken. Immediately the smile left her face and she came towards me, her face only inches away from mine as she hissed, 'Tell Madame the Countess ten o'clock tomorrow morning, or the Castle Meinhart after she has returned to it – she can make her choice.'

Suddenly she thrust out a long thin arm and next moment I found her thin clawlike fingers around my wrist, although only lightly.

'You are a pretty child, a very pretty child. Are you a secretary to the Countess or perhaps even a new friend?'

'I am her daughter's governess.'

'Is the child here then in Vienna that you are here interrogating me?'

'I have not interrogated you, madame, I have merely explained that the Countess is ill and will see you in the morning.'

She chuckled again. 'Perhaps you will tell the Countess that it is a long time since I saw her little girl. My, but she was a pretty child – a very pretty child! Such prettiness does not always last, though. It often fades – or it can be destroyed.'

I looked at her levelly in spite of the menace contained in her words, and with as much disdain as I was capable of I withdrew my arm from her clutch and walked towards the door, holding it open so that she could do nothing but follow me. I stood on the doorstep watching her shuffle down the steps and it was only when she reached the gate that she looked back and said in a firm loud voice, 'Ten o'clock in the morning, Fräulein. Tell the Countess I can come no other time.'

I closed the door with a feeling of extreme thankfulness that she had gone. It seemed that by her presence she had somehow contaminated the hallway and the room beyond and I shivered in spite of the warmth of the house. Hans was hovering at the back of the hall and came forward to meet me.

'Are you all right, Fräulein?' he asked solicitously.

'Yes, thank you, Hans, but what a disagreeable old woman! It is possible she is concerned with some charity the Countess is interested in. When she is awake I will tell her the woman has been here and also what arrangements I have been able to make for her to return. You needn't worry, Hans, you did right to question her presence here,' I reassured him.

*

219

I did not know it then, but repercussions were to come long before the time of her visit the following morning. In fact they got me out of my bed before it was light, when I was aroused from sleep by Mellina's anger and the distress of her maid. I heard their voices only distantly in those first moments after I awoke, then more plainly. I jumped out of bed and hastily threw my robe over my nightgown, thrusting my feet into slippers at the same time, and ran along the corridor towards Mellina's room where the sounds were coming from.

I found Mellina pacing the floor in a fine rage while the girl cowered behind the door with tears streaming down her face. At the sight of me Mellina turned upon me like a tigress, accusing me of interference and all sorts of duplicity, saying that she would ask her husband to dismiss me and send me back to England where I belonged. Then she bundled us both out of her room saying she would see neither of us again and that the sooner we left the house the better.

'Come downstairs with me,' I said to the weeping maid, 'I'm going to make some tea. We'll both feel better after that.'

She was sobbing, her pretty country face swollen with weeping, and although I felt sorry for her our fates appeared to be somewhat similar. She sat at the kitchen table while I busied myself with cups and saucers, milk and sugar, then I sat opposite her while we waited for the kettle to boil.

'When did all this start?' I asked her quietly.

'She got me out of my bed in the middle of the night, it was dark, and she asked me if her visitor had arrived. She wasn't properly awake and it took some time to explain that she had been sleeping all day and that it was now the next day. Oh, Fräulein, she has said I must pack my bags and leave, she has no time for a maidservant who does not do as she is told, and I don't know what to do!'

'We can do nothing at the moment, at least until she has calmed down. Leave the Countess to me, Lily – take your cup of tea back to your bedroom and try to get some more sleep.' I patted her hand gently, and sounding more confident that I felt I added, 'After I have spoken to her I am sure she will not send you away.'

Obediently she did as I asked, and left alone to sip my tea in the cold kitchen I realized that I was as near to being dismissed ignominiously as I had ever been, but I did have one trump card to play. Mellina was afraid of the terrible old woman who had visited the house the night before. I was convinced she had deliberately made herself ill so that she would not have to return to the country because she had to see Madame Pickarde, who I was quite sure was in the process of blackmailing her. Very well then, two could play at that game. I could use a more subtle form of blackmail to keep my position and to enable Lily to keep hers, and things being what they were I would not hesitate to use it.

I waited until it was light and I was fully dressed before I entered Mellina's room again.

I found her sitting at her dressing table. She was dressed and in spite of her pallor she seemed more like herself. The strain was not so pronounced under the makeup she had already applied to her face and she had brushed her hair and tied it back from her face with a black velvet bow. She appeared haughty and cold in her pale mauve gown and there was no sign of welcome on the enquiring face she turned towards me.

'May I speak with you for a moment?' I asked quietly.

'What is it, Rachel? Can't you see I am busy since I can't rely on that stupid girl?'

'She is not a stupid girl, and she has done nothing wrong.'

She glared at me. 'What do you know about it? She has disregarded my wishes and I do not intend to stand for that from a girl in my employment. She can collect her wages and return to the country immediately – maids are easily come by in Vienna. That goes for you, too – disobedient servants are expendable.'

'I told her to give you the sleeping draught.'

'You told her! What right had you to interfere?'

'Your husband gave me the right when he left me in charge. He said it was not for the servants to take care of his sick wife and that I had to do what I thought was right. It is monstrously unfair to blame the girl, and if you decide to dismiss me that is equally unfair when I was only carrying out the Count's instructions.'

221

She stared at me angrily for several minutes and then quite suddenly her eyes wavered and fell before mine and with a feeling of elation I knew that I had won. She would not send either Lily or me away and it had been the mention of Max that had put the matter straight.

'Max had no right to put you in charge,' she murmured. 'I shall speak to him about it when we get back to the castle.'

'You must do as you think fit, Mellina. I spoke to your visitor, and she is coming here again this morning at ten o'clock.'

She looked startled. 'You saw Madame Pickarde?'

'Yes, though only for a few minutes. I explained that you were ill and could not be disturbed.'

'What did she say?'

'That she would come again this morning.'

She looked at me sharply, then she looked away. 'I don't know her well, she's not really a friend, she's just a friend of a friend, you understand. I'm helping her on some matters concerned with charity, that is all.'

'Yes, she informed me that she was a poor woman and that carriages cost money.'

'When did she say that?'

'When I asked if she could come again.'

'Indeed! To my knowledge Madame Pickarde makes a very lucrative living, although one would not think so when she goes around looking like a ragbag.'

She was disturbed by that weird old woman with her veiled threats and I did not believe for one moment that either of them was concerned with charity. It was none of my business and if I had hoped she would take me into her confidence I was mistaken.

'I shall go downstairs now,' Mellina said. 'Ask my maid to bring me some coffee in the Green room at the front of the house, and I will see Madame Pickarde in there when she arrives. You can answer the door as you have met the woman before, Rachel – the servants know too much of what goes on in this house as it is.'

'Very well, Mellina. May I tell Lily that there will now be no need for her to return to the country?'

'On this occasion you may, but if it happens just once more, out she goes, and you too.' She said the last three words looking at me defiantly, and I merely nodded my head acknowledging the threat before I let myself out of the door.

Lily was effusive in her thanks, but I returned to the drawing room in a thoughtful frame of mind. Promptly at ten o'clock I heard the front door bell ring and I hurried out to admit Mellina's visitor.

She looked no more prepossessing in the light of day than she had looked the previous evening. She was still wearing the faded and greasy black gown, the only difference being that now she wore a pair of black shoes instead of the carpet slippers. As I bade her good morning she smiled, showing long teeth stained with nicotine, the gaps in them even more pronounced in daylight.

'The Countess is up this morning and will see you in the Green room. Will you come with me?'

'She is better then, the pretty lady?' she asked.

'Much better, madame, the sleep did her good. I hope you will not stay too long and tire her.'

'Why, no, Fräulein – when my business is over I shall leave, have no fear on that score. I have been worried about the Countess, and I am glad I could come if only to enquire about her health.'

I stared at her without believing one single word, then I opened the Green room door to announce the visitor. Mellina was standing looking out of the window and when she spun round to look at us I could see the raw fear in her eyes. She indicated a chair, inviting the Frenchwoman to take it.

They were not friends. Mellina had shown no evidence of friendship in her greeting, only fear and a kind of loathing. I made up my mind that I would put on my outdoor clothing and wait for the woman to leave the house, then I would follow her at a distance until I had learned a little more of Madame Pickarde.

I waited in the little park across the street, sheltering behind a broad tree trunk until I saw the woman leave the house and walk down the steps. She shuffled along the road and I could see that she was smiling, evidently well pleased with her transaction and a visit that had not been without success. I hurried across the road out of sight of the house in case Mellina was watching from the window. At the corner of the park the woman hailed a cab and I did likewise, instructing the driver to follow her and stop at a discreet distance when she alighted from it. We drove through the wide thoroughfares of the city and into the narrow streets of the old town, and it was in one of these old cobbled squares that she got out. After paying the driver and looking this way and that she shuffled across the square. I too paid my driver, then I jumped down from the cab and followed her down a narrow street of crumbling houses. Before she entered one of the shops she looked quickly up the street so that I had to jump hurriedly into a doorway to prevent her from seeing me.

I waited at least ten minutes before I felt satisfied that she was not going to emerge, then taking my courage in both hands I sauntered slowly down the street, keeping in the shadows until I could see the shop. It was a jeweller's, and I wondered what a jeweller's shop was doing in such a poor area and if he ever did any business. I was only a few feet away from it when to my consternation I heard a man's voice saying, 'You have done well, madame, we didn't expect such a gem as this one. It will be better still the next time.'

The woman cackled. 'Ah yes, she is frightened now, my proud beauty! I got as much pleasure from seeing the fear in her eyes as I did from the glow of that gem there.'

'She will not speak to her husband, not even out of desperation?'

'Not she! We are safe, my friend, there is no danger that our beautiful Countess will see the error of her ways.'

'And you were unobserved?'

'Except for the girl who admitted me. She was not a servant, that one. We should know who she is and what she is doing at the Meinharts'. She is not Austrian, that I do know.'

Again there was the man's voice, saying with a wry chuckle, 'I can tell you who she is, that pretty one with the red hair and blue eyes – she is the granddaughter of the Hungarian dancer Zara.'

There was a silence before I heard the woman's voice asking, 'What has the dancer Zara or her granddaughter to do with the noble Meinharts?'

'That is something I have yet to discover. The Countess asked Roman Sadek to make a portrait from an old postcard she had found, but there is more to it than that – an old family scandal the Meinharts wouldn't like revealed, perhaps. One never knows, there might yet be something in it for us. The girl is supposed to be a governess but she is not treated like a servant. She occupies Lady Ludmilla's room and dines with the family.'

'Frau Gessler told you all this, I take it?'

'Yes indeed, and she is known to be reliable with her information.'

'Yes indeed, yes indeed,' she chuckled, and I had to leap backwards with my heart thumping painfully as she shuffled out of the jeweller's into the street. She looked neither to right nor left as she hobbled down the street and she was chuckling to herself until she rounded the corner and I could see her no more.

For a few moments I waited patiently, then I put my coat collar up and covered my red hair with a long scarf before I ventured to peer into the jeweller's window. It was a dingy little shop, in a poor quarter of the town and on a wretched street, but in the shop window were exquisite jewels that I was convinced had once adorned the necks and hands of frightened aristocratic women. Even as I looked another ring was placed in the front of the window, a dark blue opal surrounded by diamonds that flashed and gleamed. I had often admired it on the long slim fingers of Mellina's hand.

I was deeply troubled as I walked back towards the centre of the city and the tower of St Stephan's cathedral which I could see in the distance. Mellina was parting with her jewellery to that old woman and I wondered what dreadful things she had been guilty of to allow Madame Pickarde to blackmail her.

I wondered how much, if anything, Max knew, or how much he himself was involved. Even the Abbe had not known and remembering the words they had spoken about me I shivered a little as though I too had something to fear at the hands of these terrible people.

I felt unutterably helpless. Here was I, still very much a stranger in a foreign land, surrounded by unseen dangers. More than that, I was afraid that the man I loved was not as blameless as he appeared to be. I wanted to help Mellina – not for her own sake but for the sake of the name she bore, which should have been mine. I felt I could not stand by and see it smirched, but my hands were tied. All I could do was await events.

I was more than relieved to be informed on my arrival back at the house that Mellina intended to return to Meinhart the following day.

We were alone in the dining room and I thought what a ridiculous waste of space it was as we sat at either end of the long table unable to enjoy any real conversation. She seemed withdrawn, subdued, only toying with the food served to her. I noticed that she wore only her wedding ring when normally her hands blazed with jewels. She caught me looking at them and said hastily, 'I have forgotten to put on my rings. I should really put them in the safe when I am not wearing them, I have already lost or misplaced one of them.'

'Oh, I'm sorry! Which one was that?'

'Oh, you probably don't remember it. A blue opal surrounded by diamonds.'

'I remember it very well. It was a beautiful ring.'

'Yes, well, if it doesn't turn up I shall simply have to ask Max to get me another like it.'

'If a ring is so easily replaced the original cannot have carried much sentimental value.'

Her eyes snapped at me, and irritably she rose from her chair and went into the drawing room where she lounged on the sofa drawn up in front of the fire with a book on her knee. She was not reading, however, and to make conversation I said, 'It will be nice to get back to Meinhart tomorrow. Liesel will have missed her lessons.'

'She has probably been greatly relieved by your absence. I

don't understand your determination to turn her into a bluestocking. You can't tell me that you were taught all the things you are so anxious to teach her.'

'All those things and more. I should think you were too, whenever you bothered to pay attention.'

She laughed then, her good humour partially restored. 'Perhaps you're right, but what good are such studies going to be for Liesel? She will never be required to work for her living as you are having to do.'

'One never knows what will happen in a lifetime. If my father had lived I don't suppose I would have needed to work, although I am sure I should have wanted to do something with my life. I can't think that I would have been entirely happy serving afternoon tea, shopping every day along the High Street or leaving visiting cards.'

She was looking at me intently. 'What would you have put in their place?'

'I'm not sure. Perhaps writing, or painting. I might have started a dancing school. Changes in circumstances can alter one's entire life, and it's nice to feel equipped to deal with such changes if they should arise.'

'There aren't many thrills to be found in painting, writing or dancing classes – I doubt if they would have been enough for me!'

'Can you think of more exciting activities then?'

'Oh yes, Rachel, indeed I can, but I don't have to. I have a handsome, charming husband who adores me and a beautiful daughter. I have a host of friends and fortunately my husband is also very rich and can quite easily afford to replace any petty bauble I happen to have lost. We have a good life together and neither of us has any wish to change it.'

I bit my lip and returned to my book. I was aware that she was watching me with sly enjoyment and waiting for me to retaliate, knowing she had wounded me with her statement. What woman does not long for a handsome, charming husband and a child of her own? Mellina had been unkind enough and shallow enough to show me the difference between her own life and mine.

I could not help comparing the journey to Vienna when

227

Max had been my companion with the return journey to Meinhart with Mellina. She sat in her corner of the carriage morose and obviously miles away from the golden autumn sunlight slanting through the trees, whose leaves were already turning red and bronze and beginning to fall. I thought about Max's words that to be alone in the autumn meant that one would be alone all winter long. They applied all too poignantly to me, and somehow the underlying sadness of autumn touched my heart. I turned my head away so that Mellina would not see the treacherous tears that rose unbidden into my eyes.

I found myself thinking about England. The purple bloom of the heather would have gone now and the bracken would already be brittle and golden on the slopes below the rocky tors. What had I to do with dense forests of evergreens and medieval castles, or the distant snow-capped peaks shimmering in the late afternoon sunlight? At that moment I would have given all the magic of the scene before me for just one glimpse of the moor and the distant silver line of the sea. My life before I came to Meinhart had been uneventful, but there had been a calm charm to it, a feeling of stability and purpose, whereas now I felt confused and shaken by happenings both alien and evil.

Josef came lumbering out of the gatehouse to open the heavy iron gates, handling them as easily as if they were made out of matchwood. He stood near them as the carriage swept through, smiling in a sardonic fashion, but Mellina appeared oblivious to his studied insolence. As the carriage came to a standstill in the courtyard she climbed down and swept into the house, calling after her, 'Leave the luggage, I'll send one of the servants to see to it.'

I left her luggage where it was, but I could easily manage my one case without assistance from anybody.

Liesel had heard our arrival and as we entered the hall she came bounding down the stairs to fling herself into her mother's outstretched arms, and the two of them went laughing up the stairs without giving me a backward glance. I bit my lip to stop its quivering, for I felt unwelcome and sadly alone. I had not wanted Liesel to greet me as rapturously as she had greeted her mother, but a small smile perhaps, or a word of welcome, would not have come amiss. As I was halfway up the stairs Max came out of the gun room and for a brief moment out eyes met intently before he smiled and said, 'Welcome home, Rachel!'

At that moment the sunlight invaded the sombre room, warming everything it touched with long golden fingers, or was it merely the glow which his words brought into my heart?

Thirteen

The night before the Halloween ball saw an outburst of torrential rain that swept down from the mountains to swell the angry river as it crashed between the boulders. The rain and wind lashed against the trees, bending them dramatically, as though they danced some strange primeval dance out there in the forest. I lay sleepless in my bed listening to the wind moaning along the battlements above me, rattling the ancient windows, while the rain beat mercilessly against the weathered walls. If this weather continued it would indeed be a fitting background for the night of Halloween, with the thunder rolling ominously overhead and the lightning flashing in cruel forks, lighting up the rooms of the castle.

I cowered under the bedclothes, afraid that at any moment the castle which had withstood such assaults for centuries would topple from its lofty peak and lie in ruins in the moat. When at last the storm abated the sudden stillness was as eerie and terrifying as anything that had gone before. It was nearly morning and I hurriedly put on my robe and slippers and ran swiftly along the corridors towards Sophia's room. In just a few hours she would be arriving with Ernst at the castle and it had been impossible to enter her room before. Every time I had made an attempt I had found servants in the corridors, and after dinner Liesel had involved me in some card game at which to her utmost delight she had beaten me unmercifully.

It was barely light but I managed without a candle. The room looked cold in the half-light, but filled with purpose I pulled the stool next to the wardrobe so that I could stand on it, and reaching into the wardrobe with both hands I dragged out the acoloyte's suit from the back of the shelf. I felt with my fingers that the mask was still there, though I had no wish to look at it. I hunted in one of the drawers for some paper to wrap the costume in, then, with the completed parcel in my hands, I let myself quietly out of the room. I had reached the corridor where the schoolroom was situated when I heard voices coming towards me, so hastily I opened the school-room door and went inside. I stood behind the door holding my breath, waiting for the knob to turn, wondering what I should say if anybody came in, but the voices passed on and I heaved a thankful sigh of relief.

I could not risk meeting others as I walked back to my room and it was evident that the servants were up and about. My eyes roved round the schoolroom searching for a place to hide my parcel, and finally came to rest on a cupboard underneath one of the bookshelves. At the moment it was filled with old books that were no longer in use and which I intended to return to the library, so hastily I pulled them out into a pile on the carpet and pushed the parcel inside the cupboard, piling the books up in front of it as neatly as I could. I had almost finished when the door opened and Liesel stood watching me in her dressing gown, rubbing the sleep from her eyes.

'I thought I heard somebody in here,' she said. 'Surely we're not having lessons today?'

'No, of course not, but I remembered these old books and I thought I would return them to the library so that the room would look tidy if any of your mother's guests decided to come in.'

'They're not likely to come in here,' she answered me. 'It looks far more untidy with the books lying on the carpet than it did when they were in the cupboard.'

'It won't when I've taken them back immediately after breakfast.'

'But it's only just morning. Why have you started to get them out so early?'

'The storm kept me awake, and I thought I'd rather do something than lie there shivering. Didn't it keep you awake too?'

'No, but then I love it when the wind rattles and the rain beats down, just like it did last night. I was thinking what a pity it wasn't Halloween – it'll probably be a calm night tonight and the atmosphere will all have gone.'

'Are you looking forward to it? You haven't told me what you are going to wear.'

'I suppose it will have to be that new thing mother brought back from Vienna.'

'That's beautiful, why don't you like it?'

'I don't see why I always have to dress up in pale blue or pale pink, I feel like sugar icing on top of a birthday cake! What are you going to wear?'

'That black velvet dinner gown of Ludmilla's with the sable edging, it's still one of my favourites.'

'It's hardly a ball gown.'

'It isn't supposed to be a grand ball, and I'm not really a guest either. I'm only here until they decide to send you to school.'

'The sooner the better then,' she snapped, and when I laughed a little she said, 'Not just because of you, but for all those other reasons that make me hate this place.'

'What sort of reasons?'

'Oh, like not being able to see Frau Gessler, and having Sophia here for weeks when mother spends more time with her than she does with me. Besides, I should think you'll be glad to go back to England – you hardly ever see my father these days.'

'Not seeing your father is hardly an incentive, Liesel. I came here to teach you, not to be a companion to your father. Now do go along to your room or you'll catch cold and then you won't even be able to go to the Halloween ball. Are you coming down for breakfast?'

'No, not to be shown off in front of those silly people as though I was a prize poodle or something. I shall have breakfast in my room.'

'Very well then, you can go back to bed for at least another hour,' I said, determined that she should leave the room before I did. I wanted to make quite sure that the parcel was well hidden.

*

232

I looked at Mellina's guests over luncheon with dismay. The Baroness had arrived, morose and withdrawn as always. The young man who mouthed poetry was there but nobody was listening to him, and so was the blonde who had insisted on calling me deary, and who now informed me that her husband had decided to remain in the East so that she was having to sell her jewels in order to keep up appearances. She even offered to sell me a diamond bracelet cheap and went on to complain that she had lost a valuable earring and that the one left to her was of no value without its mate. I felt rather sorry for her, and later produced the earring saying I had found it on the path outside the castle. After that, regrettably, I was her closest friend.

These people were incongruous and bore no relationship to Mellina's beauty or her life style. Amongst this ill-assorted company there were a few aristocratic names, bored, lonely people living in exile, moving from one pleasure to the next, living off money they had managed to smuggle out of the country that had disowned them. There was no sign of Max and my heart sank further when I thought of the celebration ahead with Max away from the castle.

It was early afternoon when I passed through the entrance hall in time to see another group of people arriving, and this time Ernst was there with Sophia, and to my consternation Sergei too. I leaned over the balcony hoping they would acknowledge my presence, but only Ernst looked up and smiled. Then Mellina was crossing the hall to greet her guests enthusiastically, putting one arm round Sophia and the other round Sergei and drawing them into the reception room beyond the hall. My heart sank. Ernst followed with two women I had not seen before, one young and one old, looking very much like mother and daughter, and I wondered if the younger was the girl Mellina had found for him to marry. I felt unhappy and discouraged and I wished with my whole heart that the weekend was over and that we could get back to normal living.

But not for long, I thought miserably. In two more months it would all start again with the Emperor's ball and I would have been at Meinhart for a whole year.

Quite suddenly misery washed over me and I sat down on the stairs and sobbed. I so desperately wanted to go home that the feeling was like a physical pain, and I was still in tears when Liesel found me and in her sweet childlike voice asked, 'What's the matter, why are you crying?'

'I'm being a crybaby again, thinking of home I suppose,' I muttered, wiping my eyes.

She was standing on the stairs, her pretty head on one side, regarding me out of those incredibly light blue eyes, puzzled but hardly sympathetic.

'I thought you didn't have a home to go to in England?'

'I don't, but one can be homesick without exactly having a home,' I answered her, pulling myself together sternly.

'Don't you like it here?'

'Of course, it has nothing to do with that.'

'What then?'

'Oh, I suppose it's because I don't really belong here with all these people.'

'Is it all so different in England?'

'Oh yes, Liesel, very different. Twelve months ago I was busy at my desk doing something I liked doing, or listening to Miss Frobisher grumbling about the tradesmen or the shops because they didn't have what she wanted. It was all so normal.'

'This isn't normal?'

'I suppose it is for here, but it's not my kind of normal.'

'Sophia has arrived and that Russian Sergei. Is she going to marry him?'

'I don't know.'

'He's old and fat and sinister and I don't like him, but then I don't suppose Sophia likes him much either.'

'She must do if she's going to marry him.'

She looked at me with pitying scorn for a few moments. In what could well have been her mother's most bored voice she said, 'You really are very naive, Miss Arden. Perhaps it is time you went home.'

I watched her walk down the stairs and cross the hall feeling the utmost exasperation. There was no doubt about it,

I was naive when it came to Liesel, and she was right, it was time I went home. I had lost Sophia's friendship and probably Ernst's too, I had never had Mellina's or Liesel's and I was desperately in love with a man who didn't love me. I didn't know what was in store for me at the Halloween ball, but if they expected Sophia to take her place as the acolyte, wearing her boy's costume and that terrible mask, they would have to find it first. Naive I might be, but I intended to save Sophia if I could.

The long day wore on dismally. It was dark and cloudy and the sun never once managed to break through the low heavy clouds, although the gales of the day before had completely disappeared. My sense of depression was unrelieved by any promise of joy in the evening ahead of me. I was not interested in the ball, and although there was an air of tense excitement in the people I spoke to, I had a feeling that it was not the ball that engendered it.

I looked through the window after lunch in time to see Ernst escorting the two women he had arrived with along the path towards the stables. They all wore riding clothes so it was obvious he intended to ride with them around the estate. He had made no effort to see me alone so once again I reached the conclusion that this girl was the one who had been picked out for him. I was about to turn away when I saw Sophia and Sergei also leaving the castle. They made an incongruous couple, Sophia dainty and feminine in her green velvet riding habit, and Sergei pompously strutting beside her.

I felt unutterably miserable and went along to the schoolroom to see if I could find something to do. There was no sign of Liesel and from the silence in the castle I surmised that the guests were either resting in their rooms after lunch or had gone out. The schoolroom fire had not been lit although the day was chilly, but before I left I went once more to the cupboard to make sure the parcel was still in its place. I pulled out one or two of the books making a space wide enough to insert my hand, relieved when it encountered the texture of wrapping paper.

I looked inside Liesel's room but she was not there and I then went to Sophia's room. I knocked on the door in case anyone should see me standing there, but when there was no response and none of the servants were about I went inside. Her cases lay open on the floor and no attempt had been made to unpack them apart from the riding habit, which must have been lying on top. Otherwise the room looked as unlived-in as it had that morning.

I was about to leave when I saw hanging on a hook behind the door a black silk domino. It had not been there the last time I had been in that room, and unless Sophia had brought it with her somebody else had put it there to await her arrival.

I took it down and slipped my arms into it. It covered my clothing entirely but I did not try to pull the hood over my head and I took it off extremely puzzled. I replaced it on the hook and told myself that perhaps the domino was necessary to cover that unusual boy's costume whether she accompanied the rest of them to the forest or merely passed from her own room to the old chapel. Satisfied with my reasoning I listened for a few moments for any sound in the corridor outside, then I let myself out of the room.

Fourteen

In spite of Mellina's hints that the evening was one of the highlights of the social year, I had not bothered to buy a new gown during my stay in Vienna, so I wore Ludmilla's black velvet dinner gown which seemed to me now like an old friend. It became my pale skin and dark red hair, and when I saw some of the beaded and sequinned creations around me I was glad of its simplicity, its only adornment being the rich sable fur.

Mellina, to my utmost surprise, was also wearing black, a colour which enhanced her delicate fairness to perfection, but it also emphasized the nervous gestures of her long slim hands and the eyes which seemed too large for her pale face. Her laughter seemed forced and too shrill, and she laughed too often at inanities.

Ernst had been placed between the young woman and the older one, and they were introduced as Princess Natalia and her daughter Anna – Russian, I assumed, like Sergei. Liesel sat next to her mother, beautiful as always in pale blue, her eyes missing nothing. There was a strange half smile on her lips which I felt boded no good for someone and I wondered if that someone could be me. She seemed excited, hardly touching the food on her plate, and when I looked about me I saw that other guests too were only toying with the delicious food set before them. When I glanced at Sophia she looked quickly away and once I saw her lips quivering as though she was about to cry.

We drifted into one of the reception rooms to drink coffee and it was then that Sophia asked to be excused as she didn't feel very well. I thought I was unobserved as I followed her into the corridor and I ran to catch up with her before she reached her room.

'Sophia,' I cried, 'if you are not well I would like to help you.'

Her eyes opened wide, frightened, and the next moment she was leaning against the wall sobbing while I strove to calm her.

'Oh Rachel, Rachel!' she was sobbing. 'It's all gone so terribly wrong, and now I'm afraid and there is nobody I can tell, nobody!'

'You can tell me.'

'No, no, I can't, I can never get away from them now, I know too much about them. It all seemed so innocent, such good fun at first, but now it's too late for me, it's too late for any of us!'

'My dear, you need help. Can't you confide in me?'

'I can't involve you, Rachel. You should go away while there's still time.'

There was a sound from behind us and I saw Sophia's eyes open wide with fear and felt her shrink away.

A man's voice said, 'You are ill, Sophia. I came to see if I could be of assistance.'

I turned round and found the Russian standing behind me. He was speaking to Sophia but he was looking at me out of cold expressionless eyes, polite but strangely menacing. I removed my arm from Sophia's shoulders and stood up straight against the wall so that he had to look up into my face, and I was glad that I was so much taller than he. At all costs I must not let this man see I was afraid of him, and trying to keep my voice calm I said, 'Sophia is not well, I am taking her to her room where she can rest before the ball.'

'Perhaps I should see to her – after all she is my betrothed.'

'I'm sorry, I didn't know, but I am her friend and this is woman's business. I'm very much afraid if she does not rest now there will be no dancing for her later on.'

I had won. Suddenly he dropped his gaze while I took hold of the trembling girl and drew her towards her room. She sat on the edge of the bed shivering, her teeth chattering. I poked the dull embers of the fire into some semblance of a blaze, adding more logs from the scuttle beside the fireplace, then fixing her with a stern eye I said, 'Like his master he brings you no warmth, Sophia.'

She looked at me startled for a moment, then she put her head down on her hands and sobbed again. I went to sit next to her on the bed. 'Don't you want to go to the ball, Sophia?' I asked gently.

'I must go, they'll only come looking for me if I don't.'

'Who are they?'

'Sergei and those other people. He's very rich but he knows I don't want to marry him. I don't love him, I'm afraid of him.'

'Good heavens, girl, you don't need to be afraid of such a man. This is the year 1900. Why don't you just tell him you don't want him?'

'Because I don't trust him, I don't trust any of them! I know too much, they can't afford to let me go.'

We both looked round with startled eyes and I knew that she thought, as I thought, that somebody was listening outside her door. I put my finger to my lips and crept across the room while she watched, her eyes wide with terror. All was quiet, but in my imagination I was sure that behind that door some other person was straining to hear just as I was.

I tiptoed back to the bed and whispered, 'Try to rest now, and come downstairs when you feel better. I'll come up again if you don't appear.'

She didn't answer me, she was too frightened to speak. I left her room quietly and as I turned the corner to go back to the hall I was just in time to see a black-clad figure slip through the door at the top of the corridor. I was sure it was Frau Gessler, although I had not seen her in this part of the house for several weeks.

Mellina was waiting for me at the bottom of the stairs, her face inscrutable, and with her were Sergei and Liesel.

'How is Sophia?' she asked coldly.

'Not very well, I'm afraid. She will come down when she feels a little better.'

'Oh well, I'll go up to see her presently. You can leave her to me now, Rachel, there is no need for you to concern yourself again.'

'Very well, Mellina,' I said meekly. 'I am sure she will be well looked after,' and with all the aplomb I could muster I walked away.

I did not enjoy the ball, I was bored by it. I did not like dancing with men who held me too closely, or others who poured silly flatteries into my unwilling ears. I danced only once with Ernst and that was in a quadrille, and I thought that he too seemed unlike himself, as though his mind was on other matters far more important than a ball. I expected it to go on until the small hours of the morning, but soon after midnight I became sensitive to an atmosphere of unrest amongst the dancers. There was much consulting of watches and yawns of sleepy boredom, until one by one they left the ballroom leaving only a handful of guests to dance the last waltz.

Sophia had returned to the ball, her pallor and weariness disguised by heavier makeup than she normally wore, but I had no opportunity to speak with her. Goodnights were said amongst the guests, and I went up to my bedroom where I put on my robe over my evening dress and sat shivering in front of the fire, watching the dying embers fall dismally into the grate. There was a strange unnatural quiet over the house, like that eerie dark quiet that comes before and after a storm, and I could feel by my racing heart that I was tensed up and waiting for I knew not what.

I don't know how long I sat before I became aware of vague whisperings and movements all around me. I rose from my chair and moved over to the window. It was a night of full moon, but it was hidden by low clouds and as yet I could not distinguish the path below my window. I heard a soft click from the door next to mine, and then soft footfalls as my neighbour left his room. Soon they would all come pouring out of the castle and head for the forest. I was as sure of this as I was of the full moon hiding behind the clouds, and as though aware of my thoughts the clouds suddenly seemed to scud away and the moon rode high in the sky, lighting up the castle with its cold blue light.

Now there were figures below me, moving in twos and threes towards the drawbridge, all enveloped in black dominoes with the hoods pulled up over their heads. Now and then the gleam of a woman's gown showed where the small chill wind blew the dominoes away. As they moved towards the edge of the forest their torches were lit and the firelight leaped up in a great blaze.

I hung back from the window. If they looked up they would see my curtains drawn, and I knew that in her room Sophia would be preparing for her part in the celebration and the moment when those hooded figures took their places in the old chapel.

Hoping to encounter no latecomers to that unholy procession I let myself out of my room and hurried towards Sophia's. I heard her opening and closing drawers frantically and sobbing quietly to herself, and I knew why. She was looking for her costume and was unable to find it. I opened the door and went inside.

She was in her robe, standing on the stool I had stood upon to reach into the back of her wardrobe, and in a quiet voice I said, 'It isn't there, Sophia.'

She turned to face me, her eyes wide open and staring. The pupils were strangely distended, which made me wonder if they had given her a drug to prepare her for her part in the ceremony ahead.

'Where is it?' she asked plaintively. 'I must find it and there isn't much time.'

'I took it away and I have hidden it. You can't go without the costume, so you had better get back into bed and forget you ever heard of that devil's ritual.'

I could tell that she wasn't fully understanding my words, all she understood was that the costume was not there and she had to find it. I helped her down from the stool, then I pulled her across to the bed.

'There is nothing to be afraid of, Sophia. If they come to you in the morning you just say that you left the costume in the wardrobe and that it is no longer there. Perhaps they will realize that their secret is known and that they are in danger of being exposed to the authorities.'

'They're not afraid of anything. They are rich, powerful people, and I'm afraid of what they'll do to me when they find out I have betrayed them.'

'You haven't betrayed them. You haven't done anything. Have you a sleeping draught?'

'Yes, in the bathroom.'

'Do you normally take one?'

'No, but the doctor prescribed them for me at home because I wasn't sleeping very well.'

I found the draught, mixed it with water and urged her to drink it. 'You can tell them I gave you a sleeping draught and that you don't remember anything else, and I shall say I gave it to you because you had been unwell during the evening. Don't worry, Sophia, everything is going to be all right.'

I spoke with more confidence than I felt, but she took the draught willingly enough and I waited for several minutes after seeing her eyelids flutter and close. Satisfied that she was in a deep slumber, I pulled the bedclothes over her and taking the domino from behind the door, I let myself out into the corridor.

I was not sure at first what to do. I was too late to follow them into the forest, and from the window I saw that they were in the clearing and that the strange rites I had witnessed on that other night had already begun. I put the domino over my gown and made my way down the stairs into the hall, hugging the sides of the staircase where the shadows were darkest. Now the bright moonlight shone through the windows, throwing diamond patterns on the polished floor, lighting up the suits of old armour so that their menacing forms looked as though they would step out at any moment to bar my way.

The night was cold but I was too excited to feel it, and as I stepped through the door leading into the courtyard I saw that the procession was already returning from the forest, walking slowly and looking neither to right nor left. I waited until they reached the path and passed below the castle walls, then I stepped out behind them, walking with head bowed. They seemed unaware that another had joined their ranks. They had stopped their chanting and we walked in silence.

The hood pulled over my head shaded my face, and in any case none of them seemed at all curious about their neighbours. They had done this many times before, and now the door leading into the old chapel was open and we were descending the stairs cut into the rock.

Inside the chapel I looked around me in amazement under cover of my hood, as we knelt between the rows of pews on scarlet velvet cushions. It blazed with candlelight, and what I had taken to be a tall cupboard was now open in the form of a reredos behind the altar. Black candles were lit in the silver candlesticks which now stood on a black coffin pall which covered the altar, but it was the crucifix bearing the figure of Christ hanging upside down which stunned me most.

Once again I found myself remembering my father's stolen chalices and vestments from the vestry of the old stone church in distant Devonshire, and I tried to remember all I had heard on that night about the Black Mass. On one side of the reredos was painted the lifelike head of a goat, its eyes malevolent, its horns adorned with jewels, and on the other side was painted the figure of a youth, as beautiful as a Greek god, with a face as fragile as a girl's and with eyes bluer than an alpine lake and as cold. I shuddered as they seemed to look into mine, for they were filled with all the sadness of the ages.

At that moment I knew I could not stay. God only knew what would happen in that room after the Mass was over, what obscenities, what abominations would be committed in the name of Satan. I had seen enough, and slowly, hardly moving at all, I started to back away. Then from the side of the chapel two figures emerged and I shall never know what stopped me gasping aloud in my amazement.

First came the tall masked figure of a man clad in the robes of a priest, complete with the alb and the stole, similar to those worn by my father on special feast days. But it was the smaller figure walking behind him that concerned me most and my heart lurched sickeningly as my eyes tried to penetrate the disguise. The acolyte, clad in the velvet breeches and the white lace-edged surplice, face covered by that awesome mask, turned to face the priest, swinging the censer this way and that so that the room soon became filled with thick acrid

243

smoke and the small slender figure of the acolyte grew dim through the mist.

It was impossible that this figure could be Sophia, but who had taken her place? I had watched Sophia swallow the sleeping drug with my own eyes, she couldn't possibly have been wide enough awake to carry out her part, but try as I would I was unable to picture any of Mellina's guests small enough or slender enough to wear that boy's costume. I was almost at the door now, my feet inching their way slowly backwards, but as I put out my hands behind me to feel the door, they encountered instead the softness of another hooded figure and I felt myself grasped firmly in strong cruel hands and pushed forward into the light.

The priest ceased his chanting and the acolyte turned to stare through those incredibly long black silken lashes of the mask. The hood was pulled roughly from my head, allowing my hair to fall loosely around my shoulders. I was immediately surrounded by black-robed figures staring at me through masks as hideous and obscene as any I might have dreamed of in my wildest nightmare. They were masks of animal heads, vicious and snarling, or of men and women, beautiful but depraved, hideous and sinister. I struggled, but I had no hope of freeing myself from those strong pitiless hands which held me like a vice. The acolyte dropped the censer with its gold chains with a clatter on the floor and started to run for dear life towards the door. Another figure sprang forward to restrain her and she screamed, terrified. They struggled, the small figure of the acolyte fighting like a tigress, kicking and screaming at the black figure who strove to hold her. Suddenly I saw the gleam of steel and the downward flash of a knife, and with a small chilling cry the acolyte lay still on the floor, the white surplice stained with a growing patch of bright red blood.

After that it seemed all hell was let loose. The entire chapel erupted into screams as men and women jostled with each other to get out of the door. Finally there were only a handful of people left behind including myself, all staring at that small still figure on the floor.

One of the black-robed figures stepped forward to kneel

beside it and at that moment the hood fell away to reveal Mellina's pale golden hair. She had already removed the mask she had been wearing and her face was pale as alabaster as she bent forward to remove the mask from the acolyte's face. Then she let out such a scream of despair it seemed to pierce me to the bone. It was not Sophia's face which lay staring up at her, the blue eyes wide open and sightless, it was Liesel who was lying dead on the cold stone floor. Mellina fell on the body, sobbing and wailing as she clutched it to her, while the priest knelt beside her and tried vainly to comfort her.

The hands which grasped me never relaxed their hold for one moment while all this was happening. I could feel fingers biting into my flesh until I cried out with pain. Then Frau Gessler stepped forward and if I had never seen hatred in a woman's face I was seeing it then, so raw and terrible that I recoiled before those baleful glaring eyes.

'It was you who took the costume, you!' she screamed at me. 'I saw you go into the lady's room, I saw you with the parcel! You hid it in the schoolroom and the child found it and that is why she is dead and Fräulein Sophia is alive. It is you who should be dead, it is you who made it happen!'

'It wasn't I who killed her,' I croaked, but the hands holding me only took a firmer grip. Now the priest put Mellina away from him and came towards me. I knew that in just a few seconds I would be looking up into Max's eyes, seeing in them all the anger and loathing he must feel for me, and piteously I stared up at the tall figure wearing a mask fashioned in the likeness of the youth on the reredos, the cold beautiful face of Adonis. But the eyes blazing down into mine were not Max's dark ones, they were eyes that flashed blue steel behind that sad expressionless mask, and I remember feeling one shining moment of joy before I recognized that they belonged to Ernst. That was the moment I slipped into merciful unconsciousness.

They threw cold water over me to make sure that I missed nothing of the torture they planned for me, and my captor picked me up in his arms as easily as if I had been a feather. I knew by the feel of his hands that it was Josef who held me, so easily but so remorselessly that I made no attempt to scream. None of them was blaming the man who had stabbed Liesel for her murder, they were blaming me, and I could see now that he had removed his hood and mask that it was Sergei the Russian. He was standing dazed, with his eyes on the ground, and neither Ernst or Mellina had any further interest in me. They stood around the body of the child while Josef and Frau Gessler took me down the dark corridors towards the dungeons, and I already knew that they would be pitiless and without mercy.

They were speaking in some guttural dialect I couldn't understand. Josef set me down on the floor while Frau Gessler went to light one of the torches sticking out from the wall in a bracket, and by its light I could see that another figure had joined them.

'You will stay here until morning,' Josef told me, 'then I shall come for you.'

'Where will you take me, what will you do with me?' I asked him painfully.

His bold eyes looked over me slowly so that I shrank back against the rock and Frau Gessler tittered coarsely, cruel, amused laughter as she gloated over my plight. She had detested me since that first moment when I arrived at Meinhart, and more so as the weeks and months passed and I had used all my influence to remove her from any contact with Liesel. Now I was to pay for my interference as Josef smiled down at me, saying, 'That will depend on how long you continue to please me. The master will never know what happened to his proud high-stepping beauty, but I won't keep you for long in case they come here looking for you. They will never find you in the forest, Fräulein, they never find anything in the forest. In a few short hours nothing is recognizable when the birds and the animals have taken their share.'

It was then that the third figure stepped forward, and reaching out for my hair she wound it round her fingers making me cry out with pain as she lifted my head to stare at her. I could only see her eyes glittering through the mask of a cat's head but I had already recognized the rings on her fingers. She twisted my hair cruelly, but she was looking at Josef.

'I could make use of this one. There are gentlemen from the East who would pay a high price for such a beauty.'

'But not yet, Mother Pickarde,' Josef said smiling down at her. 'See, my fine lady,' he said leering at me, 'now you have two choices. First me and then the forest, or else the soft bed of some rich Eastern gentleman with a taste for pink flesh.'

'There is to be no choice, Josef,' Frau Gessler cried. 'It is the forest for that one, nothing else while my baby lies dead in the castle there.'

'Be quiet, woman,' Madame Pickarde said, 'it is not your business.'

'It is my business to see that she pays for what she has done,' Frau Gessler shouted, but the Frenchwoman ignored her.

'Come now, Josef, what is it to be, a pocket full of gold which will buy you a dozen willing women, or one night with the unwilling girl there before you bury her in the forest?'

Frau Gessler was screaming abuse at them, threatening what she would do if they allowed me to live. Suddenly Josef struck her full in the face, sending her reeling back against the dungeon wall. Her head struck the rock with a sickening thud and she gave a low moan before she slithered down to the floor, her head hanging at a strange angle as if her neck was broken. I looked at him horror-stricken but he only laughed.

'You will have good company in the forest, Fräulein, if I decide to take you there,' he said, and then he and the Frenchwoman laughed.

'There isn't much time,' the woman snapped. 'Who knows what will happen upstairs now the girl is dead? Whatever we decide we shall have to be quick.'

'We can do nothing yet,' he muttered. 'She will have to stay here until we decide what is to be done with her.'

'Please, please don't leave me here, not with her,' I pleaded piteously, but they only stared at me. Josef reached out for two chains hanging close to me on the rock face and before I was aware of it he had fastened two thick steel bands around my wrists, so tightly that they made me cry out with pain as the metal bit into my flesh.

He stood back with a grin on his face, well pleased with his handiwork, but it was the widow Pickarde who terrified me most at that moment. With the toe of her shoe she kicked the body of Frau Gessler so that she fell beside me, her eyes wide open, glazed, but staring up at me as though they could still see.

'She is not a pretty sight, that one,' she leered, 'but she will serve to remind you that we are not engaged in playing games with you. Why couldn't you mind your own business, girl? But no, you must meddle, you must play the heroine and protect the lady. You see yourself as an avenging angel? This is where your meddling has brought you.'

'You said we must hurry, Mother Pickarde,' Josef muttered, moving anxiously away. 'It is you who keep us here now.'

'Indulge me for one moment more, my friend,' she said, cackling softly to herself, showing those incredible green pointed teeth, her face pressed close to mine so that I could smell her fetid breath against my face and the stench of her unwashed body and stained clothes.

'You were high-handed to poor Mother Pickarde when she came to the house on the Ringstrasse, were you not? Me a poor old woman with her beauty long since gone, you with your soft white flesh and your beautiful young face. Well, it is my turn now, my pretty one, and there is no one to help you. The Count is far away and uncaring, the Countess only concerned with the death of her child, and the Baron will have no pity on you for destroying his nice comfortable life, even if he did once look at you with desire.'

I was staring at her with huge horror-filled eyes, my mind so tormented I could hardly comprehend the menace in her words; I only knew that her eyes were pitiless in her evil face. Josef too was staring at her, his base peasant's brain unable to follow the subtlety of her cruelty.

'Are you not done?' he said, taking her by the arm, but she shook him off and moving back into the shadows she picked up two long rusting instruments of torture which she thrust suddenly before my eyes.

'See, my pretty, here is a branding iron that could make its mark so decoratively on that smooth white flesh of yours, and here too is another toy. They knew well, those old ones, how to make their prisoners wish they had never been born. Can you not see how easily this little tool could rob those violet blue eyes of yours of their sight for ever?'

'Enough, mother, enough,' Josef cried. 'You've had your little game, do you want them to find us here?'

Reluctantly she laid the instruments beside me, then cackling with obscene laughter she said, 'Sleep well, my pretty, very soon you may be asked to sleep for ever. We'll leave the old woman to guard you in the darkness.'

I watched them walk away from me, taking the torch with them, leaving me in the darkness and the silence, with the body of Frau Gessler only a few feet away, and I never knew if it was still night or if dawn had crept up unaware of the tragedies the night had produced.

I do not know how long I lay on that cold stone floor. Time meant nothing to me in the darkness, I was only aware of the cold and the damp eating into my bones and I struggled to ease my cramped limbs and my aching and bruised wrists. I was remembering Frau Gessler's eyes filled with hatred, now staring lifelessly at me in the darkness, but I had more reason to fear the obscene cruelty of the other woman. She was only concerned with the money or the jewels she would get out of it, she was a leech, living on the fringe of the rich and famous, just waiting for one mistake, one little fall from grace, to follow it with her threats of exposure and the increasing demands for payment for her silence.

I knew Josef would kill me, for however much he desired me he couldn't afford to keep me alive, but it was what he would do to me before he killed me that terrified me most. He would not dare to leave me in the dungeons longer than was necessary in case they were searched, but I found myself thinking about the forest as I had often glimpsed it from the drive: the dark reaches of undergrowth, the tall trees through which the sun never shone, and the relentless approach of hungry birds and animals. From one of the corners I heard a scuffle and I started to scream, then I heard the alarmed rustling and squeaking of rats and I screamed until I could scream no more to scare them away.

It seemed like an eternity before I heard voices in the darkness and saw the gleam of candlelight shining on bare rock. They were coming for me at last, and I strained back against the wall wishing that I could die of terror before they reached my side.

I heard the low sound of men's voices, unrecognizable in that first instant, and I was sobbing painfully as I heard the click of the lock releasing the bands which surrounded my wrists; then I felt them being eased away gently from my bruised and swollen flesh. I was past caring, even the unexpected gentleness brought no ray of hope, but then, incredibly, came the indescribable relief of Max's voice saying, 'Give me your hands, Rachel. Are you able to stand?'

I struggled, but I could not stand unaided, and as on that other occasion when he had found me in the crypt he said to his companions, 'Take the candelabra before us, I shall have to carry her.'

He lifted me up, keeping between me and my grisly companion on the floor. Then he carried me all along the corridors and up several flights of stairs to the hall above, while I lay quietly in his arms with my head resting against his shoulder. Neither of us spoke as we followed the flame of the candles.

When we reached the drawing room and I felt myself lowered on the couch in front of the fire I saw that the candles had been carried by Herr Pacherov and that with him was the Abbe. They both looked down at me in consternation while my hands tried to take the glass of brandy Max was holding to my trembling lips.

How enchanting was the gleam of firelight on a bowl of late autumn roses, how exquisite the glow of velvet and the bloom on a bowl of purple grapes standing on a small wine table near the window! How dear the everyday sound of a clock ticking on the mantelpiece and logs crackling in the grate, sounds I had thought never to hear again. I started to speak but Max said, 'Not now, Rachel. There will be plenty of time for talking when all this is behind you. There is a fire in your room and one of the servants will bring you some food. I want you to stay in your room until you feel better, then perhaps next week you will be well enough to travel.'

'Travel!' I echoed in a small voice.

'I will write to your friends the Liptmanns, I am sure they will allow you to stay there until you are feeling better. If it is not convenient I have a good friend who is a doctor with his own sanatorium in the mountains. The Abbe knows it well, you can be taken care of there.'

'But I am not ill, I don't need a sanatorium and there is no reason why I should leave.' I started to babble about it all being my fault that Liesel was dead and I had not known what harm I was doing, but he silenced me gently.

It was daylight when I awoke. A young maid was sitting in the chair pulled up in front of a glowing fire. She came to ask me if I felt better when she saw me struggling to sit up.

'I don't know,' I answered her, 'I don't know how I feel. What time is it?'

'Just after two o'clock, Fräulein.'

'It is Wednesday?'

'No, it is Saturday.'

'But I can't have been sleeping all that time, it's almost a week!'

'Yes, Fräulein, but you have had terrible nightmares so a doctor was called and gave you sleeping draughts. Now you will feel ready for something to eat, you have had nothing but liquids for several days.'

She went away and left me staring towards the window but I was not seeing the blue sky and the white scudding clouds. Painfully I was remembering the scene in the old chapel and my own plight in the dungeons below, and afraid of my memories I tried to get out of my bed to find somebody willing to reassure me that the events of that night were unreal, only happenings in one of my nightmares and nothing more. I slid my feet out of bed but when I came to stand on them I would have fallen if I had not clutched hold of the bedpost. I was so weak.

The maid came back with a loaded tray, and seeing my predicament she put the tray down and came to help me back into bed.

'You must not get up until the doctor says you are well enough,' she admonished me. 'Now you must eat and soon you will be well and strong.'

'I must speak with Count Meinhart, please ask him if he will see me as soon as possible.'

'I will give him your message, Fräulein, as soon as I am able. Now sit up against the pillows and eat.'

I ate some warm soup and a little lightly cooked fish dutifully under her watching eyes, then I asked if I could sit in the chair in front of the fire. She seemed doubtful, but after a while with her assistance I managed to walk to the chair, although it seemed like a mile. I watched her make my bed, smoothing the covers, pulling the rich bedspread over it, and as I watched I started to ask questions, all of which she met with a sweet smile and gently dismissive answers until I felt I could have screamed with frustration.

'The castle is so quiet!' I wailed. 'Please, please ask someone to come to me – I don't care who it is but I must speak to somebody.'

'Please be patient, Fräulein, a few hours and someone will come,' was all I got in reply.

She left me at last and as soon as she had gone I was determined to walk to the window even if I had to crawl along the floor like a child. With the help of furniture I was able to reach it and I sat staring out, unable to believe that the scene before me could be unchanged. The drawbridge still crossed the still waters of the moat studded with waterlilies and in the distance the trees of the forest stood straight and tall beyond the river. It seemed like a thousand years since I had seen those same trees aglow from the light of flaming torches carried aloft by black-robed figures. A slight mist shrouded the lake, obscuring the distant mountains, and it felt chilly away from the fire.

I had no idea how long I sat staring out of the window, my

mind filled with unanswered questions, when suddenly emerging through the mist came a group of people walking slowly along the path which skirted the lake. I watched eagerly, at first unable to recognize any of those dim figures, but as they grew closer I made out the rotund form of the Abbe and the tall gangling one of Herr Pacherov. Then my heart leaped as I saw Max. He was walking with Sophia, and although my eyes searched for Mellina she was not there. Suddenly the truth dawned upon me; they were coming from the private burial ground across the lake. I wondered miserably if this was the day they had buried Liesel.

I struggled back to my chair near the fire, shivering. My teeth were chattering, not entirely from the cold by the window, but from that other more terrifying cold that came with memories. The little maid came back and with a dimpled smile said, 'Count Meinhart has returned now, Fräulein, and I have asked Otto to tell him that you are awake and asking for him.'

I thanked her and she said, 'You are very pale, Fräulein. Would you not rather go back to bed?'

'No, but I would like to see what I look like. Will you pass me that mirror from the dressing table?'

I was shocked at my pale face and dark-rimmed eyes. I looked as though I had been suffering from some malady for a considerable time, with my lacklustre hair and haunted eyes.

'I will brush your hair for you. We did not like to waken you so nothing has been done with your hair for days.' The maid reached for my hairbrush, and for the next few minutes I let her attend to it although every brush stroke only increased the ache in my head.

There was a brief knock on the door, and the maid went to open it. With a little curtsey she went out, leaving Max to close the door behind her. He pulled up another chair and sat down opposite me. He was wearing black mourning clothes and a black cravat, and in answer to the unspoken question in my eyes he nodded.

'Yes, about an hour ago.'

'I saw you walking back from across the lake, but I didn't see Mellina.'

'No, she is in her room and has been kept heavily sedated since it happened. Are you sure you feel well enough to talk, Rachel?'

'Oh yes, please, I must talk! There is so much I have to tell you, so very much I feel responsible for. If I don't talk to somebody I'm sure I shall go mad!'

'I already know most of what you have to tell me. The Abbe told me about the mask and your visit to its maker in Vienna. He told me of your efforts to protect Sophia, for whom you had a great affection; you were not to know that Liesel would find that costume and wear it. There is no blame attached to you, Rachel, but I wish you had taken me into your confidence a little more.'

'How could I? I didn't know who were my friends or how deeply you yourself were involved. I thought at one time I could trust Ernst but then I decided I would tell him no more, and I am so glad I did not.'

'I tried to protect you as much as possible by saying I was going away and then returning unexpectedly. I did this on Good Friday and again on Walpurgis Night because I had been expecting something disastrous to happen for a long time. Unfortunately Ernst saw me returning the second time, so their celebration was brief.'

'You knew Mellina was involved with it?'

'I knew that the gossip about her was true – there would have been far more gossip if everything about Mellina had been known – but she was my wife and it was my duty to protect her, and more than her, my good name and the honour of a noble family.'

I said nothing to that, as I had no great cause to love that noble family, but after a few moments I asked, 'What will they do now that Liesel is dead? I saw the Russian stab her. Why did he do that when he thought it was Sophia and was supposed to be in love with her?'

'Sophia was expendable and they were never entirely sure of her. They could not afford to let the acolyte escape in her telltale costume in case she found someone in the castle to help her and then their secret would be out. Love, my dear, is not important to people like that. Liesel ran because she did not want to be discovered wearing the costume, and that was her undoing.'

'What is to happen now?'

'Your jailers, Josef and Madame Pickarde, are already in the hands of the police and they are searching for the others. Some of them will already have left the country. Borders are of little consequence to people with enough money to move freely from one country to another. Sergei, the Russian, has been handed over to the authorities for deportation. He will face his punishment at the court of St·Petersburg.'

'And what of Sophia and Mellina?'

'As I said, Mellina is too distraught just now to remember anything. Sophia is waiting to see you before she goes home to Salzburg this evening.'

'Yes, I would like to see Sophia. I'm not sorry I tried to protect her, she was always kind to me and I couldn't believe she had taken part in this knowingly.'

'No, but she will tell you her own story when she comes to see you.'

'I shall not be needed here at Meinhart now.'

'Alas, no, I have arranged for you to go to the Liptmanns in Vienna as soon as you are well enough to travel.'

'I would rather go home to England.'

'That is impractical. You have no home to go to in England and the Liptmanns are kind people – you can stay with them until you feel stronger and better able to face the future. Herr Pacherov is returning to Vienna, he will escort you in a few days from now.'

Max had risen to his feet and stood looking down at me. I was unable to read the expression on his face as he bent forward and gently kissed me, the kiss of a brother for a sister, a friend for a friend. Then he was gone and at that moment I believed the rest of my life had gone with him.

Sophia came, subdued in her gown of mourning, but her face was serene and untroubled now and for that I was grateful. It had all seemed like a game to Sophia, an extension of the carnival, perhaps a little wild, a little daring, riskily different, but something that had no real meaning for her. It had only been much later that she realized what she had done and then it was too late, because they dared not let her resume her ordinary happy life in case in her innocence she talked. That was when Mellina found Sergei for her, and then she became afraid.

She wept as she thanked me for my part in saving her that night, but it didn't ease my own feeling of guilt. I should have known that Liesel, with her recklessness and disdain for any kind of authority, would look for that costume after she had seen me removing books from the schoolroom cupboard before it was light.

Three days later I returned to Vienna still harassed by my feelings of guilt, believing that I was leaving my youth and my hope of happiness for ever behind me.

Fifteen

The Liptmanns were very kind to me in the weeks that followed my return to Vienna, but it seemed as though I would never recover from the listlessness that took hold of me after the nightmares were over. They tried to involve me in the excitement of the approaching carnival season but although I tried to appear interested I do not think I deceived them for a moment. I had no desire to go out into the city to join in the revelry and although I listened to Frau Liptmann's descriptions of the balls and the gowns the women were wearing, in reality my heart was weighted down with apathy and it seemed to cause me an almost physical pain when I remembered that it was only just a year ago that I was dancing in the Prater with Ernst and Sophia, unaware of the tragedies which would soon both separate and unite us.

There were times when I asked questions of the Liptmanns to see if they could tell me anything about Meinhart and the people concerned, but always they professed not to have heard, and this year there had been no mention of them in either magazine or newspaper. Mostly I lay on a couch pulled up before a glowing fire with a rug over my knees, and watched the snowflakes fall onto the linden trees outside the window. I hated the lethargy which I found so difficult to shake off and although I made great efforts to appear better when my hosts were with me, in their absence all I could think of was that fairy-tale castle on its hostile crag and the sound of sleigh bells across the snow.

I had received two visitors, Herr Pacherov, the Count's lawyer, who came bearing gifts of flowers and the good wishes of the Count for my welfare, and the Abbe, who sat in the large chair opposite the couch, smiling benevolently in my direction like a toby jug. They had both been well primed to discuss nothing of the past with me, consequently they left me more frustrated than ever and not a little hurt that Max himself had not written or called.

At the beginning of February I spoke of returning home but the Liptmanns convinced me that I must stay longer, that I made up to them for the absence of their daughter who was travelling abroad with her husband and children, or that I was company for Frau Liptmann when her husband was away on duties connected with the opera house.

It was a dismal day at the beginning of April and I was sitting in the study trying to write letters to my stepfather and Miss Frobisher in England. I was aware of the steady drip of raindrops from the trees in the garden and I was finding that I had very little to say, when the door opened and Frau Liptmann's smiling face appeared round it.

'You have a visitor in the drawing room, Rachel. Leave your letters for now and I'll have some tea sent in to you.'

For a few moments she held me at arm's length looking at me very closely. Seemingly satisfied she said, 'You are looking better, my dear. We will see what your visitor thinks.'

My heart was leaping wildly as I opened the drawing room door. How I wanted it to be Max waiting for me there! But it was Sophia, a happy blooming Sophia looking as radiant as on the day I first saw her. She came forward to embrace me.

Clad in the luxury of velvet and furs she was an exquisite picture and she was happy, so much I saw after I had recovered from that first swift moment of disappointment. Just as in the old days she chattered merrily away and I listened to her quietly with a smile on my face.

'I wanted to come much sooner, but everybody said you had to rest and seeing me might only remind you of those terrible things that happened.'

Remind me! Dear God, how could I ever forget? She looked at me tremulously, and then throwing her arms around my neck she said, 'Darling Rachel, I'll never be able to repay you, never! It was all my fault that you had to spend that terrible time in the dungeon. I was so stupid and so foolish, I don't deserve that you should ever forgive me.'

'It's over now, Sophia, and it's better if we never speak of it. I shall forget in time, I'm sure, and from your glowing face it would seem that you have already put the past behind you.'

'Oh yes, I have, it seems shallow to have recovered so quickly but my parents were wonderful. They took me to the mountains where it was so beautiful and quiet in the snow and then Stephan came to see me, and – oh, Rachel – they allowed us to be together so that we got to know each other really well and I know now that I do love him and that he loves me.'

'This time you are quite sure?'

'Very, very sure.'

'And your parents – they don't object?'

'No. They like him. He hasn't any money besides his pay from the army and I suppose deep down my mother would have liked me to marry a rich man with a title, but after that terrible time at Meinhart they're relieved for me to have found a good man.'

'So you've come to tell me that you're engaged to be married?'

'Not quite. Stephan is going to Hungary with his regiment for six months and during that time we have to think about each other quite seriously. If we still feel the same at the end of it, we are free to marry.'

'And you don't mind?'

'Not a bit. We shall write to each other and I know I shan't change my mind. Oh, I know I was flirtatious and silly, I thought life was a game and that all we had to do was play it to suit ourselves. Now I know that it isn't like that at all.'

Her eyes filled suddenly with tears and hurriedly she hunted in her bag for a handkerchief.

'I promised myself I wouldn't cry and here I am blubbering like a baby, but I keep thinking of Liesel, wondering if she would still be alive but for my stupidity.'

'Something bad would have happened to Liesel sooner or later; I don't think anyone could really have saved her from the ultimate tragedy of her life. She was a strange child in many ways.'

I wanted to ask about Max and Mellina but the words stuck in my throat. I couldn't bear to hear that tragedy had brought them together but neither could I bear to hear that it had torn them further apart. Instead I contented myself by asking about Ernst and the others.

Her face was immeasurably sad when she spoke of Ernst.

'I haven't seen him since the night of the ball. Stephan told us he was in close confinement in one of the garrison barracks but I don't know what they will do with him. It's so awful. He could be so gay and so sweet and now his career is in ruins and where will he go if they send him into exile?'

'And the others?' I prompted gently.

'Josef and the Frenchwoman are in prison, as well as the jeweller in the poor part of the city and many others who made money out of those bored stupid people.'

'And what of those bored stupid people? If they had not been stupid those other wicked people would not have been able to blackmail them.'

'They had enough money to leave Austria, they're probably a hundred miles away by now, running for their lives.'

We spoke no more about the events at Meinhart. Frau Liptmann came in pushing the tea trolley and after that we talked about other things, the weather and the latest fashion, until Sophia jumped to her feet saying, 'You look weary, Rachel. I'll come again when we get back from Innsbruck and you must come back to Salzburg with me.'

I didn't argue, but I knew that instead of going to Salzburg I would be on my way to England and the rest of my life. I was glad that Sophia was happy, she was a dear girl and I was very fond of her. At the same time I couldn't help pondering upon the injustice of life. I had suffered more than she had as a result of her foolishness, yet now she had found happiness and I had been denied it.

Spring came to Vienna with the blossoming of the lilac trees in the parks and all along the broad avenues of the city the linden trees were already bursting into tender leaf. It was the beginning of May when I told the Liptmanns that I had finally made up my mind to return to England. I promised I would remember their kindness as long as I lived and that I would write to them often, and in spite of their protests I informed them firmly that I must go home and look for work, that I could not go on allowing them to care for me and feed me indefinitely.

They looked at each other sadly, but seeing I was adamant they accepted my decision. Herr Liptmann said he would make all the arrangements for me to travel in about ten days' time. Now that I had finally made up my mind to return to England I sternly told myself that I must pull myself together, do something about my appearance and give some real thought to my future.

There were only three days left when Frau Liptmann asked after luncheon, 'Have you got everything you need, Rachel? I can't come to the shops with you this afternoon because we are expecting a visitor, but you don't have to stay in.'

'I don't need to go to the shops, but I'd like to take one last look at the Danube. I once thought I would have liked to sail on the river to Budapest but I don't suppose I ever shall.'

'Well, put something warm on, my dear, it's a chilly day for May.'

She was right, it was chilly and a low mist swirled about the river making its waters appear anything but blue.

I sauntered along the path towards the place where the steamers sailed from. One of them was already moored there while other vessels slipped in and out of the mist, their hooters echoing mournfully across the water. I stood on the quayside looking pensively down on the ship, wishing with all my heart that I could sail on her to Budapest and onwards to the Black Sea, but sadly I turned to walk away. Through the mist a small group of people were approaching, and when they reached the ship's gangway I recognized them as the party of young gypsies who had played for us at Meinhart on the night of Walpurgis.

They didn't notice me at first, and they walked up the gangway and went to sit at the stern of the steamer in the open air. It was the man who had danced with me who suddenly saw me, and a broad bold smile curved his lips as he came to the ship's rail to call out to me, 'Come with us, Fräulein! One week and all Budapest will be at your feet!'

The two younger men who had played the violins came forward to add their entreaties to his, and only the girl sat alone, eyeing me with dark hostile eyes.

I smiled and waved my hand to wish them bon voyage, then I walked slowly away. I didn't want to see them sail. I would never see them again but the sight of them had brought back all the old familiar yearnings just when I had told myself I was starting to forget.

It was quiet along the path, only one tall figure was coming towards me out of the mist. He stopped right in front of me and I looked up quickly to find myself staring into Max's dark eyes. The next moment I was in his arms, my questions muffled by his lips on mine. He released me slowly and I gasped, 'Oh, Max, you came to say goodbye! I was hoping you would, or that you'd write to me.'

'Herr Liptmann wrote to say you intended to return to England at the end of the week.'

'Yes, there is nothing for me here now. I shall go home and start looking for work. I should have done it a long time ago but the prospect was too daunting. Perhaps if you were to give me a reference it would help – the sight of a title and a family crest might prompt somebody to employ me.'

He smiled, and taking hold of my hand he said, 'I know a little coffee house where we can talk. It will be quiet at this time of day and anything we say will not be overheard.'

Gently he steered me towards the road above the steps, but we had to wait at the kerb to allow a company of hussars to ride past on their way to the palace. I looked sadly at the stranger riding at their head, and aware of the thoughts passing through my mind Max gently squeezed my hand.

We sat at the back of the coffee house in an alcove lit by candlelight, and after he had given his order he said, 'I left a great many things unsaid on the day I came to see you at Meinhart, Rachel, but at that time life was full of uncertainties. How could I tell what the future would unravel?'

'And now?' I prompted gently.

'Now I think I can tell you the whole story. I knew about Mellina almost from the first day I married her. I told you the Meinharts often married their Salzburg cousins and I had known that one day I would marry Mellina when I was still little more than a boy. I was no different from other men, I found her beautiful and amusing, and I suppose in those early days I was in love with her, but I soon realized that her beautiful face was merely a façade for a disposition that was reckless, promiscuous and entirely without a conscience. Soon after our marriage she grew bored with the country and showed little interest in the tenants on the estate and the life of the villages. Instead she would disappear for whole weeks at a time, to Vienna and Budapest, to Paris or Berlin, and she would come back feverishly gay, or listless, according to the pleasures she had found.

'After Liesel was born I thought there might be a chance that she would settle down, but instead she became more and more unstable so that I made up my mind there would be no more children at Meinhart. We grew apart, we each lived our separate lives more and more, and in those days I felt very close to Liesel – she was such an incredibly beautiful child. One day Mellina saw me riding in the park with her and when I returned to the castle she told me it was not even a certainty that Liesel was my daughter. Whether she was jealous of my affection for Liesel or hers for me I never knew, but from then on I began to see Liesel in a new light and I realized that in her there was so much of Mellina and nothing of me.'

'I could never understand why you seemed so unconcerned about her. I can tell you now that I never really liked her, although heaven knows I tried, but you were her father and I couldn't believe that you didn't like her either.'

'I couldn't help it. Apart from her beauty she seemed to embody all Mellina's worst traits, the things I had disliked in Mellina even as a child. I was never sure, there were many men in Mellina's life, men I didn't know, and then there was Josef.'

'Yes, of course, there was Josef.'

'You knew about him?'

'I saw her leaving the castle one night and it was morning when she returned, and I wondered if she had been with Josef. Why didn't you dismiss him?'

'While I kept him on the estate I knew he would keep his

mouth shut, but if I had dismissed him he might have talked about their relationship and I couldn't risk that. I decided to bide my time, but it was very difficult after you came to Meinhart.'

'Why was that?'

'Because you were so honest and normal, because you were sweet and lovely, and because I fell in love with you. I was insane with jealousy when Ernst was with you, that vain stupid young man who flirted with danger and disaster in the name of pleasure, and was accepted by all those people because of his fresh young face and his aristocratic connections. Ernst had money once, but he gambled heavily and lost most of it. He was like a puppet and all those degenerate people were pulling the strings, paying his debts, buying his clothes, paying for all his extravagances because of his nearness to the Emperor, while he in turn sold them military secrets that he had access to. Then came the ultimate form of flattery, when they made him their priest for the celebration of the Black Mass, and he hadn't the sense to realize they had bought him, body and soul.'

'Sophia told me that he was confined at the garrison but she didn't know what they would do with him.'

'He has been relieved of his commission. At the moment he is languishing under close guard until the Emperor decides what is to be done with him.'

'What will they do to him?'

'It has been known for traitors to be shot, but if the Emperor spares his life he will find himself in exile like all those other degenerates who have now scattered. One day, in some other pleasure spot, they may all come together, and then perhaps evil will rear its ugly head again.'

'And Mellina, what about Mellina?'

'Mellina is in the Tyrol at a little convent high up in the mountains. I put no pressure on her to take this step, she has decided this is what she wants for herself and the good Abbe has arranged it. She wants to spend the rest of her life there; she has refused to see me since the night I took you from the dungeons. I didn't even see her on the morning she left Meinhart for the last time. Perhaps there is hope for Mellina if she feels ashamed for the things she did.'

I could find nothing to say as I tried to imagine Mellina with all her pale blond beauty hidden by a nun's sombre veil, her zest for life for ever extinguished within the narrow confines of convent life.

'She does not blame you for Liesel's death,' Max said, gazing earnestly into my eyes. 'She blames only herself, and if you can think calmly about the past you will see that Mellina is indeed to blame, for her way of life, her friends, her influence on the child – but the Black Mass! That is sheer decadence. People of disappointed ambitions, those who have exhausted the normal joys and crave the forbidden ones, those who would sell their immortal souls for a new thrill, those who look to Satan for the gifts which God refuses, the whole body of degenerates with the blackmailers who live on them, criminals seeking accomplices, poisoners seeking protection, great ones rubbing shoulders with the riffraff of the underworld – all of them giving allegiance to the devil, who is only capable of promoting evil things safely done, and giving them hearts ever more stony and pitiless.'

I shivered as though an icy hand had suddenly clutched my shoulder. Max was watching me across the table and in his eyes was only a great tenderness.

'You haven't asked me why I am here,' he said smiling a little.

'I thought it was so that you could say goodbye and perhaps tell me about Ernst and Mellina.'

'I came to prevent you returning to England. I want you to marry me, Rachel.'

'But Max – you are already married to Mellina!'

'Not any more. At least I shan't be married to her after the end of August.'

'But how can that be? She is only entering a convent, she is not going to die!'

'I have received the Emperor's permission and also that of the Church for the marriage to be dissolved. The Emperor knows the full story and Mellina has agreed it will be the best thing for both of us. Then I shall be free to marry you – that is if you wish it.'

'Oh yes, Max, I do wish it – more than I have ever wished for anything in my life!'

'You are quite sure?'

'Quite sure! Does it mean that we shall have to live at Meinhart with all its unhappy memories?'

'You would not want that?'

'I don't know. It is beautiful and overpowering and I believe I could bear it when you are with me, but when you have to go away, then perhaps I shall be afraid of the past. I shall find myself wondering if there is still evil in those dark cold places underneath the castle and, dear Max, I am not very brave.'

'But you are brave, my darling! You were brave enough to face evil alone and unprotected, so surely you are brave enough to turn Meinhart into a home, to chase the shadows and the cobwebs away so that the sunlight can fill the corners again? What lies beneath the castle can be sealed off for all time so that it is as much a part of the past as any medieval barbarism that has gone before. Is the prospect too daunting, Rachel?'

'What would be your answer if I said it was?'

He was silent for several minutes and I knew that he was thinking seriously about my fears and about his love for the castle he had grown up in. Then as if he had suddenly made up his mind he said, 'I would shut the castle up and give it to the Austrian nation as other castles and palaces have been given in the past, so that future generations can find some sort of pride in their heritage – or perhaps even relief that life is different for them.'

'If you would do that for me, then the least I can do for you is to live in your wretched old castle and make the best of it.'

He laughed then, not the old cynical laughter that held little amusement, but the joyous laughter of a happy man. He was holding my hands tightly across the table and I could see the happiness shining in his face for all the world to see.

He only had one more question to ask of me, and it was asked with a wry smile and a touch of irony.

'So you approve entirely of the Emperor's involvement

with my marriage – you might even begin to think that it wipes the slate clean?'

I pretended to consider it seriously, then to his utmost amusement I said, 'I never knew such a man for setting other people's marriages aside! I vowed I would never forgive him for putting an end to my mother's marriage, but I think I shall forgive him for his interference with yours. Yes, I really will.'

THE CARRADICE CHAIN

Sara Hylton

Elaina Carradice was the first person I had ever totally and obsessively hated. I hated my grandmother then – on the night she took me, wailing, from my mother – and in all the years of humiliation that followed. And, God help me, I hate her still . . .

Jacintha went to live at Ravenspoint not because she was Elaina Carradice's grandchild, but because she was the daughter of the one Carradice who had defied them all – and so had to be punished every day of her life. For the chain which held the Carradice empire together was made of money, ambition, power and greed.

Raised in that lonely, eerie house, Jacintha's life became a desperate struggle to cast off the Carradice chain – for ever – and to find the love she so desperately needed . . .

DANGEROUS OBSESSION

Natasha Peters

A novel of tumultuous love by the author of SAVAGE SURRENDER

Rhawnie: she was the starving gypsy girl who wanted only to sing and dance and to be free.

She became the daring and defiant wanton who used her wit and sensuality to become a demi-mondaine in Paris, a countess in Bavaria, a singer in New York, and, above all – a survivor.

But she was possessed by one dangerous obsession – a man who brought her only degradation and heartbreak and from whom there would be no escape. Seth Garrett was her tormentor and her destiny – and fired a love so powerful and shameless that she could do nothing but surrender!

A RAGE AGAINST HEAVEN

Fred Stewart

A towering novel of passion and power, of triumph and be-trayal . . .

For the rich in Philadelphia in the tranquil year of 1860, life is an ordered and pleasant business. Lew Crandall and Elizabeth Butterfield are young, perfectly suited, the children of wealthy parents. But their gentle lives are soon to be over-taken by the inexorable flow of history . . .

In this epic novel, Fred M. Stewart masterfully recalls the years of destiny between 1860 and 1870: the Civil War from Bull Run to Andersonville, the bandit-ridden Mexico of Maximillan and the sinister opulence of Grant's Washington.

HISTORICAL FICTION FROM ARROW

All these books are available from your bookshop or newsagent or you can order them direct. Just tick the titles you want and complete the form below.

☐	THE TREASURE IS LOVE	Barbara Cartland	£1.00
☐	RAVEN	Shana Carrol	£1.50
☐	BEULAH LAND	Lonnie Coleman	£1.95
☐	NONE BUT ELIZABETH	Rhoda Edwards	£1.95
☐	A DISTANT SUNSET	Virginia Ironside	£1.50
☐	AMARYLLIS	Priscilla Jenkins	£1.75
☐	WILD HONEY	Fern Michaels	£1.75
☐	DANGEROUS OBSESSION	Natasha Peters	£2.50
☐	FAREWELL COMPANIONS	James Plunkett	£1.50
☐	THE HOT AND COPPER SKY	Bruce Stewart	£1.95
☐	A RAGE AGAINST HEAVEN	Fred. M. Stewart	£2.50
☐	ELIZA STANHOPE	Joanna Trollope	£1.50
☐	THE INCOMPARABLE MISS BRADY	Sheila Walsh	£1.50

Postage _____

Total _____

ARROW BOOKS, BOOKSERVICE BY POST, PO BOX 29, DOUGLAS, ISLE OF MAN, BRITISH ISLES

Please enclose a cheque or postal order made out to Arrow Books Limited for the amount due including 15p per book for postage and packing for orders both within the UK and overseas orders.

Please print clearly

NAME ....

ADDRESS ....

....

Whilst every effort is made to keep prices down and to keep popular books in print, Arrow Books cannot guarantee that prices will be the same as those advertised here or that the books will be available.